Praise for *The Big Door Prize*

"The ability to take what is primarily a funny, engaging, leisurely paced look at Small Town, USA, a la Fannie Flagg, and turn it into a breathless, high-stakes page-turner in the last sixty pages speaks to the mastery of Walsh's storytelling skills. . . . In the most simplistic terms, the message of *The Big Door Prize* is some variation on the grass is always greener on the other side of the fence. But the more profound lesson is the realization that the possibility for change is always present, it's just a matter of being receptive to it and a willingness to take the first step."
—*Atlanta Journal-Constitution*

"Walsh's brand of comic tenderness is the perfect soother for these troubled times. . . . Like Thornton Wilder or Edgar Lee Masters, those other masters of the small town collective portrait, Walsh probes the secrets at the heart of individual lives and reminds us to look long, listen hard, and offer compassion."
—*The Times-Picayune | The New Orleans Advocate*

"The premise [of *The Big Door Prize*] is fantastic and at the same time, simple. . . . M. O. Walsh is a gift. He is imaginative and productive. . . . Definitely one to watch."   —*Tuscaloosa News*

"*The Big Door Prize* is M. O. Walsh's long-awaited second novel and a captivating analysis of human nature, ambition, and how we chase our dreams while honoring our relationships and commitments."   —*Deep South Magazine*

"All of [the] characters are fully realized and artfully drawn. . . . From the opening line, the reader has the sense of a wise, omniscient narrator peeking into various bars, cars, and bedroom windows, a twinkle in his eye as he brings some mischief to the lives within. . . . These connections lie at the heart of *The Big Door Prize*, and what an enormous heart it is." —*Chapter 16*

"[A] big-hearted and magical novel about fate, identity, and the loyalties of a small town . . . Combining the humor and heart of small-town cozy fiction with the poignancy of literary fiction and the drama of domestic suspense, M. O. Walsh proves once again that he is a writer who needs to live on your bookshelves." —*BookReporter*

"Walsh skirts the edge of fantasy in this playful and touching tale set in small-town Deerfield, LA. . . . [He] follows these characters with humor and compassion, leading them to an ending readers will find surprising and satisfying. The novel transcends its quirky premise, offering many insights on the mysteries of the human heart." —*Publishers Weekly* (starred review)

"It's hard to believe that Walsh wrote this moving novel long before the COVID-19 pandemic, for there is eerie prescience in its soulful message that gratitude and grace are not to be taken for granted and that life can be upended in an instant." —*Booklist* (starred review)

"An eccentric, well-written small-town novel jam-packed with appealing characters and their dreams." —*Kirkus Reviews*

"*The Big Door Prize* calls attention to the ordinary, hard-won joys of real people. M. O. Walsh's second novel is a feel-good read in a down-home setting, with serious undertones." —*BookPage*

"Think of *The Big Door Prize* as a beautiful box full of all the things that compose our lives: love, fate, chance, jealousy, sadness, jokes, desire, and music. M. O. Walsh gives us all this and more, page after page, until we feel as if we know a little bit more about everything there is worth knowing. One of the most big-hearted books you'll ever read, about so much, but, in the end, really about the secret of life: the specifics of caring."

—Daniel Wallace, author of *Extraordinary Adventures* and *Big Fish*

"The lives of a couple facing their mid-life crisis and a young man coming of age intersect in this humorous and hopeful novel. M. O. Walsh has never been afraid to go down into the darkest places of the human heart, but his truthfulness is balanced by a beautiful optimism, just as his sharp humor is leavened by his genuine affection for the layered, vital characters he creates. A wise, wry, twisty, and entertaining tale. I loved it."

—Joshilyn Jackson, author of *Never Have I Ever*

"Part mystery, all charm. The big prize here is for readers: a heartwarming and eccentric page-turner in the grand tradition of Southern literature that will keep you wonderful until the very end. Walsh writes his characters with great respect to prove we're never too old to discover new things about ourselves."

—Steven Rowley, author of *The Editor* and *Lily and the Octopus*

"The characters in *The Big Door Prize* are familiar yet curious—so much like my own neighbors that I began to weave myself into the story, considering other lives I might live if I were braver, pluckier. Walsh's novel is the ideal summer read, an immersive escape as well as a brilliant examination of free will vs. determinism."

—Mary Miller, author of *Biloxi* and *Always Happy Hour*

Praise for *My Sunshine Away*
Winner of the Pat Conroy Southern Book Prize

"A tantalizing mystery and a tender coming-of-age story."

—*O, the Oprah Magazine*

"Walsh has an innate knack for plot and suspense, but the real pleasure here is his prose. This stunning and gracefully written debut novel is a total page-turner until the very end."

—*Entertainment Weekly*, "The Must List"

"A lyrical portrait of the melancholic South, *My Sunshine Away* is a sharp meditation on the passage of time and the plasticity of memory."

—*San Francisco Chronicle*

"M. O. Walsh's marvelous debut novel is so thick with searching nostalgia and melancholy, it gives the reader the same sense of authenticity and emotional satisfaction more typically associated with a good memoir. *My Sunshine Away* is the kind of novel you simply can't put down."

—*Dallas Morning News*

"A coming-of-age tale that's part mystery, part family drama, part love story, it begs to be read slowly—as languid as the Louisiana summer in which the crime that changes everything takes place. I adored this novel right down to its breathtaking last page."

—*The Huffington Post*

"[A] rich, unexpected, exceptional book . . . A gripping read that's more than a thriller, more than a traditional Southern tale, *My Sunshine Away* is a brilliant meditation on the unpredictability and the lifelong effects of childhood events and relationships."

—*Chicago Tribune*

"Just fourteen pages into reading *My Sunshine Away*, M. O. Walsh's debut novel about a boy growing up in Baton Rouge, LA., I had a thought . . . *My Sunshine Away* is . . . simply, like Lee's novel [*To Kill a Mockingbird*], a great work of fiction."   —*Fort Worth Star-Telegram*

"[A] wrenching and wondrous coming-of-age tale."   —*People*

"*My Sunshine Away* is one of the best novels of 2015. . . . From the first gripping sentence to the very last, Walsh has written a compelling novel that gets tremendous strength from the appeal of its narrator."   —*The Free Lance-Star*

"[A] haunting, mysterious debut."   —*US Weekly*

"*My Sunshine Away* made me nostalgic for a time and place I'd never lived. . . . The story hinges on a local tragedy, but it expands into so much more: teenage lust, family dysfunction, personal expectations, and Louisiana culture. It's beautifully written and almost impossible to put down."   —*BuzzFeed*

"In his stunning first novel, Baton Rouge native M. O. Walsh evokes a languid Southern gothic atmosphere, rife with a hazy, heat-drenched poetry. . . . Reminiscent of Pat Conroy's sweeping family epics and Jeffrey Eugenides' folkloric intrigue . . . *My Sunshine Away* achieves a rare feat: both a page-turning mystery and literary-quality novel, you'll be charmed, impressed, and engrossed in this meditation on memory's ambiguity and how a childhood tragedy can affect us more deeply than we consciously know."   —*Bustle*

"[A] gripping debut novel . . . Pitch perfect on details . . . Walsh [is] a master storyteller."   —*The Times-Picayune*

"Recalls the best of Pat Conroy: the rich Southern atmosphere; the interplay of darkness and light in adolescence; the combination of brisk narrative suspense with philosophical musings on memory, manhood, and truth. . . . Celebrate, fiction lovers: The gods of Southern gothic storytelling have inducted a junior member."

—*Kirkus Reviews* (starred review)

"I really loved this book. I am in awe, swept up in the quiet beauty of the prose, and in the wisdom and compassion of the narrator. . . . I can't praise it enough."

—Anne Rice

"*My Sunshine Away* is that rarest find, a page-turner you want to read slowly and a literary novel you can't look away from. At times funny, at times spine-tinglingly suspenseful, and at times just flat-out wise, this novel is also a meditation on memory, how it can destroy or damn us but redeem us as well."

—Tom Franklin, author of *Crooked Letter, Crooked Letter*

"If you start this novel, you will not put it down. *My Sunshine Away* is a riveting, suspenseful, page-turning mystery. It is also a wise, insightful, and beautifully written novel. This is an extraordinary debut."

—Jill McCorkle, author of *Life After Life* and *Hieroglyphics*

"This is literature of the highest order. Although the book snaps with the tautness of a thriller—and Walsh keeps the reader guessing until the end, as the best mystery writers do—*My Sunshine Away* also asks essential questions, like how much responsibility we have to each other, and whether we can we ever fully reassemble the pieces of broken lives."

—Matthew Thomas, author of *We Are Not Ourselves*

"M. O. Walsh has written one of the best books I've read in a long while. An outstanding examination of the way that the past and the weight of our memories shape us, *My Sunshine Away*, thanks to Walsh's verve and total control over the narrative, feels utterly original." —Kevin Wilson, author of *Nothing to See Here*

"M. O. Walsh's *My Sunshine Away* reminds us that art can be wrenching and a delight, that pain—if examined through wit, intimacy, and wisdom—can be a salve. This novel is great."
  —Darin Strauss, author of *The Queen of Tuesday* and *Half a Life*

"*My Sunshine Away* begins with a crime. But the novel is so much more than a mystery; it's half lament, half love letter to youth and to possibility. On every page, we feel complicit, perhaps even guilty. Guilty of what? For ever having been young ourselves. The magic of *My Sunshine Away* is in M. O. Walsh's extraordinary ability to make us long for the heartache of youth and its inevitable sins. This is an awe-inspiring debut."
  —Hannah Pittard, author of *Visible Empire* and *The Fates Will Find Their Way*

THE
BIG
DOOR
PRIZE

A NOVEL

M. O. WALSH

G. P. PUTNAM'S SONS
NEW YORK

PUTNAM
— EST. 1838 —

G. P. PUTNAM'S SONS
Publishers Since 1838
An imprint of Penguin Random House LLC
penguinrandomhouse.com

The Library of Congress has catalogued the
G. P. Putnam's Sons hardcover edition as follows:

Names: Walsh, M. O. (Milton O'Neal), author.
Title: The big door prize: a novel / M. O. Walsh.
Description: New York: G. P. Putnam's Sons, [2020] |
Identifiers: LCCN 2020010820 (print) | LCCN 2020010821 (ebook) |
ISBN 9780735218482 (hardcover) | ISBN 9780735218499 (ebook)
Classification: LCC PS3623.A4464 B55 2020 (print) |
LCC PS3623.A4464 (ebook) | DDC 813/.6—dc23
LC record available at https://lccn.loc.gov/2020010820
LC ebook record available at https://lccn.loc.gov/2020010821

First G. P. Putnam's Sons hardcover edition / September 2020
First G. P. Putnam's Sons trade paperback edition / August 2021
G. P. Putnam's Sons trade paperback ISBN: 9780735218505

Printed in the United States of America
3rd Printing

Book Design by Ashley Tucker

For my family:
my readout

and

for the still-singing heart of John Prine

Against all odds, honey.
We're the big door prize.

—JOHN PRINE,
"In Spite of Ourselves"

Question:

How can you know that your whole life will change on a day the sun rises at the agreed-upon time by science or God or what-have-you and the morning birds go about their usual bouncing for worms?

How can you know?

And why would you think there's another life for you, perhaps another possibility inside of you already, when the walk that you take each dawn is so lovely and safe? When the roads are all paved and the sidewalks just swept and those who move along them, like you, seem so content to re-tread the worn path that they've made?

Why would you think it?

After all, this is only Deerfield: a town so simple it is named for what you might see and where you might see it.

It is a place where storefronts hang flowering baskets, where the rocking chairs gently set on friendly porches look fit for rocking gently the friendly people who own them, as they rocked gently their friendly parents before them. And such quiet on a morning like this one, such quiet on every stormless morning in Deerfield, that the only sound above you is the rustle of venturing squirrels in the branches. Maybe, to your side, the huff of a familiar dog at a familiar fence line who muzzles your hand as you pass. And if this were not enough to comfort you, not enough to seduce you into believing that today is just another in the easy procession of days you began so long ago, the first words you hear spoken on this morning are also the first words you hear spoken on most mornings, from the manager at the grocery store you walk to for coffee who says, "Good day," and to whom you reply, "Isn't it, though?"

So, how could you know?

Perhaps you might know on this particular morning in Deerfield, in this small part of South Louisiana, because you see something new at the store. It is a simple-looking machine, sitting next to the customer service desk. It is large enough to enter through curtains, as one would a photo booth at the mall or parish fair, and promises to tell you your potential in life, what your body and mind are *capable* of doing, based on the science of DNA. Some people in town have already tried this machine, you've heard, and to surprising result. A neighbor opened up a new business after getting her readout. An old friend quit pills and got clean. Another person you know left town entirely, off on some long-dreamt-of vacation they never would have booked before. This kind of talk is enough to make you curious, to make anyone curious, the way word of a simple and miraculous new diet might do, and it costs only two dollars to try.

Today, tucked safely in your pocket, you have exactly two dollars. And you, tucked safely into your life, haven't much else to do. So, you draw back the curtains and enter the booth. You give it your money. The screen brightens.

You read a message that instructs you to take one of the Q-tips provided, to remove the plastic and gently swab the inside of your cheek, and so you do this as well and why not? No one can see you. What would anyone care? You then deposit this into the slot as directed and can't help but grin at the disclaimer, which reads there is a 1 percent margin of error in a pursuit like this, and that the company, DNAMIX, is not liable for any stress your new potential may cause.

Yet still you carry on. You wait for the result. But *why*?

That is the question.

Perhaps it is because people like you, people like us, when we are joking, say, "What is the worst that could happen?"

But when we are honest, and when we are alone, we wonder, "What is the best?"

1

The Hubbards

After thirty-nine years and eleven-plus months, Douglas Hubbard had finally had enough of being Douglas Hubbard. So, for his fortieth birthday, just last Friday, he bought himself a trombone. It was a thing he'd long wanted and, now that it was purchased, Douglas felt this object made him an entirely new man. He was so excited, in fact, he spent his entire weekend polishing the instrument until it nearly glowed, standing in front of the full-length mirror in his and his wife's bedroom, spinning aloud magical phrases like *Dizzy Douglas, Herbie Hubbard,* and *Thelonious Doug.* He dreamt up enough jazzy nicknames in the first few days alone to sustain several impressive careers and yet had not even put lip to mouthpiece. Why bother? When a person finds as much joy as Douglas did in simply imagining themselves to be someone else, the actual work required to change, along with so many other things they hold dear, can be forgotten.

But tonight, after clumsily blaring his way through his first trombone lesson at a friend's apartment, Douglas Hubbard returned home to his wife, moved aside the wooden birdhouses she'd been building those past months, and set his trombone case down on the table. "Well," he said. "It's official. I can't play a note."

"Don't be silly," his wife said. Then she began to cry.

This was unusual.

Cherilyn Hubbard was typically warm and upbeat at this hour, which she called their *wine time*, and Douglas always looked forward to seeing her. Through fifteen years of what they would both call a happy and uncomplicated marriage, she had remained redheaded and faithful, busy and beautiful in her unpretentious way, and as quick to offer love and encouragement to Douglas as she'd been on the days he first fell for her. But, on this night, she stood alone at the far end of their modest kitchen and, instead of greeting Douglas with a hug at the door, wiped at her eyes with the undersides of her wrists. She then leaned heavily against their blue-and-white countertop, which was covered in flipped-open magazines. Beside her, a pot of water boiled quietly on the stove. Near the sink, a box of macaroni and cheese stood unopened. Next to that, Douglas knew, because the day was Wednesday, two hamburger patties sizzled over low, greasy heat in the skillet.

Douglas said nothing. He instead removed the blazer he had draped over his arm and placed it on a chair, hung his keys on a hook screwed into the wall for that purpose. He then took off his hat, a brown woolen beret he'd taken to wearing since he bought the trombone, and arranged the wayward hairs on his balding head. He knew Cherilyn hadn't been feeling well. Some powerful headaches, lately, a dizzy spell or two. He'd been meaning to talk to her about this. The amount of aspirin bottles he'd found about the house, the antihistamine nose spray she'd taken to cupping in her palm those past mornings. The naps she took at odd hours. These are the minor changes to a marital landscape that can worry a thoughtful husband like Douglas. Yet he'd chalked most of it up to stress.

Cherilyn was busy of late in atypical ways. She'd signed up to sell her own handmade birdhouses at the Deerfield Bicentennial that weekend, would have her own booth on the square both Saturday and Sunday, and so had spent the past few months turning their home into a sort of avian sweatshop. There were probably a hundred of the little houses always in eyesight, each in some incomplete phase of construction, with not much time left before the event. That could make anyone nervous. Still, Douglas knew she enjoyed her crafts, had signed up for this booth herself, and so he did not press her.

There were other things it could be, of course, besides bird homes. The oncoming heat of a southern spring. The exhaustion from dealing with her elderly mother, who they both worried was losing her mind. Cherilyn's trips to check up or take her shopping had become daily. She'd therefore quit working her temp jobs around town, cut back on her volunteering, and so maybe that was it, Douglas figured. Maybe she felt her world was shrinking a bit, becoming too predictable, and, as the pre-trombone version of Douglas knew, that could get anyone down.

Still, seeing her cry at wine time was new. He tried not to overreact.

Douglas understood to take his time with the curveballs of marriage. He was a good husband, after all, a kind man, and wanted to gather what information he could before trying to brighten her mood. So, he simply approached the kitchen counter, watched Cherilyn dog-ear a few of the magazines' pages, and listened to her breathe in through her small and freckled nose. After a moment, he touched her arm.

"What's going on in here?" he asked. "You feeling okay?"

"I dropped my phone in the oil," she said, and took to her soft crying again.

"The oil?" Douglas asked.

"Olive oil," she said. "A full cup of it. Our last of it. And then when I picked it up it slipped out of my hand and hit the ground and broke. I mean, completely. I'm afraid it's totaled."

"The cup?" Douglas said.

"No, Douglas," she said, "not the cup."

Cherilyn pointed over to her phone, which stood propped and shattered in a bowl of rice like an unfortunate sculpture. "I was trying to find this recipe," she said. "I wanted to try something new and it just slipped." She rubbed her palm as if trying to re-member the feeling, to re-create the scene. "And then I got to look-ing at these magazines and there are just *so* many different dishes out there, Douglas." She paused to keep from crying again and said, "So many things I've never tried. I mean, have you ever heard of baba ghanoush? It's made with tahini, of all things. Who has ta-hini, Douglas? What *is* tahini? That's what I want to know. And eggplant, too. You know, it turns out that, in certain parts of the world, *a lot* of things are made with eggplant. We're talking about beautiful parts of the world! Why don't we ever have eggplant, Douglas? Why don't we ever have eggplant?"

Douglas rubbed her arm to calm her.

"I can't say I've ever been asked that question," he said.

"And then I saw this one for beef Wellington," Cherilyn said. "Have you heard of that? I thought, I have ground meat. I have beef. Maybe we have a roast in the freezer. But I apparently need some sort of *pâté* to make beef Wellington. Is there a *pâté* aisle at Johnson's, Douglas? Is there a *pâté* aisle at Walmart?"

Douglas had no idea where any of this was coming from, and so, instead of asking if she'd started wine time a bit early, instead of trying to calm her with a simple joke, moved his gentle hands to her shoulders. They were as warm to the touch as if she'd been jog-ging, as if she were coming down with a fever, and as Douglas be-gan his light and practiced massage he saw that the magazines she'd been reading, at least twenty of them, were indeed all opened to recipes. He recognized the magazines from a subscription they'd received as a gift a few years ago for which they made their own little shelf in the kitchen but never read. They looked to have a rather gourmet agenda, all splayed open before him now, with high-quality photos of skewered meats and bright vegetables at the top, ads for products like pomegranate juice and organic cereal along the margins. He continued to rub Cherilyn's shoulders as she closed and stacked each of the magazines carefully without ever leaving his touch, constructing a pile that reached from the countertop to her soft chin, which she then rested on it.

Douglas took a deep and obvious whiff of the air. "I love Burger Wednesdays," he said. "Who needs eggplant?"

"I know," she said, and turned to face him. "It's not that. It's not you. I'm sorry. I don't know what got into me. I'm sorry about the phone. I know they're expensive."

"Don't worry about it," he said. "We'll get you a new one. In the meantime, maybe we can string together a couple of cans."

"I just don't know what's gotten into me," she said again, and turned back to the stove. "Anyway," she said. "How was your lesson? Tell me everything."

"You sure?" he said. "Because all the evidence here suggests you're pretty upset. Exhibit A, I'd posit, is anxiety over beef Wellington. Exhibit B, I'd say, is the water leaking out of your face."

"Stop it," Cherilyn said, and flipped over the burgers. "I'm fine. I'm serious. I know you have to be excited. Your very first trombone lesson. How'd it go?"

Douglas walked around the stove so she could see him. "Okay," he said, and waved his arm as if painting the scene. "Imagine, if you will," he said, "the sound of an elephant being kicked in the balls."

"Quit that," Cherilyn said. "Did Geoffrey say that to you?"

"No," Douglas said. "Geoffrey's great. It's not him. It's just a little overwhelming, you know. I mean, that man can play twelve instruments. He's a genius."

"Well, so are you," Cherilyn said. "But enough of all this down talk. Let's have some music."

"Your wish," Douglas said, "is my pleasure."

Now, the first thing one should know about Douglas Hubbard is that he has always been, since his youth, an amazing whistler. A true wonder, really. Douglas Hubbard can whistle in any key and at any tempo he desires. The man is like a bird in the forest. He whistles confidently, whistles constantly, yet bothers no one. Not even the slouched-over high schoolers in his History classes, checking text messages beneath their desks. Not even his exhausted colleagues, sitting through another depressing faculty meeting. Not even the testy parents at the grocery store, trying desperately to keep their kids from wreaking havoc on the candy selection. And most importantly, of course, his whistling doesn't even seem to bother his wife, who, for the last twenty years of her life, has been perpetually immersed in the sound of him.

So, when Cherilyn said she wanted some music, Douglas knew where she was coming from and whistled for her "When You're Smiling" by Louis Prima, a man who had been on his mind all day. Cherilyn quietly opened the macaroni and cheese and fiddled with the knobs on the stove and, while he whistled, Douglas walked back to the kitchen table and took his new trombone out of the case. He ran a small cloth over the bell of it and reattached the slide. He handled it as carefully as one does a secret because, for many years, that's exactly what it was.

It wasn't until the night before his fortieth birthday, after all, that Douglas had finally confessed. He began by telling Cherilyn the large and emotional truth, which was that he felt he'd hit a wall in life. He believed it was time to make big-picture changes.

Since somber conversations like this were rare in their home, Cherilyn understood he was serious and sat beside him on the sofa. She let Douglas carry on in his self-deprecating and humiliated way without interruption. It had nothing to do with their marriage, he assured her, and he meant it. Yet here he was nearly bald and sporting a comb-over. Here he was soft in his belly. He had recurring and inexplicable pains in his feet if he wore certain shoes. He had no serious hobbies, he realized, no remarkable trophies on their bookshelf, and had made no permanent mark on the world. Each of these depressing observations, as if he had just read them in the papers, appeared to Douglas as undeniable facts. Even his job as a teacher, he told her, the one he now understood he'd likely have forever, was not as fulfilling as it had once been. He'd nurtured no prodigies, rescued nary an at-risk youth off the Deerfield streets, and could barely remember ever even giving a D.

It was, by all means, a crisis.

Then, after he had talked himself out and the two of them put on their nightclothes and crawled into bed, Douglas told Cherilyn the practical truth: that shaving off his mustache to become a hotshot trombonist was all that could save him now. It was what he had always wanted to be, he told her, ever since he'd seen a man playing trombone on the corner of Bourbon and Royal Streets on an eighth-grade field trip to New Orleans and felt, for the first time in his life, a love of music. It was perhaps still the reason he felt so drawn to music, the sound of it live and on vinyl, the jazz and funk masters, even the symphony, as he inevitably imagined himself one day playing those brassy notes when he heard them. And so how was he now forty years old? How had he never kept that promise to himself? To give it a try, at least? To pursue it? How had all those years gone by? With everything else in his life so admittedly happy and secure, Douglas told her, this was his only regret in the world and he could no longer deny it. Life was too short. Time was too precious. Desire was too big. It all made sense to him. He snuggled next to her in the quiet dark after he said this, wondering if she was awake, then wondering if he himself was asleep, until Cherilyn spoke, and asked him to kiss her with his mustache one last time. After that, she whispered, if he really thought it would help him blow a trombone, she would shave off the push broom herself.

And so he did this for her. And so she did that for him.

This was their marriage.

What Douglas did not know, however, was that tonight, as he sat at the dinner table polishing his new horn, his clean-shaven upper lip looked so foreign to Cherilyn that she fancied it to be made of wax. The lingering splotches of razor burn, along with the rigors of his first trombone lesson, had crested his top lip like an infection and made Cherilyn imagine her husband, for the first time in her life, a stranger. But these were not her only imaginings.

As is often the case when one person is honest, other hearts wish to be honest as well. So, ever since Douglas confessed, Cherilyn had begun some introspection of her own. What kind of life was *she* living? she wondered. What sort of dreams had she put on hold as she piddled about at different jobs, as she ran her errands, as they small-talked their way through the Sunday crossword? And were the undone things in one's life even dreams, when you thought about it? Could something even be a destiny if you don't know it exists until your life is half over? What was *her* true calling? Making birdhouses out of Popsicle sticks? Crocheting Christmas stockings? What great places had she stamped on her passport? An entire life in Deerfield? Is that what she was meant for? Why not something bigger? Something grand? Wasn't she about to turn forty as well?

Yes, she knew, she was.

Rather than talking to Douglas about any of this, though,

Cherilyn quietly turned away from him as he put together his horn. She wiped her hands on a towel and stared out of the kitchen window above the sink. Douglas kept up his jazzy whistle and, when he got to the solo, pretended to play his trombone right there at the table. He jerked the slide in and out and raised his eyebrows with each high note.

He then stood up from the table and posed for Cherilyn with the horn, as he had done several times since he bought it. He straightened his back, held the trombone at the ready position, and gave her a wink. This was something that had previously made Cherilyn smile, although not tonight. "How do I look?" he asked her and puffed out his cheeks on the mouthpiece.

"Ready to play the king's court, I suppose," she said.

"Picture it, Cher," Douglas said. "Lights down. Radio City. There you are in the front row, VIP. What do you want me to play for you? You name it and you've got it."

"You know I'm no good at this," Cherilyn said. "Play something with a lot of trombone in it, I guess. 'Seventy-six Trombones.'"

"A march?" Douglas said. "On a night like this? Not a chance. For my wife, the prettiest girl in Manhattan, I would play something romantic. Something soothing." He adjusted his shoulders and readied himself. Then he lifted his chin above the silver mouthpiece and whistled a low and vibrating tune.

"That's nice," Cherilyn said. "Something exotic."

Cherilyn moved to the stove and looked down at the boiling water. Pasta shells surfaced and dove like dolphins. Steam surrounded her face. And who could say how many worlds both invented themselves and disappeared in her mind as she let the vapor plume around her head? It was impossible, even for her, to keep count. So, she drained off the water, added milk, butter, and powdered cheese, and served dinner.

Douglas dropped a paper towel onto his lap, picked up his fork, and began to gently scrape the gray fat off the side of his hamburger patty. He shook the ketchup bottle, still thinking of his wife's mysterious mood, and said, "I sure do love your burgers."

"I was wondering," Cherilyn said. "Have you seen that new machine at the grocery?"

"I don't know," Douglas said. "You mean the one that reads your future?"

"That's not what it does," she said, and poked at the ice in her water.

Douglas knew about this machine. It was apparently a recent addition to Johnson's Grocery that sat near the big green box for people cashing in their change, but he'd not seen it himself. Yet he'd heard enough ridiculous anecdotes the past couple of weeks from people who'd played the game to make up his mind that it was not likely a fruitful pursuit. He was a history teacher, after all, and these are a hard lot to impress.

"It reads your DNA," Cherilyn said, "and then it tells you your potential, like what you *could* have been if everything would have worked out just right. What you are capable of doing, of *being*. Do you know what I'm talking about?"

"I think that's the one my students are playing," Douglas said. "Charlie Tate gave me some slip of paper the other day that said he'd grow up to be a nuclear physicist. Told me he didn't need my class anymore, just to go ahead and give him the A. Isn't that funny? Not just the idea that a nuclear physicist doesn't need history classes, which is itself a horrific notion, of course, but the idea of Charlie Tate in charge of anything. His parents would say the same. I mean, I've seen that boy eat an eraser. But anyway, yeah, I remember it now."

"You think that could work?" Cherilyn asked. "You think there is a way to know your potential like that?"

Douglas dipped a piece of his hamburger patty into the ketchup and chewed it. "Doubtful," he said. "Just by pure definition, your potential isn't written in stone, I don't think. Then there's the idea of nature versus nurture, as you know. Can't teach an old dog new tricks, et cetera. The debate's been around for centuries."

"They can do all sorts of things with DNA these days," Cherilyn said. "And you know Megan Daly started up that new sno-ball stand because her DNAMIX reading said Entrepreneur. She got the readout and just went for it the next day. Had it up in a week. That place already has a line around the block."

"Good for her," Douglas said, and he meant it.

"Do you think it's silly for people to do that, though? To wonder about that stuff?"

Douglas saw that his wife was eyeing him intensely, leaning in toward the table, the bow of her white blouse dangling above her plate. "I guess people get into all sorts of things," Douglas said. "But I wouldn't put too much stock in a video game."

"It's not a game," she said. "Why do you always have to put things down?"

Here was another small thing to make Douglas worry. He did not feel like he was putting anything down and yet she did. It was an odd experience for them to be sitting together yet feeling apart, and so Douglas set down his utensils and looked across the table at her.

"I'm sorry," he said. "I didn't know I was doing that."

Cherilyn placed her head in her hands. Her fork jutted out between her thumb and forefinger with each tine stuck through an individual pasta shell, something Douglas hadn't noticed her doing while he ate. He looked down at her plate. The noodles had been shifted around the edges and pressed to the exact height of the skillet burger, which remained untouched. "Maybe you aren't putting *me* down," Cherilyn said. "You just don't know what I'm talking about. I'm sorry. I know. I'm just tired."

Douglas longed to say something perfect, to perhaps utter some sweet turn of phrase that might recalibrate the evening entirely, but could come up with nothing. So, instead, he instilled each bite he took with a noise meant to suggest that this particular piece of her meal was even more pleasurable than the last. And when it became obvious that she wasn't going to eat her portion, Douglas reached across the table and switched plates. He forked off an edge of her patty and used it to scrape up some hardening cheese. "I'll tell you what," he said, "this meal hit the spot. I don't know what else a guy could ask for."

Cherilyn took his empty plate from the table and walked to the kitchen. "It needed tzatziki," she said. "Is that how you say it? Tatzeeky?"

Douglas nodded, although he wasn't quite sure, and began to whistle the theme to *Peter and the Wolf*.

Later that evening, Douglas sat on the couch watching a baseball game. Cherilyn had come out of the kitchen and gone into the spare bedroom, which they used as an office, without speaking. After an hour passed, Douglas walked down the hall to find her sitting at the desk and reading a large book, with her left hand inside her blouse. When Douglas pushed the door open, he saw her tugging gently at her nipple.

"Cher?" he said.

Cherilyn took her hand out of her shirt and looked up at him. "What?" she said. "I had an itch."

"What are you doing in here?"

"Your computer takes forever to start," she said. "I grabbed a book."

"You want to come watch the ball game?" he asked her. "The good guys are up in the fifth."

"I don't know," she said. "I can't keep the players straight anymore. It's like all of their names blend together."

"Just come sit with me then. Bring your book if you want. I've been missing you in there."

The book Cherilyn was reading was called *Lines of Succession: A World History.* It was a textbook Douglas used to teach to his ninth-graders before the change of curriculum. Cherilyn kept her place in the book with a pencil and followed her husband to the couch. She sat cross-legged on the cushions and placed a pillow over her thighs. She took one glance at the television. Estenitando Escarbiones was at the plate and only hitting .230.

"See what I mean?" she said, when the announcer called out his name.

"It's a big world out there," Douglas said, and began to whistle an old bullfighting song called "El Carne."

"You've got that right," Cherilyn said and reopened the book.

Douglas watched her flip through the pages, scanning over pictures of dukes and duchesses, kings and queens. "What are you reading?" he asked, even though he knew. She pointed to a paragraph on the page.

"Did you know that twenty of the world's fifty richest men are oil sheiks?" she asked.

"I did know that," Douglas said. "Or, at least, at one point that was true."

"Look at this one," she said, and turned the book around for him to see. "I can't pronounce his name, either." The man in the picture was in full ceremonial dress, standing next to a camel cloaked in a red jewel-covered blanket. "He's a prince, it looks like. He's got a big mustache like you used to have," she said. "Where do you think he's from?"

"Saudi Arabia, probably," Douglas said. "They have princes."

Cherilyn got off the couch and walked over to the wall where

Douglas had hung a map, long ago. She ran her fingers over the glass frame until she found Saudi Arabia and tapped it with her nails. "Here it is," she said. "I found it."

Cherilyn returned to the couch but didn't speak. Instead, she read the large book until her husband fell asleep. Later that night, she turned off the television and woke him up. She then led him to the bedroom and, once they were under the covers, began to touch him in the well-rehearsed way that, Douglas knew, meant she wanted to make love. After fifteen years of marriage, this was an increasingly unexpected request, and so Douglas, sleepy as he was, was happy to oblige. He recalled the most recent times they had been together, maybe three occasions in the few months since Christmas, the last a tipsy night after a school fundraiser, an impromptu session on the living room couch, of all places, and orchestrated this new scene in the way he'd so often done the past twenty years that they'd shared themselves with each other. He then collapsed, grateful and pleased, on top of her.

Life, at this moment, was not so bad.

What troubled Douglas, though, and what was truly unprecedented in the life they'd long lived together, was this:

After he finished, Cherilyn asked him to do it again.

"But maybe," she whispered. "A little bit harder this time."

2

Jacob

He had his father's face. Maybe there was some value to that.

And the face he used to share: his twin brother's. Jacob could never forget.

But what else did people think about *him*, as a person? Sixteen years old? Skinny? Invisible? That he was the *other* Richieu boy, the lesser twin, as he had always been? What had he done to stand out? Win a spelling bee? Play Pokémon? Rock out his PSATs? Bake a soufflé? Suck at basketball? That is quite the résumé. So, Jacob wondered, what could he do to better himself? To move forward? Was that even a thing that he wanted? And where was all the anger he was supposed to feel about his brother's death, all that rage he'd initially felt? And how again do you rationalize a numerator? Do you multiply both the numerator and denominator by $\sqrt{ax+b+2}$? And is today Thursday? Is it tacos or chicken nuggets for lunch? And how serious was she about him? About anything? Could he ask her? Could he be honest? Could he tell her he wanted out? What were the options before him? And how could he, the person in charge of his own thoughts, not know even the simplest things about himself?

Jacob had little time to consider these questions as, behind him, two other boys tromped in through the men's room door. He checked them out through the reflection in the bathroom mirror, registered neither fear nor simple pleasure at their appearance, and went back to staring at his own face. The boys were Randall Wilky and Brett Boone, both of whom Jacob knew in the obvious way that everyone knew one another at Deerfield Catholic, but these boys were truly non-integers, neither positive nor negative, in the math of Jacob's life. They were freshmen, as Jacob was a junior, and were so engrossed in their own conversation that they didn't even notice him.

"She doesn't actually blow on it, you idiot," Randall said. "It's just a phrase. Jesus, man."

"My point," Brett said, "was even if that's *all* she did, I would prefer she do it from a great distance."

Them, too? Jacob wondered. Even them?

He picked at a scab on his chin and washed his hands. He ripped a long stretch of brown paper towels from the dispenser and held it against his skin until the small dot of blood disappeared. He then turned to leave as the boys brushed past him and sidled up at the urinals.

"What's up, J?" Randall said. "Hey, you're a smart guy. Can you tell this dumbass what a blowjob is?"

"It's an idiom," Jacob said. "Not a phrase. Getting a blowjob is an idiom."

"All I'm saying is that I believe Brett would be an idiom not to accept Jenny's offer."

"That," Jacob said, "would be a maxim."

"And *that*," Brett said, "is a pretty good website."

The boys laughed and bumped their fists over the urinals as Jacob put the straps of his pack around his shoulders. He paused at the bathroom door before leaving. He paid no attention to the familiar graffiti sprawled across it but looked only at the top-left corner, which was still, thankfully, blank. He then left the bathroom and walked into the bustling hallway, alive with the clamor of slammed lockers and squeaking sneakers, as the two hundred and twenty-four students of Deerfield Catholic hustled to first period.

Jacob entered a classroom and walked down the second aisle to his seat in the back row, where he had been assigned by alphabet some months ago. Through the loudspeaker on the wall, the voice of Father Peter Flynn crackled, "All the time," to which the two hundred twenty-four students of Deerfield Catholic replied, "God is great." To which Father Pete replied, "God is great," to which the students replied, "All the time."

And so another day began.

Jacob put his backpack on top of the desk and laid his head on it. Each day that passed in this stretch of life seemed to be filled with new forms of misery and, as far as school was concerned, Jacob dreaded first period most of all. It had nothing to do with the course or the teacher, both of which Jacob liked in his own quiet way.

It was instead centered on the broad-shouldered girl who sat like a catatonic in the row by the window. This was Trina Todd, who many might now peg as Jacob's closest friend, if not something a bit stranger. Even Jacob, despite constantly trying, could not define their relationship. She'd been his brother's ex-something, one of Toby's many ex-somethings, and was with him on the night that he died. Not with him in the car, though, Jacob knew. Since then, she'd latched on to Jacob in curious and troublesome ways. She'd called and texted, cryptically hinting that Toby's accident was not an accident at all. People, she said, were to blame. Toby's friends, she'd told him, all the dickheads at their school, every single one of them, but offered no real evidence to back this up. It was just another binge-drunken night of high school, people said, and Toby never should have turned the key and driven.

That was everyone's story but Trina's.

Still, Jacob had listened those nights on the phone as if for no other reason than to hear his brother's name again, as if for no other reason than to continue talking to a girl who wanted to continue talking to him and, in this time, confessed to also hating the dickheads, because he did. In the weeks after Toby's wreck, he'd hated everything. But recently, Jacob felt, Trina had turned his simple confession into an alliance. She was hatching a plan, she'd said. She would take care of it. She told him they were in it together.

They'd stopped talking to each other at school nearly entirely the past two weeks, though, instead doing most of their communication through folded notes slipped into the slats of their lockers, via text message, or out in the open as they ambled the woods of Deerfield, killing the hot hours between school and dinner at the respective houses that they didn't want to return to. This was where Jacob spent as much time being interested in Trina, and as much time feeling sorry for Trina, as he did being terrified of her. She had a look that unsettled him, as if she knew so many truths he did not, and this was not a comfortable feeling. Was it really friendship, then, that put them together? Was it obligation? Was it attraction? Was it loss? Was it something else entirely? Jacob did not know. Most important to Jacob was another question, the one that clouded nearly all of his thoughts lately:

Was there a way out?

Jacob sat up when he heard the door to the classroom shut, thinking it was his history teacher, Mr. Hubbard. This guy was an unabashed pop-quiz junkie and the way he had rambled on for the last twenty minutes of yesterday's class about the possible political ramifications of the bald eagle's inevitable extinction, or something to that effect, something about things seemingly beyond our control actually being in our control and forcing us to change our national symbology or systemology or some sort of -ology, had Jacob guessing there'd be a quiz.

It wasn't Mr. Hubbard, though, who was now uncharacteristically three minutes late. It was instead Rusty Bodell, all five feet eight and near three hundred pounds of him, with his pasty white skin and ample breasts, who strutted into the classroom in the same peacockish manner he had done for the last week. He had the collar of his white uniform polo popped up to his earlobes, his shirttail untucked over a pair of navy blue Dickies shorts, and pink sunglasses on. He wore fluorescent blue Nike sneakers with ankle socks, and his legs were the color of cream cheese. His thick and freckled arms were also remarkable in their total lack of definition or even elbows, it seemed, and yet they appeared operational as Rusty lifted them to prop his red hair back into its improbable and aerodynamic shape. This was a new coif for Rusty, undoubtedly inspired by the page of a magazine at Supercuts or from some movie he'd seen, and its odd cylindrical attitude reminded Jacob of a snail shell. Regardless, there were no two ways about it. Rusty looked ridiculous.

Yet, Jacob had to give it to him. Here was a high school kid who had done the impossible. He had reinvented himself right in the middle of a semester. Not two weeks ago he was sitting alone at a lunch table using his fingers to shovel Nutella into his mouth, and now, here he was, still a kid by himself at a lunch table, sure, but dressed to the ludicrous nines and remarkably confident. So, what was the change? Jacob supposed it was all mental, in the same way other desperate kids of that age suddenly decide that they can't stand another day in the skin they're in. So, they join a new clique or try out some new sport or make up a rumor about sleeping with a substitute teacher and hope that it sticks, which it never does. Whatever Rusty's reasoning, though, he looked to be all in.

He stood at the front of the class and took off his sunglasses. "I'd like to make an announcement," Rusty said. "I want all the females in this room to know that I am currently untethered by any serious relationships. I am therefore available for long walks in the park, canoe rides at sunset, and sex marathons. But, please, ladies. One at a time."

Somebody from the back of the class threw a wad of paper at him and, in the front row, Becca Colbert said, "My God, Rusty. What is that fucking smell? Did you *bathe* in cologne?"

"That, dear Becca," Rusty said, "is the smell of your future in paradise."

"Disgusting," she said.

"I'm serious," Rusty said. "That's the name of it: Your Future in Paradise. It cost me twenty bucks."

Jacob heard a strange buzzing behind him. It sounded like a June bug or some fat mosquito going by at close range, but when he ducked to the side to avoid it, he saw that it was a small drone the size of a coaster flying by his desk. This was a remote-control job, about five inches wide, with a prop like a tiny helicopter, and it made its awkward sojourn to the front of the classroom. Jacob looked back to see Jerry Whitehouse working the remote, his back-pack opened on his desk, from where he unleashed the drone. He flew it up toward Rusty and then backed it away when Rusty took a swat at it. He laughed and floated it over his head in a circle as Rusty Bodell, in his predictable way, made a few awful jumps to snag it.

"Look!" Jerry said. "It's King Kong!" and the class let loose.

Even Jacob smiled, though he was not proud of this. Still, it had become so easy to laugh at Rusty in their years since grade school that it felt like a form of therapy. The way his cheeks went bright red as he hopped and swatted at the thing. The way he climbed onto a chair, the skin of his gut poking out beneath his shirt. No one was immune to the cruel humor, nor would the moment be lost, as half the kids in the room began recording the action on their cell phones and uploading it to the larger world. Such was Rusty's fate.

Jacob stopped smiling when Mr. Hubbard walked in. Instead of immediately taking control of the situation, however, Mr. Hubbard simply strode up to his desk and set down his satchel and trombone case. He wore the same silly hat he'd been wearing the past week and was looking at a couple of small slips of paper in his hand, receipts maybe, shuffling through them. "Have a seat, Rusty," he said without looking up.

"Mr. Hubbard," Rusty said, and climbed off the chair. "I feel like I am being discriminated against."

Mr. Hubbard continued going through the receipts and said, "What's the charge this time?"

"It's my animal magnetism, sir," Rusty said. "My classmates are having a hard time controlling themselves."

Mr. Hubbard folded the pieces of paper and put them in his pocket. He looked up at Rusty and, finally, the drone. "Have a seat," he said again and watched the drone follow him as he made his trek over the outstrewn legs of his classmates. When he sat down at his desk, the drone did a wide circle above his head.

"Look at it," somebody said. "It's like a fly on a turd."

"That's enough," Mr. Hubbard said. "Who's controlling this thing?"

"I am," Jerry said, remote still in hand. "I was thinking about yesterday, Mr. Hubbard. You know, how maybe this could be our new symbol if the bald eagle goes extinct."

He then made the drone fly up to the ceiling and do a few expert loops around the class. He started making jet noises with his mouth, letting out a whistle now and again as if it were firing off missiles. "Paint a flag on it," Jerry said. "Put it on the dollar bill."

Mr. Hubbard sat on his desk and watched the small machine make several sorties over the students' heads, to which they applauded. Then he looked over at Jacob. And it was this recent habit of Mr. Hubbard's that had begun to aggravate Jacob. The way he tried to make eye contact at the pinnacle of each lecture. The way he looked to Jacob as if only he might know the answers to the rhetorical questions he posed about history and meaning. Jacob couldn't stand it.

Why did Mr. Hubbard assume that he knew something the other kids of his age did not? Was it because he had become so predictably, so excruciatingly, Jacob wondered, the A student in all of his classes? Was it as benign as that? Or was it something else? Was it about his brother? His mother? His father? The interior walls of his life? Regardless, the manner of searching connection Mr. Hubbard had been making with him the past two months inevitably made Jacob want to tear up, which inevitably made Jacob embarrassed, which inevitably made Jacob furious.

So, he did what he often did, and broke off the gaze. He instead looked down at his desk as the other kids had their fun. They shot paper clips up at the drone, cast paper airplanes around the room, and began, under Jerry's lead, a full-throated rendition of "Off we go, into the wild blue yonder," which the choir had been practicing for the bicentennial. Their concert was to kick the whole thing off tomorrow night, along with an award ceremony for the football team, who had made the state playoffs that fall, and Jacob knew this not because he had any desire to go, but because Trina had recently mentioned this as a place where nearly every single one of them would be, all the dickheads she blamed for Toby's death. All of them gathered there, she said, like "sitting ducks." Jacob shook this thought from his head as his classmates beat their desks like drums, paradiddled their pencils on their laptops, and constructed for themselves a lasting memory. When Jacob finally raised his head, he made the mistake of looking over at Trina, his new best friend, he supposed, his dead brother's ex-something, his partner in mysterious sadness, his problem, who was staring right back at him. Her eyes were clear and gray and devoid of humor or even passion as she mouthed a string of words to Jacob beneath the noise of the classroom. Jacob looked back at her and furrowed his brow as if to say, *What?* As if I to say, *I can't understand you.*

But he knew what Trina was saying. She was repeating, over and over:

Every single one of them.

3

Douglas

After lunch, Douglas had a break.

First period aside, the rest of his day had gone sanely. No more drones, military songs, or overt animal magnetism. Still, Douglas hadn't taught well. He felt barely there. He'd lost his train of thought during lectures, let kids get away with their obnoxious snickering behind his back, and didn't think to give a single quiz. This type of mental malleability, he knew, was the ruin of any good teacher. Still, he couldn't help himself. Instead of reinventing the past for his students, Douglas had spent his morning reimagining his own recent history, at first headlined by his failure to produce the sexual encore Cherilyn had requested the night before. He'd tried, all right, as the last thing he ever wanted to do was disappoint his wife, but after positioning himself between Cherilyn's legs for the second time in thirty minutes, his body, ever so pitifully, succumbed to his mind.

What were the reasons?

Cherilyn's desire for something a bit rougher was out of character, sure, but Douglas wasn't one to be selfish. He considered himself pretty open-minded in the grand scheme of things, although life in Deerfield rarely required him to prove it, and would like very much to provide any sexual attitude Cherilyn desired. After all, Douglas figured, *he* was still the person she was asking it from, and that's what mattered. Yet this, the very fact that it was *him* she wanted it from, in its own way, became the problem. When Douglas looked down at her for the second time that night, the long, thin hairs he normally kept combed over the crown of his head fell before his eyes and he was reminded, resolutely, of his baldness. Mustn't he look silly in this pose, he thought, like some desperate traveling salesman? When he tried to forget about this and focus instead on the pleasures available to him, to look down at steady parts of Cherilyn that always kept him able, he was again distracted by the unfortunate parts of himself, the paunch of his hairy stomach, the slight sag of his middle-aged breasts, and this also discouraged him. So, despite his best intentions, Douglas had to wonder if he was the type of man who could even do it a bit harder when called upon. Now, there was a depressing thought. This made him wonder if he was able to do *anything* differently than he had previously done. And, if not, then what kind of man was he? And who would want to be with a man who, at forty years old, doesn't even know who he is? These worries, Douglas understood, were not very sexy. Yet around and around the pity pot he went until it became clear that he had nothing more to offer.

Douglas rolled over apologetically and made a few awkward attempts at pleasing Cherilyn with his hands. This well-intentioned groping only seemed to embarrass them both, though, and Cherilyn pulled the covers up over her breasts. "It's okay, honey," she said. "I don't know what I was thinking."

"I would have waited," Douglas told her. "I mean, if I knew you weren't ready. I could have waited longer."

"Shh," she said. "Just turn around. Let me hold you." Cherilyn scooched up to Douglas from behind, and the heat of their bodies beneath the covers, the stick of their sweat, was almost too much for him to bear. He kicked a foot from under the blanket. He fluffed the pillows under his head.

"You know," he said. "Biologically, men aren't really built to go twice in a row."

"I know," Cherilyn said, and gently ran her fingers through the patch of hair above his ear to calm him. "I was just enjoying it. Take it as a compliment."

"Our hormone levels drop pretty drastically is all that I'm saying," Douglas told her. "It's not about interest. You know that, right? It's about science."

"Let's talk about something else," she said.

Douglas closed his eyes as Cherilyn traced her fingertips down his neck and to his back, where she began drawing unknown shapes along his shoulders. "How about this," Cherilyn said. "Pop quiz. Are you ready?"

Douglas sighed. "I'm ready."

"Did you know," Cherilyn asked him, "that those Arabian kings, like we saw in that book, have these things called harems? And that all those women are kind of like royalty, like princesses?"

"I did know that," Douglas said. "Though that definition may be a bit problematic."

"I was wondering," she said. "How does a person get chosen for something like that?"

"You know," Douglas said, "maybe if I just got a drink of water."

"Oh, Lord," she said. "You did great. Let's get some sleep."

The two of them lay spooned together like question marks after that, each trying to match the other's breathing while Douglas stared across the room, the flickering night-light in the bathroom looking to him like a lonely candle left to peter out in a cave. After a while, Cherilyn took a deep breath and said, "I do love you, Douglas," and rolled over on her back to cool off.

Douglas did not reply but instead feigned sleep, slowing his breathing to become almost imperceptible. He continued to do this even as he felt the slight shaking of the bed beside him a few minutes later, even as he heard the quiet sounds of his wife's unmet desires that, for some reason, on this night, he did not feel the right to interrupt.

But these were yesterday's problems.

Douglas had new quandaries to consider.

For one, when he tried to leave for work that morning, his car wouldn't start. After he showered and got dressed, Cherilyn still asleep under a mound of pillows, Douglas grabbed the trombone for his lesson after school and went to put it in the back seat of his car, the door of which was ajar. He then noticed the overhead light was out. And, sure enough, when he sat in the driver's seat, the engine wouldn't turn. Crime was so uncommon in the heart of Deerfield that Douglas didn't even suspect it, instead figuring that he'd likely not shut the door hard enough the evening before, another small failing to add to his ever-growing litany. Rather than waking Cherilyn up to tell her, Douglas took her keys and her Subaru.

On the short drive to school, Douglas smelled the faint odor of tobacco coming from his wife's air-conditioning. They had both been social smokers when they met, mainly buying a pack on a whim after they'd had a drink or two and still felt young and invincible, but they'd decided to quit that whole business on their wedding day. Cherilyn was known to occasionally stray from this pact, and the scent that sometimes followed her actually comforted Douglas. It was a quick memory of their courtship, a reminder that his wife was a casual and imperfect being, complete with her own version of a small, secret life. A life similar, Douglas realized, to the one he himself had carried on in the form of a slick

and golden trombone, his name on a flashing marquee. So, who
was he to judge? Instead, he turned down the radio and took in
the scent, recalling all the good things he felt about their lives
together, and whistled to himself as he drove, a lesser-known composition by Copland.

When the smell of tobacco faded, Douglas turned down the air-
conditioning and opened the compartment on the dash to see
what she was smoking these days, to see if she had her customary
pack of skinny Benson & Hedges stashed in there, but she did not.
In it instead were a number of what he first thought to be receipts.
The papers were blue, however, and folded neatly together, not in
the way a person disposes of trash. So, Douglas became curious.
He pulled into the school parking lot and removed the small slips
from the tray. The paper was waxy like that of a gas-station pay
pump's and, after he parked, he unfolded the slips from the middle. He had seen something like this before, he sadly realized, from
the student who claimed he would grow up to play with plutonium.

At the top of the first slip was the outline of a man, arms and
legs spread like da Vinci's model. On his chest, in dark blue ink,
was a double helix: the drawing of DNA. Underneath this was the
word *DNAMIX*.

He then saw his wife's name, Cherilyn Mae Fuller, her maiden
name, and Douglas found himself the reluctant master of a puzzle.
Why he hadn't put together that his wife had tried this ridiculous
new machine at the store, and why he didn't ask her about it the
night before, became to him a looping wonder, a reason to second-
guess his every move from there out.

Listed beneath her name was a series of numbers in incredibly
fine print, as well as things such as eye color, hair color, and potential height. This is when Douglas recalled everything from the
previous night, triggered by that word *potential*, which Cherilyn

had said was the whole point. He remembered her fork and its carefully speared pasta, the way dimples showed up in her thighs when she sat Indian-style on the sofa, and the way she held him close with her ankles when he had finished making love to her that first time.

Her potential height read 5'6", and Douglas thought that was about right. The potential number of children she could have read 12, which seemed to Douglas outlandish and insulting, especially since they were childless after several early years of trying. And then Douglas saw another category, which listed Potential Life Station.

It read, in bold print: **ROYALTY**.

Douglas shook his head. How Cherilyn could put any stock into this contraption unnerved him. It seemed totally unlike her and yet, as with many surprises, he could not tell if this delighted or depressed him. He moved the first sheet aside and looked at the one behind it, an exact copy of the former. Again and again, all in all totaling ten different times his wife had entered this machine. Each one of her responses read the same: Royalty, Royalty, Royalty. One of the final slips said **SURFER**, but Douglas saw that this was not his wife's reading at all, that it didn't even have a name at the top. Still, he cross-referenced the series of small numbers of this readout with Cherilyn's and they were not a match. Why would she subject herself to something like this? he wondered. What was she hoping it would say? And who even knew how this thing worked? It was outlandish. He looked at the Surfer readout again and saw that it had been soiled, likely discarded, as Douglas felt he might do with anything that told him to jump in the ocean. Still, he folded all the slips back up and put them in his pocket. He then walked into the school building, strolled down the hallway to his class-room, and found Rusty Bodell swatting away at a drone.

Now here he was again, back in his classroom on his lunch break, flipping through the readouts once more and nursing a necessary cup of coffee. He'd decided to give Cherilyn a call and talk it over, to bridge the small gap he sensed between them the night before and approach the subject with humor, as he felt his wife's anxieties were easy to be solved. Douglas now thought it rather cute that Cherilyn had buried her nose in that textbook, trying to find a picture of her potential self. It was endearing, the way she had been poring over foreign recipes. This was something, Douglas figured, they could laugh about in the years to come. This could be simply another spud, he reckoned, in their marital pile of small potatoes. Douglas then imagined everything about the previous night smaller than it was before because, for the first time in his life, he discounted the undertow of our dreams.

He took out his cell phone and, remembering that hers was broken, dialed their home phone instead. After an unusually large number of rings, Cherilyn answered.

"Your car won't start," she said.

Douglas smiled. He wanted to tell her how glad he was that this whole business from last night wasn't serious. He wanted to say that he could go twice in a row right now if she asked him to. "I know," he said, grinning. "I took the Outback. I'm sorry. I was running late."

"What's so funny?" she asked.

Cherilyn sounded on edge, as if he'd interrupted her, and Douglas stopped smiling. "Oh," he said. "Nothing. Nothing's funny. Everything okay?"

"Well," Cherilyn said, and sighed. "I'd wanted to run some errands with Mom, but I guess I won't. We do need groceries, though. Can you swing by the store?"

"Sure," he said, "anything for you," and took out a pen and paper from his satchel.

"Okay," Cherilyn said and shuffled something around in the background. "Here goes. We need four eggplants, pita bread, a bottle of lemon juice. There may be a coupon for that in the driver's-side door. I'm not sure. Um, we also need some tahini. Just ask if you can't find it. Two cloves of garlic. I've got salt, green onions. Get some more olive oil, though. It looks like we are going to need a lot of olive oil."

Douglas took down what she said, feeling his stomach sink a bit more with each request, and wrote a question mark next to every single item. In the long history of their marriage, had he ever been asked to purchase such things? He had not. But should the addition of unexpected items in one's life even be of note? After all, that's the heart of jazz, isn't it? If he wanted to stand onstage, be a man on the scene, he figured he had to embrace a little improvisation. Yet his mood became sullen. He traced over the question marks time and time again. He underlined the word *eggplant*.

"Are you feeling all right?" he asked her. "How's your head? You sound down."

"I'm fine," she said. "I've just been watching the news. You know, the world seems kind of terrible when you watch the news."

"Should I pick up some steaks or something?" he asked.

"No," Cherilyn said. "I think that's the whole meal. It's mainly an eggplant thing."

Douglas told her he would swing by the store after his trombone lesson at four and be home around five-thirty or six. "Okay," she said.

"I love you," he said.

"Okay," she said. "Me, too."

Douglas turned off his phone and set it on the desk. He didn't even have time to whistle out some blues when, behind him, he heard a man say, "I love you, too, sugar-nuts."

Douglas looked up to see Deuce Newman, the de facto town

photographer of Deerfield, standing in the doorway to his classroom.

Deuce was a man who took up a lot of space. Although not even six feet tall, he had a certain girth about him, which, like the trunk of a tree, only seemed to grow with time. His thick face, the strange outdated haircut that swept over his ears, the two heavy and professional-looking cameras slung around his neck: They were enough to block Douglas's view of the hallway. The two of them had been classmates in high school forever ago and Deuce Newman, whose actual name was Bruce, was once an all-state middle linebacker who, as luck would have it, wore the number 2.

Now hitting forty himself, Deuce had become a somewhat legendary figure around Deerfield. After tearing up his knee in his senior year, Deuce had decided to do what many local athletes do and spend the rest of his life milking his youthful celebrity for all it was worth. At this, he was successful.

After all, Bruce Newman's story is the type a small town understands. He didn't come from much, a little two-bedroom house with a dad who worked at the auto shop, didn't have any fancy training techniques, just the old rusty tackling sleds behind the school, and yet was given, or as many in Deerfield would say, *blessed*, with outsized abilities. He'd once had a clear path out of Deerfield and into the larger world, complete with fame and riches and everything a person can dream of, until an illegal crack back block from a big-city kid quickly took him out at the knees. This was Deerfield life in a nutshell.

But Douglas didn't feel too bad for Deuce. He was ambitious in his own way and had ultimately achieved a sort of fame, after all, becoming akin to the town mascot. After the injury, he stood on the sideline with his crutches and led cheers for the fans, got pecks from the cheerleaders. Even after he graduated, the coaches still invited him to the field as a sign of goodwill, where, out of little other than boredom, Deuce took to bringing a camera with him. He took action shots at ground level, candid photos of hopeful parents in the stands, and this resulted in the local paper, *The Deerfield Bugle*, running some of his pictures, and the next twenty years of Bruce's life were pretty much set.

Yet Douglas had no idea why he was at school that day, nor why he was standing in the doorway to his classroom staring at him.

"Bruce," Douglas said. "What can I do for you?"

"I just have to know," Deuce said, "what kind of man can be married to a woman like Cherilyn and still sit there with a face as sad as a donkey's dick?"

"Lovely," Douglas said.

"That was Cherilyn, right?" Deuce said. "I'm not interrupting something secret, am I? Maybe some side honey with a teacher's pet?"

Douglas stood up from his desk and walked over to shake Bruce's hand. This type of crass and innocuous teasing was common between them, so Douglas didn't think much of it. "I think you know me better than that," he said. "It's good to see you."

Truth be told, though, Douglas didn't feel like seeing anyone at that moment. And, out of all the nobodies Douglas didn't want to see, Bruce Newman ranked pretty high. It was nothing overtly contentious, but they'd always had a sort of odd relationship, all the way back to high school, as Bruce long harbored and still maintained, Douglas would argue, an unrelenting crush on Cherilyn. The practicalities of the matter had been settled years ago, of course, as Cherilyn had never shown a lick of interest in Bruce, as she had loved and married Douglas without incident, and as the world was a logical place. But the misguided hearts of some men, for whatever reason, never waver. So, the way Bruce always asked about her, the way he would kiss her hand when they saw each other out shopping or at some event in the town square, the way he would be sure to remind Douglas how lucky he was to have her, inevitably made small talk between the two men a bit strained.

"Damn," Deuce said. "What happened to your mustache? Your face looks like a dolphin's vagina."

"I have to say," Douglas told him, "you have an impressive amount of animal genitalia similes."

"Whatever that means," Deuce said, "I thank you."

"So," Douglas asked. "What brings you to campus?"

"Bicentennial fever," Deuce said. "I've only got two days left to get all these headshots done and these damn kids don't show up to appointments. I've tried everything I could think of and then some. I figured I'd just track them down here."

The bicentennial. Of course. Everything in town, it seemed to Douglas, was about the damned bicentennial. That very weekend Deerfield was to hold what they considered to be a huge celebration. It was something the mayor and the city council imagined would be a statewide news item, maybe inject a little energy into the place, pump some tourism dollars into the local economy, although Douglas felt this to be a bit delusional. Still, the party had become a sort of homework assignment for the whole town that past year. The school band was learning new songs, banners were being printed up by the dozens, Cherilyn was making birdhouses like crazy. Even the courthouse building had been pressure-washed and repainted. Bruce Newman's role in this occasion had become prominent by his own design. He'd promised their mayor, Hank Richieu, a sort of monumental mosaic, one of those hidden-picture computer-type deals about ten feet high and five across, to be made up of a small photo of everyone in Deerfield's face. There was also to be a talent show, a parade, a gumbo cook-off, and even a fireworks display, but Deuce's mosaic of the nearly twelve thousand people in Deerfield was said to be the centerpiece. The whole thing was even kicking off tomorrow night, Douglas remembered, in the school gym. He had no plan to attend. All he wanted this Friday night, he knew, was a normal dinner with his wife.

"Actually," Bruce told him, "I still need a photo of you, don't I? How about you hop up there on your desk and give me an action shot? We'll call it 'The Teacher in Deep Thought.'"

"You know," Douglas said. "This really isn't a good time."

Deuce took one of the cameras in his hand and began fiddling with the lens. "Come on," he said. "Pucker those lips and give me a trademark Hubbard whistle. I'll get you in the middle of 'What a Wonderful World' by that fat guy."

Douglas reached down to his desk and grabbed his beret, picked up his mug of coffee that was already getting cold. "You mean Louis Armstrong?" Douglas said. "American genius?"

"That would be a good caption," Bruce said. "Stand over there by the window. I'll get you in your artsy-fartsy hat and everything. We'll call it 'Douglas Hubbard: The Professor in Repose.'"

Douglas knew he was trapped. So, rather than fight it, he walked to the window and stood thoughtfully enough, he felt, with his coffee and beret. "I'm not actually a professor," he said, and just like that, here was another thing that reminded Douglas of what he had never accomplished. No Ph.D. No stellar career. No dynamo in the sack. And this thought led him back to Cherilyn.

"Bruce," Douglas said. "I was wondering. Have you heard about that new machine at the grocery?"

"Indeed," Bruce said. "Amazing, isn't it?"

"What," Douglas said. "You believe in that thing?"

"No," Bruce said. "I meant it's amazing the shit people will buy if you shovel it."

"I'm guessing you haven't tried it, then."

"No need," Bruce said. "Why mess with perfection, am I right?

It's like you. Why would you try something like that? You know who you are. It's the same person you've always been. The luckiest man in the world."

"I don't know," Douglas said. "I imagine I could be a lot of different things."

"Whatever you say," Deuce said, and angled his camera. "Now give me a smile, Mr. President. Give me a big cheesy grin for the ages."

Douglas rested his hip against the windowsill and willed himself to smile. Before Deuce could get a shot off, however, a baseball crashed through the glass. It hit Douglas in the hand, cracked his mug, and splashed coffee all over his blazer.

"Perfect," Douglas said.

A boy named Tim Nevers quickly ran up to the window, nearly out of breath, and surveyed the damage. He looked through the hole and into the room. "Damn!" he said. "How fast you think that was going?"

Deuce picked the ball off the floor, tossed it in his hand a couple times. "Upper eighties, easy," he told him. "Nice little slurve to it, too."

Douglas mopped at the coffee with the sleeve of his blazer. "Go see the principal, Mr. Nevers," he told him. "Tell her to call maintenance."

"I'm sorry, Mr. Hubbard," Tim said. "I just found out yesterday that I'm going to be a pitcher. A Major Leaguer! Can you believe it? I didn't even know I liked baseball."

Deuce turned the ball in his hand. "A pitcher, eh?" he said. "That's what DNAMIX told you?"

"Yes, sir," the boy said.

Deuce tossed the ball back to him. "Not bad," he said.

"You may want to work on your command," Douglas told him. "And start thinking of a way to pay for this window."

"Won't be a problem," Tim said. "I'm going to be a millionaire!" And then he ran along.

When Douglas looked back up at Deuce, he saw that he was already clicking away, grinning and aiming his camera, catching shot after shot of Douglas looking grumpy and stained and miserable.

"Douglas Hubbard, everybody," Deuce said. "The Luckiest Man in the World."

4

Cherilyn

England. Luxembourg. Liechtenstein. Monaco. Morocco. Qatar!

So much royalty googled and it was not even noon.

So many stories.

Did you know, for instance, that the Kingdom of Bhutan has a Dragon King named Jigme Khesar Namgyel Wangchuck and he married a non-royal woman named Jetsun Pema and made her a queen? Just like that. Boom! She was royal. At their wedding they wore multicolored scarves and pink kimonos and he had a ponytail and she got a crown. This was something Cherilyn did not know yesterday.

It was nice to be reminded, she thought, that the Internet was useful. Although she spent a good amount of time on it, checking Facebook, looking at the things her friends either birthed or ingested on Instagram, getting craft ideas from Pinterest, she did this all from the small cloister of her smartphone. Maybe she would venture over to her news feed every once in a while to read the gossip headlines about which celebrities were mad at other celebrities about what rumored affairs they'd had at which beach house in the Hamptons or Martha's Vineyard or some such place, but Cherilyn didn't think this counted as being "online." She was not one of those "Internet people." The opposite, actually.

Cherilyn liked her phone for the conversations it *provided*, not the distractions from them. Her texts with friends when alone in the house, the way Douglas would call her on his lunch break: These were good things. If given the chance, Cherilyn would always choose real-life people over her phone, she was sure of that, and if someone were to ask her, she would likely say that this phone stuff was a big part of what was wrong with the world these days. People weren't connecting. When she and Douglas had dinner, for example, neither of them ever had their phone on the table. Not like eating over at Jeannie and Ted's house, where he was always looking up every little point they brought up to try to prove people wrong. Like that time she told them mayonnaise is actually sort of a miracle food because it's the only food that literally changes its chemical composition when mixed together. It's no longer its separate parts like other things are when you mix them. It becomes an entirely new thing. And then Ted spent five minutes at the table googling around, trying to prove her wrong, like she was some sort of idiot, and there was a person, Cherilyn thought, who could benefit from taking his head out of his ass. Even if people are wrong every once in a while, if they misremember something, that's okay. Put up your silly machine and let them wonder, Cherilyn thought. This was important.

Perhaps all this crusty philosophy was a sign of her age. Although not an old woman by any stretch, Cherilyn already felt apprehensive about the teenagers of Deerfield, who walked around the square like zombies, thumbing away at who knows what. She'd see a group of high school girls, for instance, still in their school uniforms, all walking together but each laughing at something different on their phones, and felt that, although these girls were barely twenty years younger than her, although she remembered high school like it was yesterday, she now had absolutely nothing in common with them. And what about the ones who got addicted to those games where you shoot other people you don't know while talking to them on a headset for thirty hours in a row? Now, there was a problem. She'd read that some people in Japan were just dying there in the coffee shops because they forgot to eat for like two days. Even those people who were tweeting all the time, or getting angry about what other people were tweeting: What was wrong with them? How does a person get angry about something someone they don't even know didn't really even say? That's what Cherilyn wanted to know. These were the people who lived "online," she thought. And, no, she was not that.

If anything, she felt, her phone just kept her more local, more grounded. Her Facebook feed was made up of her friends who lived down the street, same with Instagram. Her email filled only with ads and bills, maybe an uplifting meme of a possum with its head stuck in a Pringles can that she would then forward over to Douglas. She had intentionally structured her Internet to mirror Deerfield itself, she understood, but would never prefer it to the real thing because it had no sky and no love and no wind.

Yet she was surprised how much she missed it today, her phone. It felt odd to be sitting at Douglas's old computer in her bathrobe in the middle of the day. She'd already had a strange enough morning, having woken flushed and breathing heavy beneath a mound of pillows after a dream in which she ate figs off a lone tree on an island in the middle of the Mississippi River. The sweet taste in her mouth upon waking was like syrup and, when she reached over to grab her phone and check the time, she felt almost panicked not to find it. The strange reality that it was sitting cracked in a bowl of rice made her wonder if she was even awake. She looked at the clock on the dresser and couldn't believe it was nine-thirty. When was the last time she'd slept so late? Was Douglas already gone? she wondered. When was the last time she hadn't kissed him good-bye before work?

And with this thought came the memory of the previous night. What had she been thinking? Asking him to go twice in a row like that? Poor Douglas. She knew he would try to make up for it some-how. He'd probably start doing push-ups in the morning, buy a new pair of running shoes, he was so sensitive. What on earth had got-ten into her? The romance, maybe, of the royal women in that text-book had taken to dancing in her head. The strange feeling of his clean-shaven upper lip on her neck. Maybe something to the idea of being worshipped. Or perhaps it was simply the delight of their reliable sex that she had both wanted and received that thrilled her, the sex that had become less frequent those last few years, she had to admit. The simple idea of asking for more. It was intrigu-ing. She enjoyed being with Douglas, she always had, yet pleasing him was about as challenging as dropping a letter in the mailbox. Maybe she was merely looking for a challenge? She had no idea.

Despite the time, Cherilyn didn't immediately hop out of bed. She instead conducted a mental body-check in her head, something Douglas didn't know had become part of her daily routine. How was she feeling today? she wondered. Her feet felt normal, none of the peculiar cramping she'd had last week, and her legs seemed okay, too. So maybe it all had passed. All of the symptoms she'd been worried about: the strange tingling and numbness in her hands, the sometimes overwhelming exhaustion, maybe today they would disappear? Nothing to see here. Nothing to fear. Wouldn't that be nice?

She eventually got up and made a fresh pot of coffee and turned on the TV and then walked outside in her robe to sneak a cigarette, when she discovered her car was missing, along with the smokes she had stashed in there. She tried to start Douglas's car to no avail and it bothered her, she had to admit, that she found herself stranded. Was that her word for it? *Stranded*? Had she felt this way before about her own home? Since when had she become so dramatic? Come on, Cherilyn. It's not like she had anything to do anyway, she figured. She'd still get a call every once in a while asking her to fill in for someone, a receptionist at the veterinarian's office, maybe running the checkout at the church garage sale, but she'd quit most of that. And so what was on her docket today? Nothing at all. She needed to run to the store for some groceries, go check on her mom yet again, whose house she could easily walk to, but, dear Lord, maybe this lack of unpredictable options was the problem. She had the birdhouses to finish, that was true, but nothing in the world sounded quite as boring as that. And why had she chosen birdhouses anyway?

She stood barefoot in her humid carport and thought with remarkable clarity: *There is nothing at all in this town I want to do*. So, as she had the night before, she went to Douglas's computer. She had info to gather, some details she wanted to figure out.

What Cherilyn wanted most, though, was to feel better. Although everything seemed okay when she woke up, she couldn't deny that her right hand was tingling again. This was yet another in the mysterious and niggling string of symptoms she'd been trying to chalk up to aging, maybe some seasonal allergies. These occasions were also dotted by migraine headaches, though, some dizziness, and a few other obvious nuisances that had her worried. Even right now, once she thought about it, a slight burning in her neck. Had she slept crooked? Maybe a pinched nerve in there somewhere. Perhaps an ibuprofen would do the trick. Or an allergy pill. An Excedrin. What was it like to not feel like something was missing? To not feel like she needed medicine to make her right again? Did she remember?

No, she did not.

She sat and listened to their old desktop try and start itself up. Even though she turned it on last night, it still grumbled like an old man getting out of bed when she moved the mouse. A few lights on the hard drive blinked by her feet and the machine sounded like it was chewing on nickels.

Once it warmed itself up, the first thing she googled was DNAMIX. She needed to find out about this machine, maybe talk to some other people who had tried it, see what they were thinking, but her search came up empty. There was a DNAMIX.com, but this led her only to an unimpressive page that read "This Site Is Under Construction."

Who could she talk to about it? She'd not mentioned her readout to anyone yet and had heard only vague mentions of the machine from her friends. One in a text from Christine Willis, who wrote: *Have you ever heard of a sommelier?* And another from Bruce Newman that asked her directly about it. *Hey, there*, it said. *Have you tried that DNAMIX machine? Tell me what it said if so!* And it was odd the way he texted her out of nowhere, but that was always Bruce's way. As soon as you'd forgotten about him, he'd pop right up beside you. This could be annoying to most people, she knew, but Bruce was lonely and she pitied him. She did not mention this text to Douglas, though, that was for sure. She knew his thoughts on Deuce Newman, who was not a man she had any interest in, in the grand scheme of things, but a man she sometimes thought of.

She also did not mention to Douglas that the real reason she dropped her phone yesterday was that, just for an instant, she could not feel her right hand.

She began by googling "royalty" and went through them all: the pictures of palaces, the lines of descent, the estimated wealth, the beautiful clothes. Hours passed until she found herself staring at one single page, and all those feelings she'd had the night before began creeping back to her. Some sort of heat. Some form of desire. She'd come across the Al Said royal family of Oman and this rabbit hole had a strange effect. On their Wikipedia page she'd found a picture of a striking man with a silver beard and an ornamental gold-and-blue turban on his head and she stared at this person a good while. He was apparently a sultan, which, paired with the photo, now had for Cherilyn an almost erotic ring to it, *sultan*, although the only sultan she could remember seeing previously had been in the Disney version of *Aladdin*, which Cherilyn understood was not at all erotic.

She clicked on some other images, one of them of this same man handing Barbara Bush a ceramic jug, another of this man sitting in what looked to be a solid-gold chair. She then came upon a picture of the most elegant-looking woman she had ever seen, and it nearly knocked her breath out.

It was a close-up of a white woman's face, or at least she appeared to Cherilyn to be that way, wearing a black hood with a beautiful gold dragonfly pinned to the side of it. Her green eyes, her sandy-colored hair, the soft turn of her lips and nose. *Oh my goodness*, Cherilyn thought. She looked both beautiful and relaxed, not at all stuffy the way some of those British royal women appeared. But what injected Cherilyn with a type of energy, a type of adrenaline, was that she and this woman looked, very much, alike.

Cherilyn clicked on her picture and was brought to a page called "How to Live Like an Omani Princess." She gained no clearer idea what an Omani princess actually did after reading the page, but what Cherilyn most wanted to know was the woman's name, to find out if this person was a living, breathing reality, and, sure enough, she was. She was Princess Susan of Oman. And what broke upon Cherilyn as she studied the delicate freckles along her cheeks, the touch of strawberry color in the sweep of her hair, was pleasure. She felt she'd come across a sister she didn't know she had. It was not true, of course, but she felt it all the same.

This idea sent a flush through Cherilyn's chest and made her realize how alone she currently was in that house, how truly alone, without her phone to reach in and ping with a text, without anyone to question her. And, as anyone who finds themselves completely alone with their thoughts might do, Cherilyn began to wonder if she was going crazy. Why had she become so enamored with this idea of being someone important? Someone royal? Her mother's recent battiness didn't help to calm her, that was for sure. She knew the whole idea was ridiculous, that Douglas was probably right about the impossibility of it all, and yet she'd spent yesterday morning in front of her bedroom mirror, trying on the few fancy dresses she owned, ones she hadn't worn in years, which she could not even zip all the way up. And why had she dug out that old Elton John CD with the remake of "Candle in the Wind" that he'd made for Princess Diana? Was she simply bored? Was she flat-out losing her mind? These were both legitimate concerns.

Although finding a person to talk to in Deerfield would have been easy enough, where everyone chatted on the sidewalk or at the gas station, where everyone knew everyone else's business, this seemed the exact opposite kind of talk that Cherilyn needed now. What she wanted was something anonymous, where she could chat with anyone in the world, about any subject she desired. A place where she could talk without judgment. That sounded pretty nice.

So, Cherilyn went to the search bar and typed in "chat with strangers."

The first site that came up was called Omegle and she clicked on it. She had to choose if she wanted the adult chat or the regular chat and, since she wanted to talk to adults and not children, she clicked it. Two small video screens popped up next to a text bar and after she clicked "OK" she was surprised to see her own face materialize in one of them. She looked on top of the monitor and saw that their ancient webcam had lit up with a green light. They had used this device only once that she could remember, she and Douglas, back when someone told them Skype was going to change the world. So, they bought a webcam and skyped with an old college friend of theirs who now lived in France and it was a neat thing but that was years ago, before FaceTime, and the webcam was forgotten.

The other screen said it was connecting her to a stranger and suddenly a man came to vision in the little video box above hers. He looked to be in his sixties and, when the screen became clear, she saw that he was shirtless and holding a bottle of baby oil. The man typed: *Are you looking to be dommed?* Cherilyn grimaced and quickly pressed "Next."

After this came a person wearing an Easter Bunny mask and then a group of three teenage boys passing around a pipe of some sort, but what Cherilyn noticed was that she was really looking at herself this whole time. It was odd to see herself on camera. Her hair pulled back in a ponytail, her green eyes, her freckled nose, the top of her bathrobe in the little screen. It was not a bad tableau. A number of people appeared and disappeared above her as she studied herself. She liked what she saw, she realized, and then the house phone in the kitchen rang.

She got up and walked through the den, pausing to look at the television, which she had left running on the twenty-four-hour-news station. She saw footage of bombed-out brick huts in some dusty landscape and read the scrolling headline that said "Police pronounce all of the victims 'OK.'" She looked at the caller ID and saw that it was Douglas calling. She felt irritated, for some reason, that she'd been interrupted, that she'd been reminded of chores and reality and the fact that he had taken her car without asking. She answered the phone and said, "Your car won't start."

After she'd asked him to pick up a few things to make something called moussaka, Cherilyn went back to the office, where she planned to shut down the computer entirely. When she got there, though, she saw that a man was sitting in the little video box above hers. His location said "Jordan" and he was dark-skinned, with a thick stubble on his face. He looked maybe twenty-five years old and wore a red soccer jersey and seemed to be sitting at a desk. Behind him was a flag that she did not recognize. When he saw her picture come up on the screen, he smiled. He waved his hand. He was, Cherilyn had to admit, quite handsome.

He leaned forward and typed something and then a string of Arabic letters popped up on the screen. It looked, to Cherilyn, like art. She must have smiled because he smiled back and typed *English?*

She typed *yes.*

The man typed back *Not great at English. But you are very beautiful.*

Cherilyn looked at the words, read them over again, and then rose from her desk and walked to the office window. What was this feeling inside her? She looked outside to their backyard, nearly glowing green with its thick St. Augustine grass in the sunlight. Against their aging wooden fence, she saw, a dark shadow from an oak tree cast a shape like a hand. On the small table in the middle of their yard, the birdhouses made from Popsicle sticks and El-mer's glue that she'd set out yesterday to dry. And on one of the red Adirondack chairs she and Douglas had purchased last Christmas, the ones they often sat in to drink wine and watch the sun set, Cherilyn saw a plump squirrel turning an acorn in its little paws, again and again, as if it was the greatest discovery. Cherilyn watched it for a moment and reached up to close the blinds. She then walked back to the computer, loosened her robe a bit, and sat down.

The man was still there and so she smiled at him. He smiled back.

You think I am beautiful? she typed, and he nodded.

She undid her hair from her ponytail.

She swooped it over her eye like Susan of Oman.

Okay, she wrote. *Now tell me. What else do you think I am?*

5

A Crooked Piece of Time

They met mouth-to-mouth in the woods.

It had been only a minute, maybe two, since the three-o'clock bell, and Trina popped out from behind an oak, grabbed the back of Jacob's neck, and shoved her rough tongue through his teeth so aggressively that to call it a kiss at all may have been a mistake. Yet Jacob wasn't searching for words as the taste of her smoke on his lips, the remainder of her breath in his own lungs, both disturbed and delighted him to such a degree that he felt he'd gone blind, the way he'd read in Human Behavior that people sometimes did in the midst of a trauma. By the time he'd regained his sight, Trina had already pushed him away and was now thumbing the screen of her phone. Jacob wiped his mouth with his fist.

"What the hell was that?" he said.

"I'm worried you're backing out on me," she said, and turned her phone around so he could see the picture she'd just taken. It was of the two of them, selfied tongue to tongue like teen lust birds. He'd not even noticed her taking the photo, such was the shock of the kiss, which was the only one they'd ever shared, and the only one Jacob had ever received. "Aw," Trina said, and looked back at her phone. "A couple's first kiss. I'm putting it up on Instagram. Now, no matter what happens, you're implicated."

"Implicated?"

Trina hit the screen two more times. "There it goes," she said. She then knelt down and picked up a small red rock the size of a quarter. Jacob thought she might throw it off into the bayou or maybe try to peck his brain out with it, he had no idea, but instead he watched her rub her thumb over it several times, like someone does a worrying stone, and put it in her mouth.

This was the second time he'd seen her do this. The first was at his brother Toby's burial, two months ago, where Trina stood in the back and spoke to no one. Then, when people were saying their final good-byes at the casket, before they shut and lowered it into the dirt, Jacob saw Trina bend and take a small stone from the ground and close it in her fist. She then walked up to Toby's casket, waiting her place in line like everyone else, and, when she got to him, slowly placed the rock inside of her mouth. Jacob had no idea what to make of it, although he now realized that this was the beginning of everything between them, because, as Trina turned to leave, she approached Jacob for the first time in her life. She and Toby hadn't been dating long, if that's what you could call it, she'd only been at Deerfield Catholic a few months, and had never even seemed to notice Jacob before. But, on this day, she grabbed Jacob's hand and squeezed a piece of paper into his palm that he would later find out was her phone number. She then looked him in the eye without tears or remorse but, rather, with some indiscernible conviction and said, only, "This is not over."

And how Jacob wished, at that time, that his brother's life was not over.

This scene remained one of Jacob's only clear memories of the funeral, which his subconscious was trying desperately, he knew, to blur. And again today, just as she had then, Trina closed her eyes, breathed deeply through her nose, and moved the rock over to the side of her mouth like a lozenge. Jacob stared at her.

"Normal," he said.

"Let's walk," she told him. "Not much time before the dickheads arrive."

Trina took off down the path toward town and Jacob noticed that, in the few minutes since school had ended, she'd somehow altered her uniform to look as if the whole ensemble was now of her choosing. She'd pulled down the top of her jumper to hang off her hips like looping belts, untucked her shirt over the skirt of it, and rolled her socks down in a sloppy and uneven way. Her hair, pulled back at school, was nearly jet black and hung long enough to hit the middle of her back. It looked thick and waxy and so unwashed that it didn't seem to move with her.

The only alteration Jacob had made to his uniform was to pull a ball cap down tight over his head on his way through the parking lot. This was his favorite cap, one he'd ordered from a company in Japan, a black-on-black snap-back with a highly stylized picture of Latios, his favorite Pokémon, on the front of it. Latios was a sleek and flying monster with Psychic energy who Jacob admired. He could do some serious damage, especially in his evolved EX forms, but since many of his attacks required a flip of heads on a coin to work, he also required fate to be on your side. To win with Latios you had to be both determined and a bit lucky, which Jacob felt was truer to life than other attacks you might use. And, although most boys of sixteen would never dare to rock out Pokémon attire in public—the men of Deerfield normally wore LSU or Saints gear, maybe camouflaged Salt Life or PFG shirts as if a football game or fishing trip might break out at any second—Jacob's hat was so obscure and advanced, so beyond the Pikachu bullshit you saw on kids' backpacks, that most people had no idea what it was about.

And Jacob liked Pokémon. He wasn't ashamed of that. He was

no Johnny-come-lately, either. He didn't give a damn about the stupid app people played on their phones, walking around looking for monsters that weren't really there. No, Jacob was into the card game, the real deal, the outrageously strategic, deeply complicated, and crystallized stuff. It was like chess in technicolor, and he enjoyed this. He was good at it, too; had destroyed all the local competition when kids still outwardly played, and had gone on to compete in a regional tournament in New Orleans last year, which his father said seemed fair, considering how many baseball tournaments and football games they'd traveled to for his brother. And maybe, Jacob wondered in the quiet moments when people are prone to wonder, the fact that he was good at this meant *something*. Maybe he wasn't totally useless. So, wearing the hat made Jacob feel protected, both a little bit taller and a little more hidden at the same time, and that is the best thing a hat can do for a man.

Up ahead, he watched Trina sling her backpack around to the front and stash her phone. She then took the rock from her mouth, pocketed it, and pulled out and lit a cigarette in one well-rehearsed motion. She blew the smoke up toward the branches, and hers would be, Jacob knew, only the first of many trails of smoke and vapor to waft along the path that next hour.

The trail they were now on ran from Deerfield Catholic to the town square and was called the Crane Lane, as legend had it a boy had once spotted a red crane standing in the shallow waters of Bayou Ibis, which it ran alongside. This was decades ago, before the school had even been built, and the path was made by birding enthusiasts who tromped all over Deerfield after reading about this story in the paper. Red cranes did not exist, of course, and none were ever seen again, but people have a habit, Jacob understood, of too often believing everything that they read.

These days the path served as a convenient place for underaged kids to smoke cigarettes and chew tobacco and, Jacob now realized, quite possibly be mauled by the opposite sex on their way home from school. The trail was crisscrossed by oak and cypress roots, canopied in leaves and hanging moss nearly all year long. On the weekends, married couples and families took the place over, making picnics in small clearings by the water, casting a line in for bream or catfish, and watching out for the family of gators that liked to lounge on the opposite bank. It was a peaceful place between eight and three p.m. every day and that's what Jacob was hoping to enjoy. If not peace, then at least solitude.

He'd done his best to get off campus without seeing anyone, especially Trina. He left as soon as the bell rang, hustling through the parking lot with his head down as other boys hurled footballs and lifted girls onto the tailgates of their trucks, which was a scene Jacob loathed. Ever since his brother's death, Jacob felt especially insulted by the merriment that followed the three-o'clock bell. The way his classmates had originally acted sad around him, almost deferential to his presence, evaporated in less than a month and Jacob wasn't sure if this quick recovery was more a reflection on him or on his brother. Did they really miss Toby the way they said they did at the funeral? Were their lives forever changed by his accident, which Trina claimed was not one at all? Or were they, as Trina also claimed, just completely full of shit? Jacob wasn't sure. If he had to guess, he would say that their renewed sense of joy sprung from the fact that they no longer felt the need to behave in any particular way around Jacob because, just as it had been before his brother's death, they hardly even knew he was there.

The only person who always knew where he was appeared to be Trina. He'd no idea how she had beaten him to the woods, no idea if he would rather walk with her or stay and wait for the dickheads to arrive, so he just stood there, mainly wondering why a person would put a rock in their mouth.

"You see that log?" Trina called to him, a good twenty yards away. She gestured over to a fallen and hollowed oak by the water. "Remember that one," she said. "It'll be a pickup point."

Jacob reluctantly walked over, where she stood pointing at the log with her cigarette. "Pickup for what?" he asked.

"You will know at the appropriate time," she said. "It's not long now." She swung her bag back around and opened it up. "You want a cigarette?" she asked. "They taste terrible."

"You should go into advertising," Jacob said. "You've got a knack."

"I try," she said.

"Why the hell did you buy them, then?"

"I didn't buy them. I lifted them out of somebody's car when I was doing a little recon for us last night." She pulled out a long and thin pack of Benson & Hedges. "I didn't even know they still made these things."

"I don't smoke," Jacob said. "But thank you for offering me something you despise."

"My pleasure," she said, and looked him in the eye. "I mean it."

Beyond the bend in the trail behind them, they could already hear voices. Kids laughing and likely pushing on one another, some playing music on their phones. Jacob got the sense that he and Trina could stand right there, so outcast were they in the high school world together, that the flow of kids would move right past them as river water does a great stone. Part of him wanted to try this, to see if anyone even saw him, or if they might run right into him, knock him over, like he was not worth the effort to move. He was in a dark mental place these days and he recognized this. But, sometimes, the thing to do in a dark place is tape the curtains shut and see if it can get any darker. So, he decided to stand there.

"What are your opinions," Trina asked him, "on breaking and entering?"

Jacob thought about this. He smiled.

"I think, in a certain context," he said, "that entering sounds like fun."

"Oh, look," Trina said, and grabbed his wrist. "He is a virgin after all."

She tugged him toward town and walked quickly.

"What we need is a way to get materials," Trina said. "As you are aware, we are both under seventeen, so buying things without parental consent can be tricky. What I'm thinking, though, is that people have most of what we need just lying around their houses."

As they spoke, a group of four guys turned the corner behind them. They were on bikes and going fast, asses up off the seats, and, when they passed them, Chuck Haydel reached out and grabbed Jacob's hat off his head. The blow was so unexpected that Jacob said nothing, just leaned over and put his hands to his ears.

"Nice hat, dipshit," Chuck yelled, and was beyond their reach before Jacob could react. When he stood back up, his heart was pounding, adrenaline thumping from embarrassment or anger or any one of the million ready-made outrages that teenagers have access to and he balled his hands into fists. If he could, he would evolve himself into Latios right there, take off like a jet, and burn him to bits with a Psychic Blast. Destroy him completely. But he could not.

So, instead, he did nothing.

Trina put her cigarette on the ground and grabbed his chin. "Hey," she said. "Whenever you think you want out of this, I want you to think about Chuck Haydel. That fucker who just stole your hat. He was with your brother that night. You know that, don't you? He was feeding him drinks. *Making* him drink. The things those assholes did," she said, and stared at Jacob a long time. "Somebody needs to be held responsible."

Jacob spat on the ground. He felt like his face was on fire, his ears bright red, his head throbbing. And he did have fantasies about the type of justice one found not only in card games and RPGs but in movies, too, of course he did. There were things to do with a person like Chuck and he thought of them often, but he did not give Trina the satisfaction of hearing him say it. But he also didn't like hearing about the night his brother died. It made him angry in so many ways. The fact that he was not there with him, that he didn't know what really happened. Everyone but Trina had the same story about Toby that night, framed by the two cohesive facts Jacob *did* know: Drunk driving. DOA. So, what else could have happened to make Trina so angry at everyone? To blame them? She'd given him only hints and Jacob couldn't stand not knowing. He felt this anger trying again to overtake him and rubbed his palms together to calm down.

"New question," Trina said. "Do you know the motivation behind ninety percent of car break-ins in Louisiana?"

"What the hell are you talking about?" Jacob said.

"I'm asking you a simple question," she said, "to prove my theory that we live on fertile ground. Just answer, yes or no. Do you know the motivation behind ninety percent of car break-ins in Louisiana?"

"No," he said. "And I really don't care."

"It's guns," Trina told him. "People are looking for guns. Ergo, we live on fertile ground."

"Ergo," Jacob said, "I'm going home."

"Wait," Trina said, "I've been meaning to ask: Your dad's the mayor, right? Key to the town and all that? I was wondering. You think he has blueprints of the school?"

"I don't know," Jacob said. "Why the hell does it matter?"

Trina looked at him in a way so inscrutable that Jacob didn't know if she would yell at him or kiss him again. Nor did he know which one of these he wanted. Instead, though, she only said, "Hiding places, J. I think what we need are hiding places."

Trina was right, Jacob thought. A hiding place was exactly what he needed. A place to get away from her, from this town, from his life. But Jacob had decided that he was done agreeing with anything Trina said, and so he did not.

"I think what you need," Jacob told her, "is to get real."

"Why, Jacob?" she said and glared at him. "Do I look flippant to you?"

"I don't know what you look like," he said.

"Good," Trina told him. "Maybe that's the way I want it."

Jacob said nothing and started again up the path. Trina followed him until they got to the mouth of the trail that opened near the town square. People were moving about in the world they now approached, going in and out of shops, gassing up their trucks and pushing strollers. Men set up scaffolding alongside Annie's Chicken and Biscuits, where they were pressure-washing the brick front. On the far side of the street, another group of men were building a set of bleachers. The town was alive in a way it hadn't been before in Jacob's memory, all excited about the bicentennial, and yet he felt none of this enthusiasm. In a clump of high grass near the bayou, however, he saw his hat, which Chuck had apparently tried to sling into the water. He walked over and picked it up.

"Are you just going to let him get away with that?" Trina asked him. "Just let those fuckers do what they want? You think Toby would let him do that to you?"

And here again, another mention of Toby, as if she had known him better than he had. Jacob couldn't stand it. He slapped his hat against his thigh and allowed his temper, which he normally kept hidden from everyone, to unfold all over Trina. "Listen," he said. "You don't know a damn thing about my brother. What, you let him fuck you? Congratulations, Trina. He did that to a lot of girls. So, stop acting like you're all special, okay? And if you think he was so great then why weren't you in the car with him that night? Y'all went together, right? If he was so fucked up, why'd you let him drive? Why weren't you with him?"

Trina looked up at Jacob. She cocked her head.

"What are you saying?" she asked. "You wish I was dead, too?"

Jacob looked at the ground. "That's not what I'm saying."

"Maybe I am," she told him. "Maybe I'm a ghost."

"Look," Jacob said. "I'm just tired of everybody acting like they know things that I don't. I was his brother. Nobody knew him better than me. And so I'm starting to think that everything you're saying is bullshit. Whatever you think happened, and whatever sort of revenge you have planned, jumping those guys, beating the shit out of them, count me out. The whole thing is stupid. I'm sorry I ever called you. I'm sorry I even entertained it. But I'm done with all this. If you know something that I don't, either tell me straight up or leave me the hell alone."

Jacob expected to feel a tremendous relief upon saying this but instead heard a car honking at them from the square. He looked up to see a blue Toyota pickup pulling over to the side of the road. Trina ignored this and walked closer to Jacob. He was hoping that he'd hurt her with what he'd said, was hoping this might be the end of them, but she looked totally unfazed. She got right up in his face. "You want to know something *I* know that you don't?" she said.

Before he could reply Trina reached up and kissed him again, her tongue deep and fast in his mouth as if she were trying to make him gag. She then pulled away and said, "You not only look like him, Jacob. You taste just like him, too."

She poked him hard in the chest.

"And for me," Trina said, "that's a problem."

Then she turned and walked away.

Jacob looked up to see Father Pete in the blue Toyota, the school priest, who was now calling to Trina through the window. Jacob nodded at him, embarrassed, and Trina climbed into his truck without saying so much as good-bye.

After this, Jacob walked the few blocks to his house, where he found his father, the town mayor, trying to lasso a television with a rope.

6

Level on the Level

By the time the three-o'clock bell rang, Douglas Hubbard felt like a much older person than he'd been that morning. He was technically, of course, about eight hours older, but he had the sensation that years had gone by. Decades, maybe, and difficult ones. It was as if he'd gone to work that morning as *Jailhouse Rock* Elvis and emerged Las Vegas Elvis. He was not alone in this feeling. All across America, at that very hour, teachers poked their heads from dank school buildings like ancient turtles from their shells. They shaded their eyes with notebooks and binders, jingled heavy sets of keys in their pockets, and looked, as a group, generally confused as to how the sun was still out, how the day could possibly be so long. This confusion made them drop their favorite travel mugs and neoprene water bottles in the parking lot, where they watched them roll beneath cars and realized they would have to get on their hands and knees in front of students to retrieve them because these cups were some of the most expensive items they owned. Would this be the day's final indignity? they wondered. It was unlikely. Yet all they knew for sure, these teachers, was that their palms hurt on the asphalt, their backs were sore from standing, their voices hoarse from talking, and they felt well beyond their years. All of this, Douglas understood, was because teachers *are* well beyond their years.

He had a theory to explain it.

The phenomenon of high-speed aging, as particularly experienced by high school educators, Douglas had long thought, was a simple by-product of the space-time bend that occurs when otherwise reasonable adults are forced to navigate an adolescent's world. It wasn't merely the headaches teenagers caused that did it, with their nuisances, their ignorance, their bodily horrors, but rather, like everything else ironic about teaching high school, it was the way a school day being cut into fifty-minute blocks to keep it active for the students inevitably made it interminable for the faculty.

Take Douglas's day, for example: four sections of American History with two different preps (one freshmen, one junior level), an Honors World History class (for seniors with college hopes), a noisy cafeteria lunch, then a break which is not really a break at all because you need to call your wife, who suddenly thinks she'd be better off in Saudi Arabia, and then have your picture taken by a romantic rival while your window is broken by a future Hall of Famer before prepping for three more sections of World History, Civics, and Louisiana History, respectively, each of which you will try to teach while your students stare blankly at a custodian named Wilson who is trying to fit a piece of plywood into the broken window frame without any discernible tools. All of this in the same building, often in the very same room, each scene beginning over again during the same stretch of day. It was, in many respects, like going to work on a loop.

In fact, Douglas liked to think that if you tallied it all up and considered each individual class a person teaches as an entire workday unto itself, which Douglas felt it was, mentally, then a person who teaches high school ends up working for eight different days within the span from eight a.m. to three p.m. alone. This is not to mention the day they live before coming to work, with their various family, children, and breakfast scenarios, nor the one they must face afterward, with those same families and dinners and bills. Thusly, a mathematician might surmise that high school teachers actually live ten entirely different days per each ordinary day, which means they live through fifty separate days in the five-day work-week enjoyed by most human beings. Tack on the two normal days for the weekend and the typical four-month semester actually adds up to around eight hundred days in fall and eight hundred in spring, or somewhere around two years of life per semester, which, of course, means that for each year a person teaches high school they're actually doing about four complete years of living. It is therefore not unusual for a freshman, by the time she graduates, to witness her favorite teacher age sixteen years to her four. And, if that teacher were to get roped into teaching summer school as well, then, by Douglas's calculations, they might just turn to dust.

This is why even the most optimistic educators Douglas has ever known, those hired fresh out of college in Baton Rouge or New Orleans, with all their new lesson plans and pedagogies and wholly revolutionary ideas for bringing Deerfield education into the twenty-first century, often end up looking like their own grandparents before they've made it through their first year of faculty meetings. The new Social Studies teacher, for example, Betsy Miller, who Douglas had found quite attractive just a few years ago, with her bouncing pixie haircut and fashionable eyeglasses, now wore only flowered muumuus to school, her hair done up in a tight and dull bun. Young Matt Clark, as well, the English teacher with an MFA degree who had once been known to stand in the quad reciting Whitman at full throat, going *Dead Poets Society* all over the place in his snappy suspenders and pleated khakis, had twice come to work this semester alone wearing a different shoe on each foot. He had no idea he had done this, the poor guy, and his students skewered him for it. It was hard to blame them. The old are such easy targets.

Yet Douglas understood that the way the faculty tottered around campus, scribbling reminders on their own hands, shuffling around student essays like they were incomprehensible contracts, was the result of living for far more days in each single day than the rest of the world. Douglas also knew that very few of them besides Pat Howell, the school principal, had done this at Deerfield Catholic longer than he had.

It was Principal Pat that Douglas now saw as he left the school building, lugging his large trombone case with him on the way to his lesson after school. This was to be expected, as Principal Pat was known to keep a hawkish vigil over the parking lot come dismissal, making sure no one was smoking or drinking or fighting or, worse, proliferating the human race on her watch. Principal Pat was a strong and spherical woman, whose tucked-in shirts and high-waisted pants made it nearly impossible to tell where her breasts ended and her belly began, and whose large and magnified eyeglasses gave one the impression that she might be able to see everything that happened on campus, whether she was physically there or not.

"Hubbard?" Pat said. "Is that you?"

"All day long," Douglas replied. "And probably tomorrow."

She studied him for a minute and frowned. "I didn't recognize you without the mustache. When the frip did that happen?"

"Last week," he told her. "We've had two faculty meetings together since then. We spoke after lunch today about my window. That was maybe two hours ago."

"Right," she said. "That's actually what I wanted to talk to you about."

"Mr. Nevers assured me that he'll pay for the window out of his signing bonus."

"Not that," she said. "After our meeting, I started thinking about all the great work you've done at Deerfield, how dib-nab long you've been working here, how well you get along with your cock-a-poo colleagues, and how even these dribbin' students seem to respect you."

Principal Pat, one might notice, had a strange way of speaking. Her thirty years of being a Catholic school principal, complete with her own self-imposed no-cursing-on-campus policy, had given birth to an entirely new lexicon of near curse words that she alone employed with impunity. To her credit, she didn't settle for things as easy as *crud* or *dang*, as most polite people in Louisiana might do around children, but instead bequeathed her invectives with a sort of bouncy and alliterative quality that Douglas rather admired. There were *flim-flams* and *gob-nobs* and mysterious curses like *deekin-hawks* strewn throughout any conversation you might have with her, at any time of day, in virtually any setting. Douglas relished this aspect of her personality most in faculty meetings, where listening to her admonish a colleague was not dissimilar to what he imagined sitting in a jazz club might be like, hearing Etta James scat on the mic in her prime. Not everyone enjoyed this quirk of hers, though, he was sure, because even the most naïve parent at Deerfield Catholic could glean from any conversation that Pat was fighting deep-seated urges to call their child a *shithead*. In fact, Douglas figured, if a person were to substitute her invented sounds for the curse words they obviously stood for, they'd realize the school principal was likely the most foul-mouthed woman in the parish.

"You know," Douglas told her, checking his watch. "I've also been thinking about how dib-nab long I've been working here recently."

"Don't give me that bully-brick," she said. "I'm serious. You deserve some flip-floppin' recognition for all you do around here."

This conversation made Douglas uneasy. He was not at all used to being complimented at work, by his students or his peers, or by anyone other than Cherilyn, really, who, in her predictably thoughtful way, had made a sort of art form out of it. Beyond her little mentions of his looking handsome as they left the house for dinner parties or an anniversary, which Douglas miraculously believed every time she told him, Cherilyn had also taken on the role of providing for Douglas at home the compliments she felt he was likely not receiving at work.

She'd elevated this habit to such a degree that, for the last five years, at the end of each spring semester, Cherilyn held a small ceremony for Douglas at their kitchen table. She would dress nice, in a blue blouse and long white skirt he had once mentioned liking, and fix him a glass of his favorite bourbon, Basil Hayden's, which at thirty-four bucks a bottle was seriously high cotton on their budget. She would then proceed to emcee her own little private awards show for Douglas in which she held a box filled with thank-you notes that she herself had written, all in the guise of his ungrateful peers and students. The notes would thank him for a wide variety of small extracurricular services he had performed throughout the semester, ones Douglas must have mentioned to Cherilyn at one time or another. Since she often didn't know the students' names about whom he complained, the notes would be signed with things like: "Sincerely, that boy who didn't show up for his midterm but you let me take a make-up anyway because you are a caring and sensitive person" or "All my best, from the geography teacher whose class you covered when I had that 'cold' that everybody knows was actually a court date for my DUI." Each event ended with him being presented with the same small trophy Cherilyn herself had made that had a golden apple on top of it and "Teacher of the Year" written across the bottom, which she kept on a mantel in their office.

These were bighearted nights in which Douglas and Cherilyn laughed together, as lucky couples are apt to do, about her surprising and sly sense of humor in the notes, about his endless gullibility when it came to work (which he swore every year to curtail), and about the impressive imbecility of nearly everyone he came in contact with when he left their home each morning. But what most tickled Douglas about this little ceremony of Cherilyn's was the fact that these notes meant she had actually been listening to every single conversation they'd had throughout the school year, which Douglas imagined must seem to her like an endless string of very similar days. This could not have been easy to do. He often wondered how Cherilyn could retain these anecdotes that he himself had forgotten, if she remembered everything that he'd ever said to her, or, perhaps even better, if she went off and wrote the thank-you notes the very night he complained, as if she were always fashioning little presents for him in the way some parents are perpetually Christmas shopping for their children. If so, then hers was a love, Douglas knew, that didn't take a day off. And, as if proof of how hard it was for Douglas himself to listen to every detail in a conversation, he realized that this quick memory of his wife had removed him from his conversation with Principal Pat entirely, who was now coming to some conclusion about a point he had no idea she'd been making.

"So, I've decided," she said. "Who in the fudge-pop better than you to replace me?"

"I'm sorry," Douglas said. "Replace you? For what?"

"Earth to Hubbard," she said. "Haven't you been listening? It's official. I'm retiring. I'm no good for this place anymore. I am no longer, how the flake to say it, in my element."

Principal Pat then removed from a pocket, which was perhaps in her pants or perhaps in her shirt, a small slip of blue paper. Douglas recognized it immediately as being from the DNAMIX machine.

"Oh, Lord," he said. "What are we going to do about these things? Heddy Franklin told me today that she is supposed to be a samurai. She spent all of first period doing origami. And let me be clear that she has *no idea* how to do origami. You think it's time for a ban? If you say so, I support it. I second the motion right here. No need for a meeting. I'll even help you print up the papers. Maybe Heddy can fold them for us."

Principal Pat was known for her swift and unilateral action against fads. As soon as it seemed the kids found something in common, something they all enjoyed, she sent home bright pink warnings in everyone's folder that read "NOW PROHIBITED" and listed their new favorite toy. Years ago it was Silly Putty, then homemade slime and fidget spinners and, of all things, Rubik's Cubes. Despite their educational applications, if the kids liked it, Principal Pat typically got it the hell out of there.

"I'm not in the banning business anymore," she said. "That's what I'm trying to tell you. Look and see for yourself."

Douglas took the blue slip of paper, having already made up his mind about the ludicrousness of these readouts, and opened it up. It looked just like Cherilyn's, with all the little numbers and factoids, suggesting, though, that Principal Pat, unlike Cherilyn, was not capable of producing human children. It read at the bottom, in bold, Potential Life Station: **CARPENTER**.

"I've put in my two-week notice with the archdiocese," she said. "I'm moving to the country to build me a home, just like the song says. I thought you might be a good candidate to replace me."

"You're joking," he said. "Pat, this is just a piece of paper. It came out of a vending machine."

"It's not *just* a piece of paper," she said. "It's the *right* piece of paper. It hit me like a train when I read it."

Douglas set down his trombone. He looked around the parking lot as if he might be hallucinating, or perhaps being filmed for some sort of candid-camera situation. He removed his beret and wiped the sweat from the top of his head. "Just one question, Pat," he said. "Do you know anything at all in the big beeping fleeping world about carpentry?"

Pat reached into either her breast or pants pocket and pulled out a pair of safety goggles. She held them up in the air like evidence. "I bought these over at the Rockery Ace yesterday," she said. "So, I know about safety. That's one thing I know. I also know that my grandpa was a carpenter, and that the big man's son was a carpenter. I know it's mainly a hammer and nails and I also know what nobody else *could* know, which is that as soon as I saw that piece of paper, I built a house in my head. I could see every part of it: the wooden floors, the vaulted cathedral ceiling, all those nuts and bolts I could screw in and feel good about. It was all right there as if it had always been, but I just hadn't looked. And I have to tell you, Hubbard, when I saw myself in that house, all covered with sawdust and dirt, I became a different person, like the most badass momma-jomma you've ever met. Even today, I feel totally new. Heck, I'm surprised you even recognize me."

"You know," Douglas said. "There's a rumor that Phil Reed has been spiking the coffee in the teacher's lounge again. You been hanging out in there today?"

Pat didn't reply but instead looked at the parking lot as a group of seniors peeled out in their pickup trucks. To Douglas's dismay, she didn't even bother to jot down their names for detention tomorrow. "I stated in my resignation letter," she said, "that I would like to pick my replacement. I'll be giving them your name tomorrow."

"Look," Douglas said. "I appreciate the gesture, but you should know that I'm not particularly in the market for more responsibility right now." He tapped his trombone case with his foot. "I was thinking of a change of employment myself."

"Don't be flicking ridiculous," she said. "You're meant for this, Hubbard. You're good at this. Anybody can see that. Some people are no great mystery."

What Douglas wanted to tell her, of course, was that she had him all wrong. This life he'd been living in blazers and button-up shirts, this was the lie. The truth of him was an artist with talent likely too molten hot for this town to contain. He just hadn't pursued it yet. But instead of saying this, Douglas asked, "What about Father Pete? Wouldn't he make the most sense to step into a sort of emergency situation like this one?"

Douglas knew the answer to this already, which was no, Pete Flynn would not be very good at this at all, but Douglas mentioned him only because he now saw Father Pete in the parking lot, walking over to his old beat-up blue Toyota pickup.

"Please," Pat said. "The kids would eat that man alive. He'd be hitting the whiskey by noon. Men of God are too fragile to be principals."

Pat took her slip of paper back from Douglas, folded it into one of her pockets, and said, "It's a lot to soak in, I know. Talk to Cherilyn about it, be sure she knows you'll get a pay bump, though not nearly as much of a bump as it should be, if you were to ask me, and get back with me tomorrow." She then patted him on the shoulder and walked back toward the school building.

"Wait," Douglas said. "One thing I have to know, Pat, from a true carpenter like yourself: How exactly do you plumb a line?"

It was an ugly urge that made Douglas ask this, as it was a question he himself didn't know the answer to. Yet he'd heard it used in various conversations with men that had this kind of knowledge and hoped, in some petty way, he might embarrass her for also not knowing.

Pat opened the door to the school and turned back to face him. She pulled the safety goggles over her head and stretched them

out over her eyeglasses. She looked like she might be going snor-
keling. "As a matter of fact," she told him, "I don't know. But I aim
to find out. I plan to start by getting a plumb and then getting a
line and then, finally, Douglas, being happy in my own skin."

Douglas looked at the ground. "Good answer," he said. "I'm
happy for you."

"Don't lie," she told him. "This is a lot to think about. We car-
penters have a saying, though, Hubbard. When God closes a door,
we just build ourselves a window. Maybe this new job could be
your window."

"Maybe," he said. "Or maybe you'll go home and have a wrench
fall on your head and come back to reality."

"Reality!" Pat said and bent over laughing. "That's a good one."

7

Father Pete

People of God, like teachers, may also live multiple days in each day. Who are we to say?

As Father Pete would be the first to tell you, making assumptions about anyone else's situation, no matter how seemingly obvious it may appear on the outside, is to willingly close yourself off to the heart of God. He wouldn't say the word *God*, though, and definitely not *Jesus* or, even worse, *Christ*, if he was just making polite conversation. He knew the way his students' eyes would glaze over, even some of his parishioners' eyes, for that matter, when he said God's name anywhere other than Mass, as Catholics don't much care to be preached to unless wearing their Sunday clothes. So, instead of invoking the names of the Almighty God the Maker of Heaven and Earth and Jesus his only living son who was crucified, died, and was buried for our sins, Pete might simply remind them of the much less heavy and guilt-ridden saying that to "assume," if you look closely enough at the word, can make an ASS out of U and ME.

The parents at the Lenten fish fries on Fridays, the men working the BBQ booths at the school fair, they would get a kick out of something like that, but he couldn't use this same phrase with their kids. Their attention spans would snap completely as soon as he said the word *ass*, making the rest of the conversation as productive as trying to teach math to a cat. So, what *would* he tell these students if he found them making assumptions? People who live in glass houses shouldn't throw stones? Do unto others as you would want them to do unto such and such? What would he tell his own child if he had one? And why was he thinking about this again? Maybe he'd pray on that tonight. A good long prayer about giving advice to a child he would never be able to know. Hell, he figured, why not? He'd done it before.

Regardless, Peter Flynn, or Father Pete, as people called him, lived two full days in each day and he knew that. A man of fifty years old, stout in the shoulders from the fifty push-ups he did each morning at the foot of his bed along with the forty bicep curls he did in front of the mirror with his shirt off, the hair on his chest beginning to gray, Father Pete had lived in Deerfield only three short years, having been reassigned from Livingston Parish, outside of Baton Rouge, through no fault of his own. He was a good priest, he felt, a loyal friend and admirer of women and men and fishing and sports and God who didn't outwardly break any priestly vows. He just had thoughts, is all, some regrets, some resentment, which was normal. And when a person gets to his age and has the type of routine and discipline that the priesthood requires, he knows exactly how many days he lives.

So, by the time Father Pete reached his truck and waved goodbye to the school principal, who was rolling back toward the primary building in her odd sort of spherical manner, and gave a nod to Douglas Hubbard, who he liked quite a bit but never spoke much to, he was already looking forward to his second day.

He was currently one hour and forty minutes away from this day beginning, of which he was massively aware, as it always occurred, if he could help it, at exactly five o'clock. This was when

Pete, unless under some work obligation, would finally be alone in his house. This is also when Pete would take a lime out of the little hanging basket he kept near his kitchen sink and set it on top of a small wooden Louisiana-shaped cutting board that could double as a wall decoration but typically stayed right there in the drying rack on the counter. He would then take a knife from his drawer and cut the lime across its equator, turn it upright to slice it in half again and then again, until he had exactly eight identical triangles. These were squat triangles, though, more like pyramids, and not those crescent-moon-looking jobs you get when you cut the lime from top to bottom as they do at the El Sombrero Mexican restaurant in town. This was important to him, the precise manner of cutting, as were many rituals. Pete would then reach into his cabinet, where he kept a set of two crystal-clear cocktail glasses that had a frosted silhouette of the St. Louis Cathedral in New Orleans on their sides. These glasses were fancy, somehow both sturdy and thin, the set a gift from one of his professors when he graduated from the seminary, along with a handwritten note to accompany them that said only "Keep 'em clean, Pete."

Pete intended to. They were two of his favorite things.

So, at five o'clock he would take one of them down from the cabinet and hold it to the light, still clear as the day he got it five years ago, and set it near the cutting board. Then he would walk to his refrigerator, where he kept a bottle of cold soda water that he himself had made that morning from a SodaStream machine he'd purchased online to avoid any rumors that might rev up if he was seen purchasing a soda maker at the Deerfield Walmart. Sure, you could ostensibly use this device to make root beer and cola and other flavored drinks, but this was Louisiana, and people know what adults do with soda water. Anyway, he would grab the bottle of soda and open the freezer and remove for himself the fifth of Sobieski vodka he kept in the door, stash it under his arm, pluck a handful of cubes from his bucket of ice, and walk back across the kitchen. He would then drop the cubes into the glass, where they made a clinking sound that bordered on the divine, squeeze in the lime, pour just enough Sobieski to flood the bottom floor of the cathedral, and top it off with soda water so fresh and bubbling that the sound of it coming to life in the glass would fill his empty kitchen like rain.

Father Pete would then remove his collar and raise the drink to his lips, where, at this time of the day, if everything had gone just right, the falling sun through his kitchen window would light up the bottom of the glass in a way that made the lime cast its particular shade of green on every angle of ice and bubble around it. This display would look almost glowing to him as he thought of his wife, Anna, dead nine years now, and said what he always said at this hour, which was "One day closer to you." He would then bring the glass to his mouth to feel the pleasant patter and pop of carbonation on his nose and upper lip. And then he would take that first sip, that sip you can't ever get back for the rest of your second day, and would think he'd done pretty well in life, that he'd served both man and God and Anna to the best of his ability, because he'd made it back to five o'clock undeterred again, just as he promised them all that he would.

But in order for him to even have that second day today, Pete needed to go to the liquor store. It would be fine, of course, if Pete didn't have this moment tonight, it wouldn't be a huge deal, as there have been plenty of nights when he hasn't, but he would prefer it. And as he was a working adult, and as he didn't need to coach the school cabbage-ball games or attend to anything else at the rectory, he was going to get what he wanted. So, he backed his truck out of the parking lot and cut up Iris Lane, where he then planned to drive past the square and up Highway 61 toward Clessy's Package Store, over in the neighboring parish.

He'd no need to go that far, as the good state of Louisiana allows liquor to be sold basically anywhere that has a cash register. Gas stations, convenience stores, Johnson's Grocery, Walmart, even the Deerfield pharmacy sold beer and wine, but he was wearing his collar and didn't want to go all the way home to change and, you know, maybe the drive out to Clessy's might do him some good, allow him to think about some things.

One of the things he needed to think about was not a thing at all but rather a person, whom he now saw standing on the side of the road. It was his niece, Trina, the daughter of Pete's tragically AWOL sister, who'd had, he knew, a hard couple of years. He also knew Trina was having trouble adjusting to Deerfield Catholic after moving here last fall, as Pete had endured no less than four conversations with Principal Pat about her seemingly strange and antisocial behavior. He had vouched for her each time, explaining that her mother had become addicted to pills and run off to who knows where, that her father was also of no account, and that, as surely Pat recalled, the Bible says, Bring us your weak, your feeble, your in need, and the lot of it. Or was that the Statue of Liberty?

Regardless, Pete was the reason she'd come to Deerfield Catholic in the first place, once he found out she was no longer showing up to classes over at the public school. He'd negotiated a family discount on her tuition and paid that, as well. So, he understood that he was somewhat responsible for her behavior. And, truth told, she was an odd bird, for which he worried. She hardly spoke to him or to anyone, it seemed, especially the past few months. But the entire community had been saddened by the Richieu boy's death. It was a tragedy in that real way something is a tragedy when a child of God is seemingly taken before their time. Pete had heard rumors about her relationship with the boy, seen a few disparaging remarks about her scribbled on the boys' room wall at school, which he bleached out after school hours, but, try as he had, he could never get a straight answer out of her.

So, wasn't it strange, Pete thought, that she was now standing by the road with the other Richieu boy, looking so similar to his brother in the face if not in the body that it appeared as if this same exact scene could have unfolded months ago? Was she now dating this boy, too? He didn't want to assume, of course, because you know what the word *assume* can do, but he pulled over to the side of the road anyway and gave her a little toot with his horn. "Hey there, stranger," he said. "You need a lift?"

Trina lived a few miles up 61 with her father, Lanny Todd, a man who made it difficult even for a priest to see God in. He had been the undoing of many other people's lives, Pete's sister Amanda among them, and lived in a run-down rancher on a plot of land he'd inherited from his family right at the edge of the parish, which Pete would, perhaps providentially, he thought, be passing on the way out to Clessy's today. Maybe this was the man upstairs at work yet again?

The surviving Richieu boy, whose name was Jacob, Pete remembered, looked up and nodded respectfully when he honked, but Trina didn't acknowledge him at all. Instead, he watched her reach up and kiss that Jacob boy right on the mouth in plain sight, full on tongue-to-tongue as if they were chewing the same food for a while, and then stop and poke him hard in the chest. It did not appear, from his angle, to be much of a loving gesture.

"Katrina," Pete hollered from the car. "Let that boy have some oxygen. Come say hey to your uncle."

Trina slung her backpack over her shoulder and walked toward the truck without looking at him. The boy then shuffled off in his own direction and, instead of just leaning in through the open window, as he thought she might, Trina opened the door of the truck and sat in the cab.

"It's hotter than that made-up place in your favorite book out there," she said. "I'll take the ride."

"Nice to see you, too," Pete said. "Why are you walking anyway? Doesn't your daddy pick you up?"

"Normally, yes," Trina said, "and it's such a joyful experience, let me tell you. But, alas, he couldn't find his car this morning. My theory is that he sold it for drugs but doesn't remember. My reason for thinking this is because I watched him sell it and now he doesn't remember. Still, there's no use arguing with him."

Pete pulled back onto the road, waved his hand at the car behind him to let them know he appreciated their slowing down, and headed for the highway.

"You can always call me if you need something," he told her. "You know that, right? I know your dad can be trying to live with. I'm here for you."

"Oh, but you have plenty of other souls to save, Uncle Pete," Trina said. "Trust me. Plus, making me come to this shithole school has been help enough, thanks."

If there was one thing to admire about Trina, which Pete was always looking for, it was that she let you know where you stood with her. Ever since her mom had run off and Pete had begun checking up on her, ever since he had moved her to Deerfield Catholic, Trina had been outwardly aggressive toward him. He saw some of his sister in this and was sure that his reputation had been somewhat poisoned for the girl since her youth. His sister Amanda was not a bad person, as Pete felt very few people were, but she was not well. Ten years younger than him, she saw his entrance into theology after Anna's death as a reproach to her own selfish partying ways, a sort of one-sided trouncing of her in the sibling-rivalry arena, and acted as if, since her brother was now going to be free of sin, she might as well double up. Pete missed her, and worried about her, but it would be a lie to say that they were ever close. He often wondered if this, a sort of feeling of lost kinship, is why he had taken such an interest in her daughter.

After he'd convinced Lanny to let her enroll in the private school, bringing the sheriff along with him to explain Louisiana truancy laws, and promised Lanny that he would cover her expenses, that Lanny wouldn't even have to get off the couch, Pete took Trina to the Young Fashions outlet to get her uniforms for the year. Trina wore a black tank top to this store that seemed not to have any back at all, pimples dotting her broad shoulders, a patch of dark hair, he saw, in her armpits, and openly ridiculed every item in the place. When he'd finally gotten her all the various requirements from the list Principal Pat had given him, she walked out of the changing room in her plaid jumper and blouse, her socks pulled up to her knees, her black-and-white Mary Janes unlaced on her feet, and said, "So, is this what God makes women wear in heaven, too? What does he have, some sort of fetish?"

The man working the counter looked over at Pete and Pete simply handed him his credit card. He looked back at Trina and said, "I'll wait for you in the truck." And once inside his truck he prayed for her, as he was apt to do.

She was wearing that same uniform now, but Pete noticed she had undone it in various ways since school let out. She put her Mary Janes up on the dash and they were dirtied from the trail he knew she'd just walked.

"How'd you get to school this morning, then?" he asked her. "If the car was gone."

"Tessa brought me," she said.

"Who's Tessa?"

"She's the whore that lives with us now."

"Trina," he said. "That's no way to talk about a person."

"But wasn't Mary Magdalene a whore, too?" Trina asked, doing a really wonderful impression of a person feigning interest. "And, if so, then aren't I potentially giving her, like, the greatest compliment? I mean, maybe she could one day grow up to be Jesus's favorite whore!"

"That's enough," Pete said. "What you got going on with that other Richieu boy? Aren't you a little young to be swapping DNA out on the street? You dating him now, too?"

"Dating?" Trina said. "I don't *date*, Uncle Pete, especially not boys. I am what they call polyamorous. Boys, girls, men, women, mixtures of those things in between. Straight, gay, lesbo, transbo: All of God's possibilities are open to me. Does that bother you? Am I going to hell, Uncle Pete? Does God hate it when I like other people?"

"All right," Pete said. "I was just making conversation."

They drove a few minutes in silence until Trina said, "I'm also thinking about getting an abortion, you should know. Then I plan to donate to Planned Parenthood and maybe do some porn work on the side."

"A person's choices are their own," Pete said, and grinned. "But, if that's the case, how about we get you home before you get gonorrhea all over my truck."

"Ouch," Trina said, and smiled for the first time since she'd hopped in the cab. "You're going to have some rosaries to say for that one."

Pete reached up and rubbed the rosary he had hanging from his rearview mirror. "I'm on it," he said.

When they got out past the gas station and onto the open road, Pete saw what looked to be Phyllis Vernon pedaling a bicycle on the shoulder. Outdoor recreation took many forms in Deerfield, such as fishing, hunting, four-wheeling, and, hell, even some amateur archery, but, as a general rule, you didn't see a lot of people riding bicycles unless they were either between the ages of six and seventeen or were one of the patrons of Getwell's Bar who had long ago lost the state's confidence with regard to their responsible operation of motor vehicles. This was not the type of town, in other words, where you saw people exercising in public. It was just too damn hot for that type of thing. All of these social and geographical factors were part of what made Phyllis stand out, sure, but what Pete most noticed was her outfit.

Phyllis Vernon, age sixty-two, with a rear end that had taken on a sort of legendary status to those who saw it slowly spread itself across two chairs over the last twenty years at Heroman's Flower Shop, was wearing what appeared to be a neon-pink spandex onesie with black racing stripes down the side. She had on a yellow bicycle helmet with reflectors pasted on the back of it, the sort of laceless shoes a person might wear if they planned to go swimming in a public pool, and was moving that bicycle down the road at a speed of approximately two miles per hour.

Pete rolled down his window and slowed the truck. He liked Phyllis a great deal. She was a good Catholic who had what he imagined was an untreated eating disorder combined with simple human sadness caused by the loss of her husband nearly three decades ago. She'd talked about her eating in Confession with Father Pete on several occasions, detailing the nearly always surprising number of empty ice-cream tubs she found in her own trash bin, and he felt for Phyllis.

When he got beside her, Pete saw that this was no ordinary bicycle she was working on. This thing was gleaming and brand-new and had its own suspension system in both the front and the back. The name Gary Fisher was embossed on the frame and since Pete had no idea who Gary Fisher was, and since this was the most interesting bicycle he'd ever seen, he figured it was probably expensive.

"Let's just say hey," he told Trina, and leaned his head out the window as he drove.

"I can't wait," Trina said.

"Hey, young lady," Pete called. "I'm looking for an old broad named Phyllis Vernon. Have you seen her around here?"

Phyllis turned her head to look over but did not smile and did not, Pete was surprised to see, stop her pedaling. Her face was nebula red, brighter than the hottest sun, riper than the ripest beet, and he was suddenly afraid that she might have a heart attack right there on the street. Yet still she kept going. He thought to get out and walk beside her, such was her top speed, but instead he kept cruising.

"My God," Trina whispered, looking over. "Is she going to die? And, if so, can I have her outfit? I've been wanting to build a hot-air balloon."

Pete cut Trina a look and said, "Be nice."

He noticed that the reason Phyllis Vernon had not spoken to him was that she had a tube running from her mouth to what looked like a pouch attached to the back of her onesie. She was drinking water, he figured, which was good, because she looked very thirsty. "You all right, Ms. Phyllis?" he asked her again, and now that she seemed to see him more clearly, she gave him a thumbs-up. Luckily, the glove she was wearing opened up at the thumbs and fingers and allowed her to do this. She then let the tube fall from her mouth and began panting enthusiastically. She tapped the side of her helmet, where Pete saw, underneath one of the nylon straps that went across it, a folded slip of blue paper.

"Doing great, Father," Phyllis panted. "Can't talk now. Lot of work to do."

She then looked back at the road before her and continued her labored pace upon it. Pete glanced over at Trina, who was no longer watching any of this but instead typing something on her phone. Phyllis's breathing was loud enough to sound like she was in the car with them and so Pete said, "All right, then. See you Sunday," and lightly pressed the accelerator to move back over into his own lane.

"What do you think it said?" Trina asked him.

"What's that?" Pete asked.

"Her readout. That thing she pointed to. What do you think it said?"

Pete knew about these readouts but wasn't sure what to make of them. Two different confessions last week hinted to the blue pieces of paper, a kind of new way of looking at the world, but he'd not had much time to think on it.

"I'm betting it said O-Blimpian," Trina said. "Or, maybe, Steamroller."

"That's that new game, is it?" he said. "Some sort of fortune-teller?"

"According to some," she said. "According to others, it's just simple science. Much more reliable than things like, I don't know, prayers, for instance."

As they approached her house, Trina started moving around in the cab. She reached down and unzipped her backpack and took out a pack of cigarettes. She rolled down her window and lit one without even asking, which Pete found wildly inappropriate for many reasons. Yet he was so struck by the swiftness of her movements, the sudden change from her looking relaxed to looking nervous, that he didn't say a thing to stop her. He just put on his blinker and eased off the highway onto her gravel drive.

"What about you, Joe Camel?" he said. "Have you gotten one of those readouts?"

"No," she said. "But I know what mine would say." She put the backpack on her lap and blew smoke out of the truck window. "I'm thinking, Potential Life Station: Scalpel."

As soon as Pete pulled into the driveway, Trina hopped out of the truck.

"It would probably be best if I didn't invite you in," Trina said. "My father has been known to, you know, despise you."

"I understand," Pete said. "I don't want to get him riled up. I'm just glad you made it home safe."

She closed the truck door and turned around to face him. "Is that what I look like to you?" she said. "Safe?"

She turned and took a few steps toward the house before he called her back.

"Katrina," he said. "I meant to ask. You heard anything from your mom lately? Any word at all?"

She took a last big drag of her skinny cigarette and stomped it out on the gravel. "No, Uncle Pete, I haven't. What about you?" she asked. "You heard any word from God?"

"I believe I did," he said. "The moment I saw you standing on the side of that road."

Trina stared back at him without any emotion at all. Her eyes were so blank and gray in response to his compliment that it scared Pete a bit. What was going on with that girl?

He watched her walk up to the porch and into the house without so much as a good-bye and Pete thought about the house she lived in. It wasn't a bad place, structurally. It was brick with aluminum siding. It sat on a solid slab. Back when it was built, Pete figured, probably in the 1940s or so, it was likely the pride of the whole Todd family. No mansion, no big stucco Acadiana-style thing that people keep throwing up around Louisiana, but a big broad house with three bedrooms and two bathrooms. Enough land to have some chickens if you wanted them or to plant some shade trees. You could easily put a flower garden right there in front of the porch. That would brighten things up a bit. You could take the rusty tractor that hasn't been used in thirty years out of the yard, as well. That would free up some space. It probably wouldn't hurt to remove the discarded camper top that served as a doghouse for

Lanny's strange sort of Laplander–pit bull mix that he kept chained up under there, too, but, in all, it was a good house. It just needed some attention and maybe, Pete thought, a little prayer. He sat there thinking about these things for so long that he eventually heard the squeaking of Ms. Phyllis Vernon's mountain bike behind him. And this must have been too long to sit in another man's driveway praying about another man's house because, after he watched Phyllis inch by in his rearview mirror, he looked up to see Lanny Todd walking toward him. He was predictably shirtless but, unexpectedly, toting a shotgun.

Whatever this was about, Pete prayed, he hoped it would be over by five.

8

Oh My Stars

Oof. That was a record.

Well, in the last twenty years or so. There had been that time in high school when Cherilyn's mother left her alone in the house for a weekend, sure, but she had really just discovered it then. What was she, fifteen? Sixteen? Regardless, it was totally normal. Plus, she'd watched that movie with Patrick Swayze and Demi Moore in it about ten times (who knew a pottery wheel could be so exciting?) and probably hit the double digits in her own fun. But since then? Maybe once every two weeks or so, quickly in the bathroom, more languidly in the shower if Douglas was off at work. But three times in a day? Three times *since noon*, really, now that she thought about it? And the one last night when Douglas was sleeping?

What had gotten into her?

She'd thought of other men before, of course, but always in the sort of generalized way that Cherilyn imagined most adults with working parts thought about other adults with working parts. There were various skin colors and muscle tones, multiple attitudes, a different jawline or set of hands than she was used to. There was the muscled V of a younger man's back, maybe, a body without a face, or maybe a face without a body and, depending on her mood, perhaps even some long and luxurious hair instead of (yes, it was true in some of these fantasies, although she hated to admit it) a balding head with those freckles on the top like she was used to. Maybe even a tattoo, something colorful across the broad chest and shoulders but of what design or message she did not know nor care because these were not real people she was thinking of. They were just little imaginary cruise ships floating by. Little Love Boats, if you will. And they existed in so many different scenarios and locales that the whole process became a blur and caused her no guilt at all because it was not as if she was thinking specifically of one *particular* man, one other man besides her husband, was she, and it was not as if she were cataloging these things for display for someone else anyway. So, what did it matter? Nope, these thoughts were hers alone. And to her credit, she thought, these thoughts nearly always circled back around to nice memories with Douglas.

For these fantasies to *feel* as if they could actually happen, after all, for them to take her to the places she wanted to go, Cherilyn eventually had to imagine herself in them. Not a fantasy self, but her real body, both her physical being and her emotional being, and whenever she imagined this person feeling comfortable enough to share real pleasure with anyone, that person was always Douglas.

She had done this today, as well, the first time. It was a scene she often remembered, back when they were first married, in their mid-twenties, when they went tubing with some of their college friends on the Tickfaw River. They were both so young and happy and new and all the men on the river were shirtless and laughing and diving and splashing and she was in a bikini, of all things. Yes, there had been that version of her. She'd worn bikinis without a second thought until her thirty-fifth birthday, when she saw that picture Douglas had taken out in the backyard when they were sunbathing. Nope. No more two-pieces after that. There just comes a time, you know? She was sort of okay with that. But in this memory of the Tickfaw there was a moment when they found themselves alone in a bend of the river and they had locked their legs together beneath the water, her and Douglas, floating outside of their tubes but still holding on to them and how did it even happen? What were the physics of it? She remembers the kissing and how it was her who had first pulled his swimsuit down beneath the water, how she was just being playful, testing him, and how at first she didn't think it would go any further but then how pleased she was to feel his hand pulling her bikini bottom to the side. And how impetuous and fun to be doing this invisibly beneath the water, continuing even as they heard their friends around the bend, as if they couldn't stop once they had begun and the way they drifted joined together like that, the strange rush of water, the mix of heat and friction and the blazing sun above them, the memory of it toasting their cheeks and collarbones as they looked at each other, eye-to-eye that entire time, grinning and enjoying themselves and her biting her bottom lip for the first time in a way that Douglas still loves, she knows, that he still mentions to her on occasion, while nobody knew their secret. Yes, yes. She thought of this often.

But, full disclosure, she sometimes recalled her other times and other men. Three others, to be exact, before she began dating Douglas, and three was a perfectly fine number, she thought, and remembering is a natural thing. And there had been that incident with Deuce that she thought about once in a blue moon, but that was nothing, really. Still, she thought of it sometimes. It was harmless, not even an indiscretion in the biblical sense, but something a person thinks about. But not today. No, today there were new things to wonder.

Her conversation with that man on the computer, for example.

The curiosity of this would be hard to deny. They'd chatted for only a few minutes, and what had they even talked about? He had spoken of her beauty. He complimented her robe. Then he told her how warm it was in his room, that he had been playing soccer and was sweating, and asked if it would be okay if he took his shirt off.

And she had typed, *You may.*

Okay, so, if a person were to really study the situation then they might find it a pretty strange coincidence that she had broken her record on a day that she'd talked to this other man, but it isn't like she actually *knew* him. He was no more real than her thought boats. But something had happened. Yes, okay. Something had started her up. Had she been unfaithful? Was that what she had been? No, of course not.

Yet the way he stood before her, there was something in that. She watched him scoot back in his chair and rise and hook his thumbs into the neck of his shirt and pull it over his head and the cartography of his body was something to see. Flat lines of muscle beneath his collarbone, his strong pecs and shoulders. The dark hair on his chest, the musculature of his stomach and the way this definition seemed to make two rivers that led into his shorts where there were undoubtedly other things to explore. He was no super-model, no artificially tanned and waxed gym rat, and that was good. He was merely a man standing before her and he did not, at first, sit back down. He allowed her to look, to appraise him, and she did.

Studying his body, Cherilyn was struck by the image of men running. Not just this man but all men, grown men, perhaps running around a soccer field like the high school boys in town. Did she know any men who played soccer? Of course not. Had she ever seen a grown man run in real life? She thought about this. Not on the television, not in a football uniform, but right there in front of her? Had she seen this? Had a man ever run past her? Had she felt the air move in his wake? Smelled him go by? Not that she could remember.

The men of Deerfield sat in boats and shot guns. They hunted and drank and yanked at the cords of lawnmowers and were manly enough, sure, but they did not run. They did not play soccer. And so she imagined this man, fit and sweaty and fast, just as she imagined all running men must be and, truth told, she may have also imagined all of these imaginary men taking off their shirts for her and her alone and, so, when he sat back down at the desk and smiled at her, when he was obviously willing to do anything she might ask of him, when she felt her heart begin beating in an unfamiliar way, Cherilyn leaned forward, touched the mouse, and clicked "Next."

She then quickly shut down the page and turned off the monitor as if to make sure nobody saw it and was left looking at her own reflection in the dark screen. Again, not a bad tableau. She put her hand to her face, traced her finger down to her collarbone. She looked down at her robe. This was the most comfortable thing she owned. It was blue and thin, with felt at the collar, some discoloration where the hem hit the floor, and had a mismatched flannel tie around the waist. It was the literal opposite of sexy. She had worn it a thousand times, as if it were her morning uniform. But today it appeared transformed to her and she looked at herself again in the monitor. *Hello, there,* she thought, and hooked a finger into the edge of the robe, tickled her own skin with the back of a fingernail, and pulled the robe gently to the side. Half of her there. Hello. Yes, half of her there to see.

After this she'd had her first bit of fun right on the office chair. Then the phone rang again in the kitchen and, expecting it to be her mother, who would probably be confused as to why she hadn't answered her cell phone or who had perhaps forgotten to turn off the stove and set her house on fire, Cherilyn got up and answered it, not even bothering to check the caller ID. Instead of her mother or even Douglas, though, it was Geoffrey Mallow, who was looking for Douglas to confirm their afternoon lesson. And after they had chatted for a few minutes and she'd thanked him for being so kind to Douglas, who was very excited about this trombone business, she went back to the bedroom and unexpectedly had her fun again on top of the sheets and then again one last time in the shower and, throughout all of this, she did not feel bad. Not guilty. Not sick. Not worried. Not at all.

But now she was leaving her house.

It was already three-thirty and she was usually at her mom's house by noon. She'd been sure to close out her Internet session by clicking all the little X's she could find until the screen was back to their home page. Then she'd thought to open up a game of solitaire and leave it on the screen, as if that is what she'd been playing all day, and went out their front door, not bothering to lock it, and headed down the sidewalk toward her mother's house. She carried a plastic grocery bag with a Tupperware bowl in it, containing the leftover burger and mac and cheese from the previous night and figured her mom could eat it as a late lunch or for supper tonight if she wasn't in a cooking frame of mind.

When she got to the end of their street, she saw Stacy Pitre in front of her house pulling weeds. She waved Cherilyn over to complain that her azaleas weren't blooming, although she'd seen the ones over on Maycomb Street starting to bud, and said she was worried that her husband had cut them back too late in the year because, you know Dan, he's never done anything on time in his life, but what were they going to do, she worried, if they had to go through spring without their azalea blossoms? Could you imagine?

Cherilyn was not quite sure if she replied to Stacy that *yes* she could imagine or *no* she could not imagine, which both would have meant the same thing in this scenario, because she'd again begun to feel the day's heat in the distracting and bothersome manner that was still new to her.

Far from the young woman tubing down the river in her memory, letting the sun bake her skin and face, the Louisiana heat had recently become an enemy of hers. It affected her head lately, always in negative ways, making her almost dizzy, feeling totally exhausted and out of it. It may have been the case, in this particular instance, that part of her was still busy rearranging what had happened with that man on the computer. So, maybe she was only distracted? After all, had she done something wrong? That would be unlike her. But why, then, had she put the solitaire game up as if she'd been playing it? Was that a lie she had told, in the way that lies can so often be silent? Had she just lied to her husband without even saying a thing? She did not like that idea at all.

Regardless, she decided that she would most certainly *not* be going to that Omegle place again, now that she'd had some time to think on it, because it was not appropriate for a stranger to look into her home, nor was it appropriate for her to look into his. So, she would just wash her hands of that. It was in the past, and everyone has a past. Time to move on.

But the way Cherilyn was having a hard time literally understanding what Stacy Pitre was saying—something about the flowering cells in azaleas having to travel from the root of the plant to the tips, how they have to regenerate every year—the way the words themselves didn't make sense to her, felt undeniably physical in nature. She was suddenly gripped by the fear that she might be acting very strangely in front of her neighbor, staring blankly at her mouth as she spoke, although Stacy didn't seem to notice. And when Cherilyn finally left and began again down the sidewalk, knowing she only had to go another mile or so to get to her mom's place, maybe a ten-minute walk, her legs felt so heavy beneath her, as if she were wearing gravity boots, that she honestly didn't know if she could make it.

But Stacy was right. Things were beginning to bloom around town, and maybe that was it. Allergies. Had she taken a Claritin this morning? Done her nose spray? Changes in weather could do physical things to a person, everybody knew that. Even the paper reported on pollen and such. She would give it another week, maybe. If it wasn't better then, she'd make an appointment with Dr. Granger.

Or maybe she would just be straight-up with Douglas and tell him how it's worse than she's been letting on, how it's more than just the headaches, how there's some other things she's been worried about. Maybe confess to him the true reason she'd dropped her phone. And, while she was at it, maybe she'd even tell him that she had been on the computer today and learned a lot of interesting things about royalty and would he ever want to visit one of those places?

"Mrs. Hubbard?"

And maybe she would also tell Douglas, by the way, I am supposed to be a queen myself. Or maybe a princess. A royal person. And I have proof. Isn't that funny?

"Yoo hoo, Cherilyn."

And maybe she could go with Douglas to do this machine, too, and maybe his readout would say that he was also destined for something great and so they could go off and be great together. Why couldn't they?

"Going once," the man said. "Twice."

Cherilyn stopped walking. Who was talking to her? She looked over and saw a black Lincoln Town Car driving slowly along the curb. The window was rolled down and the man inside was smiling. She recognized him immediately.

This was Tipsy Rodrigue, who everyone knew.

"Oh," Cherilyn said. "Hey, Tipsy. How long have you been there?"

"About four houses," he said. "Want a ride?"

"I'm just going to my mom's," she said.

"I know the place," Tipsy said. "Plus, I've got A/C. Hop in."

Tipsy Rodrigue, among his other distinguishing features, was missing some important teeth. This was not necessarily uncommon for a man in his fifties who, like Tipsy, had made a slurry of questionable choices in life but, unfortunately for him, he was missing his two front teeth. So, no matter what he was talking about—baseball, fuel efficiency, marine life, climate change—his countenance lacked a certain credibility. Still, he was a nice guy who was doing his penance in Deerfield, and so not many people turned down a ride when they saw that gap-toothed smile from the Lincoln.

"It *is* hot out here," Cherilyn said. "I'll admit it."

Tipsy leaned over and opened the door. "Well, come on, then," he said.

Above all else, Tipsy Rodrigue was a man-about-town.

As the only cab driver in Deerfield, he held a sort of monopoly on the transportation-for-hire scene. However, since he didn't charge any money, you didn't hear people complain. His venture was not for profit. Tipsy instead just drove around town all day and night, offering people free rides. He didn't need money since he'd gotten that big settlement from the slip and fall at Walmart a few years ago, but it was that hip injury and the settlement money that most people said caused his drugging and drinking, which then led to the DWI and head-on collision he'd had with the front of Tony's Donut Shop two years back. This accident had not only removed his front teeth but could have been, everyone knows, much worse, as the Donut Shop was normally full of children at the hour in which he struck it—eight a.m. on a Saturday morning—and can you imagine the tragedy that would have been if Tony's was not closed that day for maintenance? Yes, everyone could imagine.

Tipsy himself had imagined this tragedy-that-almost-was to such a degree that he'd publicly sworn, in a letter to the editor of *The Deerfield Bugle*, that he would never drink and drive again. He also would not get fake teeth so that he, too, would always remember.

After giving it a few weeks, though, and realizing that drinking was not really a thing he was likely to give up on his own, Tipsy had decided to simply begin driving all the time. This was the only thing he could find to help keep him sober. He began to pick up couples on their way to church, scoop his old friends as they stumbled out of Getwell's, and even ferry nice married women over to their mothers' houses. In this way, he had remained true to his word and so the town of Deerfield held him close, took his rides when offered, and appreciated how he was somehow paying them back for the tragedy he almost caused.

Cherilyn liked him, too, mainly because he always had the good gossip. He was a living Deerfield newsfeed.

Cherilyn sat down in his car and shut the door. "How have you been, Tipsy?" she asked.

"Busy, busy, busy," he said. "I'm telling you, Mrs. Hubbard, with the bicentennial and all, this town is *a-buzzing*."

"Is that right?" Cherilyn said and leaned her head back on the leather seat. The frigid air from the A/C was like heaven as Tipsy automatically rolled her window back up, sealed them inside the car. He had the radio tuned to the local talk station, where someone was reporting on the amount of speckled trout that were apparently biting that spring.

"So," Cherilyn said. "What's the news?" She tried not to let on how she was feeling, just figured to make some small talk and let Tipsy carry on in his usual way, as she knew this would be a short ride. She blinked her eyes, looked at her hands, and tried to focus. She rubbed her right palm with her thumb. Was it cramping again?

"National, regional, or local?" he said. "Do you want political? Celebrity? Illicit? You need to narrow it down a bit."

"Well," Cherilyn said. "Don't tell me anything that's going to hurt my feelings. I know just about everybody here, you know."

"Is that too cold for you?" Tipsy asked, and fiddled with the A/C. He had the nicest car in Deerfield, with black leather seats and this sophisticated climate control that could keep, according to Tipsy, the four different passenger zones at four discrete temperatures based on the riders' preferences. He also had seat heaters, which never got used, and tinted windows. He was proud of his car, proud of the things he'd accomplished these last two years, and had even ordered a bumper sticker for his back window that read "The Goober Uber."

He was hard not to like.

"Let's start with celebrity," Cherilyn said.

"Okay," Tipsy said. "Well, they say Britney Spears is making a comeback."

"Is that so?" Cherilyn said. "Good for her."

"She's so talented," Tipsy said. "And from right up the road in Kentwood, you know. If she could just keep her underpants on, she'd probably be all right. I can't help rooting for her."

"I feel the same way," Cherilyn said. "So, how about political?"

"All-righty," Tipsy said. "Did you know there is a final city council meeting tomorrow about the bicentennial?" Tipsy lowered his voice as if keeping it secret. "And word on the street is that Deuce is going to make a play for Hank's job. Going to say he's no longer fit to serve due to, you know, his personal losses."

"That's not news," Cherilyn said. "Bruce has wanted to be mayor since he was seventeen years old. He's harmless. Plus, everybody loves Hank. It was a tragedy what happened to his boy, but he'll be okay with a little time and prayer. Let's stay local, though. What else do you have?"

"Well," Tipsy said. "Did you know Alice's Costume Shop is doing bang-up business? I mean, *bang*-up. I've been bringing people there every day. People buying firefighter outfits, police outfits, old fluffy dresses. You can't hardly fit in the store."

"Really?" Cherilyn said.

Cherilyn knew Alice well. They used to craft together, share a booth at the Fish Festival, and Alice had even invited Cherilyn to partner up for the costume shop whenever that was, some ten years ago now, probably. And why hadn't Cherilyn done it? Douglas had encouraged her to, she remembered, but why hadn't she done it?

"Why do you think that is, Tipsy?" Cherilyn asked. "Is it just people getting ready for the bicentennial? Is there going to be a fancy party?"

"No, ma'am," Tipsy said. "I believe it's because of these."

Tipsy leaned forward and pressed a button on his dash. A compartment slid open without noise, as if every single joint of this vehicle was motorized and lubricated, and it was beautiful to witness in its small way. When Tipsy pulled from it a stack of blue receipts, Cherilyn felt her heart drop.

"Oh," she said. "I've heard about those."

But what Cherilyn was really thinking at this moment was, *Where are mine?* Oh my God, she thought, they are in the car with Douglas. They are in the car with Douglas.

"Miss Alice says nearly everybody coming in her shop is coming on account of these. Trying to get the right clothes, I figure, for what they know they can be now. Trying to dress for success, as the expression goes."

"What are you saying?" Cherilyn asked. "Other people in town, they believe these readouts? People don't think they're crazy?"

"Shoot yeah, they believe them," Tipsy said. "How could you not? It's science, Mrs. Hubbard. Plain and simple."

Tipsy took one of his readouts between his fingers and held it out to Cherilyn. It read: Justin Paul Rodrigue. A series of meaningless numbers. Then, Potential Life Station: **DRIVER**.

Cherilyn wanted to cry.

"I told Miss Alice I'm just lucky mine doesn't require any fancy paraphernalia, you know? I'm lucky doing what I'm already doing. But maybe it's not luck at all, Mrs. Hubbard. Maybe the fellow upstairs just works in kooky ways."

"So, your readout was right?" Cherilyn said. "Is that what you're telling me?" She went to hand it back to him. "Some of these are right?"

"You keep that," Tipsy said. "I've written my phone number on the back. It's my new business card. As if a person might need any more proof that I'm done boozing. Here's my proof. Clear as can be. You can count on me."

Tipsy stopped the car and put it in park. Cherilyn looked up to see they were already at her mother's house. She stared at the orange brick front with its gray roof. She looked at the rusty screen door, the Oldsmobile parked in the driveway.

"Looks like somebody's been waiting on you," Tipsy said, and then Cherilyn noticed her mother standing at the open door to her garage, peering out at them. She wore a pink jogging suit with sparkles along the shoulders and, just by the look of her hair from here, Cherilyn knew she was not having a good day.

"Thank you, Tipsy," Cherilyn said, and folded the blue slip of paper into her hand. What tremendous evidence this was, she realized, what a great moment. "I am very, very glad I got in your car today."

"That makes two of us," Tipsy said.

"And you keep me posted on this Britney Spears comeback story, okay?"

"Will do," he said. "You know, they say she's opening up a new restaurant in Kentwood."

"Is that a fact?" Cherilyn said.

"Yep. It's going to be called Hit Me Baby, with Some Fries."

Cherilyn looked at him. Tipsy smiled.

"It's a joke, Mrs. Hubbard. I've been kind of trying it out."

"It's a good one," Cherilyn said, and shut the door.

Cherilyn walked up the driveway with her grocery bag and held it up in the air for her mother to see, as if to start off their conversation on a good foot by giving her a present.

"I brought food," she said.

Her mother looked like she had just gotten out of bed, which Cherilyn knew couldn't be true. Still, the bright white hair that she was so vain about, that she normally spent an hour fixing up in the mirror, was as flat and unkempt as if she'd slept on the couch.

"Where have you been?" her mother said.

"I'm sorry," Cherilyn said. "The car wouldn't start and I got tied up at the house."

"I've been waiting forever," she said. "I called and called."

"I broke my phone," Cherilyn said. "Why? Is everything okay?"

"No, of course it's not okay," she said.

"What's the matter?" Cherilyn asked.

"It's my daughter," she said. "She's trapped in the attic. She won't come down."

"Oh," Cherilyn said. "Mom."

And all those feelings.

Fear. Illness. Worry.

Were they all coming back to her now?

Yes, they were.

And how long could they stand there together, these two women, a mom and her only daughter, on opposite sides of the door, with each of their minds in some mysterious disarray? And what were the worries between them? Were they all the same? All different? In what directions were they headed? And are all daughters destined to become their mothers and mothers destined to become their daughters? And, if so, was it true that life was buzzing for them both in that moment, that something big was about to happen for each of them, but in totally opposite ways? Could they feel it? What was about to happen.

The future.

Could they feel it buzzing?

9

Slide of Hand

Douglas pulled into Geoffrey Mallow's apartment complex on time, parked near the green dumpster on the side of the building, and stared blankly through the front windshield. He was doing all he could to erase from his memory the conversation he'd just endured with Principal Pat. He'd tried calling Cherilyn to tell her about it, the outrageous notion that he become principal of Deerfield Catholic because his boss had purchased a pair of safety goggles, but she didn't answer. He figured she must have walked down to her mother's, but since she didn't have her phone, and since Douglas didn't have the energy for a conversation with his mother-in-law, whom he loved but who was undoubtedly losing her mind, he decided he would just tell Cherilyn the whole mess tonight. This was probably better.

After all, they had a lot to talk about. There was the business of that ridiculous machine, after all, which he would need to mention in regard to Pat's sudden change of vocation. And this topic, if arising as he and Cherilyn consumed the suspicious amount of eggplant and olive oil she'd asked him to purchase, would undoubtedly bring up Cherilyn's own DNAMIX reading, which she likely didn't know Douglas had seen. And how would he react if she told him? How *should* he? He worried that, for the first time in their lives together, he may need to pretend to be happy about something that he wasn't happy about, that he might have to act like someone else in front of her instead of just being himself. And all because of a little slip of paper. But it wasn't just eggplant and amateur carpentry, was it? It wasn't only Cherilyn and Pat, but also the Major League pitcher and origami girl, perhaps all of his students and colleagues, the whole town newly adrift in doomed daydreams. What was Douglas to do? How could a rational person, he wondered, express the silliness of these readouts, of Cherilyn's readout especially, without making Cherilyn herself feel silly? How could he bring her back to normalcy? How could he branch out from his own?

There was much to think about for a Thursday.

But, for now, his lesson.

The Scenic Wetlands Apartments and Balconies was the only complex in town. A decade ago, its construction was a pretty hot topic, as the old guard of Deerfield believed that apartments, or any multifamily homes, really, were destined to become crack houses and brothels. This notion was ludicrous but understandable. Change is hard, especially in the South. Douglas understood that. And since everyone else in the history of Deerfield had seemed perfectly content living with their own families in modest ranch-style houses separated by ample yards that either lined the highways or sat quietly along neighborhood roads, each equipped with a two-lane gravel or oyster-shell driveway with grass growing along its middle that led to a covered two-car garage with a tin or shingle roof, what possible reason, people wondered, would anyone have to live on top of a stranger?

The idea of apartments, much like the idea of public transportation, seemed to offend some deep sense of southern freedom to the older generation of Deerfield, but, as Douglas knew would happen, the apartments were eventually built and occupied not by prostitutes and drug addicts, but by normal people who just didn't want to do any yardwork.

The building now sat as quietly as the rest of town, where the only weekday sounds you might hear were the persistent hum of lawnmowers and Weed Eaters, maybe a UPS truck rattling by on occasion. It therefore became part of the normal and innocuous Deerfield soundscape, where it would be hard to find any place that wasn't generally, almost excruciatingly quiet, unless you counted Getwell's Bar on LSU football Saturdays, or the Straight Pin Bowling Alley whenever they had that eighties cover band for the Fourth of July. So, like most worrisome things in the history of Deerfield, it turned out to be nothing to worry about. It was not a drug den, not a strip club, and not the end of the world.

The brick front of the Scenic Wetlands Apartments and Balconies was also unremarkable. It was two stories high, with maybe twelve apartments total, all with dark gray doors. There were rusty guard railings on the second floor, mosquito screens on all the windows. Not much to look at, really. The view from the back balconies of these apartments, however, was what gave the place its charm. The complex was situated at the northernmost reach of Bayou Ibis, along a watershed known to attract wading birds like egrets and spoonbills whenever the water rose. Even in the dry times, when the bayou was low, this area was covered in white and pink flowers, and so legend had it that this was actually the best place in town to sit and have a glass of wine, maybe play a little soft guitar or saxophone, light up a citronella candle, and watch the long-legged birds go about their gentle pacing.

So, Douglas took a deep breath, turned off the motor, and got out of his wife's car. He pulled his trombone case out of the back seat and felt so exhausted by his day that if this were any other obligation in the world, he might have just canceled it. But this

new forty-year-old version of Douglas would never cancel a trombone lesson, not only because of what it might mean to his future
career, what it might metaphorically suggest about his commitment to the art form if he was already making excuses not to practice, but also because, even though he had a lot on his mind, he
actually did want to practice. He did want to learn and get better.
All of that was true. Yet the real reason Douglas would never cancel this lesson was that it gave him a chance to hang out with
Geoffrey Mallow.

In the way that aspiring novelists might like to imagine their
work someday being discussed in a sophomore literature class, the
teacher enthusiastically tracing their literary influences back
through the canon, or the way philosophers like to chart the evo-
lution of thought from Socrates to Plato to Jay-Z, or even to the
way athletes like to thank God for helping them sack a quarterback or run a quick forty-yard dash, Douglas also liked to imagine
himself one day becoming part of some traceable lineage. He could
picture his story inserted on the margin of a textbook he used in
his own History classes or maybe spread across a Wikipedia page
made by one of his fans. If it was a quick sketch, Douglas imagined, the bio might say something simple like "Musical Influences:
Miles Davis and Geoffrey Mallow." Or, if it was an interview, Douglas might take the time to thank the little-known musician from
Louisiana named Geoffrey Mallow, who taught him all he knew.
Or, if it was a full-on biography, that sort of Pulitzer Prize–worthy
investigation into his life, the author might write something like
"Douglas Hubbard, when it was all said and done, idolized Geoffrey Mallow."

This would be true.

Geoffrey Mallow was, in Douglas's estimation, the coolest man
walking the planet. Tall and graceful, about 6'4", with long fingers,
short graying hair, and a meticulously trimmed goatee, Geoffrey

Mallow was everything Douglas wanted to be. Descended from a
family of New Orleans musicians, Geoffrey could make any instrument sound as if it were made for him. Douglas had seen this at
the variety of talks Geoffrey had given at Deerfield Catholic since
he'd moved there the previous year, where he also gave private les-
sons and solo performances at various school assemblies. For most
people, it may have been the simple fact that a talent like his was
so rare in Deerfield that made Geoffrey stand out but, for Douglas,
it was something deeper. It was Geoffrey's polished confidence he
most admired, the way he walked around town in any type of
hat—porkpies, ball caps, a fedora—dressed in whatever attitude
the day suggested to him, talking to people in the easiest and most
self-assured manner. It was the way you might see him playing
chess at one of the outside tables of the Butter-It-Better Café,
sometimes against himself, at other times with whoever had
stopped by for a game. It was the way he would take off for a week
or two to gig around New Orleans, show back up at a high school
football game and nonchalantly read the paper as if he hadn't just
done the coolest thing Douglas could imagine. And it was also, of
course, the reason Geoffrey had moved to Deerfield in the first
place that Douglas admired.

Upon their first conversation at school, after Geoffrey had performed a one-man show in which he played a medley of spirituals
and gospel songs on no less than five different instruments (saxophone, coronet, clarinet, oboe, violin!), Douglas asked him why
anyone with that sort of talent would move to a place without
even one decent nightclub. Geoffrey told him that he had been
gigging all his life, made enough money through studio sessions
and sporadic touring that he could retire or, at least, begin to live
life on his own terms. "I don't need much," he'd said. "All my
instruments are paid for. Now it's just me and my breath. Me and
my hands." The sentiment was charming and lovely but also

confusing to Douglas, who, like many people on the planet, understood New Orleans to be the epicenter of everything brass. "Won't you miss the scene, though?" Douglas asked him. "I mean, nothing happens in Deerfield." Geoffrey smiled in the kind and gentle manner a person does when they have absolutely nothing to prove and said, "I can always find some noise if I want it. What I'm looking for is quiet when I need it."

Douglas felt a grand and benign jealousy upon hearing this, not dissimilar to the way an attorney may feel a college professor lives the good life, with their summers off, their leisurely strolls around campus, when viewed in comparison to the attorney's world of endless briefs and soulless schmoozing. Or perhaps the way a college professor may feel an attorney lives the good life, with their stacks of money and cruise vacations, in comparison to grading essays on the weekends and navigating the cesspool of departmental politics. It was, in other words, the way that people are so quick to think without knowing, to assume without understanding, and it felt natural.

So, when Geoffrey asked Douglas if he played any instruments, Douglas answered honestly that he'd always felt a certain kinship with the trombone but didn't play it. "If you ever want to learn," Geoffrey said, "I can teach you. It's just like everything else. All it takes is endless practice and frustration and then, if you are open to it, joy."

"To be honest," Douglas said, "I can whistle a bit, but I don't suppose that counts as an instrument."

"Everything is an instrument," Geoffrey said. "Lay it on me."

And so Douglas, who, for the first time in his life, felt nervous about his whistling, puckered up and went for the Charlie Parker sax lead on "Summertime" from his complete *Master Takes* album circa 1949 right there in the middle of the school cafeteria. Geoffrey stood wordless until he finished, then put his hand on

Douglas's shoulder. He looked as if, during some point of the song, they had become old friends. "You told me nothing happened in this town," he said. "That's not true. *You're* happening, man. That was beautiful."

Douglas felt both deeply pleased and embarrassed by the compliment. His heart beat in an unfamiliar way. "It's Charlie Parker," he said. "I've got the record at home, on vinyl."

"Nope," Geoffrey said, and pressed his hand to Douglas's chest. "You've got that record right here."

This simple gesture made Douglas fall into a version of love with this man, or at least the idea of him, and now here he was, almost a year later, finally taking Geoffrey up on his offer. He walked to the corner of the apartment complex and climbed the metal stairs with his trombone at his side. When he got there, he saw Geoffrey standing on the breezeway in front of his apartment door. He was dressed, unexpectedly, in a tuxedo and top hat. He looked handsome, intriguing, and sharp, like a figure cut from an old-time magazine.

"Whoa," Douglas said. "Look at you."

Geoffrey grinned. "That's right," he said, loud enough to project past Douglas and into the parking lot. "Look at me closely." He held out his hands to show his empty palms. "And then ask yourself this question: Can you really believe your own eyes?"

At this, Geoffrey threw something onto the ground in front of him. It sparked and popped on the pavement, emitting a cloud of blue smoke so thick that it made Douglas take a step back and cover his mouth. When he finally waved the smoke away and opened his eyes, Geoffrey was gone.

"Okay," Douglas said. "That was unexpected."

Although he was certain Geoffrey had just walked back inside his apartment, which he'd been standing right in front of, Douglas had to admit he hadn't heard the door open. He also hadn't seen the smoke become disturbed by the draft of air that his rushing back inside would cause, and so he slapped the side of his leg in a makeshift applause. "Not too bad," he said, and walked to Geoffrey's door.

When he opened it, Geoffrey was sitting in an armchair and reading a magazine, dressed in khaki pants and a black Zildjian drums T-shirt. He looked up as if nothing at all was abnormal.

"Hey, Hubbs," he said, and checked his watch. "You know, if there's something else to admire besides your whistling and extensive knowledge of history, I'd say it is your punctuality. You're right on time. That's rare in the jazz game." He stood and approached him. "As the saying goes, most of us operate on six-eight time, meaning if you want us there by six, we show up at eight. But this is good. I'm glad you're here."

Douglas stared at him. "Okay," he said, and pointed to his new outfit. "I'm impressed." He then looked around the room for the tuxedo, which he imagined Geoffrey had peeled off and thrown in a corner, but it was nowhere in sight. "I'm also confused."

As far as Douglas knew, Geoffrey Mallow was not one for tricks. Yet as he shook his hand and scanned the small apartment, Douglas began to experience a rather unfortunate feeling of déjà vu. On the coffee table, he saw three small cups set beside a red rubber ball. Stacked on the sofa, where last night there were milk crates full of jazz records, there now sat several old boxes of magic tricks, a series of manuals, and a small plastic wand with white tips.

"What's going on in here?" Douglas asked.

"Wait," Geoffrey said. "Don't move."

He looked over Douglas's shoulder as if there might be a spider or flying insect about to land and then reached behind Douglas's ear. When he brought back his hand, as if it had been sitting there the whole time, he held a small slip of blue paper.

"Oh, Jesus Christ," Douglas said.

"I have had," Geoffrey told him, "the most extraordinary day. Set down your horn and make yourself a drink in the kitchen. Let me tell you."

The story went, of course, that last night, after Douglas's first lesson, Geoffrey had gone over to Johnson's Grocery. "Have you seen that thing?" Geoffrey asked him. "I'm telling you, man, it's like a miracle. I haven't even slept since then. I don't feel like I need to."

Douglas dragged himself over to the kitchen, poured an iced tea, and felt himself toggling miserably between anger and outright depression as yet another person spilled their imaginary guts to him, for which, Douglas presumed, he was supposed to be happy.

"A magician!" Geoffrey said, and plucked a stack of cards off the coffee table. He shuffled them around in his hand, scissored them expertly between his fingers. "You have to understand. Out of all the things that machine could have said, *that's* the one that got me. I mean, *got* me. I cried in the middle of the produce section. I forgot why I was even there. Speaking of, did you know Johnson's set up a box of tissues by the checkout now? He said so many people been crying in there after getting those readouts, he figured why not. People are just crying from joy, he says. Joy, my man! The good stuff! Well, most of them, anyway."

Douglas said nothing in reply, simply chugged the glass of tea and poured himself another. He then put the pitcher back on the counter and returned to the living room, where Geoffrey was now running a long red scarf along his palm. He gestured over to the couch.

"The thing is," Geoffrey told him, "you see all those boxes? All those magic books? I've had them since I was a kid."

He leaned over and picked one up, handed it to Douglas. It smelled of attics and footlockers, that old library smell, and had a picture of a magician pulling a rabbit out of his hat on the front. It was made by Mattel, copyright 1974. "These were gifts from *Santa*, man. That's how old they are. My folks only wanted me to practice sax and piano, and I dug that, too, but as a kid, I always wanted to be a magician."

"Is that so," Douglas said, and sank down into the chair.

"And I just popped into that DNA machine for kicks, you know? It's only two bucks. I figured I'd try it out for a laugh." Geoffrey pulled the scarf between his hands, balled it up in a fist, and, with a shake, promptly made it disappear. He then leaned closer to Douglas, lowered his voice to almost a whisper, and said, "But when I got my readout, I was like, *how could it know?* It's like that old joke about a thermos. You remember that?" He looked at Douglas, who sat without expression.

"Humor me," Douglas said.

"You know the one," Geoffrey said. "A kid asks a scientist, 'What's the greatest invention in the world?' And the scientist says, 'The thermos bottle, because it keeps things hot in the winter and cold in the summer.' And the kid says, 'Wow,' then sits and thinks for a minute. Then the kid raises his hand again and says, 'But, but, teacher. *How do it know?*'"

"Is that the whole joke?" Douglas asked.

"Yes. It's a classic. But, anyway, that's my question, too, Hubs. How the hell do it know?"

Douglas set the box back down on the couch, took a deep breath, and pressed his palms against his eyes. He felt himself sliding into teacher mode here, which he recognized as a mistake, as it was the worst and most pitiful part of his personality. This was a mode all teachers have access to, where nothing more than rampant depression and boredom made them want to destroy any argument volleyed forth, even if by a child. This was an aspect of his character Douglas usually forbade himself to unleash around other

adults, but there was a part of him, on this day, that felt he might
be losing his grip.

"Geoffrey," Douglas said. "Not to be a wet blanket, but isn't that
a pretty typical desire for a kid?"

"What do you mean?" Geoffrey asked.

"I mean, for example, if there were to be a poll that asked kids
what totally romanticized occupation they might like to have
when they grow up, regardless of whether the child has any actual
knowledge about what that job might entail, wouldn't 'magician'
rank right behind, oh, I don't know, 'Spider-Man,' 'police officer,'
and 'firefighter'?"

Geoffrey smiled. "I will ignore your condescension," he said, "for
a more illuminating anecdote."

"I'm not trying to be condescending," Douglas began, but Geoffrey quickly waved his hand to the side, as if making that whole
line of conversation disappear.

"Do you know how many times I've moved in my life?" Geoffrey
asked him. "I mean, from one little shithole apartment to another,
living with folks in whatever band I was in, sleeping five people to
a room? I've lived with *drummers*, man! Drummers! I've seen some
shit. Anyway, my point is: I've left stands behind, sheet music,
amps, all sorts of truly valuable stuff, just because I didn't have the
energy to move it. But I never left these behind. That's what I'm
saying. I couldn't tell you why, but I always kept these magic tricks.
All my life, I felt like they were important. And now, here we are. It
all makes sense."

"It's simple nostalgia," Douglas said. "I still have the complete
set of 1988 Topps baseball cards my uncle gave me when I was a
kid. It doesn't mean anything."

"Maybe it doesn't," Geoffrey said. "Maybe it does."

"But Geoffrey," Douglas said. "You're what, fifty years old? You're a world-class musician. You're a genius. Don't you think you've pretty much met your calling?"

"I hear you," Geoffrey said. "And I appreciate it. But I'm really good at this, too, Hubs. It feels natural to me. And what I'm thinking is, maybe music *is* a type of magic. And maybe that's what's carried me through. Maybe that's why I've always been happy enough, because I've always been close to my calling without even knowing it."

Now, here was something Douglas couldn't argue with. Music was a type of magic. This was undeniable even in teacher mode. It was something Douglas felt every time he put on an old record, closed his eyes, and let himself be transported out of Deerfield and into the horns of strangers he would never know, but who somehow felt like brothers and sisters to his own soul when they played. And this recognition, along with the light in Geoffrey's eyes as he sat across from him, made Douglas think about Cherilyn, how she was obviously taking this readout as seriously as Geoffrey was, as Pat was, as seemingly everyone was, and the culmination of all these faces made Douglas feel a strange and rare sensation.

Maybe he was wrong.

This was not an easy thing to consider. Countless geniuses throughout the history of human thought have sabotaged themselves in their unwillingness to be wrong. Politicians. Parents. Husbands. Men. They've gone down on ships strewn with holes of their own making since before the word *stubborn* existed. And here was Douglas. Maybe he was wrong about this machine? Maybe he was wrong about a lot of things. Maybe the odd distance he'd felt between he and Cherilyn was not because of her and her readout at all, but because of him: his own stubbornness, his closed-mindedness, his predictability. Maybe there was something to this science, regardless of how outlandish it seemed, how out of reach some of these readouts may be for people. Maybe there was something deeply true about DNA, something exciting and heretofore unknown that Douglas had just not afforded himself the chance to consider.

This idea made Douglas feel an immense and corkscrew-shaped guilt about his conversation with Cherilyn the night before, the way he had attempted to assuage his wife's mysterious longings with grunts about her skillet-fried burgers. The way he had not truly engaged her at all as she leaned across the table and asked him what he believed possible in the world.

Weren't these the *real* conversations of love, after all? Conversations about possibility? Talks about maybes? And isn't closing oneself off to possibility, even in its most simple and generic form, whether due to familiarity or expectation, the true danger of something like a marriage? That was not the kind of husband Douglas wanted to be, a sort of stone wall to his wife's potential, nor was it the kind of husband he felt he had ever been. And so, above all things, Douglas suddenly longed to be with Cherilyn. He wanted to apologize to her, to speak with her or, rather, to *listen* to her speak to him about what was now taking life in her heart. He thought about the way he'd stood before her with his trombone that night before, her sweetly offering up "Seventy-six Trombones" as a tune she might like to hear on his perfect day, and he had an idea. He stood up, walked back to the door where he had set down his case, and brought it to the table.

"Geoffrey," he said. "Can you teach me how to play a song?"

Geoffrey leaned forward and put his hand on the case. He closed his eyes, muttered something under his breath.

"Of course," he said, and looked up at Douglas. "But first you have to learn something else." He then sat back and crossed his legs, stroked his goatee. "You have to learn how to be *willing*. How to be *open*." He nodded at the case. "Go ahead," he said. "Take a look."

Douglas reached down and unlatched the case, raised the lid.

Inside of it, nestled beneath the straps of his trombone case, sat two playing cards that had not been there before, each facedown. The effect of this trick on Douglas was near visceral. He felt goosebumps on his arms, a chill at the back of his neck.

"Okay," he said. "How'd you do that?"

"That's not the question," Geoffrey said. "Turn them over."

So, Douglas did, and the first card he turned over was a seven. The second one, a six.

Both of them hearts.

"The question," Geoffrey said, "is how did *you* do that?"

10

Home on the Range

Jacob was drenched by the time he got home. He'd not even been running. It's just so damn hot around four o'clock, when it isn't so much the sun bearing down as it is the heat rising up from the sidewalk. There's no escape. Stick to the shady side of the street all you want. Walk with an umbrella. Wave a fan in your face. It doesn't matter. When the temperature and humidity both hit 95, you're walking around in a sauna. It's like even your eyeballs are sweating. It makes you wonder why people would live in a place like Deerfield.

Jacob often wondered this, too.

He knew from school that sociologists might argue people don't notice this type of thing, the peculiarity of their own environment, if they've been raised in it. Things like weather, language, attitudes: Why would it seem strange if you've never known anything different? This is why people with accents don't know they talk funny until they move out of town. Why people from Maine don't know you don't often eat lobster in Louisiana, why people from Louisiana don't know you can't get crawfish in Maine, and so forth. Yet Jacob had lived his entire life in Deerfield and never made peace with the heat. Whereas most kids looked forward to summer—water-skiing out on Lake Maurepas, fishing at Lake Verret—Jacob dreaded it.

The heat made his back break out in a rash. This made him unwilling to take his shirt off, which inevitably made the rash worse, and so, in the lifelong battle of shirts versus skins, Jacob was either shirts or did not play. Toby, of course, was always skins. Jacob's face, too, in its teenage splendor, stayed greasy and slick and never tanned. His neck itched around his collar, his shorts chafed around his bony hips, and he smelled pretty ripe no matter what he sprayed in his armpits. The saying goes that the heat brings out who you truly are in Louisiana and Jacob knew this expression was true. The problem was, he was not always a fan of this person.

As such, he'd spoken to no one since leaving Trina at the mouth of the trail. He instead shoved in his earbuds and kept his head down, cursed his own life in an increasingly familiar way, and blared whatever playlist he'd already had queued on his phone. He got no pleasure from this music. He was so lost in his thoughts about whatever was happening with Trina that he couldn't tell you one song he'd played. Something heavy, is all he remembered, before it was interrupted by the ding of a text message that read:

I can still taste you/him/y'all

Jacob did not reply.

What would he even say? He felt so lost as to Trina's intentions with both him and the world that it frightened him. Ever since he first called her, just a few nights after the funeral, and she began her hinting around about how the dickheads had caused Toby's death, little about Trina made sense. Even at the most basic level of human interaction. She was edgy and dark from the moment she first came to Deerfield and yet had partnered up with Toby somehow, who was nearly the opposite of this. He was athletic and popular, always surrounded by guys laughing and slapping his back or girls he barely knew grabbing his strong shoulders, as if they just wanted to get a feel of him.

Nobody, up until today, had wanted to feel anything of Jacob's. And for the first one who did to be Trina? What to make of that kiss? he wondered. Why was it a "problem" for Trina that Jacob resembled his brother? Was she so attracted to Toby that she now found Jacob attractive, too? That was a disappointing notion. And why did someone like her go after a guy like Toby in the first place? Didn't he have enough attention? Why, Jacob wondered, wasn't she first attracted to him? What sort of invisible magnet did Toby possess that his own twin brother could be so obviously deprived of? And again, Jacob thought, why wasn't she in the car with him that night? He couldn't figure it all out.

And though it was true that this exact form of confusion had basically sustained Jacob the past two months, listening to her plot some vague revenge for Toby's death, having her pay him such strong attention, letting the whole scenario become a sort of dark and wonderful distraction from his reality, he'd had enough. His plan now was to cut her off completely. He would ignore her texts. He would turn her into the authorities if she didn't leave him alone. He would have her committed.

Why? Because she was either full of shit or she was batshit. Had to be.

Why had Jacob bought into it? Perhaps it was simply the timing.

In the mad days after Toby's death, when Trina first suggested Toby's friends were behind it, forcing him to take shot after shot as if being initiated into the idiocy of manhood, to chase beer after beer just to prove that he belonged on a fucking varsity baseball team, of all stupid things, Jacob was still so angry that his conscience was bent. He acted unlike himself. He kicked a hole in his wall. He told her he hated them, too, all of the dickheads, and

wished that they'd driven off the road instead. He bounded between the icy poles of sadness and anger like all of those saddled
with loss. And the loss *was* big, wasn't it? His brother. His twin.
His friend. His competition. His backup. His pride. His nemesis. In
many ways, himself. All of them gone in one day.

So, he was justified in these feelings and, like any person adrift
in anger, had so many options as to who to get even with. He could
take revenge on God through antipathy. Revenge on Toby's friends
through action. Revenge on the whole damn town. Yet he was out
of his mind in those moments, it was true, and Trina fed into it all.
He had taken her initial promise that "This is not over" to mean
their talk of Toby was not over and used it as a selfish way to stay
close to his brother. Jacob understood that now.

But as the weeks have passed and his anger has dulled, how every interaction he's had with Trina inevitably made him feel worse
instead of better, Jacob was finally starting to feel like himself
again. Things were becoming clear.

Trina was not mentally well. This was a fact.

The first piece of evidence for Jacob was that the closer he physically got to her, the farther away she seemed. This feeling shared
no kinship with the way he felt about other girls he'd tried to come
close to. They were easy enough to understand. He liked them but
they did not like him. That is the simplest math. So, it wasn't because Trina was especially coy or aloof but, rather, Jacob feared,
because there wasn't anyone at the core of her to know. This also
frightened him. And yet the kiss, he had to admit, the strange
physical attention she'd paid to him these last weeks, was another
story. Perhaps it, too, was about his brother, in some twisted way,
about remaining close to him through Trina or maybe even steal-
ing something from him. Or maybe it was because of the generic
her, the fact that Trina was a female and Jacob was a male and the
way he thought of her was much like the way he thought of other

females of his age and it was nice and curious and natural and so why shouldn't he like it? Why should he always have to be different? Why should he have to feel guilty about something nearly everyone else of his age was doing? He shouldn't. He wouldn't.

Still, he was headed for trouble with Trina. He knew that.

So, it would be simple. He would cut her off. He would ignore her. He would back out. He would not give her what she wanted.

That was the plan.

When Jacob rounded the corner at Oxbow Street, he saw the door to his garage standing open, a truck he didn't recognize parked in the driveway. It was an old Ford pickup, white with a brown stripe down the sides, and had a flatbed trailer attached to it.

Whatever this was about, Jacob had a feeling it wouldn't be good. His dad had been off his rocker since doing that stupid DNA-MIX machine. His readout was ridiculous and his reaction to it pitiful, Jacob knew, but it was hard for him to blame his dad for anything these days.

His father was a man who'd now lost both a wife and a child, not to mention his parents, years before, and was not yet sixty years old. All he had left was Jacob. All he had left was the mirror. How much can one person take? Life had been hard for Jacob, too, but even he knew that losing a brother did not equal losing a child. There are no equal signs for that.

Jacob walked up to the trailer and studied it. It was full of wood scraps, one large stack piled up as if tossed there. He took off his Latios cap and wiped his head. It looked like simple wood paneling, most of it, the kind you see on men's room walls at a restaurant, already used and scratched up. Beside this laid a pair of swinging doors off their hinges, a row of 2x4s. Beneath it all, one long piece of something nice, oak or cedar, maybe, stained to a deep lacquered red.

In the front yard stood a pyramid of plastic tubs that Jacob did recognize. These were the bins he and his dad bought at Walmart, when the two of them finally tried to organize Toby's stuff. They didn't get very far, packing only some of the clothes from his dresser one afternoon, his baseball mitt and cleats, before his dad went quiet. Jacob looked up to see him fingering the green Ziploc bag the police had given him on the night of the accident. It was full of Toby's minor possessions, he figured, the stuff from his pockets, and his dad did not open it. He instead simply turned it over, where it sat on Toby's desk, as one might do the page of a book they weren't sure if they wanted to read. He then said only, "Son, I need a break," and went off to his room alone. Later that night, Jacob heard his father moving these bins to the garage, where most of them remained empty. After this, he heard him close Toby's door for good.

Now, though, Jacob heard a different noise. It sounded like a shelf coming down, some breaking glass, and so he took out his earbuds and walked to the garage to see. He found his dad standing there, in full regalia, twirling a lasso over his head. On the floor behind him, a broken blue vase lay shattered across the concrete.

"That," his dad said, "was an accident."

He then hurled one end of the lasso across the room. It hit off the wall and fell gently over Toby's old television, which was sitting on a wooden chair.

"Yaw!" his father said and pulled the rope tight. "My best go yet."

Jacob looked him over.

Hank Richieu was built like his sons. You could see Toby in the shoulders, strong and physically capable like Toby had been, and yet Hank stayed as skinny as Jacob in the gut, no matter what he ate. He had the kind of posture that made your hips poke out in front of you, your back stay straight. He looked like a person you could trust, and you could. There was no one in the world, in fact, that Jacob trusted more than his father. And today, as he had for the last several days, Hank wore faded blue jeans and cowboy boots. He had on a western-style shirt with pearl buttons, one of a set of twenty he'd recently ordered online, with a leather vest on top of it. On his head, the enormous cowboy hat he'd taken to calling "Phil."

"Did you go to work today?" Jacob asked him.

"A fine howdy-do to you, too, pardner," his dad said.

Jacob rolled his eyes in a way so well rehearsed it looked as unremarkable as his breathing. He watched his father loosen the rope, flip it off the TV, and reel it back in at his hip. He had obviously been practicing. He was wearing what looked to be a holster.

"Did you at least go to the grocery?" Jacob asked.

"I rustled up some victuals, I reckon," Hank said.

"Dad," Jacob said. "This isn't healthy."

Hank stopped looping his rope and looked over at his son. And in the time that they considered each other, any manner of conversation could have sprouted between them: long-overdue talks about Toby, perhaps, about the mother Jacob never knew, about what seemed like bad luck all around them. But none of these conversations happened. The space was there, and Jacob could feel it, but he cut off the opportunity.

"Whose truck is that?" Jacob said.

"It's mine," his dad said. "I traded in the 4Runner, even steven. It's a beauty, isn't it?"

The truck could have been thirty years old. It had rust on the hood, an empty gun rack in the cabin. The antenna was bent. The hubcaps were dirty. His father, Jacob knew, had turned in a perfectly good family vehicle for a much worse option. "It looks like the world's crappiest Hot Wheel," Jacob said.

It was the kind of truck Jacob could imagine being interesting to collectors, maybe even a valuable antique if you fixed it up, but it was wholly impractical. It was reminiscent of a different era, where people used pickup trucks for work instead of style, and Jacob figured that's what this new version of his father liked about it, too. This meant ironically, though, that his father was also going for style when he made this trade, cruising around town to project a different personality than the one Jacob loved so much and this infuriated Jacob in one of the few meaningful ways a father can ever truly anger his child; it made his father seem pathetic.

Jacob looked at him. "For the last time," he said. "You are not a cowboy. This is not a ranch. It's time to get over it."

"Well," Hank said. "That may be true now, but you know what they say. A cow's ass ain't its head, either, until you cut it off and put it there."

"Literally no one says that," Jacob said. "That has never been said by a single person."

"And now it has," his dad replied. "That's my point."

"I'm going inside," Jacob said, and walked toward the door. "You might want to turn that lasso into a noose, though. You've got company coming up the street."

Hank looked out through the garage door and saw Deuce Newman's truck pulling up to the curb. It was an enormous and new Ford F-250, black and gleaming like it had just come off the lot. Despite how new it was, though, as if by nature, Deuce had already done a few things to decrease its value. It had a tall CB antenna mounted to the roof, a bumper sticker that read "If It Flies, It Dies" on the back window, and a pair of rubber testicles hanging from the trailer hitch that swayed obscenely as he put the truck in park and stepped out.

Hank turned back to Jacob and tipped his hat. "Much obliged, Son," he said.

Jacob shut the door.

Once inside, Jacob slung his backpack on the table and headed for the kitchen. There was homework to do, some math, some reading for History, but it could wait. Jacob was thinking of dinner. He walked to the fridge and opened it up to where the contents produced a familiar dismay. As it had that last week, the shelf contained only four primary food groups: A gallon of milk. A six-pack of Lone Star beer. A pack of sausage. Two T-bone steaks.

Jacob shut the door and went to the pantry. This also looked similar to previous days. On the middle shelf, a row of about twenty cans of pork and beans. A bag of rice. Some baking potatoes. Cartons of oatmeal. Beef jerky. On the floor, a jug of Texas-style BBQ sauce. This was undoubtedly a cowboy paradise. It was also Jacob's new hell. He was going to need to work for some flavor.

He walked to the sink and washed his hands and through the kitchen window saw Deuce Newman waddling up their driveway. He had a long garden hose slung over his shoulder and some sort of machine in his hand, a camera, maybe, a projector. Deuce was, in Jacob's opinion, the town asshole. There was something about his ubiquity that unnerved him. Deuce was at every high school event, at every restaurant and around every corner, it seemed, and came to their house at least twice a week to gripe to his dad about something Deuce claimed his father was doing wrong. It was, in all, creepy, and his complaints about Jacob's father were unfair. Town halls, Rotary Club dinners, Sewage and Water Board meetings, ribbon cuttings, church on Sundays: The demands on a small-town mayor were constant, Jacob knew, and his father tried hard to keep up.

It seemed, however, that Deuce was taking Toby's death as an opportunity to usurp his father's job. In a way, Jacob understood his reasoning. His dad had clocked out just when the town needed him most. Jacob couldn't give two shits about the bicentennial but knew it was a lot on his dad. The phone rang constantly, even at home, from unusual callers. People looking for permits to set up food stands and shops, locals lobbying him for improvements from the general fund, people asking where the expected profits would go, people complaining about the noise in town. One time, Jacob overheard an hour-long conversation with someone debating whether Mylar or plastic balloons were more appropriate. What man could stay sane in such a routine? If he and his father had anything in common those days, Jacob thought, it was that they were both waiting, both begging, really, for something to be over.

Jacob looked out of the kitchen window to see Deuce turn on the water hose. He got his father to spray it against his own truck, where the mist made a great plume off the glass. His father kept turning off the nozzle, though, pretending to holster it as if in a duel, and Deuce was obviously becoming irritated.

"Just hold the gad damn thing!" he heard him say. He fiddled with his projector. "Let me show you this, Hank."

Jacob went back to the stove. And here, of all places, he found his little dominion. Jacob had been the de facto cook for his family since he was fourteen. He was okay with this. His father cooked serviceably enough but without any joy, heating up microwave dinners and turning out boxes of mac and cheese as if they were nightly specials. Toby never complained. He was a high school athlete and so all he needed was calories and lots of them. Food, for Toby, was merely the vehicle these calories rode in on and he would eat anything placed before him. What Jacob needed, however, was pleasure, from something, from anything, and he got this on top of the stove. He opened a can of beans and poured them in a pot. He then added some BBQ sauce, a little chili powder to spice them up. He remembered a small carton of mushrooms he'd bought himself last weekend and pulled them out of the drawer in the fridge and sliced them. He threw them into a skillet with some butter and Worcestershire sauce, found a hunk of cheddar cheese to cube, and set them atop and watched it all cook down. This was a dish with no name, a little invention of his, and Jacob liked it.

When he turned the heat low, he heard the door from the garage open and shut. Deuce Newman walked inside. His shirt was wet from the hose, Jacob guessed, and he sat at the kitchen island like he belonged there.

"Son," Deuce said. "I think it's official. Your father has lost his damn mind."

Jacob said nothing, only grabbed a box of toothpicks and plucked a mushroom out of the skillet. He popped it into his mouth and it wasn't bad at all.

"Let me ask you something," Deuce said. "Have you ever been to Disney World?"

Jacob looked at him and chewed. He shook his head.

"That's this town's problem," Deuce said. "Nobody has been anywhere. Let me tell you, I've been to Disney World. It's all water and light these days. All water and light. That's what your daddy needs to understand. We have to be progressive. Hell, we just need to catch up! I can't do this all on my own. I'm so far behind I probably can't even make the damn choir tomorrow night, and that would be a paying gig for me. I just need some assurances, is all, that we'll be good to go on Saturday. That's only two days from now, which is something your father seems incapable of understanding."

Deuce leaned over and grabbed a toothpick, plucked himself out a mushroom. He chewed and said, "Damn, Jake. This is pretty good. You taking Home Ec or something?"

Jacob put a lid on the skillet and slid it away from Deuce. "You know," he said. "I think they stopped offering that class after women got the right to vote."

Deuce stopped chewing and looked at him.

"Do *you* know," he said, "there's a difference between being smart and being a smart*ass*? You might want to keep that in mind."

Jacob felt the creep of a familiar fire. A tingling in his neck. A bubbling anger. It was a feeling he'd had not long ago, when Chuck Haydel knocked off his hat. It was the feeling he'd had when his brother died, when he first started talking with Trina, and it was a feeling he tried to keep down.

"Is there something I can do for you, Mr. Newman?"

Deuce stood up, wiped his hands on his wet shirt. "First things first," he said. "I need a picture." He pulled out his phone and aimed it at Jacob, who did not smile. He clicked. "Secondly, I need to get you to help me," he said. "You need to talk some sense into your father. This cowboy shit," he said. "I didn't expect for it to make him even more stubborn than he already was. He doesn't listen to me at all anymore. You just need to tell him that, unless he gets his ass in gear, we're coming for him tomorrow at the town hall. We've only got one more day to get ready. It's now or never. It's time to piss or get off the pot."

With this comment, the way Deuce took aim at his father, Jacob felt an almost uncontrollable urge to do some sort of damage to this grown man in his kitchen. It nearly consumed him. He would be throttled, he knew, if he tried this. Deuce outweighed him by a hundred pounds. And was it even Deuce he was angry with? Can a thinking person truly be angry with an idiot? Or was it the way it seemed his entire world had shrunk these last months to become a sort of straitjacket? In every direction he turned, he felt only frustration. His father. Toby. Trina. Deuce. How could a person's world be so small? What could he do to expand it? To explode it?

"No offense," Jacob said. "But our family suggestion box is full at the moment. Maybe you could find somewhere else to put your complaint."

Deuce leaned on the counter and looked him in the eye.

"Does your daddy know you talk to your elders like that?" he said. "Maybe you should get your own readout done. Maybe it would tell you to have some manners."

"My dad knows how I talk," Jacob said.

"I bet he doesn't," Deuce told him. "I bet he also doesn't know who you're palling up with over at school, either. I know what goes on over there. It was bad enough your brother took that Todd girl for a ride, don't you think? Bad enough she was the one with him that night. You going to go chasing her tail now, too? You think he wants to be reminded of all that?"

Jacob's heart shook at the unexpected mention of Trina, the presumptive nature of this man in his kitchen. "You don't know anything about me," he said.

Deuce pulled out his phone again. He thumbed the screen and turned it to Jacob and said, "Don't I?"

Jacob saw the picture Trina had taken of them in the woods, now up for display on Instagram. "I know a hell of a lot more than you think I do," Deuce said. "Trust me on that. You kids think what you do on Twitter and all that is some sort of secret, but it's just the opposite. You're the most obvious generation that's ever been. You don't have any secrets at all. It's sad, really. But, look. Just tell your dad to get his shit straight by tomorrow, okay? One last chance. I say that as a friend."

Deuce left the kitchen and walked back to the garage. Jacob's heart thumped as if he'd been sprinting and he picked up the empty can of beans and threw it in the sink. It clanged against the metal and splashed its thick juice on the wall. This was something Jacob would have to clean up, he knew, and this pissed him off even more. He grabbed his backpack to go do his homework but, when he got to his room, merely slung it violently onto the bed.

He walked back to the kitchen and looked out the window to the street, where Deuce was now pulling off in his truck. His father had apparently tied his lasso to the set of rubber balls on the hitch and it moved like a snake behind the truck as Deuce drove off. Hank slapped his hat on his thigh and laughed as Deuce stuck his hand out the window and flipped him the bird. These were the adults, Jacob thought, these were the fucking people in charge of his life, and he ran back down the hall past his room and to his father's office. The door was closed, as it always was, and Jacob opened it. The place was a mess, but Jacob knew what he kept in here. It was like an outpost of city hall. On the wall, shelves stuffed full of building permits and tax codes, fake keys to neighboring towns, wooden plaques. Boring shit, all of it. But among these documents, Jacob knew, because he had seen them before, was the blueprint of Deerfield Catholic.

He riffled through the shelves and found it. He went to put it on the table, where he saw a gun his father had been given. It was in a glass case, some commemorative pistol and old-timey bullet his father received at some ridiculous occasion for some ludicrous reason that had previously been hung on his office wall those past few years. It was one of a hundred meaningless things in that room. Jacob moved it to the side and unscrolled the blueprint. He was acting unlike himself, he knew, being in there without permission, giving in to Trina yet again, but there are times when being unlike yourself is the only way to get away from yourself, and so he took his phone out of his pocket, quickly snapped a few pictures, and put the blueprint back up where he'd found it.

He then left the house through the garage, still angry at everything he saw, where his father was now hammering a piece of wood paneling into the wall.

"Hey, Son," his father said. "Here's a shot in the dark: You have any idea where a man could get his hands on a player piano?"

Jacob stared at him but said nothing. Then he took off down the street.

He looked again at his phone and quickly loaded the pictures into a text message.

You fucking want it? he typed. *You fucking take it.*

He hit send.

Trina replied, almost immediately, with a face that had hearts for its eyes.

11

I Hate It When That
Happens to Me

Douglas left the parking lot of the Scenic Wetlands Apartments and Balconies with as much bravado as any man driving his wife's Subaru Outback can achieve. He was full of adrenaline, lit up like a witness to magic should be. He was also reminded brightly of the love he felt for Cherilyn, for the world, even. Learning new things always did this to Douglas. This was why he'd gone into teaching in the first place. It made him feel fresh, sort of expansive and interesting to gain new knowledge, as if his was now a mind on the scene. Geoffrey had taught him only the most basic imitation of "Seventy-six Trombones" in that last hour and Douglas was admittedly terrible at it, but he'd puckered his lips and blown all the same. He'd moved the slide in and out, puffed his cheeks, and filled that apartment with rambunctious and unpredictable noise. He would get it, eventually. It would take him a while, he knew, like everything worth a damn did, but he would get it.

He drove back through the Deerfield square with his windows down, the evening beginning to fall, and blared the jazz station from New Orleans. He took off his beret, let the air whip his spindly hair around, and felt magnanimous and wise, more certain than ever that he was on the right track. If there were any panhandlers in Deerfield, Douglas would have given them his money at that moment. He would have given them a lot of it, maybe *all* of it, and told them not to give up on their dreams. If he'd seen a child, he would have tousled their hair, produced from his pocket a piece of candy, and relayed to them the secrets of life-long happiness. Even if he was in front of his class, yes, even if he was *working*, this energy would have brought forth the type of lecture that becomes legend. He would have blown minds, changed futures, won awards. That's the kind of mood he was in.

This mood also made him feel more certain than ever that he and Cherilyn could get clicking again. He was going to be a jazz musician. He was going to spice up their lives. He would tell her tonight. Any interest she had in being someone else, someone royal or important, was not because of any lack on her part, he'd say, because she was already the most important person in his life. Instead, he would argue, the desire she felt for something new was probably because he himself had become stagnant. Whistling the same old songs. Trudging off to work in the same old classroom. His blandness had become contagious, he figured, infectious. He saw it now.

And he was about to cure it.

He pulled into the parking lot of Johnson's Grocery and reached over to the passenger seat to grab the shopping list. He flipped the top flap of his satchel and found the notepad he'd written the list on, with all of its question marks and underlining, all of Cherilyn's endearingly exotic requests. He scanned it over as he looked for a parking spot. *Absolutely,* he thought, and ripped the page from the pad, *let's eat some damn eggplant. Let's eat all the eggplant in the world, my love. Put some tahini on my trombone, place a little garlic in my mouth. Let's live a little, shall we? Come closer. Sign me up. Call me Twice-in-a-Row Joe.*

Douglas found a spot at the back of the lot and parked, more cars than usual on a Thursday night. He shut the door and walked toward the store with his hands in his pockets, whistling like a man who'd just gotten a raise. He tipped his beret to Claire Sanderson, who was leaving the store with a cart full of flowers. He said hello to Dave Austin, who was sweeping the entryway by the propane tanks. "Turning into a beautiful evening, isn't it?" Douglas said.

"I'm sweating like a pig," Dave said.

"Pigs don't sweat, my man," Douglas said without slowing down. "No glands. That's just a wonderful idiosyncrasy of our speech. Sweating like a pig. Raining cats and dogs. It's just another reason people are interesting!"

Oh, yes, Douglas thought, he was on fire tonight.

The doors of Johnson's slid open and Douglas entered the cold and well-lit store as if he owned the place. He grabbed a handbasket and walked to the produce section looking for eggplant, and there they were, a whole pile of them. He checked his list. How many did Cherilyn want? Four? Well, then, he would buy her eight. Spare no expense. Douglas stacked them in the basket and headed for lemons. He whistled all the while, a Stevie Wonder tune now, tossing each lemon into the air and catching it.

He even found the tahini easily enough where it sat in the ethnic foods aisle next to the Sriracha and soy sauce. Had shopping ever been so easy? He then grabbed a bottle of wine, a twelve-dollar bottle, which was as high as he and Cherilyn went on birthdays and anniversaries, and headed for the checkout. As Douglas reached for his wallet, though, the outside world returned to him. He noticed how empty it was in the store and how quiet, despite all the cars in the lot. Had he seen anyone in produce, even? He looked at the checkout line. Only one register open, nobody waiting.

He walked toward the register and, once he cleared the tall rack of potato chips and beef jerky, saw where everyone was. A line of people, probably twenty or so, over by customer service. The people were of varying ages, adults and teenagers, some of whom Douglas had never seen before, all standing quiet and single-file. Many of them thumbed at their phones, others picked at their nails.

Douglas set his eggplant on the conveyor belt and said, "Hey, Sheila," to the cashier. She'd been a student of his a few years ago, a bright person, and he always enjoyed seeing her. He remembered specifically that she'd written a proposal essay about removing Confederate statues from government land before people were actually doing this and she'd gotten an A. These were the student papers that Douglas remembered, like finding little jewels in a sandbox. She was now pregnant and looking well, and carefully piled his eggplants atop of the scale.

"What you making, Mr. Hubbard?" she said. "Eggplant fries? Some tapenade? I've been hearing eggplant's good for a baby."

Douglas motioned to customer service. "Y'all giving away hundred-dollar bills?" he said. "Looks like a crowd."

Sheila smiled and, before she could speak, a man in the store began shouting. The voice came from some unseen place in the line and Douglas couldn't tell if the person was dying or cheering. Then Douglas saw this man appear from behind the curtains of a large box.

"Unreal," the man said. "*Unreal!*".

This man was in his fifties, probably, well dressed like an attorney or insurance salesman, and was not anyone Douglas knew. He stepped out of the box and turned to face the line behind him. He held up his hand and waved a blue ticket in the air and said, to no one in particular, "Ain't this some shit?"

The man then pulled off his necktie and threw it the garbage. "Not one more day in that tie," he said. He bent down and plucked off his loafers. "Not one more day in these shoes." He then pulled off his blazer, swung it over his shoulder, and strolled out of the store with a grin, dropping his shoes in the donation bin for the Salvation Army by the door.

Douglas looked back at the box he'd stepped out of. Of course, he thought, the DNA machine. How could he forget?

The people in line shuffled ahead and a woman pulled back the curtains and entered the box that, Douglas now clearly saw, read "DNAMIX." Even from this distance, it was far less impressive than he'd imagined. The whole thing looked to be made of plywood or pressboard, not even sanded to smooth corners at its edges. The logo could have been stenciled by one of Douglas's least gifted students, it was so rustic. Still, Douglas tried not to be cynical. He was on a mission to have a good night.

He looked back at Sheila. "So, that's what all the fuss is about?"

"Thirty-four dollars, Mr. Hubbard," Sheila said, and held out a big paper bag.

"Yes, ma'am," Douglas said, and swiped his debit card. "What do you think about that machine?" Douglas asked. "You tried it yet?"

"No, sir," Sheila said. "I already know what I'm going to be." She rubbed her belly with her hand. She gave it a pat. "In about two months from now," she said, "I'm going to be tired. I don't need to know any more than that."

"That sounds like wisdom," Douglas said. "I'm impressed."

"I also don't want to spend the two dollars," she said. "I'm saving up."

"And that sounds like smarts," Douglas said. "You're the total package."

Sheila smiled and blushed like Douglas recalled her doing when he'd praised her at school. "Thanks," she told him. "I miss your class, by the way. I miss school, in general. I don't get a chance to read as much anymore, what with work and all."

"Luckily," Douglas said, "it's kind of like riding a bike. You can start back anytime you want."

Douglas left the register and headed for the door, having already made up his mind that he would not be joining the line. It would be almost redundant, he thought, after his lesson with Geoffrey, after he'd become more convinced than ever that he was on the right track. Plus, he wanted to get back to Cherilyn. He had some loving to give.

On his way out, though, Douglas saw Jacob Richieu, one of his best students, standing in the line. He held a grocery bag in his hand and wore a black cap pulled low and Douglas noticed he'd been growing darker recently. It wasn't that gothy stuff, really, but he was just kind of sullen and withdrawn, maybe a little angry. Who could blame him? And who knew if it would last?

As a high school teacher, Douglas had borne witness to hordes of teens staking their unfortunate claims to style at that age, sophomores and juniors, mainly, prematurely casting themselves in the movies of their future. And what would Jacob's movie be? He had that skinny look of a whiz kid. He wore the Pokémon hat of a gamer, of a loner, and maybe that's what he was since his brother died.

His brother. Toby.

Not as sharp a student as Jacob, Douglas remembered, but he was a charming guy, a nice enough kid, even though he ran with some of the jocks that Douglas wouldn't trust with a pair of scissors. Still, his death was a tragedy, no doubt. That had to account for some of Jacob's darkness. Being the son of the mayor could be hard, too. And that girl he was now palling around with, that Trina. Douglas felt she was the type that might know *exactly* what to do with scissors.

"Jacob," Douglas said, walking toward him. "How are you?"

Jacob stood near the front of the line. He looked almost

embarrassed to be found. He glanced around the store as if he'd forgotten where he was and pulled his earbuds out of his ears. "Hey, Mr. Hubbard," he said. "I haven't done the reading for tomorrow yet, if that's what you're going to ask."

Douglas smiled and said, "That's okay. I know you're on top of things." He looked at the woman behind them in line and nodded, just being polite. "So, you going in this machine, too?"

"No," Jacob said. "I just love standing in long lines."

"Ouch," Douglas said. This new attitude from Jacob: What was behind it?

"I'm sorry," Jacob said. "I've just been standing here for an hour. I should go home."

"Yikes," Douglas said. "Does it take that long?"

Before Jacob could answer, they heard the curtains open back up and the last woman who'd entered step out. She had been crying in there, Douglas could tell, and said nothing as she left the store, merely crossing herself as if leaving Confession.

"It only takes a minute," Jacob said. "I just haven't been able to pull the trigger. I keep going to the back of the line."

"Understandable," Douglas said. "But I'm not convinced about this thing, myself. What are you hoping it will say?"

"No clue," Jacob said. "I think that's my problem."

Another person stepped into the machine and Douglas realized Jacob was next.

"No matter what it says," Douglas told him, "I wouldn't worry too much about it. After all," he whispered, "it's made of plywood."

"I'm sure it's just a beta-testing case," Jacob said. "You have to start somewhere. I mean, the first airplane was made of paper, wasn't it? The first car was a horse."

Douglas looked at Jacob and felt a familiar ache for this boy. He'd felt this way in class before, whenever Jacob gave an answer that was somehow sharp, worldly, and wistful. Complain as he may about high schoolers, Douglas knew some of his kids had much older souls than they should, much larger inner lives than he gave them credit for. And if he'd had a son of his own, maybe that was the feeling, if he had a son of his own, he might like him to have a mind like Jacob's. This made Douglas think more deeply into the boy's life, about his mother who'd passed when he and his brother were born, about the way his father had raised them by himself while also suffering so much, and the way his father still gave so much to the town. It was empathy Douglas felt, he supposed, whenever he looked at Jacob. It was respect.

In front of them, the curtain pulled open again and the woman stepped out.

She held her blue receipt and said, "Five years ago. Where was this thing five years ago?"

Douglas then watched her hobble out of the store, the right leg, below her knee, a prosthetic.

"I guess you're next," Douglas said.

"Nah," Jacob said, and handed Douglas his two dollars. "You take my place. I'll see you tomorrow." Jacob then walked out of the store, not bothering to hop back in line.

Douglas stood there with the two dollars in his hand and looked back at the woman behind him. She had her eyebrows raised, as if waiting for him to say something, and Douglas realized that all the people in the line were looking at him.

"Well," one of them said, "if you're going to skip, you might as well be quick about it."

The woman behind him nudged Douglas ahead. "Don't worry," she said. "It ain't gonna bite you."

"Oh," Douglas said. "I'm not really interested."

"I've got two kids in the car," the woman said. "Let's giddy-up, okay?"

So, as if succumbing to nothing more than peer pressure,

Douglas stepped inside the machine and closed the curtain behind him. He turned around.

What did we have here?

The machine looked built by a child. In front of him, the display screen appeared to be little more than a simple computer monitor mounted in plywood, along with slots cut into the wood beneath it. One was recognizable as a place to put your money, the kind you might see on an arcade game or ATM, and another appeared to be the place your printout came through. To the side of that, another slot read "Deposit Sample Here."

With all the visual evidence before him, Douglas couldn't help himself. He cracked up laughing. This machine had a serious ethos problem. No credibility whatsoever. So, what he would do was simply this: He would put in his money and get his readout just to say he did it. He wouldn't even look at it. This way, depending how his conversation with Cherilyn went, he could show her he tried it and they could laugh over whatever silly thing it had spat out. Or, perhaps even better, they could rejoice together when it said what he knew it would say, which was: **TROMBONIST. JAZZ MASTER. EXTRAORDINAIRE**.

He slid his two dollars into the slot and watched the screen brighten. *Welcome to DNAMIX*, it read. *Please begin by swabbing your cheek*. Douglas looked down to see a pile of Q-tips set in a basket. *Ridiculous*, he thought, but still he followed the prompts to remove the plastic and swab the inside of his cheek. He then slid the Q-tip into the prescribed opening, where it seemed to just drop from his hand. *Your receipt is ready*, the screen read. *Thank you. Remember that there is a 1 percent margin of error. DNAMIX is not liable for any stress your potential may cause. Have a nice day.*

Douglas watched a blue slip of paper print out from the slot. He ripped it loose and stuck it in his pocket without looking. He then turned and exited the machine and saw the people in line eyeing him expectantly, as if he might click his heels on some good news. So, Douglas felt compelled to say something. He held up his grocery bag.

"Wish me luck, everyone," he said. "I am off to eat eggplant."

Douglas left the store and, before he even got to his car, felt his conviction beginning to waver. The possibility of his readout crept upon him like gossip, and it was difficult for him not to be interested. The little paper in his pocket. What could it be? He realized he was touching it, rubbing it between his fingers, and it suddenly reminded him of Tolkien's precious ring from Middle-earth, which was another thing, he teacher-moded to himself, that was total fantasy.

He got into his car, put the groceries on the floorboard, and quickly folded his readout into the same compartment that Cherilyn had stashed hers. "Ludicrous," he said, and put the car in reverse.

Yet he didn't take his foot off the brake.

"It's made of plywood and Q-tips," he said, and shifted the car back into park.

Then drive again. Then park.

Thereabout went his next five minutes, starting and stopping, his hand and foot operating against each other in the same way his mind was combating itself. And it is difficult to win an argument with a History teacher, so, when it was all said and done, Douglas relinquished to a phrase he often told his students, which was, "There is no shame in *not* knowing something. The shame, instead," he would say, "is in having the *opportunity* to learn and choosing ignorance." He'd made that one up, as far as he knew, and it often worked for a couple of weeks as far as class discussion was concerned. It was logical. It was pretty passionate. And so Douglas reached for the readout.

What he wanted, he'd decided, was for the readout to say

something random, something outlandish. If it told him to be a **QUARTERBACK** or a **PALM TREE** or even a **HYPOTENUSE**, then that would settle it all. He could talk Cherilyn off her royal cliff and the thing would be done with. He could tell her that she had always been his queen and he would mean this as he said it and maybe that would do the trick. He unfolded the slip of paper and read it.

Douglas Alan Hubbard. Yes, that was true.

A long series of numbers. Eye color brown. Hair color brown. Potential height 6'2".

Douglas put down the paper. He straightened his back and looked in the rearview mirror.

"Six-two?" he said. He was five-ten at best.

He picked it up and read further. Potential weight 195. No potential children listed, and then, beneath all of this, he saw "Potential Life Station." Unlike the single proclamation he'd seen on the other readouts, however, his had two words written in bold:

WHISTLER. TEACHER.

He stared at it awhile.

WHISTLER. TEACHER.

This was unexpected.

It was also, Douglas felt, awfully specific.

He did not like this readout at all.

He felt his chest tighten as if he was about to get in a fistfight, and he did not move an inch. And who knows how long Douglas could have sat there glaring at that little piece of paper if his phone had not gone off in his pocket. This made him look around the car absently, as if there might have been someone else in it who'd suddenly disappeared. He did not check his phone but instead crumpled the paper up in his hand, threw the car into gear, and said, *"Please."*

He pulled out of the lot without slowing down for the speed

bumps and felt himself growing hot. His ears burned, the back of his neck tingled, and, rather than experiencing any sort of excitement or humor, Douglas felt an overwhelming sense of fear taking hold of him.

How could that be? he wondered. *Whistler? Teacher?* It was likely a joke. The whole thing was preposterous. But what about Cherilyn and Geoffrey? Why wasn't their readout what they already were? What the hell is DNA, anyway? Six feet two? How could *Whistler* even be an option? Do they have one for *Thumb Twiddler*, too? Insanity. Maybe they get your Social Security Number and then your W-2, he thought. There's no privacy anymore. Everybody knows that. Hackers can get anything they want. That could explain the *Teacher* part. But why was *Trombonist* not on there? Why not *Musician*? Why not *Artist*?

It was, Douglas believed, complete and utter bullshit.

This machine had nothing to do with potential, and it definitely had nothing to do with dreams. What did this printout even mean? What was the suggestion? Even if you granted it the least bit of credibility, what was the implication? That Douglas had already become the best version of himself that he could be? That didn't seem right. He ran a stop sign. Did it mean that if things would have gone perfectly, he would still be the exact same man he is today, only a slightly taller version of himself? This idea angered him, too. It seemed grossly unfair. Insultingly surface. Hell, it even seemed undemocratic. Worst of all, it seemed to immediately pry the gap between he and Cherilyn even wider. The only thing he wanted in life, he realized, more than any glowing trombone, was to feel as secure and comfortable with Cherilyn as he had just a few days before. Before he knew about her readout. Before she'd begun feeling sick. Before she had requested something of him which he failed to provide. He wanted all of this back, and yet seeing his own readout made the possibility of their reconnection seem more remote than he had ever imagined it. He entered his neighborhood and drove right past his house. He then made the block and drove past it again. For the first time in his life, he realized, he felt ashamed to face his wife.

So, he stopped the car and pulled out his phone and, seeing that the last call was from Cherilyn's mother's house, did not even check the voicemail. It would be from Cherilyn, he knew, and what could he say to her now? That he was maxed out? That this was the best her life would ever get if she continued to slum it with him? That he could offer nothing more than he'd already given? No. That wouldn't do. That wouldn't do at all. So, instead of calling her back, he did something that he had never done before. He dialed his own house, knowing that no one would answer, and lied to the family machine.

12

I'm Taking a Walk,
I'm Just Getting By

The walk back to town wasn't all bad.

Would he have rather had his truck? Possibly. His work uniform, with its starched black shirt and pants, wasn't exactly comfortable. His black sneakers, though, special-ordered from the Catholic Warehouse in New Orleans, were okay. Nice padded soles. Extra wide. Good laces. Still, you couldn't deny the heat. Pete could do without the heat. Yet when Lanny had rested his shotgun on his shoulder and leaned on Pete's driver's-side door to ask, "Now, Pete, what would your bossman do in a situation like this one?" Pete knew he had a point. It reminded him of one of his favorite moments from seminary, actually: a day when Pete grilled one of his professors about charity and its relationship to knowledge.

Here was the hypothetical, as Pete had drawn it up in class:

Say you came to a stoplight and saw two men standing on opposite sides of the road—one to your left and one to your right—and the man on your left asked you for a dollar. Say you recognized this man from church, from Confession perhaps, and *knew* that he was a drug abuser trying to get clean. Maybe he had a family, kids counting on him, all that. Let's say you also knew that the man on your right was a drug *dealer*. How could you have known this about him without assuming? Well, let's say he was blatantly waving a bag of drugs in his hand and yelling across the street to the man on your left that he would sell him this bag of drugs for only one dollar, which was, perhaps not coincidentally, the exact amount of money the drug abuser had asked you for. Let's *also* say that you could clearly see a needle and syringe sitting on the little cardboard box or lawn chair or whatever it was the man on your left had been begging from. Now, you know the man could use more than a dollar. He could use a good meal and a shower and so you offer him that. You offer to take him into your own home, even, but he declines and says nope, that he only wants the one dollar and he needs it right away, please, before a golden opportunity passes him by.

Now, Pete continued, you understand that charity is supposed to be blind. We all know that. However, in this particular situation, you yourself are *not* blind and you know (you aren't assuming, remember, you actually know) that giving this man a dollar will unequivocally enable him to do the very thing that destroys him.

"So," Pete had said, "I guess what I'm wondering is, in this hypothetical situation, would you still be obliged to give it to him? If you had hard evidence that one-dollar bill would go straight into his arm, would that still be charity? Would that be willful ignorance? Or," Pete asked, "might that possibly be some form of malice?"

His professor let the question hang in the air for a while, the way all the good ones do, so that it could gather its proper importance from the physical space it was allowed, so that the slower thinkers in class could catch up, and then said, placidly, "Are you asking what Jesus might do in a situation like this one, Mr. Flynn?"

"I suppose I am," Pete said.

"Well," his professor told him. "I imagine Jesus might be curious to know how you still had a dollar left to give when you pulled up to that stoplight."

This answer kicked something loose in Pete. It wobbled his brain. It filled his heart. The purity of it. The bold simplicity.

How had he not seen it coming?

He'd long been the one in class to take a more practical, living-world view of the priesthood, so these types of back-and-forth with his professors were common enough. While others might have sought some type of spiritual enlightenment or perhaps even bookish confirmation of their faith from seminary, Pete had distinguished himself by seeking answers to how he could apply his belief. After all, he had clear goals for his priesthood. He had people he needed to see again. This wasn't some philosophical pursuit. He'd therefore gone through dozens of these mental exercises both in school and with his younger peers at coffee shops, but the answer to this affected him like none before. It was as if a new picture, some clear and physical drawing of God, had been projected for him on the whiteboard.

"Total charity," Pete replied. "It is about total charity."

"Charity before the need for it," his professor said, and moved on.

Pete said nothing for the rest of the class.

Memories like this helped ease the walk back to town from Lanny's house, helped ease the doubts he sometimes had about himself, about people in general. This version of charity remains to Pete the most challenging demand he's ever heard, and it thrills him to consider it. It was another reason why Pete felt his job was pretty wonderful, when you thought about it. It was not for the weak. But it was also the way that particular anecdote unfolded that Pete admired. It was the way it allowed you to *think* you knew your problem (should I or shouldn't I?) before Jesus ambled up and broke the whole thing open (why haven't you already?) that he loved. Jesus did this a lot, which is another reason why he, too, Pete thought, was pretty wonderful. But it was also the way the story fit so nicely within Pete's own personal version of godliness that gave him comfort. This was not a dogmatic *I am right and you are wrong* way of thinking, but instead a holistic understanding that there is both a *before you* and a *before now* in the physical sense and an *always you* and an *always now* in the metaphysical sense. It was the way that we are eternal in our own consciousness, if not in our earthly bodies, and how every choice we make today is an extension of, and an opportunity arisen from, the choices we have previously made and *will* make in the future that defines us. And it is how this boundless aspect of our existence, when all the chips have been counted, is likely the way that we are most constructed in God's own image.

Yeah, man. Yes indeed! Pete liked this idea a lot.

It felt to him like proof.

So, he was glad to be walking, as it had led him to this nice memory, and he was glad he didn't protest when Lanny said he could really use his truck, maybe just for a day or two, because his own had gone missing. Pete didn't care that he was being baldly manipulated. He simply gathered his wallet and house key, looked around the cab for any school papers or other correspondence he might need, and got out of the car. Why should Pete have a truck anyway, when other people could use it?

"No rush," he told Lanny. "Just give me a call when I can pick her back up."

"Let's maybe give it a week, then," Lanny said. "I have several items on my shit list that I'd like to scratch off."

"Deal," Pete said, and felt good about the situation.

It wasn't as if Lanny had threatened him. The gun had just kind of been there, like one of Lanny's appendages, and when Pete asked him about it Lanny looked as though he didn't even realize he was still holding it. He said he kept it around in case any "unsavories" came by but had mainly just been out back of the house shooting squirrels, he said, and had "popped off sixty-five of the little fuckers" since February, all in the same exact spot of his yard.

"Sixty-five?" Pete said. "Wow."

"All in the same damn tree," Lanny said. He then looked past Pete, as if to the horizon, and said, "Oh, to be a realtor in the land of the squirrels."

Lanny was high. Pete knew that. His skin was pasty and slick on his bare chest. His eyes weren't right, either, as if he'd been playing with his eyelids for a while, and Pete imagined pills, as that's what most people in Deerfield's Confessional seemed to be dealing with. However, the way Trina had asked him if he thought she looked *safe* worried Pete that it could be something more. The fact that Lanny's car was gone. The fact that there was a woman living with him that Pete had never heard of. These were troublesome signs.

But Pete also knew that confronting Lanny about his lifestyle choices at that particular moment was not going to lead to anything fruitful. So, instead he asked a few simpler questions, like:

"Does Trina seem all right?" to which Lanny replied, "You'd know better than me."

And, "Any word from her mom?" to which Lanny replied, "Last I heard, she was in Natchez with a midget."

"In Natchez with a midget?" Pete asked, to which Lanny replied, "Is there gas in this thing?"

"Should be," Pete told him, and that was it.

Lanny sat in the truck, put it in gear, and drove it about fifteen more yards up the driveway. He then parked and got out and walked back in the house without saying a word. Pete stood there until Lanny's dog appeared from under the camper top and took to growling. "Okay, okay," Pete said. "I'm going."

Once he hit the highway, it didn't take long for Pete to be

recognized. People pulled over and offered him rides but he kindly refused them. He wanted his walk to look intentional, he supposed, or else he just didn't want to get into specifics. He was feeling good about himself, after all, so good, in fact, that he regretted his decision not to walk over to Clessy's for that bottle of Sobieski before he made the trek home. He really would have appreciated that about now. A little personal charity, if you will. A little tip of the cap to Father Pete.

It was near six o'clock by this point, and the sun was heading down. It took him an hour and a half to do what he could have done in ten minutes in his truck and, rather than making him rueful, this thought made him feel appreciative of trucks. Miracle machines. Such engineering. Such a blessing! Yes, Pete was on a thankful roll today, and so was also thankful when he saw Getwell's Bar right there on the corner.

Pete lived on the opposite side of town, another twenty minutes' walk. And since he wasn't in a rush to get home, since he'd left Mayfly outside with plenty of water, Pete figured Getwell's was as good a place as any to stop. So, he took off his collar and put it in his pants pocket, unloosed the top two buttons of his black shirt, and stepped inside.

13

They Ought to Name
a Drink After You

Although it was rarely what one might call busy, a person didn't go to Getwell's to hide. You knew you might see a former student or employer or friend and have to stay and chat awhile, else you come off as rude. But it was also not a place people went to "be seen," either. It was, at its wood-paneled heart, whatever bar you wished it to be, a place where people generally let you do whatever type of drinking you came there to do. Getwell's could *feel* the people that walked in there, it seemed, could somehow sense the pulse of the whole town, and adapted its environment to suit that mood.

In winter, for instance, the dusty Christmas lights strung over the bar seemed festive and, in summer, whimsical. The Mardi Gras beads hung on the antlers of Ronnie, the mounted deer by the entrance, could look either carefully placed for regal effect or, if you were feeling spontaneous yourself, just kind of flung there. Whichever way you preferred Mardi Gras beads hung on the antlers of dead animals to look, that's what you got. It was a magical place, in that way, as only some bars ever are.

What Father Pete first noticed when he walked in was not the décor, however, but the temperature. The A/C enveloped him completely, and here was yet another thing to be thankful for. He sat at the bar and took a wad of paper napkins and dabbed at his head. He pulled at the front of his shirt and let some of the heat escape his chest. He spent a good minute cooling himself down, not looking at anybody, not saying anything, just sort of regulating his body temperature.

When he felt ready for human interaction, he looked up to see Cauley Thomas, the woman who owned the place. She was sitting on top of a barstool behind the bar and doing a crossword, resting the paper on top of her legs. She was young, in comparison to Pete, probably thirty-five, and had some of the more interesting tattoos in town. Pete didn't know her well but liked her, had spoken to her at a few funerals over the last year, seen her at the grocery store like everyone else. He'd had only one meaningful conversation with her, though, when he once noticed that the tattoo spread across her shoulders like wings was that of an angel and asked, "Is that Gabriel? I had no idea you were religious, Ms. Cauley."

"I've read the Bible, Father," she'd told him. "That's probably why you don't see me in church."

Pete appreciated the honesty. Give him that over bullshit sanctimony any day. He had no doubt she would recognize him in the bar and, when he looked up at her, she shifted her weight to the side a bit, as if her bartending skills had become so acute that she could physically sense a person needing a drink without even having to look. She wrote down one more answer and stood up from the stool. She placed the crossword by the cash register, laid the pen across it, and lifted her eyeglasses on top of her head.

"Well," she said. "This is unexpected. What can I get you, Father?"

"Hello, Ms. Cauley," he said. "I am wondering if you have any glasses here, like real drinking glasses, you know, not just plastic cups."

Cauley smiled. "Just wait until you hear this," she said, and reached under the bar. She pulled up two cocktail glasses. "Not only do we have glasses, but they even come in different varieties." She lifted each individually to make her point. "We have, what we like to call, tall ones and short ones."

"Incredible," Pete said. "Thank you. Now that we've established that, I'm wondering if you could take that short one and put some ice and fresh soda water in it. Make sure it's fresh, though, please. Lots of bubbles."

"I can do that," she said.

"Wonderful. Could you possibly squeeze a lime in there for me, as well? Right on top," he said. "Just a short piece of lime, though, not one of those big wedges."

"I could also do that," she said. "I have been trained in the art of mixology, after all."

"Perfect," Pete said. He then leaned forward in his stool to look behind the bar.

He saw plenty of bottles he recognized; Taaka and Smirnoff, mainly, which wouldn't do. He might as well go home if those were his choices. He wasn't a desperate man, after all, he just wanted some refreshment. And what is the point of refreshment if you aren't going to enjoy it? He saw one bottle with a gold top that he liked pretty well. It wasn't his Sobieski, but it would do just fine. So, as Cauley went to grab the soda gun, Pete said, "One more thing, if you don't mind, Ms. Cauley. Could you maybe pour a little bit of that vodka in there for me, too?"

Cauley looked at him. "This isn't going to get me in trouble with the big guy, is it?" she said. "I've only got one strike left, you know."

"No, ma'am," Pete said. "This is a fair ball. Perhaps even a home run."

Cauley made his drink and set down the glass and Pete lifted it to the Christmas lights. It was not a bad glass at all. He could see the bubbles making their playful way to the top, could see the delicate spray above the rim of the glass, and turned it around in the light. "One day closer to you," he said, and took his sip. He felt the patter on his lips and nose, just as he'd hoped, and the cold drink around his tongue and down his throat in a way that cooled him completely. It had the perfect burn when he swallowed, the perfect hint of lime. It was as if he had made it himself and, *oh, man*, he knew he'd made the right choice by stopping here. He closed his eyes. *Trina. His truck. Lanny.* All of these things could wait until tomorrow. He set down his glass and let out a deep exhale.

"I might need me one of those," Cauley said. "If that's the effect."

Pete smiled. "I've been walking a long time, is all. And not in the metaphorical sense."

He reached for his wallet and pulled out a ten. He'd no idea what the drink might cost him, so infrequently did he drink on the town, and so infrequently did he pick up the tab when he did. He couldn't go down to Dot's Diner without somebody buying his pancakes, and this was okay with Pete. As he reached in to pull out another five, just in case, he looked down the bar and saw someone familiar.

It was Douglas Hubbard, sitting by himself and wearing a beret.

Pete knew Hubbard from work, had chatted with him a few times at school functions, but nothing much past the surface. Still, he liked him. This may have been on account of his generally good disposition and, what used to be, a wonderfully thick mustache, but it could also be on account of Pete's experience with Douglas on the third Friday of every month, when the faculty took their turn in his confessional booth. The effect this session had on Pete was always the same.

"Forgive me, Father, for I think I might have sinned," Douglas would say, in textbook fashion.

But this generic opening would be followed by some minor

transgression that only a decent man like Douglas Hubbard could be disappointed in. Things like, "I know my wife likes me to stack my clothes on my own side of the closet but last week I was in a rush and I just sort of threw my T-shirt up there and I saw it fall down on her stack of clothes but I didn't do anything about it. I meant to straighten it up later, Father, but I forgot. She didn't say anything to me about it but, still, I know she appreciates having her personal space. I should have apologized."

Pete therefore spent much of his time in the Confessional with Douglas smiling and, he realized now, building a secret fondness for him. This, of course, wasn't always the case in Confessional. And why do men like Pete like the minds of men like Douglas, anyway? This was something to consider. This usually, it seemed to Pete, happened when there was a fundamental aspect about the other man to admire, when they had some clearly uncommon trait. The enormous and vulnerable love for a woman, which Douglas displayed so blatantly, was nice to witness, and definitely qualified as uncommon in Pete's Confessional. Maybe that was it.

In the bar, however, Pete was surprised by the focused manner of Hubbard's drinking. He hadn't lifted his chin at all, unless it was to take a sip. Otherwise he stared down at his hands, where he seemed to be flipping something over. It could have been a wallet-sized photo, a Post-it note, a credit card, Pete couldn't see. He did notice the two empty martini glasses in front of him, though, one of which still had an olive in it.

Pete scanned the rest of the place. It was quiet. He could hear a few other people in the back, where the bar opened up to a couple of booths and a dartboard, but he couldn't make out what they were saying. So, he took another drink. When Cauley had settled back to her crossword, Pete figured he might as well be friendly, say hello to Hubbard, see if maybe he needed some counsel, and so he walked over. He remembered seeing him with Principal Pat that afternoon and also remembered how Pat had told him she was retiring.

"Did you know," Pete said, "I hear you and I might be getting a new boss?"

Douglas looked up. It took a moment for him to refocus his eyes, and he reached out to shake Pete's hand. "I did know that," Douglas said. "That might account for this second martini, now that you mention it."

"And what was the occasion for the first?" Pete asked.

Douglas folded up whatever was in his hand and stuck it in his pocket. He raised his martini glass. "The human condition," he said.

"Understood," Pete said. He raised his own glass. "And let us also celebrate," he said, "The Air Condition."

"Hallelujah," Douglas said. "And amen."

They sat for a minute as Douglas ate his lonely-looking olive.

Behind them, the bar door opened and the light that came with it was purple and surprising. Still some sun left on the horizon somewhere, which was easy to forget in Getwell's. Through the door walked a man neither Douglas nor Pete immediately recognized. He looked to be from a different era. He had on a cowboy getup, with a big brimmed hat, and his boots clicked the concrete floor as he strutted up to the bar. It was an unnatural walk, there was no doubt about it. His legs were parted in an odd manner, spread a bit too far, as if maybe he was trying to scratch an itch without his hands. He sidled up to the end of the bar and hooked his thumb through his belt loop, did a little scan of the place, and tipped his hat to Cauley, who stood up to greet him.

"Miss Cauley," he said.

"Mayor," she said.

"It's just Hank tonight," Hank told her. "The working day is done."

"That must be nice," she said.

When the bar door closed and the dimness returned, both Douglas and Pete recognized that the man was Hank Richieu and Pete waved him over. Hank obliged.

"Hank," Pete said. "You sure do look festive."

Hank shook his hand. "Father," he said.

"It's just Pete tonight," Pete said. "But, I have to admit, you're making me feel a bit self-conscious. I'm the only guy in here not wearing a hat."

The three men appraised themselves and this was true. Hank in his Stetson, Douglas in his beret, and Pete there in the middle. They made a little landscape of possibility lined up like that, as if, as a unit, the picture of them could exist nearly anywhere and at any time in history. Had Deerfield ever held such promise? Who could know?

"You know Doug Hubbard?" Pete asked. "He teaches History at the school. One of the actual geniuses in this town, from what I hear."

Douglas leaned over to shake Hank's hand. He was becoming outwardly drunk, this was obvious, and looked a bit put out at this unexpected amount of social interaction.

"I know Hubbard," Hank said. "Sure as shootin'."

"I forget that everybody knows everybody here," Pete said.

"Or," Douglas said, as if making a profound statement, "they like to *think* they do."

Hank pulled a coin out of his pocket and tapped it on the bar. "So, what are you fellers drinkin' tonight?" he said. "I need a suggestion."

"I, for one, recommend alcohol," Douglas said.

From her stool, without looking up, Cauley said, "I second that."

"Hubbard," Hank said. "You teach History, right? I have a question for you. How about you tell me what kind of drink would be historically accurate for a cowboy to order?"

Douglas felt his teacher mode coming on again. Was even the mayor a witless victim of that stupid DNA machine, which Douglas had been privately stewing about the past hour? Could that account for his ridiculous new accent? His asinine hat?

"Why do you ask, Hank?" Douglas said. "Are you suddenly under the insane impression that you're meant to be a cowboy?"

"Naaah," Hank said, although the way he said this made it obvious that this was perhaps the exact impression he was under. "I've just taken an interest, is all. Call it historical curiosity."

"Well," Douglas said. "I don't know how to answer your question, since the term *cowboy* isn't really a historical reference. I mean, it's not a time period, Hank. It's a person's occupation."

"That's true," Pete said, and tried to get Cauley's attention by clinking around the ice in his glass.

"You know what I mean, though," Hank said. "*Real* cowboys. Wild West types. *True Grit. A Fistful of Ugly. The Fast and the Furious.* All that stuff."

"Can I have another one of those soda waters, Ms. Cauley?" Pete said.

"Just like I made it before?" she asked.

"Please," Pete said, and laid another ten on the bar.

"That's some expensive soda water," Hank said.

"Charity," Pete said. "Before the need for it."

"Well," Douglas said, "*A Fistful of* Dollars is set in the 1870s or so."

"Is it?" Hank said.

"It takes place during the Civil War," Douglas told him. "That's a major part of the movie. That's not hard to remember."

"A war amongst ourselves," Hank said. "What a dadgum tragedy."

"Amen to that," Pete said, and lifted his empty glass. "Never again."

"So, what'll it be, pardner?" Cauley asked, and set down Pete's drink. She smiled. "Don't ask me for moonshine, cactus juice, or rotgut. We're plumb out."

"Whiskey," Douglas huffed. "Get the man some whiskey."

"Yessir," Hank said. "Whiskey for my horses and water for my men."

Hank held up three fingers to order three shots and, for whatever reason that neither Pete nor Douglas complained when it was set in front of them, the rest of their night began.

A few pleasant hours passed as they discussed everything but what was truly on their minds, watched Cauley walk to the back to serve the other patrons, and told a few jokes. Douglas's generally good disposition returned, so far distracted was he from his troubles, and he took to trading stories and laughing.

They'd eventually gone through three shots each, eaten every variety of potato chip that Cauley had access to, lost track of who was paying for what, and Pete realized he had forgotten how much he liked whiskey. It was delicious, if appreciated. And what are we here to do, he reasoned, but appreciate the world around us? He also knew the way it made him feel in the morning, though, and had privately prescribed a number of penances for himself to complete come sunrise. Twenty extra push-ups. Maybe a jog. Three Hail Marys.

Hank was also feeling cheerful, and led a rambling conversation that could be summarized like this:

"A horse walks into a bar," Hank said. "And the bartender says, 'Why the long face?'"

To which Pete replied:

"How manly was he? Let's just say, if he wanted to lose any weight, he could just shave his back. If that didn't work, he'd just set down that moose he'd been chewing on."

To which Douglas replied:

"You know, I bought a thesaurus the other day to expand my vocabulary, but I don't think it's any good. I mean, not only is it terrible, but it's also terrible."

The men had begun to roll with a sort of inexplicable laughter at this point, the kind totally unwarranted by the quality of their jokes but also one that felt glorious to inhabit, so removed were they from their current worries about bicentennials, nieces, wives, sons, jazz.

"I've got one," Pete said. "A priest, a mayor, and a History teacher walk into a bar. The priest looks around and says, 'Hey, have you heard the one about us?'"

This was the capper. The men fell over one another, laughing and patting one another's shoulders as if they had always been the best of friends. And maybe they were now. The joke immediately memorialized the night for them, it seemed, assured them each that this would be a moment they could recall to one another at whatever future space they found themselves together and, in that way, it added new scenes to their life story and was therefore like the foundation of a million similar friendships. The men felt good, beyond good, and then they heard another man's voice behind them.

"What do we have here?" he said. "Some sort of triple-M *ménage à trois*?"

They looked up to see Deuce Newman approaching with another guy none of them recognized. These had apparently been the people Cauley was serving in the back and they also looked a bit high on the feel of the evening.

When Deuce recognized that Father Pete was among the group, he stopped grinning. "I'm sorry, Father," he said. "I didn't mean to offend."

Pete raised his glass and gave him a wink. "Deuce," he said. "I hereby pardon your French."

As good as the joke was, Deuce's sudden appearance had quietly sapped a certain energy from their conversation. Although they could not know this about one another, another thing these men had in common besides this evening was a mutual distaste for Deuce Newman. Douglas had a lifetime of reasons, primarily centered on Deuce's tongue-wagging at Cherilyn, and felt himself nearly angry at his presence, the way he'd made him to look a fool in his photo that morning. Hank, on the other hand, couldn't stand Deuce's constant presence, the way he was always asking for more, always seemed to be angling for his job. Pete, of course, would never admit to disliking anyone, but a permanent seat in the Confessional can make some people hard to admire. For Deuce, it wasn't any awful sin that he'd admitted to but rather the way he seemed to use Confession to fish for compliments. He would confess to doing some good deed, going the extra mile for someone, and his need for attention rivaled only that of Douglas's need for the love of his wife.

Regardless, Hank shook Deuce's hand. "Seems we can't get away from each other these days, don't it?"

"Which reminds me," Deuce said. "Shouldn't you be working? Preparing for tomorrow's meeting?"

Hank stared at him, lifted his glass, and finished his whiskey in one dramatic gulp.

Pete said, "Who's your friend, Deuce?"

"This," Deuce said. "This is nobody y'all would know. Just an entrepreneur like me. Someone looking for opportunities."

Douglas felt his neck growing hot. "That is a really mysterious answer," he said. "What's the man's name, Bruce? We didn't ask about you."

"My name is Jack," the man said, and nodded to everyone. "I'm from up in Oxford, working for the Mississippi Tourism Board.

Deuce was just telling me about all his plans for the bicentennial. That mosaic idea is amazing. All of it done up in water and light!"

"I told you, Hank," Deuce said.

"I've not signed off on that damn fire hose," Hank said.

"Just so you know," Cauley said from the bar, "if anyone says 'Hotty Toddy' in here, they will be asked to leave."

"Understood," Jack said, and raised his glass to the bar.

"Fire hose?" Douglas said.

"Seriously, boys," Deuce said. "What's the occasion? Hubbard, I can't say I've ever seen you out without Cherilyn. And on a school night, no less. Don't tell me there's trouble in paradise."

"Cherilyn's home," Douglas said. "Things are fine. I appreciate your outsized concern."

"You be careful leaving a beautiful woman like that home alone," Deuce said. "My buddy Wick . . . do y'all know Wick Bart? He started working a night shift a while back. Said his wife went crazy." Deuce leaned in to whisper. "I mean, like *sex* crazy. Took to shaving her pubie hairs, changing things around, you know, in the bedroom, which Wick was initially excited about. But it turns out she'd been running around with another man those nights and he was just sort of getting the collateral benefits of her newfound *joy de vivre*, I guess you could call it."

Pete knew, of course, that Deuce was full of shit. He had heard the real story from Wick in Confession, and the truth was that he had been destroyed by his wife's infidelity, which Pete knew was likely not sparked by the late shift at all, but by Wick's impotence, which he'd been suffering from for years. He'd long been concerned that this would make his wife wander, and so Wick's story was not at its heart a funny anecdote to be shared at a bar, but rather a man's recognition that his trainload of nightmares had finally pulled in. Such is the awful knowledge of priests.

"Deuce," Pete said. "I'm not sure how appropriate it is to discuss another man's problems without him here to tell it himself."

"Understood, Father," Deuce said. "I apologize. I'm just saying that one should look out for any sudden changes in a person."

At that point, all of the men looked over at Hank. Was he wearing spurs?

"Thanks for the tip," Hank said.

"So," Jack said. "I'm wondering. Have any of you guys tried that DNA machine? Deuce showed it to me over at the grocery today. Seems pretty exciting."

Douglas finished off his own whiskey and said, "If by 'exciting' you mean ridiculous, futile, impossible, and dumb."

"Don't listen to Hubbard," Deuce said. "He's above all that. He already knows what he is. The luckiest man in the world, right? Some things you can't change."

"Listen here," Douglas said, but Pete put his hand on his shoulder.

"I think we're all pretty lucky, in the grand scheme of things," Pete said, and looked over at Hank, who he realized, after saying this, was not lucky at all. He had suffered so much, he knew, losing a wife and son. So, Pete tried to backtrack. "I mean, in the really grand scheme of things. We're not living in a basement being tortured by a psychopathic uncle is what I'm saying."

"I guess that's true," Hank said.

"We ain't living in Iraq or Kuwait or any of those places, either," Deuce said. "We ain't eating rice in a river of our own sewage."

"My God, Deuce," Douglas said. "That is an incredibly ignorant thing to say."

"Anyway," Pete said. "My point was that I'm lucky to have a job that starts in about eight hours. I should hit the road."

"We're leaving, too," Deuce said. "A lot to do. Opportunities everywhere for ignorant folks like me, Hubbard. Not much time to capitalize. I'll see you at the meeting tomorrow, Hank."

Hank tipped his hat as the men walked out, Deuce putting his arm around Jack's shoulder and throwing his beer bottle in the trash can by the door.

"If I wasn't in the presence of a priest," Douglas said, "I might have a few choice words."

"Well," Cauley said from behind the bar, "you are in the presence of a priest, and you are also in the presence of a woman who's ready to go home. It's closing time, boys." She set three odd-looking shots down on the bar. "I've called Tipsy to come and get you. Here's one more for the road."

With Deuce gone, the men tried to shake off their newly soured moods, to get back to better times that now seemed long ago. "Well, my trusty horses," Hank said. "What do you neigh? I'm game for one more if you are."

The men smiled and reached out for their shots and Douglas asked, "What is this, Cauley?"

"It's called a three wise men," she said. "It's best not to think too much about it."

And so the men clinked one more time and took it down, all with varying degrees of success. After they each managed to swallow, to shake their heads and cough a bit, Hank said, "I've been meaning to ask, do either of you guys know where I can get my hands on a player piano?"

Then the door to the bar swung open and Tipsy Rodrigue walked in. "Gentlemen," he said. "Your chariot awaits."

The men stumbled out of the bar and into Tipsy's Town Car before Douglas had to get back out and fetch the trombone and bag of groceries from Cherilyn's Outback. "Sorry," he said, and sat in the back seat of the car, where he cradled them both.

"Hey," Tipsy said. "Have y'all heard that Britney Spears is opening up a new restaurant?"

"Hey," Hank said. "Have you heard the one about us?"

The mention of this sent the men back to their smiling, back to feeling comfortable in their heightened spirits, and Pete said, "Hubbard, is it true that you're some sort of expert whistler? That's the rumor at work."

"Is it *true*?" Tipsy said. "Have you never heard this man whistle? My goodness, it's like a songbird from heaven."

"Give us something, then, pardner," Hank said. "Give us something for that old dusty trail."

Although it wasn't in Douglas's typical nature to perform like this, he figured he had more energy left to whistle than he did to withstand the endless nagging he'd get if he refused. So, he leaned back, pulled his trombone case tight to his chest, and whistled the opening bars of *The Good, the Bad, and the Ugly*, which all the men recognized. But Douglas didn't stop there. He went on to whistle the entire theme song, composed, he knew, by Ennio Morricone, full of the little trills and bass tones that required him to hit a flurry of different notes, to do a number of things he loved, and the men didn't say a word to interrupt him.

Instead, they each fell quietly into their probable futures. Douglas wondered what Cherilyn was doing right now, if she was already asleep, what he would say to her about why he hadn't come home, and about what he had learned from his own disastrous DNAMIX reading, what he had learned about hers. Could he tell her? If so, how? Hank thought about his sons, both the physically missing and the emotionally missing, and how he needed to make some repairs. He needed to get his hands dirty, he felt, mending the mess of his life that seemed to grow more solitary each year. He could do this, couldn't he? He had to. For his part, Pete looked out of the window and thought of nothing much at all besides the beauty of Douglas's song, his tremendous gift. And he would have been happy to stay in this state of appreciation forever but then saw what looked like a person climbing out of a window of one of the houses they passed. They moved like a thief in the night, this person, like one of his favorite verses from Thessalonians, which says, "The day of the Lord will come like a thief in the night," and Pete didn't say a word to the other men in the car about it. He knew he should. Of course, he knew he should.

But he did not because he knew it was Trina.

14

Things That Go Bomp in the Night

Is it true that she was first dreaming of elephants?

Cherilyn believed it to be, and upon that dream canvas stood on an endless road of dust. Not Deerfield, not gravel, not oyster shell, not even dirt, but a soft talcum dust the color of great pyramids. She was in a place she had never been to and could not name because it had no name and no purpose but for her alone to stand tall and straight and covered in red silk and gold thread, wrapped in a dress so long and fluttering that it behaved more *of* the wind than in it. Stretches of time since she'd stood there, she felt, with nothing else in sight, and it was undeniably her. Between the flitting red scarf, below the jewels on the woman's forehead, she saw her own unmistakable eyes. Not the green she saw each morning in the mirror but a green strong enough to pull life from that dust, strong enough also to pull her own consciousness inside of that dream body where she became more than just a voyeur to this vision but now lived inside of that person, as well. She was on the outside and the inside of this dream, both the director and the actor, and then heard the thunderous noise from behind as a caravan approached. She felt the ground shake, the bells on her ankles sending song to her ear as two rows of elephants flanked past her now, their wide backs adorned in blue blankets and diamonds, their faces masked as if in military uniform. She reached out her hands to gently tip their thick skins with her fingers and each animal raised its strong trunk to bellow gratefully at her touch. Such a strange and joyful noise, and yet Cherilyn remained placid and calm in this dream because she knew it was for her that they sang. The sound of their calls like new music, the upward turn of their tusks like swords, their progress upon the ground like earthquakes. Louder now, as if to announce her, as if to tell the world of her majesty and march beyond sight into the unknown plains of her life to foretell the story of what was to come. The constant blaring of their horns. Or, no.

The blaring of one horn.

To tell her that Douglas was home.

Cherilyn opened her eyes and looked at the clock. It was after midnight and yet she had just fallen into that deepest part of sleep that knows you. Why had she stayed up so late? She could say that it was worrying about Douglas, and this may have been partially true (out drinking on a school night?), but was that really what kept her up? In the living room, she heard it again. The sudden blast of his trombone. The semblance of one note and then another with no obvious relation between them. And then one final noise that had an unfortunate and deflating sound, as if Douglas had lost his breath in the middle of blowing it. She sat up in bed. She heard the strange shuffle of uneven footsteps. Then, a crash.

She heard Douglas say, "Welp."

Cherilyn felt no need to run.

She understood her husband well enough to know that if he was blowing a trombone in the house at midnight, he was extremely, as her mother would say, *tooted*, and had likely just lost his balance. Douglas didn't get this way often. He might sip a little whiskey before dinner, split a bottle of wine with her on the couch, but they'd never laid down any sort of expectations about each other's drinking those last twenty years because there had been no need to. And what a luxury that was. Douglas stayed in his lane throughout all of life's moods and that was a comfortable thing about him. Plus, they both used to cut pretty loose in their day, so who was she to judge? She still smoked cigarettes, after all, didn't she? She was not perfect. And so Cherilyn didn't worry in the way that so many spouses must worry.

Douglas was unfailingly fun in these moods, Cherilyn thought, and she pitied her friends whose spouses turned cruel or depressing when drunk. What kind of life would that be? No, she and Douglas had struck a good balance with their partying, for which Cherilyn was grateful, because anytime Deerfield offered up an open bar they could get their money's worth without guilt. And it was no wonder she liked this version of him. Douglas merely morphed into an exaggerated version of himself when they drank. And that was some advice she could give a young person, she thought. If you're going to marry a man, make sure you like the drunk version of him, too. You're marrying more than one person, she'd say. That's what some couples don't realize. When you get married, you're marrying a thousand people.

Yet Douglas not only remained friendly and kind when he'd had a few but also seemed younger, somehow, the kind of drinker genuinely interested in everyone around him. He'd talk to strangers or call up old friends and say smart and encouraging things. Instead of seeming teacherly, which, Cherilyn had to admit, he could sometimes do, he'd instead have this brand of enthusiasm that made you feel like you were learning along with him. It felt contagious, like you were sharing in his amazement at some new aspect of the world and this was always nice, Cherilyn understood, no matter who you shared it with. And if they were out on the town and there was a jukebox or band Douglas would dance with her and whistle along and inevitably threaten to play some invisible instrument when they sat back down at the table to rest. Just for a second. Just to tease her. Just to let her know that he was still the type of guy this might actually play some wicked air trombone right there in front of everybody. To let her know that, just because they'd been married so long, that didn't mean he was above embarrassing her. And he would do this just long enough for Cherilyn to look at him, for her to smile as if she could indeed still be mortified after all these years by anything he might cook up, and then he would stop. And Cherilyn loved this about him, so she would grab his hand at the table, where she knew Douglas would squeeze hers back in return, again and again, in perfect time with the music.

When she didn't hear anything else from the den, though, she did worry he might have hurt himself and so she put on her robe and left the bedroom. She turned on the light in the living room and saw Douglas lying facedown on the carpet, the trombone by his feet, a basket he'd knocked off the coffee table overturned on the floor. He was facing her direction and opened his eyes with the light. He looked up at her without moving his head. He smiled.

"Oh, hi there," Douglas said.

"Hello," Cherilyn said.

"I think I might have tripped," he said.

"Is that a fact?" she said.

Cherilyn approached and knelt beside him and saw that Douglas already had a little knot on his forehead, reddening above his right eye. It wasn't anything serious, she could tell, but it would leave a bruise. She looked at him a minute and all those worries that had kept her from sleep were temporarily gone. Her sweet Douglas and his unexpectedly drunken smile on a Thursday. Where had this come from? An excellent trombone lesson? Was this a bit of happiness for Douglas? The idea pleased her, and she patted his back.

"I didn't mean to wake you," he said.

"You were playing a trombone," she said.

"I suppose that's true," he said.

"I'll get you some ice," she said.

"Oh," Douglas said. "That would be splendid."

Cherilyn went to the kitchen, where she saw Douglas had kicked off his shoes by the pantry, put his socks by the phone, and set his belt on the stove. On the counter, an open box of cookies. Next to this, Cherilyn saw, the bag from Johnson's Grocery. She looked inside it. Eggplants and olive oil. Lemons. Tahini. A bottle of wine. At least that was something. Dependable Douglas.

She returned to the den and knelt beside him. She placed the ice pack on his forehead and he opened his eyes.

"Well, there's an interesting sensation," he said.

"You have a good time tonight?" she asked him.

"I did," Douglas said.

Cherilyn looked him over and smiled. He was splayed out like a chalk drawing of himself, arms raised above his head as if he'd been fleeing in terror when he hit the floor. A foot away, she saw, sat his beret, where it had apparently popped right off his head.

"You're not paralyzed or anything, are you?" she said.

Douglas wiggled his pointer finger. "Check," he said. A moment later, he lifted his heel. "I'm just a little sleepy, I think."

Cherilyn gently pet his back. "You want to come to bed or you good out here?"

"You know, I believe I'm good right here, honey," Douglas said. "Thank you. And how are you?"

Cherilyn smiled again and touched his cheek. "I'm okay," she said. "I'm glad you're home."

She then pulled the blanket off the couch and laid it on top of her husband. He would indeed be fine right there and, rather than try to convince him otherwise, Cherilyn understood the kindest thing she could do was let him be.

She stood and put the basket back on the table. She then looked down at him and wagged her finger playfully. "No more of that rock-and-roll music, young man. You hear me?"

"Ten-four, good buddy," Douglas said, and closed his eyes.

Cherilyn turned out the light and went back to bed.

She did not sleep well after that. She first thought of her husband and his little surprises. A trombone after midnight? A belt on the stove? Ten-four, good buddy? These were all nice thoughts. But, when they ran out, Cherilyn had to return to what she herself had been doing that evening.

She'd spent a few hours at her mom's, cleaning up a bit, calling Douglas to see if he might also pick up some wine for dinner, but got no answer. Her mom had been joking earlier, she claimed, about thinking Cherilyn was trapped in the attic. She was just giving her a hard time. But Cherilyn had seen that strange look in her eyes, the one that made it seem as if her mother was perhaps watching two different movies at once and puzzling out which one to focus on. She said she was fine, like she always said she was fine, but it was honestly so hard to tell. It exhausted Cherilyn to think about. And as they sat on the two ancient recliners in her mother's living room, watching TV, not saying much, Cherilyn was overcome with guilt for talking to that other man on the computer. She could rationalize it all she wanted, that it wasn't that big of a deal, that she hadn't done anything that a million other people do every day, she was sure, that she hadn't cheated in any sort of legal or even technical way, that no jury on this planet could convict her. Yet her heart kept twisting around it.

So, she decided to dig through her mother's cabinets and pull out some candles. She heated her mother some soup and put the candles in the same bag she'd used to bring her leftovers that afternoon and then walked back home, determined to make a night of it with Douglas. She would cook her new dish and he could help her out with it, chopping or slicing, and she could light the candles and they could have wine and talk about his trombone lesson. They could watch baseball if he wanted. Read together in bed. Perhaps even do other things in bed and she would not ask for an encore this time. She would instead bury herself in their wonderful normalcy, which she found herself missing, for some reason, and wipe the start of that day away. Maybe she would even tell him, if the moment was right, about her readout. About Tipsy's readout. And how maybe there was something to this.

But instead she got home to hear a message on the machine that Douglas was having drinks with Geoffrey and so she fiddled around with her birdhouses, made herself a simple meal, and soon became dizzy. This was not a happy feeling. It was instead the awful and increasingly familiar dizziness that made her nauseated, the sudden and unpredictable one that caused her to nearly swerve off the road those past weeks. So heavy in her limbs that she felt pulled to the earth. And when this feeling came, as it always did, it dominated all else. She steadied herself on the table and took deep breaths until it eased. She then popped an Excedrin and walked a glass of water to their computer. She clicked her cursor onto the search bar and typed in "WebMD."

This was one of the only other sites besides Etsy she'd spent much time on, but never out of her own curiosity. It was instead concern about her mother that had previously led her there. Douglas sat beside her on that occasion and they quickly diagnosed her mother with just about every illness known to man, which Cherilyn found insultingly easy to do when you typed "forgetful," "erratic," and "female" into the search bar. Douglas had warned her of the hypochondria this site could cause.

"You know what they say," he told her. "WebMD: Where You See Things You Can't Unsee."

So, Cherilyn didn't put much stock into what it said about her mother. There were just too many options to choose from: dementia, Alzheimer's, blood clots, menopause, pregnancy, dehydration, normal aging. A person could be as sick as they chose to be.

This time, though, she was looking for herself in those pages. She typed in symptoms like "dizziness," "migraines," "tingling," and "cramping," and such a wealth of horrific options appeared that she decided she would make an appointment with Dr. Granger tomorrow. Enough was enough. Yet all those terrible options followed her to bed, where she opened her husband's book about royal families and stared right through it until she fell asleep and awoke to the sound of elephants.

When morning came and the birds started up, she found Douglas standing beside the bed, fully showered and dressed for work. He smelled wonderful, Cherilyn thought, the masculine scent of his soap and cologne, just as he always did at this precise moment of their mornings together. His thin hair was combed neatly over his head, and below his right eye, where the blood had drained, was a big purple bruise.

"Ouch," Cherilyn said.

"You should have seen the other guy," Douglas told her. "He was a basket."

"You don't look so good," she said.

"I'd pay to feel as good as I look, if that tells you anything."

"I'm sorry."

"I think I've gone blind," he said. "It's like my eyeballs have stopped working. How did we used to drink like that all the time?"

"We were young," Cherilyn said. "We skipped class the next day."

"You're still young," he said. "Just wait until you hit forty. That's when it all goes to shit."

"I'll be sure to live it up until then," Cherilyn said.

Douglas went to the dresser and picked up his beret. Cherilyn shifted in the bed to watch him. He looked at himself in the mirror and put it on. What was that face he was making? So serious, it seemed, when he looked at himself. What pose was he hoping someone would find him in? Who was he trying to impress? Did she do the same? Douglas then fished out a pair of sunglasses from the bowl on the dresser and slid them over his eyes.

"Class," he said to the mirror. "Today, we are going to talk about hangovers."

Cherilyn rolled to her side. She hugged a pillow between her legs.

"Hey, Cher," Douglas said. "Sorry about last night. I know you were hoping for eggplant. I'm not sure what got into me."

"It's okay," she said. "I had spaghetti. I was more just wanting to hang out with you. Talk to you about some stuff. Do you feel like we haven't talked in a while?"

"We talk every day," he said. "I spilled my entire guts to you last week." He studied his face in the mirror. "Hence this weird-looking upper lip. I still can't get used to it."

"I guess that's true," Cherilyn said. "I don't know what I'm thinking. I just feel like we have stuff to talk about. I feel kind of distant."

"That's my fault," Douglas said. "But I know what you mean. We *should* talk. I'm sorry. I should have come home."

Why did it bother her, his answer?

Cherilyn felt immediately irritated with Douglas but had no idea the reason. He was being kind, she knew, taking the blame for something he didn't even do wrong. But maybe that was it. Couldn't it be something that *she* had done? Couldn't Douglas allow her to be wrong for a change, to be distant, to be at fault? Doesn't everyone have a right to be wrong?

"Let's talk tonight," he said. "We can eat all the eggplant and talk about all the stuff. I have to get to work, though."

"Okay," Cherilyn said.

Douglas leaned over the bed and kissed her on the forehead. He moaned as if this was too much movement for anyone in his condition and then told her he loved her. After he left, Cherilyn lay on her back and looked up at the ceiling. She began her body check: Feet, okay. Hands, okay. Head, okay.

After a moment, Douglas rushed back into the room. He was nearly out of breath.

"Here's a problem," he said. "I don't have a car."

And then, as if to answer him, the doorbell rang.

15

Up in the Morning,
Work Like a Dog

Pete never made it to bed.

He'd grown quiet since seeing Trina through the car window and said little other than good-bye as Tipsy dropped off the other guys on his way to Pete's house, where he agreed to pick him back up in the morning. Pete thanked him and stumbled inside with his head down. He kicked his shoes off in the laundry room and went straight to the back porch, where Mayfly was waiting with her nose pressed to the screen door. Mayfly was a beige-and-white mutt, a gift to him from a friend after Anna passed. She was part Black Mouth Cur and part Lab, he was told, and was a good dog although old now and, Pete suspected, not too bright. This, however, is a decent attribute for a yard dog, and Pete admired her simple nature. Mayfly required little other than access to food and water and for Pete to occasionally throw a ball in one direction so that she could bring it back in the other. Pete could provide this for her and so Mayfly loved him, which is the great and selfish comfort of owning a dog.

Pete opened the screen door a crack and sidled his way out so Mayfly wouldn't run in. He said, "I know, I know," and watched her uncoil into a bundle of energy. She turned in circles and wagged her tail and licked Pete all over his hands when he tried to pet her. "Settle down," he said, and this is what Pete meant by her not being too bright. He could tell Mayfly missed him. He knew she wanted to be petted. She got so damn excited, though, even after all these years, flapping around like a fish and staying just out of reach, that it made the very thing she wanted impossible. "Calm down, now," he said and clicked his tongue. "Daddy's home."

Pete patted her hard on the side and scratched her back end and then sat heavily into the lone lawn chair on his porch. He looked out to the yard. The dim porch light above afforded him only a glimpse of the dark grass, the outline of the oak trunk that stood by his fence line, and Mayfly buried her head in his lap. Pete took a deep breath. The frogs were singing. Bugs bounced around the porch light. This was a welcome scene. He scratched Mayfly behind the ears until she grew satisfied enough to run off and find the ancient tennis ball she adored. It was a nasty-looking thing, turned brown and nearly bald long ago. He'd often tried to give her an upgrade, buying her some fancier toys with squeakers, some of them running upward of ten bucks at the grocery store, but she quickly eviscerated them to get the squeaker out. The more expensive the toy, it seemed, the faster Mayfly destroyed it. It was inevitable. And on these days Pete would come home to find her in the yard, the space-age rubber ball supposed to last a lifetime scattered like a plane crash at her paws, and say, "You know, this is why we can't have nice things."

Mayfly returned from the dark and set the tennis ball beside him. Pete looked at her. Her ear was cocked to the side, her tail straight out as if frozen. "What are we going to do about that girl?" Pete asked her. Mayfly did not respond. So, Pete leaned over to pick up the ball and almost fell off the chair. He then sat back up and chucked it mightily into the air where the ball went too high and knocked out his porch light. The naked bulb popped like a firework and sprinkled its light to the ground like rain.

"Careful, now," Pete said, "there's glass," and fell asleep in the chair.

He awoke covered in dew, Mayfly still in his face. Had she even moved? He had no idea. He swept up the bulb and showered and dressed and the memory of Trina lurking outside of that house returned to him like regret. He said his morning prayer and did his penances, twenty extra push-ups, thirty extra curls, but had no time for the jog as he fought back a familiar but not insurmountable headache. Pete then went to the kitchen, made a fried-egg sandwich with hot sauce and mayo, and picked up the phone. He'd decided to call Lanny's house, to see if he could talk to Trina before school. He hated that he didn't have her cell phone number. If he could catch her early enough, though, maybe they could set up a meeting in his office, have a talk. He could give her a chance to explain.

Lanny answered.

"This better be Publishers Clearing House," he said.

"Morning, Lanny," Pete said. "Pete here."

"Shit," Lanny said. "Has it been a week already?"

"I'm not calling about the truck," Pete said. "Is Trina there?"

"Took her to school," Lanny said. "Why else you think I'm up at this hour?"

"A lot of people are up at this hour," Pete said. "It's the daytime."

"Speaking of," Lanny said. "You know you got a little wiggle on your front end, don't you? Alignment's all off. You must have hit a mighty big pothole. Probably going too fast, I'd guess. Maybe driving without your headlights."

Pete looked at the clock. He understood Lanny had likely done something awful to his truck in the short time he'd had it but was more struck by what Lanny had said. "Seems early for her to go to school, doesn't it?" Pete asked him. It was seven-thirty. "Morning bell's not until eight."

"Some sort of assignment," Lanny said. "She was all up in my face about it. Started on me last night."

"I'll catch her there, then," Pete said.

"When you do," Lanny said, "tell her she owes me ten bucks."

Pete turned off the call and put on his collar. He then drank a glass of milk and took Mayfly outside to fill up her food and water. When he got back in, he heard Tipsy Rodrigue knocking on the door. He was right on time. He opened the door and they shook hands.

"A guy could get used to this," Pete said.

"Don't I know," Tipsy said.

They got in Tipsy's Town Car and drove the couple miles to Douglas Hubbard's house. Pete hadn't seen it in the daylight before, at least not knowing it was the Hubbard place. It was a one-story rancher, like most of the houses in that neighborhood, brown brick, with a small front porch and a yard. It had a nice little row of azaleas in the front, some mulch in a flower bed, and what looked to be about a dozen birdhouses hanging from the eaves. You learned a lot about people from their yards, Pete knew, and he pictured Douglas and Cherilyn outside pulling weeds together on the weekends, doing all sorts of chores, for a nice yard like this took attention. He pictured Cherilyn in a sun hat, Douglas pushing along an electric lawnmower. Why an electric mower in this fantasy? Pete had no idea. Douglas seemed sort of progressive to him in that way, he supposed, like he was a person who thought about big-picture things like the environment, the coast, human rights, and other obvious stuff that some people in town didn't seem to think much about. This vision of the two of them in their marital teamwork, for whatever reason, made Pete like the Hubbards even more.

He sat in the car as Tipsy went up and rang the bell, and when Douglas finally emerged he looked rough. He had his beret pulled low on his head and a set of what looked to be cheap gas-station sunglasses over his eyes. He held his satchel in one hand instead of resting it over his shoulder and carried his trombone case in the other as if it was some unexpected burden. He seemed pale from this distance, nearly green, and slouched toward the car. Pete smiled. Here was the zombie version of Douglas Hubbard, he thought, dressed in Hubbard's clothes and heading to work.

Douglas opened the door and sat in the back. Pete leaned over and shook his hand.

"Pete Flynn," he said. "I believe you may have met my evil twin brother last night, Errol Flynn. My apologies for anything he may have said or swashbuckled."

"I feel like I'm blind," Douglas said. "I'm serious. I haven't been this hungover in decades."

"You *look* like you're blind," Pete said, and motioned to the sunglasses.

Douglas lifted them to show his bruise. "Let's just say that a 'three wise men' is a misnomer," he said.

"Yikes," Pete said. "What happened there?"

"I plan to tell my students I got this by reading their essays," Douglas said. "In reality, though, I just forgot how to walk."

Tipsy sat in the car. He adjusted his rearview and smiled at them both. "Not to worry, gentlemen," he said. "Douglas, I'll get you to your car. Father Pete, we're off to the rectory, and I've already dropped off Hank. We'll have everyone in place by the morning bell."

"Take your time," Douglas said, "I mean it," and looked out the window as Tipsy drove.

If this were a normal day, Douglas would be backing out of his driveway right about now and waving at Dan Pitre, who'd be out watering his lawn in pajama pants. He would honk at Bill Kelly, who'd be sitting on his front porch with the paper. He'd give a nod to Tanisha Summers, who'd be walking her three designer dogs. Yet Douglas saw none of these familiar things. He instead saw Justin Ashbaugh installing a basketball goal over his carport. He saw Lynn Pritchard chipping golf balls into a bucket. He saw Remy Esteve juggling apples. At the corner of Bertha and Jackson, Ben Shields was chain-sawing a tree in some careful way, making a type of sculpture from the trunk, it looked like, maybe a pig or a cow. On the next street, Willy Ennis shot arrows into hay bales from his wheelchair. There were three new "For Sale" signs in his neighborhood alone. And so this, Douglas understood, was not a normal day.

"How's Miss Cherilyn doing today?" Tipsy asked him.

"Enjoying not being hungover, I imagine," Douglas said.

"Hey," Pete said, and turned to face Douglas. "I was wondering. You have my niece, Trina, in any of your classes?"

Douglas groaned. "I do," he said. "First period. How's she holding up, by the way?" he asked. "I can't get a read on her."

"She hates it here," Pete said. "But she hates everything, so it's hard to gauge. She's not had it easy, you know."

"She living with her dad? Out there on sixty-one?"

"Yeah," Pete said. "That's part of the problem, I'm sure. I'm afraid he's mixed up in some rough stuff."

"That's what I've heard," Douglas said. "It's too bad. That man was a hell of a singer."

"Who?" Pete said. "Lanny?"

"My God, yeah," Douglas said. "I went to school with him. We were in choir. He always sung the solos. He had this sort of falsetto none of the other kids could hit. But then we went to high school and I guess he got tired of being the choirboy and sort of went the opposite direction. Had a rock band for a while, I remember, the

Broken Clocks, or something like that. I haven't seen him in ages but, when we were young, he had a voice that made the parents cry."

"I didn't know that," Pete said. "We've never been close. He married my sister, but we weren't really close, either."

"I'm sorry to hear that, too," Douglas said, and leaned back in his seat. He sighed, as if being required to talk in this state exhausted him. "It's good of you to help her out, though, Pete. Trina, I mean. All the faculty thought so. You're a good man, besides just being a priest."

"I second that emotion," Tipsy said.

"Sometimes I wonder," Pete said. "I hate to see anyone so miserable."

"Hey," Douglas said. "If you could get her to do her assignments, you'd make my life a lot easier. I'd be afraid to give her an F. She's got a certain look about her. No offense."

"None taken," Pete said. "Trust me. I know that look. You mind if I pop in there today, though? Maybe I could have a word with her?"

"Fine by me," Douglas said and closed his eyes. "One less student to vomit on."

"I gave her a ride yesterday, you know," Tipsy said. "Over to her mother's house."

"Who?" Douglas said.

"Your wife," Tipsy said. "She looked like she was baking out there in the street, so I just scooped her up. Such a nice lady. She feeling okay? She seemed a little beat by the heat."

"She is," Douglas said. "A nice lady, I mean. And, yes, she is feeling okay. Thanks for doing that."

"Anytime," Tipsy said.

Although he didn't say so, this information didn't sit well with Douglas.

Cherilyn was in this very car yesterday and he didn't know about it? This was an odd feeling. It wasn't a thing to make him jealous or angry, of course, as Douglas was not insane, but it was curious to him, the little pockets of life we don't see of each other. Where had she sat in this car? In the front seat? The back? He knew Cherilyn did things without him, of course, as he did things without her. She lived nearly half of her days outside of his presence and he imagined this part of her life filled with art and friendship. He pictured her at work on her crafts, popping in at her various jobs, calling up friends to chat, helping her mother. What struck him now, though, was that he always felt he knew where she *physically* was when he left her, and these were limited spaces. He pictured her at the breakfast table or in her Outback, at the grocery, inside her mother's musty house, all places that he, too, had been. And so, when he found out Cherilyn had been to a new place without him, this sleek and well-air-conditioned car, he felt a strange need to tell her about Geoffrey's apartment, as well, where he had been without her that past week. He wanted to describe it. He wanted to take her with him.

"Would you look at that," Tipsy said. "Is that Jud Chaney in a tuxedo?"

Douglas looked out the window and did indeed see Jud Chaney, a forklift operator with a chest like a beer keg, walking around his yard in a tux. He had trimmed his long beard, gotten himself a haircut. He bent over, picked a flower from a pot, and put it in his lapel.

The sight made Douglas feel sick.

What outlandish readout had Jud received? he wondered. Oil Baron? International Spy? What in the world could be changing for Jud Chaney? And why didn't the DNAMIX machine afford Douglas a new vision of himself? The injustice of it angered him. What ridiculous possibility could make a man put on a tuxedo before eight a.m.? Douglas secretly hoped that it was doomed, whatever it was, that Jud would fail in this new pursuit, and did not like this jealous and pessimistic version of himself. He thought miserably of his own readout now, and Cherilyn's, and how he could broach the subject with her. Instead of the gracious conversation he'd envisioned the night before, Douglas now thought of logical arguments against the machine. He thought of ways to *not* tell her what his readout said. He thought, in other words, of ways to lie, and he practiced the conversation in his head, like, *Maybe you can have an idea of something, Cher, of greatness, or royalty, perhaps, without it being a total black-or-white thing? Like Maybe this could be an interesting vision for us to consider and dream about, but it was not true, in the way that so few things are ever "true," because these readouts are not accurate.* It was a novelty game in Johnson's Grocery and nothing more, wasn't it? *We'd be hearing about it on the news, don't you think, if it were true? Places other than Deerfield, for sure. New York City. Los Angeles. It would be the talk of the world.* And so, *Maybe we can go back to our lives and just kind of remember this as an interesting thing we once experienced, that we let run its course, Cherilyn, don't you think? That moment when we thought we might be someone else? We can talk about it. We can laugh about it.* Because that's not the view of life we even want, is it? The idea that a machine could tell us something about our fates? That the life a person has willfully chosen, that they had chosen together, could be a mistake? That it could be a disappointment? It was a horrible thing to consider. *I love you for you,* he would say. *No piece of paper can make me think we aren't meant to be together. I don't care what it says.*

And so, in the quick fire of his mind, the matter was settled. He would skewer the machine tonight and be done with it.

Tipsy pulled up to Getwell's. He parked next to Cherilyn's Outback and Douglas hauled out his satchel and trombone and thanked him. He then looked across the street to the gas station and saw Deuce Newman gassing up his ridiculous truck with its oversized tires, and the fact that Deuce would be one of the first people he saw on this shitty day made a certain awful sense to Douglas. Still, he was steadfast in his pursuit of normalcy. He had all the arguments laid out in his head. This DNAMIX business. He would debunk the whole thing. He would blow it to bits.

Then Tipsy rolled down the window and stuck out his hand.

In it, he held a blue slip of paper.

"Hey, Hubbard," he said. "Before you leave. Let me give you my card."

16

My Picture in a Picture Show

One "like" out of twelve followers?

Such antipathy was hard to achieve. It wasn't the low number of followers that surprised Jacob, though; that Trina would cultivate an incredibly small list made sense. She was by all evidence cruel, and denying people entry to your social media is one of the easiest ways to be cruel. You don't even have to get dressed. But only one of the twelve even "liked" it? Most people hit the empty heart out of habit, just to fill it, scrolling through their feed. Jacob was one of her twelve followers, though, and he certainly didn't "like" anything about it. He hated mainly the way he looked so scared of the kiss, his eyes squinted up like he was chewing a lemon. You could see Trina's hand on the back of his head and she was pulling him. It was obvious. She was dominating him with her tongue and he supposed this could look sexy to any number of Internet freaks out there, but it did not look sexy to him. Worse, too, he thought, was the one "like" the picture had received. It was from Deuce Newman.

Why had Trina allowed him, of all people, in her twelve? It sickened him to think about. Deuce had once requested to follow Jacob on Instagram as well, months back, as he had nearly everyone in Deerfield while trying, he said, to gather pics for his project. But nobody under the age of thirty accepted his request, Jacob was sure. It was a joke.

Jacob swiped the app closed and put the phone in his pocket.

He now stood again at the boys' room mirror, doing his ritual face check before first period. He turned on the water and washed his hands and heard a flush from the stall behind him. Rusty Bodell undid the latch and walked out. He hefted his Dickies and popped up his collar and stood next to Jacob at the row of sinks. He tossed something the size of a hockey puck onto the sill beneath the mirror. It was likely a tin of dip, Jacob thought, Grizzly or Skoal, but saw instead that it was hair product called Killer Edge Shaping Wax. Rusty's new coif apparently required accessories. Jacob watched him rinse his hands in the sink and pull a bottle of cologne from his pocket. He pressed a few squirts on his wrists and rubbed them together as if making a paste.

"Man, I'm telling you," Rusty said, and dabbed his wrists to his ears. "This weekend is going to be good for business. A lot of *talent* from out of town, if you know what I mean."

Jacob looked at him. He'd known Rusty nearly all his life but hadn't had a meaningful conversation with him since they once played Pokémon together back in seventh grade. Rusty battled with a premade deck he'd just bought that day and Jacob destroyed him with one of his weakest custom decks made of Water and Plant energies, of all things. Not even one EX. Yet Jacob didn't gloat. Rusty was obviously out of his league, as most kids were against Jacob. He looked totally out of his mind now, Jacob thought, primping his hair in those bright new sneakers.

"Actually, Rusty," Jacob said, "I have no idea what you mean."

Rusty smoothed his eyebrows in the mirror, checked his teeth for morning litter.

"I'm talking about girls," Rusty said. "*Talent!* Starting tonight for the bicentennial, man. This place is going to be crawling with every shrimper's daughter in the state. And you know what shrimpers' daughters do out there in the swamp, J? They don't think about shrimp, man. They think about getting out of the fucking swamp and meeting dudes their daddies don't know. And this weekend, guess who'll be here waiting?"

Jacob acted as if he didn't know the answer.

"Who?" he said.

Rusty pointed his thumbs at his chest. "This guy," he said.

"Rusty," Jacob said. "Can I ask you a serious question? What the hell is wrong with you?"

"Not a thing," Rusty said. "I'm just living the dream."

"I've seen you cry when you didn't get a ticket to the first showing of *Rogue One*," Jacob said. "I've seen you down an entire bucket of cheese balls while writing fan fiction for *Firefly*. What makes you think that any human female, no offense, would allow you to come near her physical body?"

Rusty turned and looked at him.

"I would prefer," he said, "that you not put me in a box."

Rusty reached into his pocket and pulled out a blue slip of paper.

"Read it and weep," he said.

He held out the paper and Jacob read it.

Rusty Bodell. Potential weight 400.

Potential Life Station: **LOVER**.

"Well, that's insane," Jacob said.

"Laugh all you want," Rusty said. "You can't deny science. Plus," he whispered, "it *does* make sense." He gave Jacob a little wink. "I mean, I'm like a mule down there, man. I'm like an untapped resource."

"Thank you for the horrifying visual," Jacob said, "but what's insane is your name. Rusty Bodell? You have red hair and your legal name is Rusty? They named you that before they knew you'd have red hair? That's a weird coincidence."

"That's not my *legal* name," Rusty said, "but that machine knows things, man. It's above and beyond." He turned to the mirror and pulled a comb from his back pocket. "You know, J," he said. "I'd expect a more open mind from a smart guy like you. Go get your own readout done and you'll see."

"What will I see, Rusty? Am I supposed to be a porn star?"

"Shit, I don't know," Rusty said. "And you don't, either. That's the point. But it'll be something better than high school. I know that. Now do me a favor, will you, and hand me that hair jelly?"

Jacob grinned and handed him the can. "I'm rooting for you to break all sex records," he said. "Just so you know. Best of luck."

"Don't need it," Rusty said. "It's in my DNA. It's written in the stars. It's like a big banner in heaven that says 'Rusty Will Get Laid.' It's like justice."

Jacob turned to leave but stopped when he saw the top-left corner of the bathroom door. He felt a quick sink in his chest, a nervy heat like fire up his neck. There were now three numbers written in the corner, where it had been blank yesterday. This was the spot Trina once told him to look when the time for action came, and he couldn't pretend he'd not seen them. The number was 687, which he recognized immediately. It was his locker.

Jacob walked out of the bathroom and down the hall. He checked his phone and he still had five minutes until class. He went to his locker and studied it. It looked the same as nearly all the rest, beige metal with a combination lock and a master key slot for daily inspections. Deerfield wasn't yet the type of place that made kids wear clear backpacks or use bulletproof pencils. They were more likely to try to arm all teachers with AKs and rocket launchers or some other backward notion, if Jacob had to guess, but they were coming around to the dangers, as they should be. As such, Principal Pat was vigilant in her daily strolls through the halls and you could hear her randomly opening and shutting lockers from whatever class you sat in. So, as smart people are apt to do, the kids moved all their secrets to their phones, kept their weed pens and vapes in their shoes.

The only locker allowed to look any different was the one right beneath his. It was Toby's old locker that the school had turned into a makeshift memorial. Kids had taped cards and crosses and ribbons all over it. It looked like something you might pass on a highway, existing only to say "someone died here." The sight of it had broken Jacob down the first day he returned to school after Toby's funeral. This was a day in which he walked in, stood in front of the locker, and found Trina there waiting for him. She looked at him and then down at the memorial and said, "This is all wrong, Jacob. That's what people need to understand. That's what we need to show them." Jacob was so awash in grief he had no idea how to reply and so merely walked right back outside, where his dad was still parked in the lot as if he'd expected it. "We'll give it another shot tomorrow, bud," he said. "School's not going anywhere."

Jacob thought about taking the memorial down again today, as he had on every other day, just so he wouldn't have to be reminded, but he did not. Instead, he looked through the slats in his locker to see if he saw a note, something from Trina, but he didn't. He dialed in his combination and opened it up and, inside, saw a blue duffel bag that was most certainly not his.

He looked around and then carefully picked it up. He had no doubt that it was from Trina, but how? Had he given her his locker combination? He had not. The bag felt light and empty and this was a great relief. And what had he expected, exactly? A gun? Surely she was not that serious. Yet why didn't he stop her when she mentioned guns yesterday? Why had he sent her those blueprints? What was he thinking? Who *was* he? Why was he always making mistakes? He pulled out the bag and unzipped it. He stuck in his hand and found nothing. Still, this was far enough, he thought, and threw the bag back into his locker, slammed the door, and spun the lock.

He then walked to first period, where he imagined Trina there staring at him but, instead, saw Mr. Hubbard at his desk with his feet propped up on a trash can. He had a pair of sunglasses on and looked asleep.

"Morning," Jacob said.

"Is it?" Mr. Hubbard said without moving.

Jacob walked past Trina's empty desk. Her absence bothered him. She often ran late but Jacob had the strange vision that she was not showing up at all today, that perhaps she was never coming back, and how would he feel about that? He sat down and took out his textbook.

After a few minutes, Mr. Hubbard sat up.

"Class," he said. "Today we are going to talk about fate. And we are also going to talk about utter bullshit. And we are going to come to some very logical conclusions about how to distinguish between the two."

Jacob looked around. His classmates laughed into their hands and made faces. This was undoubtedly the first curse word any of them had ever heard from Mr. Hubbard, or any teacher at Deerfield, and they seemed unsure what to make of it. Jacob was also unsure of what to make of the adults around him lately. His father and Deuce and now Mr. Hubbard, all seeming so silly in their maturity. He thought back to the night before when he'd heard his father stumbling in after midnight, singing a song apparently titled "I'm an Old Cowhand from the Rio Grande," and rumbling through the pantry and den. He heard his boots clicking down the hall, the opening and closing of doors. At one point, the sound of breaking glass. His father was drunk, he knew, and Jacob left for school without even seeing him.

"You doing all right, Mr. Hubbard?" Becca asked. "You look a bit different today."

Mr. Hubbard stood up from the desk. He took off his sunglasses and had a wicked-looking black eye.

"I'm glad you asked that, Becca," he said. "Because, you know, I *feel* different today. But we're all supposed to be different these days, isn't that right?" he said. "Look at Rusty Casanova over there, for Christ's sake. Look at Heddy trying to make a swan out of an index card. Is that a swan, Heddy? By God, I can almost make out the neck! Congratulations on realizing your life's true calling. I bet everyone in here is doing amazing new things, am I right? Tell me, class. Who in here feels *different* today?"

A couple of students raised their hands.

In his pocket, Jacob felt his phone vibrate.

"This is what we're going to do," Mr. Hubbard said. "I want everyone in here who feels different today to pull out their readings from that DNAMIX machine. We're going to do an experiment. If you've done it, pull it out."

Some of the kids began going for their pockets and backpacks, apparently too afraid to ask this new version of Mr. Hubbard what happened to his eye, and Jacob pulled out his phone. He had a text from Trina with a video attached to it.

Jacob clicked off the sound and hit play. His heart sank.

The video showed him at his locker just a few moments before and Jacob watched himself remove the blue duffel bag and dig around in it. He watched himself look up and down the hall, and the sight of this gave him chills. It looked like security footage or maybe a hidden camera, as if shot from up in the ceiling, somehow, through a vent. Was there a camera up there? How would Trina have access to that?

Jacob looked up at the ceiling.

Holy shit, he thought. *Was Trina in the air ducts?*

THE BIG DOOR PRIZE **195**

Beneath the video, a message came through.

Destined for Instagram? it read. *You tell me.*

Jacob put the phone back into his pocket. He felt a bead of sweat drip down his side. In one quick flash he had the horrifying notion that everything he thought about Trina was untrue. That the connection she felt to him was not one Trina was seeking to strengthen, but instead one she sought to exploit. But for what possible purpose? His heart beat heavily in his chest and Jacob tried to calm himself by being logical, by taking a deep breath, and by focusing on what was in front of him.

He watched Mr. Hubbard snatch a student's readout from their hand and hold it up to the light.

"Well, now," Mr. Hubbard said. "What do we have here?"

17

There's Flies in the Kitchen, I Can Hear Them A-Buzzin'

Cherilyn felt a shadow cross her window.

She'd been off in la-la land, leaning against the kitchen sink and listening to the familiar racket of their coffeemaker gurgle and cough, looking down at her hands where they gripped the edge of the counter. She studied the various veins and wrinkles and freckles, the way her finger had grown swollen around her wedding ring. They were beginning to look like her mother's hands, she knew, becoming an old woman's hands, and Cherilyn thought of how strange it was to one day look down and think, Wait, these are not my hands at all. Whose hands are these? And then the room darkened, as if there had been an unexpected eclipse, and she felt the rumble of the truck before she saw it. It shook her insides, the engine in her driveway, and then it stopped.

Cherilyn looked out to see Bruce Newman open the door of his truck and step down. She felt an immediate sense of panic. What on earth was he doing there? What would anyone be doing there at this hour? Cherilyn had various daytime visitors, of course. Friends would stop by to chat, neighbors would ask if she'd seen their dogs or children, the mail person would slip envelopes through the door, but it was barely nine o'clock. She was still in her robe. She wasn't even wearing a bra.

She cinched her robe and went to the laundry room to look for one. No luck there and, before she knew it, she was checking her reflection in the mirror by the coatrack. It was automatic. She pressed her hands to her face, crinkled her nose, and smoothed down her hair in the back. She was disappointed in how she looked. More disappointing than this, though, was the disappointment she felt in herself for being disappointed. It shouldn't matter a bit how she looked to Bruce Newman. Of course, it shouldn't. But it mattered, in a strange way, because of him.

Among all the poorly kept secrets in town, Deuce's crush on Cherilyn was likely the worst and she knew this. A number of women were even jealous of Cherilyn, she'd once heard, for taking up that space in his heart. He would be a decent enough catch, she supposed. He was country smart and ambitious, good with tools and computers and cameras, handy around a house. He wasn't attractive, necessarily, but had a girth about him that some women liked. He resembled a clumsy black bear, she thought, which could have a certain appeal. Hell, she knew plenty of women who had settled for worse. And, because of this, Cherilyn privately felt obligated to look her best around Deuce. She'd felt this way for years, like some mentor may feel about an adoring student, as if not letting them down was important, and she was not proud of this. It made her feel vain and sort of duplicitous, but what she never liked to admit to herself was that it also made her feel powerful. She enjoyed the way Bruce looked at her. And who wouldn't? It was nice to feel attractive, wasn't it? It was pleasurable to feel wanted, even if she didn't want anything in return.

And so, any time she and Douglas went out to a party or social function where she knew Bruce might be, Cherilyn spent a bit more time at the mirror, a bit more time staring into her closet. This was, in its way, an onerous thing. She could wear no makeup at all, hit the town in a grocery bag and leggings, and Douglas would still love her. She knew that. He was unshakable. But around Bruce, for whatever petty reason, Cherilyn wanted to look her best. She understood this was not her best quality.

She hoped to sneak off to her bedroom to change but, before she could turn the corner, she saw Deuce at the back door, standing in their garage. He was wearing a suit, of all things, ill-fitting and boxy, and looking at himself in the reflection of the glass. He saw her and smiled.

Cherilyn held her robe together and walked to the door. She opened it with her left hand and kept the robe to her chest with her right. "Bruce," she said. "You lost or something? It's nine in the morning."

"You know me," he said. "I'm never lost."

Cherilyn shook her head and tried to look perturbed. He had no business being there and he knew it, she was sure of that. "Well, what's going on?" she said, and nodded at his clothes. "Did somebody die?"

Deuce looked down at his suit. He tugged at the sleeves as if to try and make them longer. "No," he said. "Big meetings today, is all. Trying to look my best. What do you think?"

"I don't think any of those meetings are scheduled in my garage," she said.

"No," he said. "No, they are not."

"So," she said. "What can I do for you?"

"Oh," Deuce said, and stepped back. He put his hand on his heart like he'd been shot by an arrow. He smiled. "Don't ask me that question. Please, you know better than to ask me that."

"Bruce," she said. "You know very well what I mean. What are you doing here?"

"Maybe I'm not here for you, Ms. Smarty Pants," he said. "Maybe I'm looking for Douglas. Is he around?"

"No," Cherilyn said. "He's at work. Today's a school day."

Deuce looked at Douglas's car. "Well, how'd he get there?" Deuce said. "His car's sitting here and yours is over at Getwell's."

"His is dead," Cherilyn said. "It's a long story. Is that really why you're here?"

"I saw him there last night, you know. Looked like he was really tying one on."

"He's an adult," Cherilyn said. "He and Geoffrey just went out to have a few."

"Geoffrey?" Deuce said. "Is that what he told you?"

Cherilyn squinted her eyes in a way that, she knew, gave away too much. It was no business of Bruce Newman's what Douglas had been doing, but had Douglas lied to her about it? For what possible reason? The idea was so peculiar to her that she had a difficult time recalling the last time she'd wondered it. Mainly in her nightmares, really, dreams where Douglas was hiding some sort of secret from her, not paying attention to her, or loving someone else. Terrible versions of her life in which Douglas did not care about her at all.

"Anyway," she said. "He's not here right now."

"Bummer," Deuce said. "I was going to offer him a ride to pick up the Outback. See if I could bend his ear little bit on the way. But, since he's not here, maybe I could offer you that ride?"

"That's either very chivalrous or very inappropriate of you," she said. "But I don't need a ride." She pointed at Douglas's car, a ten-year-old blue Honda Accord. "Maybe if you could get this one started, though."

"Cherilyn Mae Fuller," Deuce said. "Are you asking me to jump you off right here in your very own garage?"

She sighed. "Can you do it or not?"

"I can," he said. "You want to watch?"

"No," she said. "I want to get dressed. Fix that car, though, and I'll fix you a cup of coffee."

"Deal," he said.

Cherilyn shut the door and walked back to her bedroom. And in the same alarming way it had done ever since she got that readout, her mind went in an unexpected direction. Maybe she *was* meant to be royal, she thought, maybe she *was* meant to be coveted. She had someone at her house doing her bidding right at that moment, didn't she, and so what would a queen do in this situation? To what extent could she exercise her power? What could she get him to do if she asked him?

She went into the bathroom and stood in front of the mirror. She swooped her hair back on her head like Susan of Oman and dropped her robe to the floor. She looked at herself, her living body, and this was not a bad thing at all. She felt the cool wind of the A/C on her back, felt it on her bare chest and thighs, yet remained incredibly warm, as if from the inside out, almost glowing with the power of her physical shape, and she pressed her back to the wall. It was cold against her skin and she placed her palms to the wall. She spread her fingers. She then turned her head to the side and closed her eyes as if bracing herself. But for what? she wondered. For what?

Cherilyn then threw on a bra and T-shirt, a pair of shorts, and very intentionally didn't do another thing to gussy up. That would be his punishment for showing up unannounced. She wouldn't do a single thing. When she got back to the kitchen, she stopped and looked to the garage, where Deuce's truck was parked and idling. It took up the whole window. Both engines in her garage were now running, and what a strange sound that was. Is this what her home would look like if she had married Bruce Newman? A big shiny truck in her garage, if nothing else?

If Cherilyn ever decided to take him up on his offer from long ago, the one that she sometimes thought of, is that what it would be? That night when he caught her alone in the gymnasium hallway and gave her a key to his house. When he was near crying in his dumb earnestness and said, "Anytime. I mean it. Now or in fifty years, even if we're just old bags of bones. If anything changes, this is it. You can have it. You keep it. You know where to find me."

"Oh, Bruce," she'd said.

"You would turn," he told her, "my house into a castle."

Now, truth told, Cherilyn couldn't remember if he'd actually said that last bit about the castle or if it was her new wonderings that added it in, but she still had the key, she knew, just like she still had other things she rarely looked at, shoved in a box at the back of her drawer. A bracelet from high school. A pendant with her friend Jennifer's picture, who'd died those years ago. A ticket stub from *Les Misérables* from a date she and Douglas went on where she'd sworn to herself that she would dedicate more time to her art. It was just a little box of things, just like Douglas had his own little private lockbox he kept in the closet. They were people, she understood, and not just spouses, and people have secret things.

Back in the kitchen, Deuce opened the door and wiped at his head. "I just have to know," he said, "what kind of man doesn't keep a set of jumper cables in his trunk? I looked everywhere. I had to use mine."

"Come on in," Cherilyn said. "Sit at the table. Cream or sugar?"

"Neither," Deuce said. "I take it *au naturel.*"

Deuce took off his blazer and aired it out, set it on top of a chair. "Does he even know how to fix a flat?" he said. "I didn't see any tools in there at all."

"We have Triple A," Cherilyn said, and walked to the kitchen.

"Triple A to fix a tire?" Deuce said. "What in the hell is wrong with this country?"

Cherilyn poured him a cup and walked it over. "The Triple A is my choice," she said. "It makes me feel safer."

"Well, it's a great American company, that's true," he said and took the cup. "Thank you."

Cherilyn went back to pour herself a cup and Deuce sat at the table. He picked up one of the birdhouses she'd worked on the night before and began turning it around in the light. "Damn," he said. "You made all these?"

"I'm sorry," she said. "Just move them aside, if you like."

"These are *ornate*," he said. "You've really come a long way."

Cherilyn sat down at the opposite edge of the table and watched him study the birdhouse. It was true that she'd come a long way with her crafts. She wasn't revolutionizing anything, of course, but lately she'd started shaving and wetting her Popsicle sticks so she could bend them into different shapes, which had opened some possibilities. The one Deuce held had two little sets of spiral staircases going up the façade, which she was proud of. It had taken her a long time. Plus three different holes for windows. It was a home that was meant to be shared.

"This is like a bird *estate*," he said. "Makes me wonder what kind of bird can afford a place like this. A doctor bird?" he said. "A lawyer bird?"

"Don't make fun of me," she said.

"I'm serious," he said. "These are great."

Cherilyn looked at him. "Thank you," she said. "They're for the bicentennial."

"I bet you sell out in ten minutes," he said. "So, what's the news? What else have you been up to lately?"

"Not much," she said. "Taking care of my mom, mainly. She's losing it a bit, I'm afraid. She never much gets out of the house."

"I'm sorry to hear that," he said. "I worry I won't be able to tell when my mom starts to go. She's been crazy all her life."

"And what about you?" Cherilyn asked him. "I hear you've been busy."

Deuce set the birdhouse down like it was a fragile thing and said, "You have no idea, Cherilyn. Things are about to change for me, I have a feeling."

Cherilyn straightened the other birdhouses on the table, repositioned some of the twigs she had bundled up like a wreath on one of their doors. "Well, change is good, right?" she said.

"See?" Deuce said. He slapped his hand on the table. "That's one of the things I like about you. Not too many people in this town say change is good. It's like they're all stuck in the mud."

"Speaking of change," Cherilyn said. "Why'd you text me about that DNAMIX machine? Have you tried it?"

Deuce smiled. "It's the talk of the town, isn't it?" he said.

"It's certainly the gossip of the town," Cherilyn said. "I've been hearing some weird things. Is it true that Judith Freeman is becoming a Buddhist?" she asked. "Somebody told me that the other day and I just laughed it off. But now I wonder if she'd done that machine. I mean, aren't some of the readouts kind of bizarre?"

"I heard Jamie Mize has started digging a pool," Deuce said. "His told him he would be an Olympic Swimmer."

"That old pork chop?" Cherilyn said. "He'd sink like a stone."

"That's what I thought, too," Deuce said. "But it's good he's getting off his couch. It's good when people can see what's out there, I think, even if it might not make much sense sometimes."

"And what about you?" Cherilyn said. She wrapped both hands around her cup. "What did yours say? What's out there for Bruce Newman?"

"Let's turn the question around," he said. "What do you *think* mine would say? What answer could I give you that might change your mind about me?"

Cherilyn sighed again. "So, you haven't done it, then," she said.

"I didn't say that," Deuce told her. He placed his palms flat on the table and leaned toward her. "I'll make a deal with you," he said. "I'll show you mine if you show me yours."

Cherilyn smiled at him.

"Sorry," she said. "I haven't done it. I'm not sure if I want to."

"I'll tell you one thing," Deuce said. "You are a terrible liar."

"Well, then, what do you *think* mine would say?" Cherilyn asked him. "If you're so sure."

Deuce leaned back and blew a big breath through his mouth. "Wow," he said. "So many options. Derelict. Vagabond. Heartbreaker."

"Stop it," she said. "I'm serious. Take a guess."

Deuce looked at her intently. Cherilyn felt him studying her face, her neck, even her fingers as she twirled around the coffee mug on the table. "Something important, is what I'd think," Deuce said. "Somebody special."

Cherilyn felt her heart do a strange shaking thing, but instead of letting on how his comment made her feel, she just stared right back at him. They held eye contact in a way that felt competitive.

"Wrong," she said.

"Well," Deuce told her. "I bet I know what it didn't say." He reached out and put his hand on top of hers. "I bet it didn't just say *Mrs. Douglas Hubbard.*"

Cherilyn leaned back in her chair. She went to tighten her robe even though she was no longer wearing it.

"You know, Bruce," she said. "I think it's time for you to go."

Deuce didn't move.

"It's awfully quiet in this house, Cherilyn."

Cherilyn felt her eyes begin to well but she had been crying enough lately, she thought. She would not do it today, and she would not do it in front of him. "I mean it," she said. "I have things to do."

Deuce stood up.

"Me, too," he said. "Things to do. Always busy, you know. Big town hall with the mayor. Finalizing some stuff with my mosaic. I have a million things going on."

He picked up his blazer and put it over his shoulder and Cherilyn was possessed by the wild notion to keep him there. He was the only one she had talked to about this machine, she realized, and perhaps the only person who wouldn't find it crazy if she told him. And the way he had looked at her when he guessed what it would be. It was like he knew. It was like he would have believed her. Damn it to hell, she thought. Damn it right to hell. She didn't want him to leave.

She got up to walk him out and had to resist grabbing the back of his suit coat to ask him to stay. Another cup of coffee, maybe, just to let her feel that way a little bit longer, because she was back in her dream now, in the land of fine sand, and if she could just be noticed that way, if she could just share that vision with someone, maybe that would make it all go away. But was its going away even a thing she wanted? And, if so, why was she following him outside?

Deuce opened the door and climbed into his truck.

"Bruce," Cherilyn said, and put her hand on the door. "About that mosaic. Don't you still need to take my picture?"

He looked at her a long while. "I guess I do," he said. "I don't have my good camera, though. Later today?"

"Okay," she said. "But not here."

18

The Caravan of Fools

General George Custer. Benedict Arnold. Michael Dukakis. The Buffalo Bills.

Many men throughout history have stared into the mouth of utter defeat and so Douglas was not alone in his mood. Only halfway through first period, his plan to expose his students' DNA-MIX readings as self-aggrandizing slop had gone poorly. He had taken off his blazer and begun pacing up and down the rows between desks. All of his logical arguments against the machine were falling on ears as deaf as a majority congress, and Douglas seemed almost maniacal in his pursuit of at least one unbeliever. From outside the door, he likely looked passionate. He snatched another blue ticket from a boy's hand in the second row and held it up.

"A Puppeteer?" he said. "Now, here is a perfect example. Joseph Weems, answer me honestly. It's the goddamn twenty-first century. Do you have any interest at all in being a puppeteer?"

The boy was nervous, as was the rest of the class, since Mr. Hubbard, cursing with a black eye, no less, had begun his odd crusade. He stammered as he spoke. "Well," he said. "As a kid, I always sort of liked Elmo."

His classmates burst out laughing. One of them did an Elmo impression and said, "Hey, guys. I'm Elmo. I have no penis."

"Cut it out," Douglas said. "Y'all used to like Elmo, too. Don't be idiots. You forget I've seen just about every one of you sitting on your mother's lap since you were born. But my point is that this, Puppeteer, is a totally random occupation that's just been sort of suggested to you. Y'all understand that, right? You know how I always tell you history is written by the winners? It's just a matter of perception."

"Maybe so," Joseph said. "But ever since I got this, I've been sort of fiddling around with stuff." He reached into his backpack and pulled out a puppet about the size of a glove. It had long brown hair, big blue eyes, a checkerboard dress, and resembled no living human being. "And this puppet business," he said, and placed his hand inside the doll. "Well, it lets me put my hand right up her skirt, Mr. Hubbard. This is sort of like the farthest I've gotten."

Douglas looked at him.

"Puppet proctology is not a destiny," he said. "Now put that abomination away and seek counseling. Who's next?"

Douglas turned around to find every student avoiding his eye contact but one. It was Jenny Clarette. This was one of the nicest kids he knew. He reached out and snatched the readout from her hand and read it aloud. "Hopeful?" he said. "My God, Jenny, that's not even a noun. That's an adjective!" He looked at her. "How are you going to grow up to be an adjective?"

Jenny Clarette played on the volleyball team. She was a straight-A student and a member of the Fellowship of Christian Athletes. There was an article in the school paper last year about how she spends her weekends collecting canned goods for children in Rwanda. She was a counselor, Douglas knew, at a youth summer camp. She looked up at him with the largest, most openfaced smile he'd ever seen. Her teeth were in perfect alignment.

"I just plan to try my best," she said.

"Well, shit," Douglas said. "Of course you do!"

"I don't know why you're wigging out about all this, Mr. Hubbard," a girl named Shaina said. "I mean, they're all good. Why not be happy?"

Douglas turned on her like she had insulted him. His teacher mode had now expanded beyond idle hostility to become a sort of weapon. "Who says they're *all good*?" he asked her. "What, in the history of mankind, has been *all good*?"

"Well, look," she said, and held hers out. "Mine says Baker. Now, I've never cooked anything in my entire life." She reached into her backpack and pulled out a Ziploc full of cookies. "But I got my dad's recipe for homemade peppermint cookies and I just sort of added some stuff." She held out a cookie. "You should try it," she said. "My dad says they're even better than his mom's."

"I will not," Douglas said.

"Try the cookie," she said, and then other kids began doing the same. In less than a second, they'd started a chant: "Try the coo-kie. Try the coo-kie. Try the coo-kie."

Douglas was sweating.

"I will not eat that goddamned cookie!" he said.

He looked over to see Principal Pat standing at his classroom door, holding a drill in her hand. He had no idea how long she'd been there.

"Class," she said. "Y'all are dismissed."

The students immediately began slamming their books and stowing their phones and, as they trudged past him out the door, one of them said, "You know, Mr. Hubbard. I'm with you. I don't really think it matters what it says. I think it might be more about the way you interpret it than anything else. It could be just some sort of random algorithm spitting these things out, maybe some sort of facial-recognition software." He took his readout from his pocket. "I mean, mine says Glue."

Douglas looked at it.

"Your parents must be so proud," he said. "Thank you for enlightening me."

Douglas grabbed the few late papers students handed him as they tried to sneak out without conversation and said, "Okay, class. I want to thank you all for providing me this glimpse into the utter abyss. On Monday, we will have a quiz on television psychics, tarot cards, and divining rods. No need to prepare."

Douglas circled around his desk and sat in his chair. As the students filed out, thumbing at things on their phones, he thought of how, for most people, it would be time to go home. He had suffered through first period with a blinding hangover. Wasn't that enough? He had worked an entire day in his head, had been enraged for nearly an hour, and was just getting started. He had also, he knew, been busted breaking Pat's no-cursing policy and prepared himself for a dressing-down. As the last of the students walked out, Pat revving her drill at each one of them as if in mock mutilation, Jacob Richieu approached his desk.

He looked pale and nervous. Something about his face that Douglas saw differently now, though. It was in the chin, maybe, or the manner in which he pinched at his eyebrows, and Douglas realized that Jacob resembled his father, who he'd been with the night before. Much of Hank in the boy, which Douglas knew was a good thing.

"I just want you to know," Jacob said, "that I didn't do it."

"I know, Jacob," Douglas told him. "That's why I didn't call on you. Actually, your two dollars may have started this whole thing."

"No, not that," Jacob said. "Something else."

"Excuse me, Jacob," Pat said, and revved her drill a few more times. "I need to speak to your teacher here."

Douglas looked at Jacob. "It appears I'm about to get screwed," he said. "Can we talk later? I'm in here after lunch. My door is always open. Actually, that's a rule instituted by your esteemed principal right there, isn't it?"

"It is," Pat said. "Pat Howell versus the Board of Sleepy Teachers."

"I just wanted you to know," Jacob said, and walked out.

Pat stood at Douglas's desk.

"Well," she said, and pointed at his eye. "I'm guessing by the look of you that Cherilyn didn't take the news too flipping well."

"Oh," Douglas said. "This old thing?"

"Don't go cracking up on me now, Hubbard," she said. "I sent in your name today."

"But I haven't even talked to Cherilyn about it," he said. "I'm leaning toward turning you down."

"I'm not too worried," she said. "I've been making guesses about people for thirty years. You are what they call a safe bet. Take it as a compliment. That's not the whole reason I'm here, though."

"I'll pay my fine to the curse jar," he said. "Buy yourself a nice hammer."

"Was Trina Todd in your class today?" Pat asked.

Douglas shook his head. "She was a no-show."

"Look," Pat said. "Harold said he saw her coming into school this morning holding some sort of long blue duffel bag. Now, I'm not the type to overreact to things but Harold is, and he said this is on the list of things we are supposed to look out for, in terms of Code Reds and the like."

"Well, she doesn't really fit the profile, does she?" Douglas said. "I mean, she doesn't have testicles."

"Yeah, but I think there might be a bit more to her story than we know about. I've been hearing rumors about what happened that night Toby died. You know, things that went down with her and some of those boys before it happened."

"Shouldn't you be telling Pete about this?" he said. "Or her dad?"

"I will," she said, "but it's not going to be easy. Like I said, men of God are fragile, Hubbard. That's one thing I've noticed. Anyway, I'm telling you all this bric-a-brac because, starting next week, this is likely to be your problem instead of mine. And I hate to even have these conversations. You know, I don't think these kids are really any flipping different than they were when I started. It's just their role models have changed, you know? It's the adults who have changed."

"That's certainly debatable," Douglas said. "But what are you asking me to do, exactly?"

"Just textbook stuff. Be on the lookout for anything suspicious. On the one hand, you'd think this weekend might make the school a high-profile target. That's Harold's take, at least, since everybody will be tromping over here for the opening choir concert tonight and such, but he's sort of a conspiracy guy. On the other hand, though, it wouldn't make much sense to do anything illegal this weekend because we'll have more cops in town than we've likely ever had."

"You know," Douglas said. "You're making this promotion sound less and less appealing."

"Don't I know it," she said.

"On a different subject, let me ask you this," Douglas said. "If I was principal, would I be in charge of the curriculum?"

"Of course," she said, "with certain limitations. We are a Catholic school, you know."

"What if I wanted to start a jazz studies program? Or maybe teach a Jazz History class once in a blue moon. Could I do that?"

"You'd have to take it up with your boss," she said. "Which would be you."

Pat revved up her drill and did a little told-you-so with her eyebrows.

"See, Hubbard?" she said. "God has opened you a door. So, now I'm going to fix your window."

Pat walked to the broken window and removed the piece of plywood Wilson had lodged in there. She took four screws out of either her breast or pants pocket and lined them on the sill.

Douglas heard a knock on the classroom door. It was Pete.

Pat looked back at him.

"Father?" she said. "Don't you have Reconciliation today?"

"I do," Pete said. "I'm just looking for Trina."

Pat returned to the window. She put on her safety goggles and drilled noisily into the frame.

"Well," she yelled. "Join the frippin' club."

19

Never Will Go Out of Fashion, Always Will Look Good on You

For the first time she could recall, nothing in her house would do.

Cherilyn took nearly everything out of her closet and laid it on the bed. She tried dresses and nice blouses and eschewed anything Douglas adored. It struck her as hurtful to wear something he liked to meet Deuce and, aside from that, she didn't want to look like her regular self anyway. She wanted to be impressive. More impressive than she ever had been. If this was to be the picture broadcast to the rest of the town, if it was going to live on forever, she wanted to look her best and now believed, perhaps paradoxically, that the best version of her had likely never been seen. She'd always been too safe. She's always been too Deerfield. This would be her coming-out party, Cherilyn figured, a stunning photo, a way to tell the town who she was without having to say it, maybe even a way to tell Douglas.

It was already past ten o'clock and Cherilyn noticed another thing about her day. She didn't feel too bad. Not nauseated, no headache, no cramping. She felt like she could run a mile if you asked her to. Maybe this little adventure was exactly what she needed. Maybe it was all she needed? So, she took a shower and put on a T-shirt and jeans and got into Douglas's car. She missed her own car and could go for a cigarette about now. She could also go for holding her readouts again, just reminding herself of what they said, that they actually existed, that she wasn't crazy.

She pulled out of her driveway and was soon overwhelmed by the activity on the street. Look at Justin Ashbaugh shooting hoops! And Nan Shepard over there, as well. Now, who would have thought to play tennis in a driveway? *So proud of all my little subjects and their inventiveness*, she thought. *So proud!* She had the urge to roll down her window and say, *It's a new day, people! Frolic! Play! Live!*

Oh, Lord, she thought. *I am going insane.*

Cherilyn got to the end of her neighborhood and passed Ben Shields, who looked to be chain-sawing some sort of a sculpture out of a tree trunk. It was a Shetland pony, maybe, a pot-bellied pig, and isn't that awfully clever, she thought. She then took a right and headed out toward Alice's Costume Shop to see if what Tipsy had told her was true, to see if she might have something for her to wear. And so much bustle on the way! She drove past a work crew hanging a banner that read "Welcome to Deerfield!! Two Hundred Years of Peace and Quiet!!" She passed a group of police parked in a circle at Tony's Donut Shop, all of them standing outside of their cruisers and joking around. One of them held out his arms like he was carrying an enormous and invisible ball, and Cherilyn smiled. She passed through the town square and saw the wooden bleachers, people hammering down signs that pointed to the Crane Lane, and Cherilyn felt like she hadn't been to town in years, although this was obviously not true.

When was the last time she had been out? Besides to her mother's place? It was when she went to Johnson's and got those readouts. That was a sort of fateful day, she now realized, and so maybe the town hadn't changed, but she had. This idea became hard for her to ignore.

"Good gracious," she said, and pulled into the grassy field beside Alice's Costume Shop. The regular lot was jam-packed and now three rows of cars sat in the grass. So, it was all true, the booming business. It was all positive. And good for Alice. The shop itself wasn't much to look at, just a big metal warehouse, really, still the same light blue color it was from when it used to be a tire shop. Today, though, people stood outside of it, sweating like crazy, where Alice had put out a series of racks. Cherilyn got out and walked over the grass lot between two rows of cars, shading her eyes from the sun.

A man stepped in front of her and held out his palm. He said, "Halt, Earthling!"

The man wore a space helmet, the kind with a golden sheen to the mask, and Cherilyn couldn't see who it was. He then pressed a button that flipped open the visor and Cherilyn saw that it was Mel Beacher, a taxidermist she knew from church.

"Let me guess, Mel," Cherilyn said. "You're an astronaut!"

"I will be," he said. "I signed up for space camp over in Huntsville this morning. I had to tell them I was fourteen but I'll just explain it when I get there, I imagine."

"To infinity and beyond," Cherilyn said.

"The final frontier!" he said.

Cherilyn smiled and walked past him and looked at the racks of clothes. There were Confederate general outfits, Union soldier outfits, a uniform for the Harlem Globetrotters. Was that Chewbacca? Two small children scurried out from beneath one of the racks and bumped into her. The girl said sorry and then chased after the boy. She had a stethoscope in her hand.

"I ain't finished yet, Luke!" she yelled.

Cherilyn nodded and said hey to a few people she recognized and they all smiled back at her and this seemed to Cherilyn like maybe the happiest place on earth. When she walked into the shop, it was more of the same. Long rows of clothes and costumes, cases of jewelry, and three women she'd never seen before working a cash register.

She then saw her friend Alice coming up one of the aisles.

"Look who has finally graced us with her presence!" she said. "If it isn't Cherilyn Hubbard."

Alice gave her a tremendous hug. "I am so glad to see you," she said.

Alice was one of the most energetic people Cherilyn had ever known. She had a voice that seemed two octaves too high, as if everything she said was excruciatingly exciting. If you met her only once, you might think she was being sarcastic, such was the volume of her pleasure. But she was not.

"Alice," Cherilyn said. "This place looks incredible."

"I know!" she said. "I bought out two thrift stores in Jackson and one in New Orleans. I said, just send me everything you've got. I can hardly keep anything stocked."

"That's great," Cherilyn said.

"I'm so glad you're here," Alice told her. "I've been waiting for you!"

"You have?"

"I told Marian the other day, just you wait. Cherilyn Hubbard is going to come in here."

Alice called over to one of the girls.

"Marian," she said, "this is Cherilyn. Didn't I tell you, Cherilyn Hubbard is going to come in here with some fantastic readout?"

Marian had three clothespins in her mouth. She took them out and said, "It's true. She did."

"So, cough it up," Alice said. "What is it?"

"I'm just here to browse."

"Stop it," Alice said. "What did it say? Your readout. I'm hoping it said Co-owner of Costume and Crafts Shop. This whole place was really your idea. I haven't forgotten that. I still don't know why you didn't join me."

"It was both our ideas."

"Well, the offer still stands, you know. Fifty-fifty. We'll sell your crafts and my costumes. Hell, you're the one with the talent. I just order shit from other people."

"Thank you," Cherilyn said. "That's not true but thank you."

"So, what *did* it say? What are you just browsing for?"

Cherilyn looked around. "Well, let's see," she said. "Do you have anything sort of, maybe, foreign? Kind of exotic?"

"Oh, God," Alice said, "don't tell me you're a Geisha. I wouldn't believe that for a second. You've always had the men following you, not the other way around."

Cherilyn felt herself blush in front of the other women. They were looking at her in a new way, it seemed, and Cherilyn delighted in the fact that Alice had mentioned her to them. She smiled.

"I don't know what you're talking about," she said.

"Marian," Alice said. "Look at how beautiful this woman is. Look at those gorgeous green eyes. That red hair is her natural color, too! Would you just look at her? And not only is she beautiful and kind, but of course has the most precious husband with this fluffy sort of mustache. Nicest guy you'd ever meet. But she is also so talented. What are you bringing to the bicentennial, anyway? You doing those pens again? I could sell a hundred of those today just by putting them at the register."

"Birdhouses," Cherilyn said. "That's all."

"Well," Alice said. "I bet they are fucking *awesome* birdhouses."

"Actually," Cherilyn said. "I've been thinking about this particular dress. A sort of flowing one with a head scarf."

"That's it!" Alice said. "You're a Genie, aren't you? That would make sense. As long as I've known you, your every wish has come true."

"I don't know about that," Cherilyn said. "I still feel full of un-fulfilled wishes."

"Well, that's good," Alice said, and put her hand on Cherilyn's shoulder. "Because we're not done living yet, are we?"

"No," Cherilyn said. "As a matter of fact, we're not."

Alice took Cherilyn by the hand and led her to the register. "Marian, can you please show Mrs. Hubbard our nicest saris? I have to go tell Mr. Lowry that we are out of stiletto heels and, by the look of him, he's not going to take the news well."

"Come on," Marian said, and led Cherilyn down one of the aisles. "We have something in the back you might like. Are you thinking like full-on headdress or just some sort of scarf?"

"Something that can flow in the wind, is what I'm thinking."

"Are you thinking, like, Princess Diana or Princess Jasmine?"

"Which one is that again?" Cherilyn said.

"Disney," Marian said. "*Aladdin.*"

"Oh, Lord," Cherilyn said. "Would it be weird if I said yes?"

"On the Richter scale of weird I've seen in here the last two weeks, honey," Marian said, "you are barely moving the needle."

Marian led her to a big pile of dresses near the back of the store. They were layered on top of one another, just about every color Cherilyn could imagine. "Take your pick," she said. "Haven't had a chance to hang these up yet. I'll go grab some head scarfs."

"Okay," Cherilyn said. "Thank you."

Cherilyn stared at the pile of clothes and knew, without a doubt, that she would find what she was looking for. She bent down and fingered the fabric and each flowing dress she turned over made her nervous for the next one, such was their delight in her hands. Then, Cherilyn found it.

She stood up and held the dress to her chest. It was red and light with gold trim and draped over the floor. She could feel the cool fabric all over her.

Marian returned with her hands full. "That's gorgeous," she said. "Alice was right. You're beautiful."

"I've never worn anything like this," Cherilyn said.

"Want to try it on? There's a dressing room right back there."

"I do."

"Here," Marian told her. "I got you a scarf." She riffled through the scarves in her hand until she found a red one to match.

Cherilyn took them both and headed toward the dressing room.

"Wait," Marian said. "You want to kick it up a notch?"

"Yes," Cherilyn said, and turned. "I think I do."

Marian smiled.

"Have you ever heard of henna?"

20

Practically Everyone Was There

Listen. Can we get this meeting started?

Is everybody here that is going to be here?

I believe we can. Shoot.

Listen. This is how it goes.

Throwing a party this size is a form of *Art*, Hank. You understand.

Yes, Hank says, he understands, and rubs his temples, which is why they've been planning for a year. It takes more than just a few invites, as Francine Benoit tells him, more than a couple news articles. And, as Leo Blitch points out, you can't just throw up some hot dog stands and think you've done enough. Remember that Little League fiasco in '08? Yes, of course, they all remembered that. Listeria, was it? Food trucks is what Jim Bennett suggests, because they are really hot right now in *real* cities. You can get genuine Mexican tacos, the kind with pork in them instead of ground meat, with corn tortillas instead of flour, real *street* tacos, out of a truck in Charlotte, North Carolina, of all places, and that ain't even close to Mexico. Jim has been to North Carolina and so he knows and is it too late to get some of them for the weekend? There's even a show about them on the Food Network, Betty Retz says, as her way of agreeing. She binge-watches shows like that when she's in one of her moods, she says, and is always open to suggestion if anybody knows any other good shows because she has Netflix now. And Kent Williams says it's telling about the pitiful state of our culture that there is an entire show dedicated to tacos, but it turns out that the show being referred to is about food trucks, not tacos. Rachel Anne checks the minutes and that's right. And that's what we need, Jim says, food trucks, not just tacos, because the young folks from other cities like New Orleans or Jackson might expect something like food trucks and if we aren't even meeting the standards of children, then what the hell are we doing? Hank also wonders, but does not say, this very same thing.

You also need to have good security, Hank. That's true.

People don't have any respect anymore and nowadays you have psychopaths running around with machine guns at Bible schools, just because they are so evil. Not that people shouldn't be allowed to have guns, of course. Don't get Willy Trudeau started on that. You give up your guns and the next thing you know the country might be overrun by some tyrant who doesn't respect the Constitution at all. Well, there might be some irony there, Hester Evans says, but, you're right, let's not get started on that. And don't forget, Celia Starnes points out, that you can get your head chopped off by one of those terrorists, too. That's why it's good to live in a little town like Deerfield that's full of good people who don't go around chopping people's heads off. That's true. A lot of people don't even fly anymore. Did you know that? Ned Herchel won't fly because there is so much beauty to see in the United States. Why would he ever need to go to another country, he wonders, when there is so much America to be explored? But Hank reminds them Sheriff Bates has already called in some extra officers from the parish over, and they've hired one of those security companies that stand around in yellow shirts and smoke cigarettes, so everything will be fine. The whole square will have security and even the school has cops for the concert tonight, not that anyone expects any trouble. And did you know that Phyllis Vernon quit, by the way? Quit what? Smoking. Check the record. Didn't somebody mention cigarettes? She quit? Cold turkey. Who mentioned cigarettes? She's got a whole new attitude. Got herself some fancy bicycle. Well, good for her.

You also need a main event.

A bicentennial is one thing, and something to be proud of, for sure, but even a birthday party has a cake. We will have fireworks. That's true. We will have a parade. That's true. You *have* to have a parade. This is Louisiana, after all. But how do we not have a king and queen, Sarah Centola wants to know. Because it doesn't seem right, does it, Hester Evans reminds her, to put a couple of people above everyone else? This is still a democracy, after all, last time she checked. Some parades invite celebrities. That is true. We don't have the money for that. Plus, something about *that* doesn't seem right, either, does it, Hester Evans points out, to put people who aren't even from Deerfield above those of us who are? That's true, too. And what celebrities are from Deerfield, anyway? None, of course. But have you heard that Britney Spears is opening up a new restaurant? Everybody's talking about it. We will have a live band. That's true. And the kids from the school choir are doing something tonight, don't forget. I hope everyone can go. A lack of programming is not the issue, Hank says. But isn't what everyone is really forgetting, Deuce Newman wants to know, is that they *will* have a main event? We're talking about twelve thousand pictures, here, Deuce reminds them, all forming one image, as big as a wall. He's not sure they understand what all goes into something like that. Plus, the water and light they need to make it really spectacular, which, he points out, will require more help from the mayor than he's been willing to give. And has anyone else noticed that the mayor has been a bit absent lately? How many phone calls have gone unanswered? This week of all weeks, to boot. There's maybe some truth to that, Hank admits, and apologizes, but then reminds them that he is not absent now. Debby Harris would prefer a book to a mosaic, she says, sort of like a yearbook for the whole town. Frank Casiddy tells her what she is thinking about is a newspaper and they already have one of those. But Debby means a nice leather-bound book like they got back in high school. Maybe they could throw them out of the floats along with tossing beads so everyone could get one. The party is tomorrow, Hank reminds her, and many agree, although they don't say so now, that Debby Harris unfailingly offers up the worst ideas at these types of events and so, later, as they summarize the meeting for their friends and families, will say, "Throwing books at people. Can you believe it? That's what she wanted us to do."

You have to allow for some spontaneity. Lord knows.

If you plan everything down to the minute, you can't have any fun. And Jeannie Crisp wonders if she could set up a booth to do palm readings because she recently found out that she would be very good at that. Well, then, she should just register and pay her goddamn fee for the booth like everyone else and she can do whatever she damn well pleases, Ted Crisp tells her. And it is hard to have two divorced people like Jeannie and Ted at the same meeting, many of them think. So many divorces, too. Have they heard about Joe and Barbara? About Donald and Lydia? Yes, but who didn't see that coming? And maybe the deer will show up at Parker Field, Libby Jones suggests, and so people can see how the town got its name. We can at least hope they will, right? We are leaving Parker Field open, Hank reminds them, just in case, but I wouldn't plan on it. Arnie Gilder says they could always just truck some deer in. Says he saw a company on the Internet that does that. Let them loose for a while. And who wouldn't love that, Greg Berdon says, as it would just provide them with more deer come hunting season? And did you see that twelve-point he bagged last year? Mainly deer sausage. A nice roast of the backstrap. Jeannie Crisp says she has a bunch of plastic deer that she *used* to use for Christmas decorations, back when *certain people* still cared about holidays and relationships. And Ted says that they are not putting goddamned Rudolph in the middle of the bicentennial, and this, everyone agrees, although they rarely agreed with Ted and thought he was to blame for everything that happened between he and Jeannie, would not make the town look very good. But, if Jeannie was wanting to get rid of them, Wendy Peterson says her kids would really love something like that and can they text each other later to talk about it?

It also needs to have an ending. A capstone, if you will.

You can't just let people carry on however long they want to. And have you heard that Ben Shields has been doing nothing but making chain-saw sculptures in his front yard the past week? Is that what those are? Yes, and they are terrible. He told Kate Holden he was trying to carve Snoopy out of a tree trunk but she thinks it looks more like a leprechaun than a dog. And Deuce Newman also thinks it needs an ending, that nobody in this goddamn town listens to a damn word he says, and he wishes he could end a lot of things right now, such as this meeting, just to prove them all wrong, and he is so tempted, although he doesn't say this, to show them the blue slip of paper in his breast pocket and be done with it.

21

We Ate Turkeys and Pistols

What to do with the guilty?

Do you divide them from their own bodies? Does $x \div x$ = justice? Was that Trina's math? If so, then why *every single one of them*? Or, does $y \times \infty$ = justice? And justice for what, exactly? His brother driving drunk off the road? His brother being forced to drink, maybe? Being hazed? How many athletes had survived it before? Countless, Jacob knew. It was one of a million idiot high school traditions. And was Toby really one to just do whatever people told him to do? To be that out of control of his own actions? If so, did that mean Jacob was also this way? Was something hardwired in his DNA destined to make him a follower? He was second born and always second fiddle to his brother, it seemed, who was himself perhaps second fiddle to some C-student senior shortstop. How depressing was that? Yet Jacob was also second fiddle to Trina, he knew, and whatever she wanted. So, was this the one true thing about him? The thing people would always remember? Jacob was trying to piece it together. Or, rather, he was trying to pull it all apart, in the same way he was deconstructing the nasty lump of mashed potatoes and gravy on his lunch plate.

He sat at a corner table, alone for now, though the cafeteria was filling up. In the center of the room he saw Chuck Haydel and the dickheads. They joked and pushed against one another and seemed to operate as if the world had no context but themselves. They were loud and fit, their muscles visible beneath their uniform shirts, all of them athletes who lugged around jugs of water as if succumbing to dehydration was the only thing that might upset their future. They seemed to be playing numerous games with one another all at once, two of them laughing at something on a phone, another two rolling a baseball back and forth across the table. They ate ridiculous portions of turkey.

What was it about the sight of them that made Jacob's lungs grow hot? What was it that made him want to render them all empty, to embarrass and dethrone them? Was it merely the way Chuck had knocked off his hat the day before? The way he was so presumptuous, to think he had any right to touch Jacob's body, his clothing? Maybe he *was* guilty of important and invisible things. Maybe they all were. Every single one of them. Maybe Trina was right. What did they *not* feel the authority to touch, to grab, to take? Or was it simply their gluttony in the lunchroom that irked him, the way they got double portions from the servers without even asking, the way they constantly consumed PowerBars, Gatorades, gallons of water, and, on the weekends, liters of booze. Was it the way they acted as if what everyone else received was not enough for them, that they deserved and would take more, and that no one would ever call them on it? And for what reason? Because they were born tall and athletic or that their fathers were born tall and athletic? So much consumption. Taking the food, taking the air in the room. Where, Jacob wondered, did it eventually come back out? In what fashion? To what result?

Or was the reason Jacob could not stop feeling sick at the sight of them, not stop hating them, because he knew that's where Toby would be sitting if he were still alive?

More than this, Jacob wondered, could Toby still be alive if Jacob had chosen to be the type of person to also sit at that table? If he had gone out for football or baseball or been able to either ignore or fight through the crushing boredom that he felt every time he entered a weight room, which seemed one of Toby's favorite places to be, would Toby still be there? Could he have watched out for him that night? Had his back? Driven him home? Couldn't he have done that for his brother? How much was that to ask? They were twins, after all, supposedly bonded more tightly together than anyone else, almost the same person biologically. Had he abandoned his brother?

After so many years of getting the same presents from relatives, so many pictures taken of them wearing the same clothes, was Jacob, he wondered, the one who first pushed himself out? And, if that was true, if he had *chosen* to not be like Toby, the one who seemingly everyone liked, the one with the friends and the girls and the social life, then what lot in life had he chosen for himself? And, if so, how could he trust that person to choose anything for himself again? Where was the line, Jacob wondered, between being independent and being alone? Who draws it for you?

Jacob's head was full of questions with no answers.

Yet he missed Toby at that moment, he had to admit. He believed perhaps Toby could put him at ease about Trina, could laugh it all off in the way he seemed to laugh everything off, and in doing this make Jacob feel less alone. And so, despite their differences, despite the way he despised his friends, Jacob missed him. Whereas he could often feel his brother looking at him from the center table, where they would sometimes make eye contact and give each other the simple recognition of *hello*, of *I see you there*, Jacob now saw only Steven Garrett looking back at him. This was someone both he and Toby were friends with when they were younger, but who had also made his own decisions about who to show allegiance to along the way. When Jacob made eye contact with him now, Steven only pressed his lips together as if to say *I'm sorry* and looked back down at the table. Jacob turned again to his plate, using his fork to make tiny rivulets at the top of his mashed potatoes, and heard a paper sack hit the table beside him.

This was Denny Cadwalder, one of Jacob's few friends, and a person allergic to nearly everything. Peanuts, gluten, eggs. You name it. Jacob had seen him have no less than four unfortunate reactions at school over the years and Denny had now given up on cafeteria food entirely. He seemed to eat nothing but seaweed and gummy bears and sat down at the table across from him.

"Riddle me this, J," he said. "I stayed up all night streaming an entire season of *Pokémon* and I just have one question."

Jacob inwardly cringed at the subject. Although he liked Denny, he also knew that Denny was so blatantly desperate for his friendship that he constructed nearly his entire identity to match Jacob's interests. He'd spent a fortune on Pokémon boxed sets and amassed an even more extensive collection than Jacob's, though not more impressive, Jacob knew, because his binders were full of duplicates Denny was unwilling to trade. He didn't get the spirit of the game and never would, which bothered Jacob. As an example, Jacob had even told Denny about the company in Japan where he got his Latios cap and Denny showed up the next week wearing a purple cap with Meowth on the front, of all monsters. It was not a good look. Still, anyone who would choose to rock out the whiny cat Meowth, when given their choice, deserved pity instead of scorn, and so Jacob humored him. Any conversation, he thought, would be a welcome distraction from Trina.

"Which season?" he asked.

"Sun and Moon," Denny said.

"Okay," Jacob said. "What's your question?"

"I don't get Pikachu, man," Denny said. "I mean, why does Ash keep him around? He loses every battle. It's like the battle starts and Pikachu does some sort of weak-ass Electroblast and then the other Pokémon attacks and Pikachu ends up on the ground with little spirals in his eyes. I get that he's cute with his little 'Pika! Pika!' shit all the time, but it seems like Ash would just realize he's weighing him down."

Jacob stared at Denny.

"Is this a serious question?" he said.

Denny peeled off the top of his plastic tub of seaweed. "It is," he said. "That dude never wins anything."

"Think about the story, Denny," Jacob said. "Ash is a stranger everywhere he goes. He's just a kid, like our age. Pikachu is the only one he can trust. It doesn't matter how powerful he is. Ash will always go to him when he needs help. It's the same reason a lot of great players keep a Pikachu in their deck. It's not really to do damage. It's more about having someone that can help you absorb a blow when you're figuring everything else out."

"All I'm saying," Denny said. "Is that it's highly illogical."

"Says the guy eating dried seaweed crisps from Walmart."

"Anyway," Denny said, and reached into his backpack. "I've decided I'm done with that little yellow fucker." He pulled out a binder full of Pokémon cards and opened it on the table. Two full pages of duplicate Pikachus. "Take them if you want them. I'm offloading them all."

Jacob knew most of the cards were worthless, but immediately saw one he liked. It was what he called a "misfile," and had everything written in Japanese instead of English, though it was sold in America. Jacob loved these cards, as something about the mystery of their translation interested him, the idea that two cards with identical pictures could be saying something entirely different, and he slipped it out of its plastic sleeve.

"Keep it," Denny said.

"You know," Jacob said. "Principal Pat will get rid of all these cards for you if she sees you with them."

"No shit," Denny said. "That's why I have them in here. She's doing locker checks right now. I heard she was just walking down the hall, opening every single one. Not sure what she's spooked about."

"Wait," Jacob said. "She's checking every locker?"

Denny picked a green square from his teeth. "That's the rumor," he said.

Jacob took up his plate and threw his backpack over his shoulder. "I gotta run," he said, and headed out of the cafeteria.

When he got to the school building, it was mostly quiet, with half the kids at lunch and the other half still in class. He was sweating as he approached the main hall, looking in the windows of each classroom to see if Pat was in there, and she was not. When he turned the corner to where his locker was and saw that hall empty as well, he worried that he might be too late. Perhaps she had already opened it? But what would she even find, really? An empty duffel bag? What was he so worried about? He'd tried texting Trina since first period, looked for her in the halls, but to no avail. Maybe she had taken it back out? Maybe it wasn't even there.

Still, Jacob nearly ran to his locker. He quickly dialed in his combination and opened it up and the bag was still there. He grabbed it and stuffed it into his backpack. He had no idea the reason. He thought, *Maybe I can erase myself from this entirely. Maybe I can remove every trace. I can delete all texts. Shred all notes. Throw this bag in the bayou. I can be done with it all.*

He shut the locker and zipped his bag and saw Principal Pat rounding the corner toward him. "Mr. Richieu," she asked him. "Aren't you supposed to be at lunch?"

"I am," he said. "I mean, I was. I'm not feeling very hungry."

"What is it," Pat said, "Turkey day? I don't blame you. I'm afraid this place has ruined me on Thanksgiving."

"Yes, ma'am," he said.

"You sure you're okay? You look like you're sweating."

"I'm not feeling all that great."

Pat looked down at his brother's locker. They both studied the makeshift memorial. After a moment, Pat placed her hand on Jacob's shoulder.

"You know," she said. "I'm realizing now that we probably should have asked how you felt about this, huh? I think people's hearts were in the right place, but we never asked you, did we? I wonder if it makes it harder for you, now, coming to school and seeing this locker done up like a flipping pageant every day."

Jacob looked up at her and felt exactly like he did when Mr. Hubbard singled him out in class. Some sort of searching in their eyes. What did these people want from him? What did everybody want from him? The truth? About what? Where would any sort of truth he had access to begin? Why would they think he would know it?

"It's okay," Jacob said, and looked back at the locker. "I believe I'd be thinking of him either way."

"I bet," she said, and patted him on his arm. "How's your father holding up, by the way?"

"Okay," Jacob said. "Busy."

"I'm sure he is," she said. "So, you haven't seen anything suspicious today, have you? I'm sort of on the lookout for a blue duffel bag."

"No, ma'am," he said, and pressed his backpack against the lockers.

"What about Trina? You two are close, right? Have you heard from her?"

"I haven't seen her today," Jacob said.

"Okay, then," Pat said. "Get better. Don't want to be sick for the big weekend."

"I'll be fine," Jacob said, and stood there as Pat walked down the hall jangling her keys.

Jacob was struck, not only by her mention of the blue duffel bag, but by her question about Toby's locker. It was true. Why had nobody asked him how he might feel? Had they even considered it? He looked at the cards taped across the locker and had a terrible realization. He and Toby used the same passwords for everything: their lockers, their phones. It was their four-digit birth date, the month and the year.

He wondered if Trina knew this, too, if that was how she got into his locker earlier, and Jacob checked up and down the empty hall. He then leaned over and dialed in the code to Toby's locker. He lifted the latch and opened the door.

Inside the locker sat an envelope with a single rock placed on top of it.

This was not good.

Jacob knelt down and examined the items as if they could be booby-trapped, somehow, connected to invisible trip wires or lasers. The idea was ludicrous. Still, the awful experience of seeing himself on video remained fresh enough to make him question everything, and so he was careful as he reached into the locker and pocketed the small rock and envelope.

He then walked quickly to the bathroom and locked himself in a stall. He pulled out the rock and ran his thumb over it. It was thin and flat and beige as gravel, with only the thinnest veins of color running through it. It had the oval shape of a skipping rock. He put it back in his pocket and pulled out the envelope.

This item was also nondescript and plain white, the flap tucked in instead of sealed. Jacob unfolded the flap with his finger and looked inside. He reached in and pulled out a single slip of blue paper.

This paper was meant to look like a DNAMIX reading, he could tell, but it was not. Jacob had seen enough of these to know, and he'd held Rusty's just that morning. This one, however, was fashioned out of a different material and appeared homemade. It felt as thick as construction paper and, when Jacob turned it over, he saw that it was written by hand and not by a printer. All capital letters, very small and neat, that read:

Jacob Richieu
Potential Life Station
Toby Richieu

22

You Forgive Us and We'll Forgive You

Look. I've read about bees, Father. And you know all those bees are dying because of cell phone towers or satellites or something like that and it turns out that we need bees just to live because they pollinate everything. It's not just about the honey, is what I'm saying, although that's important, too. Anyway, we're redoing our porch. The whole house needs an upgrade, really, but we're starting there. So, I knocked down this column on the porch and there was this beehive in there, Father. You wouldn't believe it. It was bigger than anything you've seen on TV, I imagine. And my wife is allergic to bees, you see. And she was off at work and I didn't want her to come home and see them because Lord knows what kind of fit she'd throw. We'd probably end up living at her sister's place. And no telling how long they've been there, too, you know, without us even knowing. But it sort of floored me, Father. I mean, I just watched them crawling over one another. I just watched them forever. And I thought about all that stuff I'd read. I thought about how sort of beautiful it all is, the whole shebang. How we're all connected together. About how something little like a bee ends up putting food on my plate and lets me and my family live but, not only that, how they depend on other little things like flowers to do it, too. How there is this whole grand design to the deal where nothing's wasted. But I also thought about my wife, you know, and how I told her I'd get this porch redone, how I could handle it and we didn't need to hire nobody to charge us three times what I could do it for. And so, I guess what I'm telling you, Father, is that I gassed them. I killed them all. It's not sitting well with me. So many of them, Father. After the gas. They just kept falling.

Forgive me, Father, but I don't really have much to confess. I'm only fifteen and I don't have a car and I'm at school most of the day and I do my homework at night and I don't get out much on the weekends so I don't have that many opportunities to commit any really spectacular sins. Anyway, I got this readout saying I am supposed to be a priest, too. I'm not all that psyched about it, but my parents are. I just sort of figured, well, that's typical. Of course that's what mine would say. I'll be a virgin forever. Anyway, they wanted me to ask you, like, how does that happen? Is there some sort of school you go to? What's the pay like? Any health benefits?

Look, Father, this ain't easy to talk about. But I go to a lot of websites, you understand. Websites for *adults*. They've got all sorts of stuff out there, I'm telling you. American ones and European ones and Mexican ones. A lot of stuff out of Prague, it seems. I mean, I feel like I've visited most of Prague at this point. And I'm married, you know, and so I steer clear of all that stuff that's trying to get you to meet up with local women and the like. I don't mess with all those horny-local-MILF-type things. I mean, I have boundaries. I just look at those ones with videos of people I'll never meet. It's all on the up and up, is what I'm saying. I don't do anything wrong. There's nothing illegal about it, is what I'm saying. But what I'm trying to communicate here is that I go to these websites *a lot*. Hell, you can get them on your phone if you want. Now, I don't really want to put a number on how many times I've gone to these various sites but I'd be willing to bet that it is pretty surprising. I'll be at work sometimes. Or I'll go into the kitchen when my wife's asleep. Anytime she leaves me alone at the house, really. And I think it's been a good thing, in the big picture. I think it's helped me to stay faithful, you know, to be able to sort of relieve myself when I need to. Because God knows my wife doesn't always want to stop her life every time I get a notion, and I understand that. I'm not mad about it. I probably wouldn't want to sleep with me, either. So, it's not about her at all, really. The problem, though, is that I'm forty-eight years old and I've been doing this awhile and I think I've finally seen every single video out there that interests me. I'll just go from site to site now, sort of aimless, and there isn't anything I haven't already clicked on. I can't find anything I like that I haven't already seen, is what I'm saying. It's all just the same body parts over and over doing the same up-and-down motions and it makes me sort of scared, Father. Does that make sense? I guess it's got me thinking: Well, now what?

Forgive me, Father, but I don't know how much I should say. I mean, there are definitely some things that went down a few months ago with the team that nobody is really talking about. Some pretty terrible things that I saw and was sort of involved in, I guess, but I didn't think it would go that far. They were like, I guess, we, were sort of like animals now that I think about it. It started off fun enough, but you could tell that she, I don't know. I feel terrible about it, honestly. And then he died that night, though, so everybody was kind of distracted for a while, I guess. But it keeps coming back to me. I'm sort of worried that she'll try to get us back, somehow. No. No. I'm not like filing any report or anything. I thought this was a sort of safe space. No. I don't want to give any specifics. I mean, I think, at some level, it's probably a legal matter. That's why I can't say too much. We took a sort of oath. But I guess what I'm really wanting to ask you about is forgiveness, Father. For a person who did something. Is that a real thing?

Forgive me, Father, for I have committed the sin of lying. I have faked no less than fourteen orgasms with my boyfriend since my last confession. But, you know, that was a while ago so I'm not sure if that's a lot or, maybe, like, right in the middle.

Forgive me, Father, but I got this readout. Just the other day, and do you know what it said? I'm sorry, I don't mean to cry. But do you know what it said? It said Ballerina, Father. Ballerina! Just when I'd almost forgotten. I'm sorry. It's just that when I was a little girl and all through high school, if you only knew how hard I worked. How hard I trained. The money my parents spent. I guess it just reminded me. I'm sorry. I'll stop. I promise. But I guess it just reminded me, you know, of how I never wanted children. We were so young and stupid and this has never been my life, really. I'm sorry, Father. But all of these years, you know? So many years. My own children. It made me remember. I've never wanted them.

Forgive me, Father. I skipped in line. I'm in a rush. Anyway, I heard a rumor that Principal Pat is retiring. Is that true? If so, you have *got* to talk her out of it. It's the middle of the semester, for goodness' sake. The kids have PSATs coming up and district playoffs and the silent auction and the prom. And as a volunteer member, and I should stress *volunteer* member, of the DCH Mother's Club, I've got to tell you that we just can't handle any more work. We've already been worked to death with this bicentennial business. And so you just need to tell her please, if you will, to cool her jets. She just needs to wait until the end of the term, is all. Thank you. I should also mention that I now have thirty-three thousand dollars in credit card debt. No. No. He still doesn't know about it.

Forgive me, Father, but I am ridiculously hungover. What makes it worse, of course, is that I got drunk with a priest last night. Now, I've always heard the Catholic church was pretty loosey-goosey when it came to alcohol, but you should have seen the shots this guy put away. I mean, *yowza*. Do they teach that in seminary, Father? Me and the mayor couldn't hardly keep up with him. Yes, he was corrupting our town mayor, too, if you can believe it. But this priest was pretty good at telling jokes, I have to admit, and seems like a nice person, so it was a good time. But, anyway, this priest, maybe you know him, he had to hitch a ride home, he'd had so many. He didn't even have his truck there, now that I think about it. Maybe we drank it? I'm not sure. Anyway, I'm just realizing, Father, that it was rude of me to not offer him a ride to school when Tipsy dropped me off. We were going to the same place, after all, but I was just so hungover and sort of lost in my thoughts that I didn't even consider it. It was rude and I apologize. But, anyway, it's three-fifteen now, Father. It's quitting time. And I guess what I'm wondering is: Do you need a ride somewhere?

23

The Yield Went Around,
and Around, and Around

After Confession, the men hatched a plan.

Douglas would drive Pete over to Geoffrey's place so he could make his lesson at four o'clock. Then Pete could take Douglas's car, which was, of course, actually Cherilyn's car, out to Lanny's to check on Trina, who they'd never found at school. He could be back in an hour, Pete told him, no problem. It was just something he needed to do.

"You ever get one bad feeling about something?" Pete asked him. "And then you look around and it seems like there's just bad feelings all around you? Like they're multiplying?"

"I get that feeling every time my seventh period Civics class walks into the room."

"Look," Pete said. "I've been sitting in the booth all day so, you know, I'm sort of in the mood to confess something myself. After the bar last night, when Tipsy was driving us home, when you were whistling, which was beautiful, by the way, I think I saw Trina outside somebody's house. I saw her crawling through a window."

"You think she's got a boyfriend?"

"No, it didn't look like that. I'm afraid she might have been robbing the place."

"Uh-oh," Douglas said, and hit his brake. They'd reached a four-way stop outside of the square and the traffic was at a standstill. He'd never seen so many cars in Deerfield, delivery trucks and pickups loaded with tent poles and folding chairs, and, as he sat there, Douglas realized that he couldn't wait for this whole thing to be over. He looked at the car to his right and saw the person in it look to their right, and that person look to theirs, not merely out of politeness, as it might have on any previous day in Deerfield, but rather because none of the cars had anywhere to go. Deerfield, it seemed, was completely full.

"I just want to go see her, is all," Pete said. "I just want to talk to her."

"You sure?" Douglas said. "Shouldn't this be more of a police matter? Or maybe something for you to tell Lanny about?"

"I know," Pete said. "I just want to give her a chance to explain first. She doesn't have many people in her corner, including her dad. He's in his own corner, I believe."

Douglas finally got a chance to pull up and then immediately stopped again on the other side of the intersection. "Oh, Jesus," he said, and then regretted it, realizing he'd lackadaisically broken one of the Ten Commandments right there in front of a priest.

Pete didn't mention it, though, and the reason for this was soon obvious. He was looking out of the window and trying not to cry in the passenger seat. Douglas could feel it. There was a different energy in the car now, a sort of dark electricity. When Pete finally did speak, he had to clear his throat first and had a little hitch in his voice. "I don't know," he said. "I mean, I read these things about her on the restroom walls and it hurts." He pressed his fingers to his eyes.

Douglas cut a right and went through a parking lot to break free of the traffic. He looked over at Pete and then back to the road. "I understand," Douglas said, but what he meant by this was that he understood that Pete was crying over there now, and that the thing one man does when another is crying is to sort of open space for them, to not interrupt, to not offer any advice. To watch a man cry in front of another is a rare thing, like seeing the place where lightning begins, and it doesn't need comment.

"I'm sorry," Pete said, and took a sharp breath through his nose. "But Reconciliation weighs on me. It always has. Especially with these kids. It's like I hear their voices in there one week and they're a kid and the next week they've done something and suddenly they're a grown-up. It happens so fast and I can *hear* it. It makes me sad. I feel like we had this whole stretch of sort of in-between time when we were coming up, you know? And now I hear it in their voices so quickly. It's regret, I guess. These kids do something they regret and then it's over. Boom. All of a sudden, they're just like the rest of us."

Douglas drove without speaking as the two of them, although they did not acknowledge it, began to do what many men do when presented with enormous and unsolvable problems. They tried to solve them. What would they do if they were parents? they wondered. How would they fix this issue? Maybe they could be stern, or honest, or maybe give their kids a little more understanding, a little more forgiveness. Whatever they did would work. Or else, of course, it would fail. Those were the odds of good intentions.

"I sometimes think that my being a teacher would help," Douglas said. "Being around kids so much. It would help me understand them. But, in some ways, I think it does the opposite."

Pete breathed in through his nose. He straightened his posture in the car as if trying to change the subject. "Did y'all not ever want kids?" he asked. "You and Cherilyn."

"No, we did," Douglas said. "Tried for a few years. Got tested and everything checked out. My boys can swim, as they say, and everything is in working order for her, as well. But then you reach that point where it's either spend all your life savings chasing after it, sort of make your whole life about it, or else you let it go."

"Some things aren't that easy to let go of," Pete said.

"I know," Douglas said. "We saw couples like that at the doctor, doing all these treatments, young couples like we were then, giving each other shots and making all sorts of schedules and we saw the fear in their eyes when it wasn't working. It was like you could see them thinking, Why am I even with this person? I know Cherilyn would be a great mother. She's the kindest person I know. But I never wanted us to be like that, planning everything around some dream that may never come true. Always thinking of what we don't have instead of what we do."

"You know what they say," Pete said. "There's only one way to make God laugh."

"What's that?" Douglas asked.

"Make a plan," Pete said.

Douglas smiled at the saying, but this idea immediately made him consider his own plan from that morning. Sitting Cherilyn down to destroy her newfound desire. Is that really what he wanted to do? What kind of person would that make him? he wondered. Would he still be a husband, or even a friend, if that was his tactic? Or would that make him, too, like Trina, some sort of thief? He turned on to Willow Street and headed toward Geoffrey's.

"What about you?" Douglas asked. "I'm assuming you never wanted any since you're not allowed to, you know."

Pete looked at him.

"Not allowed to what?" he said. "Do the hokeypokey?"

"I was going to say 'marry.'"

"Well," Pete said. "I was married. A long time ago. Before seminary."

"Did I know that?"

Pete smiled. "I don't know," he said. "It's not really something I broadcast."

Douglas thought of the possibilities of a once-married man becoming a priest and none of the ways through which this could happen were good. He had a feeling that a priest couldn't be divorced, and that knowledge limited the unfortunate options to one.

"I'm sorry," Douglas said. "I didn't know."

"That's the reason I got into this business, to be honest with you," he said. "If I can be honest with you."

"Would you prefer I put a little screen up between us?" Douglas asked. "Make you feel more at home?"

"No," Pete said. "I'm good. It's just that we thought she was pregnant. I don't tell many people this, but we wanted to have kids, too, you know. And we thought she was. She was gaining weight and all, and we were excited. But it turned out it wasn't a baby. The whole thing happened pretty fast after that."

"Jesus," Douglas said.

Pete looked over at him. "That was my thought, too," he said. "It was either Jesus all the way or become the type of person I couldn't recover from."

"Can I ask her name?" Douglas said.

"Anna," Pete said, and leaned his back on the seat. "Her name is Anna."

"Okay," Douglas said.

"Anna," Pete said again.

"Anna," Douglas said, and was overcome with a feeling of respect for Pete at that moment. It was a feeling he did not know the reason for. Was it his faith? His honesty? His choice to do something positive in the wake of a horror that Douglas could not even bring himself to consider: the loss of Cherilyn. What would it do to him? He already felt like an emotional train wreck and he and Cherilyn hadn't even spoken about their readouts. They'd not even had an argument. How could Pete survive something like Anna's death? The idea awed him.

They drove in silence until they pulled into Geoffrey's apartment complex. "You know," Douglas said. "The more I talk to you, the more I realize I have like a thousand different questions to ask a priest. I mean, not like spiritual questions, although I have some of those, too, but more like day-to-day questions."

"Anytime," Pete said. "Shoot."

"Okay," Douglas said. "For starters, does the collar hurt? Is it kind of like a necktie? I can't stand to wear a tie."

"Nah," Pete said. "I forget it's there sometimes."

"Okay, then. Since you do Mass so often, do you ever just, like, totally space out and forget what passage you're reading?"

"No," Pete said. "It's the Holy Sacraments. I consider it pretty important to stay tuned in."

"Fair enough," Douglas said. "So, what about God? Does He ever talk directly to you? Like, do you have some sort of special link?"

"Yes," Pete said. "But it's probably not any different than the way He speaks directly to you."

Douglas parked.

"Last one," he said. "My favorite part of Mass, ever since I was a kid, is when the priest holds up the wafers."

Pete smiled. "The Body of Christ?" he said.

"Yes, sorry. When he holds up the Body of Christ and the bells are ringing and he sort of sings that line, 'The myssssterrryyyy offfff faaiiiiitthhhhh.'"

"Yep," Pete said. "That's a good one."

"The priest before you did it differently, you know. His was sort of low and yours is sort of wistful, which I prefer. I love the way you do it, actually. It's like this little one-line song I find myself whistling sometimes. And so, my question is: Can a priest just sort of decide how they want to do that? I mean, is that something you practice?"

Pete smiled again. "Maybe," he said.

Douglas looked at him. "So, all over the world, there are, like, hundreds of up-and-coming priests just standing in front of the mirror and singing? There's like this whole choir of them practicing, all alone, 'the mystery of faith'?"

"That's a nice way to think of it," Pete said. "You want to hear it?"

"Yes, I do."

"Try it with me," he said.

Pete pulled down the visor of the Outback and flipped open the mirror. "It feels good," he said.

And so Douglas did the same, pulling down the visor of his wife's car to take a look at himself. And then the two of them, together, in the parking lot of the Scenic Wetlands Apartments and Balconies complex, sang, "The myssssterrrrrryyy off faiiiiith."

24

We'll Record It Live, That's No Jive

Douglas heard them before he was halfway up the stairs.

It sounded like "In the Mood" or "Sing Sing Sing" or maybe something by Basie or Miller. Some steady and low percussion, a jazzy guitar riff, a horn keeping the flavor on simmer. The sound already, Douglas knew, within the first few seconds, had a chance of turning his day completely around. Such is the power of ears.

Yet it was not a record or even the radio. The sound was too hairy and live. Douglas checked his watch to see that he was on time and wondered if maybe Geoffrey had taken on some new students. This was better than the nightmare scenario Douglas worried about the night before, in which Geoffrey would move off to Las Vegas to pull rabbits out of hats, his fear that there wouldn't be anybody at his apartment at all when he showed up today. He looked back over the railing and watched Pete pull off in Cherilyn's Outback. He then straightened his beret and knocked on the door.

The music didn't stop. Douglas knocked again.

Before he could reach the handle and try it himself, the door opened on its own.

Geoffrey stood in the middle of the room, on top of his coffee table. He wore the top hat from yesterday and a T-shirt and jeans.

He danced in small perfect steps to the beat all around him, much clearer now through the open door, just one foot forward, one foot back. He looked to be living completely within the pocket of the song and smiled. He then took off his hat and twirled it in his hands. He opened his arms as if to say, *Welcome home, Hubs.*

Douglas entered the room to see four other musicians in a circle around him. Geoffrey hopped down from the table and shook Douglas's hand. He turned to the band as they continued to play and said, "What did I tell y'all? This man is always on time."

Geoffrey then held up Douglas's watch, which he had somehow slipped off his wrist without Douglas noticing. He dangled it in the air like evidence.

"Hey," Douglas said. "How'd you do that?"

"Some magic," Geoffrey told him, "is born out of necessity." He tossed him back the watch and said, "Come on in, man."

Douglas closed the door behind him and put his trombone case down on the floor. The beat stayed in its low holding pattern and the musicians said nothing to him. "Hubs, meet the Bedknobs and Broomsticks," Geoffrey told him. "This is my old set. They're playing center stage tomorrow at the bicentennial. I invited them over."

Douglas nodded at each of them, but they didn't stop playing. It was a low beat, three-quarter time, Douglas figured, and the group looked more as if they were merely practicing their instruments together in the same room rather than playing any rehearsed song. It felt as though they were waiting, maybe, or hoping, for a signal to come back together.

"Bedknobs and Broomsticks?" Douglas said. "Like the kids' movie?"

The drummer looked up. He had a deep raspy voice, from somewhere south even of Deerfield, and said, "We started out as the Isle of Na-Boom-Boom. It just kind of evolved from there."

Douglas scanned the place. The best he could figure, some be-
neficent creature had replaced the small apartment he was in yesterday with a version of heaven. The music kept its low net and the
drummer, now that Douglas studied him, appeared to be blind. He
held the snare between his legs and worked it over with brushes.
He twitched his head to the side as if trying to shake some water
out of his ear and it was, undoubtedly, one of the coolest things
Douglas had ever seen.

To his left, the upright bass player stood at least six feet four.
She was skinny as a light pole and wore a flannel shirt with no
sleeves. Her arms were covered in tattoos of Asian peacocks, and in
her breast pocket, Douglas noticed, she had a fancy boxlike vapor-
izer, similar to one he had once confiscated from a student. She
kept plucking around a bouncy walking beat, looking down at her
fingers as if to see what they might do next.

The guitarist sat across the room in an armchair, sixty years
old if a day, and wore a weathered fedora that Douglas felt immediately jealous of. He slid his hand up and down the neck of a big
hollow-bodied Gretsch, the guitar plugged into an amp no bigger
than a coffeepot at his feet. It was all barre chords, his movements
as light and graceful as if he wasn't touching the strings at all. He
looked up at Douglas and nodded.

To Douglas's right, a saxophonist stood without playing a note.
He had his eyes closed and a long black ponytail down his back
and fingered the pearl buttons of his horn. Douglas could hear the
light clacking of the valves and knew the man was soloing in his
head. The look of concentration on his face, his lips on the mouthpiece without air, the way his eyebrows shot up as if he was somehow surprising himself. Douglas could tell that this man was
tearing it up in his mind.

Douglas looked back at Geoffrey and imagined this is what

doing hard drugs must feel like on your first go-round. It was an unexpected bliss.

"Should I not be here?" Douglas said.

"Are you kidding?" Geoffrey said. "This is for you, Hubs. I told them what you were up to. Now put together that horn and let's jam."

Douglas opened his case and nervously put together his trombone as the music seemed to get a tick louder, grow a notch tighter in the room. "Now, listen," Geoffrey said. "You remember what I taught you yesterday?"

"This is 'Seventy-six Trombones'?" Douglas said.

"You can call it whatever you want to," Geoffrey said. "I'm talking about that first note I showed you. Down low. Lips together, hard blow from your stomach."

Douglas set the trombone on his shoulder and blew. The note was off, he could tell, but nobody even looked at him. They just kept playing.

"Harder now," Geoffrey said, and picked up his wand off the table. He tapped it against his own belly. "It's got to come from here. You ain't no church mouse. This ain't no faculty meeting."

Douglas took in a deep breath and blew it again and there it was.

"That's it!" Geoffrey said. "That's the only thing you need to play, okay?" He twirled the wand in his hands. "Every time I point at you, hit that note. You're going to slide right in."

Douglas took a deep breath and put the horn to his mouth. He could feel the band coming back together now, returning from all their private journeys. The drummer looked up at the ceiling as Geoffrey went back to his simple dancing, as if conducting them all with his feet. He turned in a little circle, giving Douglas time to feel the beat, and he *did* feel it. It was coming around to him. He tightened his grip on the horn and, sure enough, right when he anticipated it, Geoffrey spun and pointed his wand and Douglas blew.

By God, it sounded good.

Geoffrey made no comment and did no further coaching but simply let it come around again. He pointed his wand and *bomp*, there was Douglas, ready and waiting for it. Douglas could feel it now, the whole design. He would be the low note. All he had to do was be steady and dependable and his horn would become the tree the rest of them could branch out from. Douglas felt he had this under control, that he could play this note on this beat into a song that never ends.

He began to bounce on his heels and his dress shoes thumped the linoleum floor of the apartment to become just another aspect of their obvious rhythm. *Bomp*. He hit it again. And once he had established that he was reliable, Geoffrey stopped pointing at him. He instead leaned over a deck of cards on the coffee table and waved his hands over them in time with the music. *Bomp* to *tat-tat*, *bomp* to *tat-tat*, and the beat became more like fact than a sound. As it did this, Douglas watched the top card of the deck begin to move. The rhythm picked up as Geoffrey danced and the card lifted invisibly off the top of the deck as if pulled by a string. It hovered in the air beneath Geoffrey's hand and Douglas hit the note again. He felt as though he wanted to cry.

Geoffrey then clapped on the downbeat, the card fell back to the table, and the saxophone leapt into its solo like a sound they'd all been waiting on.

Douglas could not describe the joy that broke over him upon hearing his partnered horn, as it is a joy reserved for musicians. The sound of the sax filled the room like foreign bells and each musician looked up from their instrument, even if they could not see, to watch him play the very thing he had been dreaming of.

Geoffrey tapped his wand on the table and pointed at Douglas, "Okay, now," he said. "Your turn."

Douglas bugged out his eyes as if to say *Please, no*, and hit his low note again.

"Not with that," Geoffrey said, and pointed to his own lips. "With that."

Douglas looked disappointed. He lowered the trombone.

"Whistle?" he said. "I don't know."

"I told them about you," Geoffrey said, as the band kept on. "That's what they want to hear. But not Charlie Parker's 'Summertime.' Do your own thing. Just let it go where it goes."

That this was the easiest request Douglas could imagine fulfilling surprised even him. Ever since he had stepped foot on the stairs outside and first heard the beat, as soon as he'd entered the room, he'd had whistled scales of possibility running up and down his mind. He did not know the names for these scales nor where they even sprung from in his imagination, but he had them. He could do this with his eyes closed. And so that is what he did.

Douglas shut his eyes and whistled a note, low and punctual like he had done on the trombone, just to let them know he was there. The sax wound down its solo and Douglas hit that low note again, but this time he added two quick taps a bit higher, a little something on top, like he was knocking on the door.

The sax went up a scale to lay out the red carpet and Geoffrey reached over and took the trombone from Douglas's hand. Douglas opened his eyes and smiled. He hit that low note again and wet his lips. He heard the guitar player add a quick double hitch to his strumming, as if keying everyone into what was about to happen, and watched Geoffrey lift the trombone to his own shoulder. He gave Douglas a wink, readied himself to blow, and said, "Let's do this," and, all together, they did.

Douglas came in high and wailing and picked up that same dream the sax was unspooling. The band jumped a chord to match him and Geoffrey took over that backbone, playing with skill that the moment afforded. Douglas hit all his notes on command, contorting his face and bobbing up and down on his toes, and when he went down low, so low as to blat like a baritone sax, his tongue trilling inside of his mouth as he whistled, the drummer, who was not even looking his direction, yelled, "Yeah!"

Douglas dipped in and out of standards. He called up little pieces of "Basin Street Blues" and "Swing Time" and then finished with a flurry of his own, until, just at the moment he was nearly out of breath, Geoffrey lifted his trombone and took his own turn playing lead.

The song went another three minutes, a graceful eternity, as Douglas snapped his fingers and played the backbone again with his whistle. He danced in place, the music all over him, until his phone went off in his pocket.

Douglas pulled it out and, just like that, the song ended in a final rim shot.

"Well, holy shit," the bassist said. "The man can blow."

Douglas smiled as they congratulated him and saw that the call was from Cherilyn's mother's house. This also delighted him. He could not remember the last time he felt so good and, like any person in love, wanted to share this feeling with Cherilyn. He held up his phone and said, "One second," and stepped out of the door onto the walkway.

Douglas grinned as he heard the bassist start up a new beat inside and whistled a little accompaniment while he accepted the call on his phone.

"Is this my lovely lady calling?" he said. "My cat's meow? My butternut squash?"

"Douglas?" she said. It was Cherilyn.

"What's happening on the flip side?" Douglas said. "What's jiving out there in the crazy old world?"

"Why are you talking like that?" she said.

"I'm at Geoffrey's," he said. "There's musicians here. I've been jamming. You wouldn't believe it."

"With Geoffrey?" she said. "Well, maybe I shouldn't believe it."

Douglas was barely listening. He felt pulled back to the beat and began whistling into the phone, a little melody over the bass player on the other side of the door. He hoped Cherilyn could hear it with him, could join in this fun.

"What are you doing?" she said.

"I'm whistling," he said.

"Well," Cherilyn said. "Can you please stop?"

So, Douglas did.

With that simple phrase, it was as if his worried world had doubled. Had she ever asked him that question before?

"Look," she said. "I know we were supposed to talk tonight, but I might be a little late."

Douglas didn't say anything in return.

"I'm at my mom's," she said.

"Okay," he said. "Is everything all right? You need me to come over?"

"No," she said. "You have fun. I just didn't want you to wait on me."

"Will you be home for supper?" he said. "I've got the strangest craving for eggplant."

"I'm not sure," she said.

"Everything okay?" he said. "You sound weird."

"Well, maybe I *am* weird, Douglas," she said. "Maybe you could consider that."

"I don't understand," he said. "What's going on?"

"Just don't wait on me," she said. "I'll heat something up when I get there."

Cherilyn hung up the phone and Douglas put it back in his pocket. Whatever was happening, he knew, was not good.

Before he could think too much about it, he looked down to see a kid standing on the walkway beside him. She was maybe ten years old. She held out a blue slip of paper.

"I live downstairs," she said. "My mom told me maybe I should come up here."

The paper read **SCOUT**.

25

Got the Windows Rolled Up,
but My Mind's Rolled Down

Pete had to admit, the Outback could handle.

He'd not gotten it over twenty-five miles per hour since he left the Scenic Wetlands Apartments and Balconies but he'd taken a few sharp turns. Well, three sharp turns, if he were to be honest, and one dicey maneuver.

The maneuver was a quick zigzag right out of the gate. As soon as he left Geoffrey's place he had to cut left to avoid hitting a squirrel and then cut back right when he saw the squirrel was being chased by a dog. Pete didn't particularly want to annihilate any of God's creatures with an automobile but he might have lost his heart completely, such was its current state, if he'd hit a dog. So, he went for a sort of *Jesus take the wheel* moment and closed his eyes and grimaced, inexplicably hit the gas instead of the brake, and felt the car react as if it, too, were a type of animal. It pounced ahead as soon as he goosed it, the tires gripping the road and handling the quick turns as if they had claws. When Pete opened his eyes, he crossed himself and said a quick prayer. He'd not heard or felt anything hit the car and when he looked in the rearview mirror saw the squirrel on one side of the road, skittering up a chain-link fence and into a pine tree and the dog on the other side, scratching at his ear as if unable to remember what he was doing there by the road anyway.

Pete's first sharp turn in the Outback came shortly after this, when he saw how backed up Maycomb Street was and cut a quick left to try out a shortcut. The tension in the steering column was a small revelation in how tightly bound it seemed, how intentional, as if you could drive this thing through the different rooms of a house, it was so nimble. He'd not driven anything but his truck for the last twenty years, he'd realized, and the steering in it was so loose you had to make a couple revolutions of the wheel before the front end changed its mind. In it, he felt more like a riverboat captain than a driver.

He'd had that truck since Anna, had held on to it since Anna, or *because* of Anna, you could probably say, and Pete couldn't deny that she was still all over his mind since he'd mentioned her to Douglas. He was grateful to be reminded of her. When was the last time he had spoken her name to someone else? It had been too long, he realized, as bringing her up to Douglas felt to Pete like Confession. And what was his reason for telling?

Douglas hadn't asked him directly about her or even his past, really, but had merely brought up the idea of children, and Anna came spilling out of him. More than just her but the sense of what could have been with her, potentially with the three of them, of what *should* have been, Pete often felt. Yet the way he kept this feeling of injustice inside of him and bent it to the shape of his faith assured Pete that it was something that *had* to be and, in many ways, had always been, so that he could be the person he now was. The idea that she had perhaps died so that he could help others remember how lucky they were through God, through even the idea of God, and how lucky *he* had been to once know Anna and to touch her, to feel the love of a physical person, to feel their hands, their tight and grateful hugs. He had to remember this, he felt, in order to get back to her.

Plus he was glad Douglas was the person he'd shared this with. Pete had the sneaking suspicion that he had made, in the last twenty-four hours, a new friend. This was not as common an occurrence as he would like it to be, as it does not take any priest long to find out they are not first on the guest list to the best parties in town. He had other things he wanted to say to Douglas, as well, he now realized, about how much he admired him. How much he admired his marriage, his honesty in Confession, and the way he sort of wore his love. What was it about this obvious affection? Pete did not exactly know but wanted only to tell Douglas that he admired him. Men did not often tell one another such things, Pete thought, and this was one of the dumbest habits of men.

The second sharp turn in the Outback was genius, if a bit sneaky. Pete thought of a way to cut through a back alley behind a row of houses to avoid the traffic and he wasn't normally one to disobey the law in this way. The alley wasn't paved, was not really meant for cars, but Pete knew he didn't have much time. Douglas had given him an hour and it was twenty minutes each way to Lanny's on a normal day.

The Outback didn't seem to mind. It cruised over the grass and root beds as if it long expected this time would come, its tires bouncing up and down on the shocks like pistons and not disturbing the cabin at all. You could have sipped a cup of coffee without spilling a drop if you wanted and Pete made a note to mention to Douglas just what an impressive automobile this was. And then, after only two minutes in the alley, Pete was already pulling into the back parking lot of Johnson's Grocery. If he could just whip around the front of the store and out the other side, he would have successfully bypassed nearly all the downtown traffic and could cut up 61 toward Lanny's.

The third sharp turn came unexpectedly, though, even to him, as he pulled the Outback into a parking spot. Pete had an idea.

He turned off the car and hopped out and checked his back pocket for his wallet. He wanted to bring Trina a present. Not a bribe, really, just a peace offering before asking her to sit down and have a talk with him. Or, better, before sitting himself down to have a listen.

Several people nodded to him as he walked toward the store. So many, in fact, that he got the sensation he was going in through the out door. He walked inside and headed straight for the customer service desk. Nobody else was in line so he went right to the counter to see Cal Johnson, the guy who owned the place, restocking the spools of lottery tickets.

Cal looked at him over his eyeglasses. He was an old-timer, eighty or so, but was healthy and kind and would likely work that place until he or it disintegrated.

"Pete," he said. "I'm sorry to be the bearer of bad news but that old girl is out of order."

Pete smiled. "Who's that?" he asked.

Cal ticked his head to the side where Pete saw the big DNA-MIX machine hung with a sign that said that exact thing: "Out of Order."

"Believe it or not," Pete said. "I have an even stranger request. I'm wondering if you sell Benson and Hedges cigarettes. You know, the skinny kind."

Cal took off his glasses and leaned on the counter. "We do," he said, "but I have to admit, Father. I never took you for a smoker."

"They're not for me," he said. "I'm picking them up for a friend."

"I didn't mean to pry," Cal said, and turned to grab a pack. "Lord knows if I started judging people for everything they bought in here I'd have gone out of business and into depression a long time ago." He set the pack on the counter.

Although Pete wasn't sure, it looked close enough to the brand he'd seen Trina pull out in his truck that he reached back for his wallet to pay. "One more thing," he said. "What's that gum people chew on if they want to quit smoking?"

"Nicorette?"

"That's the one," Pete said. "Could you grab me a pack of that, too?"

Cal smiled and took a few steps to his left to get the gum. "I have to say," he said, "you might be sending your friend some mixed messages."

Pete pulled a twenty out of his wallet. "What I'm trying to do is give them options."

Cal rang him up and Pete looked around the store. It had almost completely emptied. He saw Dave Austin restocking the produce, watched a guy come in and take a picture of the "Out of Order" sign with his phone and walk out, and saw a pregnant woman working the checkout, rubbing her belly and reading a book.

"It's quiet in here all of a sudden," Pete said. "Guess you better get that machine up and running again."

"Suits me just fine," Cal said. "It's not helping business any. People come in and either laugh or cry and then leave without buying much. Nobody says hey anymore. You got people like Shelly Swanner and Deuce Newman and a couple others who come here every day and do that dang thing. They used to stop and talk awhile." Cal pulled the change from the register and counted the bills in his hand. "Not anymore," he said. He looked at Pete. "Some days I get the feeling they might just be using me for my future-telling capabilities. It makes me feel sort of cheap."

"You know," Pete said, "I sometimes get the feeling people might use me for that exact same purpose."

"I bet you do," Cal said, and counted the bills onto the counter. "Here's your change." He then dropped the cigarettes and gum into a paper bag and slid them toward Pete. "And here's your options."

Pete picked up the bag and pocketed the bills.

"I'll tell you a secret," Cal said, and leaned toward him. "It ain't really out of order."

"It's not?" Pete said.

"I just got a call a little while ago telling me to shut it down. Some folks are apparently coming to move it to the square for the bicentennial tomorrow. I guess they figure to make some real money from the tourists."

"Who's 'they'?" Pete said. "Who owns that thing?"

"I don't know," Cal said. "They just told me DNAMIX like they knew what they were talking about so that's fine by me. Hell, I don't even remember how it got here. I never signed off on it. I figured my manager must have but she split town the day it showed up and she did her own little reading thing. I haven't seen her since. I hope she's okay. She has kids and everything."

Pete studied the machine. "So, it's still on right now?" he asked.

Cal raised his eyebrows and looked around the store. "I'll run interference if you want to hop in there and give it a go."

"Have you tried it?" Pete said.

"Shit, no," Cal told him. "I've been restocking groceries for over fifty-five years. I've got a pretty good idea of what I have and what I don't."

Pete looked at his watch. Thanks to his shortcut, he was still on schedule.

"You won't think less of me if I give it a try, will you?" he said. "It only takes a minute, right?"

"I'll cover you, Father," Cal said, and nodded for him to go ahead.

Pete felt, at that moment, as if his feet were not his own. He was utterly compelled to enter the machine, but why? He'd not thought much of it at all before. He figured it might be something about the newness of this day, its utter originality, that made him willing to try it. His need to help Trina, the overwhelming reminder of his wife, his friendship with Douglas. Maybe all of these things had been in him before but, as he approached the machine, they all seemed to bud in unison and Pete felt good.

After all, he already knew what it would say.

It was possible that some other fate could be waiting for him on that blue slip of paper, but Pete doubted it. More so than he had in a long time, Pete got the sense that he knew exactly who he was and that he was okay with this person. So, he entered the machine and followed the instructions and had to take only one quick glance at the paper to know he was right. And then he prayed and thanked God in the sincere way only the rarest humans do.

He put the slip in his pocket and left the store and went out to the parking lot, where he saw a moving truck backing up to the entrance. That fellow he met the night before at Getwell's with Deuce, Jack, he thought, or maybe it was Jim, was directing the few passing cars to go around the truck and he waved Pete across.

The two men nodded at each other in a way that suggested neither could remember the other's name and Pete opened the door of the Outback and sat in. He was going to have to swing around the moving truck if he was going to get out on the side he needed to, but Jack or Jim, or whatever his name was, would just have to deal with it. Pete had places to be, maybe even a soul to save, and had to get there in a hurry.

He cranked up the Outback and revved the engine with his foot.

"Okay," he said. "Let's see what this sucker can do."

26

Little Pictures Have Big Ears

After school, Jacob walked home like a ghost. He spoke to no one, looked at no one, made no sound at all. When he rounded the corner at Oxbow Street, he saw his father tooling around in the garage, hammering away at a couple of 2x4s, but didn't have the courage to face him.

What would he even say? *I'm caught up in something, Dad, that I don't understand.* What would he confess? *I've entertained horrible thoughts, Dad. I've let things get out of hand.* What was his reason? *The world after Toby, Dad, did not feel real. I was so confused. I was so angry.* What was his problem? *The world we are living in now, Dad, the one with Trina in it, with the dickheads in it, with questions in it, with me in it, seems even worse.* What was his solution? *I want out, Dad. I want back in. I want to be left alone. I want to be included.*

The simple truth, Jacob knew, held too many truths within it.

And how would his father reply?

Yippee ki yay?

That wouldn't do.

Yet Jacob was not good at lying. He had his father's honesty. Perhaps people would recognize that. As such, he'd spent the last few hours at school in a panic, sitting through the remainder of his classes with his head on his desk, his arms wrapped around his stomach as if it were cramping. He was sweaty and nervous and the opposite of inconspicuous, he knew, despite the fact Principal Pat was looking for the very thing in his backpack, the very thing he was on video handling. Jacob couldn't help it. He wanted to play it cool, to wear some sort of unreadable poker face until he figured things out, but he did feel sick.

What did it mean, anyway, for Trina to suggest that Jacob could be his brother? To leave that note in Toby's locker. Did she plan for him to find it or not? Had Jacob outfoxed her, somehow, outsmarted her? Or, he worried, did she now have yet another thing on him?

He had no idea.

Was her handmade readout, so obviously considered and carefully written, some dream of hopeful potential for Jacob or some sort of threat? All of the fear he'd felt upon seeing himself on video became muddied by more positive notions. Is *hope* why she'd decided to befriend him in the first place, Jacob wondered, to kiss him, to trust him, because he might turn out to be like Toby? Is that why she'd said their similarity was a "problem"? Did she feel so attracted to Toby that Jacob, just by looking like him, made her feel the same way? And if that were true, was his best version, then, just a stand-in for someone else, a reflection? To put it in mathematical terms: Was Jacob a victim of the associative property? And, if so, what did she want him to copy about his brother? Not his gregarious personality, surely, not his musculature. What could he even mimic if he tried? Or did Trina perhaps believe that their similar DNA made them the exact same person, as if one day Jacob would emerge from his dark cocoon to finally become the Toby version of himself?

If so, then why did she draw him into her scheming? If Toby's friends really did have something to do with his death, if they hazed him into the darkness: Was that it? If the dickheads had done something to Toby, did Trina believe that the closest thing to justice would be for Toby himself, or at least the most similar version of him possible, to get his revenge? Toby and the girl that nobody else liked? Was she just making sure that Jacob couldn't say no when the time came?

Every single one of them, she'd said. *Every single one.*

The more Jacob thought of this, the more awful sense it made. But how could he explain it to his father? To anyone? He could not.

So, Jacob kept to the far side of the street and swiped open his phone to see if Trina had written back, but she hadn't. His unreturned texts to her now read to him as embarrassed and needy, morphing from *WTF? You spying on me now?* to *Lol Howd u film that?* to *Please don't post. Seriously. Lets talk.* to, finally, *Where are you?*

Trina was apparently nowhere.

He put his phone back in his pocket and saw that the trailer his dad parked in their driveway was now nearly emptied of wood. No telling what awful project his father had conceived. So, Jacob walked past their house and doubled back to enter through the front door, the way only strangers did. Once inside, Jacob comported himself as such. He did not go to the kitchen to make a snack or start dinner or click on the TV as he usually would. Instead, he walked down the hallway, past his own room and directly to Toby's.

Toby's door had been shut since the day he and his father tried packing his stuff and, when Jacob placed his hand on the knob, he had the outrageous idea that he was about to enter a place he'd never been before. In this way, Jacob wished more for the world. He wished for it to be less reliable in its indifference, less predictable in its offerings, less disappointing even in its physics. Why couldn't it be a world where he opened this door to a previous time? Why not open the door to a memory of he and Toby wrestling with each other on the floor, rolling over LEGOs and knocking books off the shelf like two pups in their play? Surely this day had existed and, if so, why could it exist only once? Was the world so limited, so unimaginative, that it could not be revised? And if that was too much to ask, to go back so far, then why not a less ambitious stretching of time? Why not a scene from just two months ago, on the night Toby was killed, for instance. Why not a chance for Jacob to make him stay home or, if not that, to at least say good-bye? Why can we not be afforded in life the simple luxury of edits, of knowing then what we will inevitably know now? Jacob thought he might be able to handle this world, to navigate it, if all its possibilities were suddenly new.

The room he entered, however, was only a room.

Nothing magical had fallen into its place.

Dresser drawers lay opened like tongues. Shoes littered the unmade bed. Posters of athletes palmed the walls, a row of trophies sat atop the bookshelf. It all looked so familiar, yet Jacob had the feeling he was trespassing. He took off his backpack and sat on the edge of Toby's bed and sensed that he might be breathing different air now, thicker in that room than in any other place in the house, as if unchanged and unfiltered those past months while waiting for someone to open the door. Jacob wondered if this air was so old that he might be breathing in bits of his brother in some microscopic way, all of us wrapped up in our dust.

He looked around the place. Could this have been his own room, as Trina's readout suggested? Could he have been this person? *Should* he have been this person instead? Would people be happier if it was Toby who still were alive? Trina, surely, Toby's friends, yes, but what about his father? The idea was too obvious to ignore and Jacob's eyes began to ache. His throat tightened. He took deep breaths through his nose and when was the last time he'd cried? At the funeral? In his restless sleep? He gripped the edge of his brother's bed and rocked back and forth, trying to hold it in. From any distance at all, Jacob looked like he was preparing to jump.

But he did not.

He instead sat that way for minutes, breathing heavily, fists clenched on the sheets, until he felt his phone go off in his pocket. *Finally*, he thought, *Trina*.

He pulled out his phone to check the text, but it was from Denny. *Yo J*, it read. *Whats up with yr Twitter feed? All ok?*

Why was Jacob, Jacob wondered, surrounded by idiots?

He quickly thumbed back, *Not on Twitter*, and this was true. He'd fiddled around with it some but found everyone's tweets so grossly ignorant or self-righteous with virtually no space in between that he'd gotten off it altogether. He'd not opened the app in a year and felt a sort of pride in being Twitter free.

Denny typed back. *Then whos @j_richieu2?*

Jacob had no idea. He thumbed his way on to Twitter and searched it. Sure enough, there was a @j_richieu2 that had been active for only two weeks. The profile photo was a picture of Incineroar, a fire-type Pokémon that Jacob had no love for. His profile description was the Pokémon slogan *Gotta Catch 'Em All!* which made Jacob wonder if it was a bot, a totally random account that had somehow matched his name. After all, this was not a phrase he had ever uttered aloud in his life, as it was more for the Pokémon cartoon and app and not for the card game. If anyone thought this was Jacob from merely the profile, then they obviously didn't know much about him. The account had nearly one hundred followers, though, a number Jacob never reached when it was actually him, and it followed no one. Jacob checked his followers and most of them were kids he knew from school, Denny among them, with an awful Meowth profile pic of his own. He saw that the account had tweeted a dozen or so times and, when he opened them up to scroll through them, the sink in Jacob's stomach returned.

It was no wonder people thought it was him.

Nearly his entire feed, what looked like a tweet per day, read only: *RIP Toby.*

He punched the tweets that had replies, the most active being the very first the account had sent out. His *RIP Toby*s were answered by classmates with meaningless emojis of praying hands or crucifixes, some with yellow crying faces. Some of them said *Never Forget* or *Always my bro* but, as the days went by, the enthusiasm waned and turned to what everything else turned into on Twitter: a sort of smoldering and ironic open-mic session. One reply read *What do you expect when you get hammered and drive?* Another said *God is in the fact that no one else was hurt.* This was followed by a gif of a hand dropping a microphone, posted by someone who obviously agreed that Toby had gotten what he deserved. Jacob had no idea who had posted this reply but was tempted to track them down, turn them inside out in front of their families, and deposit a mic where he could best fit it. This awful urge only reminded him of why he got off Twitter in the first place, though, and so he moved on.

He scrolled down to see a change in the tweets. The last few read differently. One said *3 days left. Enjoy them.* The next said *2 days left.* Jacob looked at the dates and realized they were counting down to today and this is when he knew things would not end well.

A tweet from this morning had a picture. It was a blue duffel bag, unzipped and opened on some unknowable floor. Inside of it, clearly visible, the barrel of a shotgun.

The tweet read: *Off you go, into the wild blue yonder.*

The only reply to this was from Denny, who had posted a gif of Ash, the main character from the *Pokémon* cartoon, sweating and chewing his nails in his frantic anime way, with the line *Did you go off yr meds, homie?* beneath it.

Jacob turned off his phone and put it on the bed. What the hell was Trina up to? If she was framing him, then for what possible reason? He thought they were in this together. And what were they even *in*? He'd never agreed to anything. He considered trying to reach her again but had a different idea. He looked over at Toby's desk, where sat the green Ziploc bag the police had given them with all of Toby's stuff from the accident, the same one he'd seen his father briefly consider before going off to his own room.

He walked over and opened it up. It held a thin pack of gum, some pocket money, a small roll of condoms, a vape pin. Most important, though, the bag held Toby's phone, the thing Jacob was looking for.

Jacob pulled out the phone, the same model that he had, with only a different cover. Instead of the Poké Ball on Jacob's, a baseball on Toby's. Same shape, different reality. Jacob found a charger on Toby's desk and plugged it in. The phone booted itself, the little apple on the screen like a warning, and Jacob felt, he supposed, like a parent.

When the lock screen came up, Jacob punched in his own passcode, the month and the year, and it worked as he knew it would. He saw icons for every social media app he could think of, apps for sports teams, ESPN, and a background photo of Toby himself playing baseball. Jacob stared at this a good while. When was the last time he had seen his brother? Toby stood before him now in midswing, the ball still visible in its violent journey out to a place, Jacob figured, it would never be caught.

How was it possible, Jacob wondered, that this person no longer existed? Why are we made of such fragile material? The idea that Toby, who was so confident, so active in smashing his way through the world, could have been a victim of anything made no sense to Jacob.

So, he touched the photo icon and looked for the reasons.

Toby had more than a thousand photos on there, hundreds of

videos, and Jacob opened the first one that caught his attention. It was a picture of Toby and Trina and, with this sight, an odd feeling of jealousy arose in Jacob, because, for one split second, he thought the picture was of himself. This was not as common an occurrence as one might imagine with twins. Although nearly identical, there were a number of differences between them that anyone looking at them as individuals and not some grouped pair could easily identify. Jacob was right-handed and Toby was left-handed. Jacob had a little mole on his neck, just above the collarbone, and Toby did not. Ever since they were allowed to make such personal choices, they had styled their hair differently, as well. Jacob's was always neat, combed left to right, while Toby let his do what it wanted. He would shave it close every few months and apparently not think much of it again. The thick mass of it gave him the look of some budding party animal ever since he was old enough to ride a bike. The most noticeable difference between them, though, was their smile.

Toby's was nearly perpetual, broad and confident, while Jacob's, whenever it appeared, gave one the impression that it took a tremendous effort to do so.

It therefore did not take long for Jacob to recognize that it was not himself in the photo, but perhaps because Toby was wearing a baseball cap, perhaps because the lighting was not great, he had experienced that moment of confusion usually reserved for schizophrenics and drunks when they see pictures they don't remember posing for. That odd feeling of, *Well, there I am. But, if that was me, then where was I?*

As strange a sensation as this was, it was rivaled only by the other half of the picture, which showed Trina smiling. Had Jacob ever seen this? He had not. On what planet had it occurred? The both of them looked drunk and glassy-eyed in the photo, and by the angle of his outstretched arm, you could tell that Toby had taken the picture. He had his arm around her neck, looking at the camera, while Trina, on the other hand, was looking only at Toby. This broke off a piece of Jacob's heart. He felt he was now looking at a photo of two people, not just one, who no longer existed. Trina was still sharp-edged and dark in this photo, sure, she was no cheerleader, but her smile surprised him. She looked not only devious but hopeful. She was plotting something in this photo, as well, Jacob could tell, just like she had been plotting something in every conversation he'd ever had with her. The difference was that whatever she felt herself close to achieving here seemed to hold the opposite promise of what she had hoped to achieve through Jacob. She had liked Toby when this picture was taken, in the simple way that girls sometimes like boys, and it was obvious. Jacob felt terrible for spending so much time wondering why they were together. Why shouldn't she be allowed to like whoever she wanted? Who else's business was that but hers? It was no one's.

This reality infected him with an overwhelming sense of guilt. The thoughts he had entertained about him and Trina, about her somehow being his now, about her tongue in his mouth, returned to him as if toxic. He felt duplicitous in his dealings with her, almost predatory, as if he had been trying to take something which was not being offered at all.

The more he looked at the picture of Toby, though, the sicker he felt. He had his arm too tight around Trina's neck, it seemed, as if he were holding her there instead of embracing her, as if she couldn't have gotten out of the hug if she tried. Whether or not she wanted out, at that particular moment, was beside the point. Toby's smile was too broad, Jacob thought, his eyes too distant, and Jacob had the strangest revelation that perhaps what everybody believed about this couple was entirely wrong, completely backward. The way Deuce Newman had warned him to stay away from Trina, for instance, the way the other kids at school scorned her.

Jacob had the sense, instead, when looking at the photo, that if he were a parent, it was his brother he would have warned his daughter about.

This feeling did not sit well with him. If that were true, and if they were nearly identical, then what did that mean Jacob himself was capable of?

All of these feelings were compounded by the fact that Jacob knew when the picture was taken. It was dated from the night of Toby's death but, more telling than that, Jacob also knew *where* it was taken. In the background of the photo stood a light pole with the sign "Swim At Your Own Risk" posted to it. This was at a place called Toup's Landing, about fifteen miles out of town at the lowest reach of Bayou Ibis, right past the parish line, where generations of teenagers had gone to escape their realities. It was here the most raucous high school parties went down after games or school functions, where kids acted as idiotically as possible, Jacob thought, until inevitably scattered by local police, who wrote underage-drinking citations so toothless that these kids would return the very next weekend. Jacob already knew this was where Toby had been that night, as his crash had occurred along the stretch of highway between Deerfield and Toup's Landing, where he had missed his turn completely, the police said, going above the speed limit, undoubtedly, and wrapped his car around an oak tree stronger than people.

Jacob remembered what Trina had told him in the days that followed. *You have no idea what they did*, she'd said. *This isn't over.*

Jacob had been to Toup's Landing only once and, like a fool, he now thought, going to see a girl he liked but who did not like him. Going to confirm again the simplest math. And when Jacob realized this girl had no interest in talking with him, in even standing near him, and that his ride was unwilling to leave, he walked by himself to the water by the boat launch. He stood there for hours doing little other than skipping rocks. So many of them there, he remembered, by the launch.

Jacob pulled out the rock Trina had set on top of the envelope in Toby's locker and looked it over. He ran his thumb over the face of it, smooth and gray and likely as old as anything else he had ever touched. It could very well be, he knew, from this same place. Jacob closed the photo and swiped to the next image in the queue, which was a video.

He hit the small arrow and immediately regretted it. It was hard to tell what was happening at first, as the video was dark and shaky and then illuminated, it seemed, by Toby turning on the flash. The phone wobbled back and forth until it settled on what looked like hair, a head of hair. Trina's hair. Then, Toby saw her face, looking up at him as if interrupted.

"What are you doing?" she said, and she was smiling. In her hand, now, Jacob saw what she held. Beneath her knees, he heard the shifting of rocks.

"It's just for me," Toby told her, his voice like some unfamiliar ghost. "Don't stop."

Trina did not stop with her hand. Instead, she said only, "Promise?"

"Hell, yeah," Toby said. "I'll send you a copy."

The twist in Jacob's stomach as he watched her return was as severe as anything he'd previously felt. He was about to turn it off completely when he heard other voices in the background. A group of guys, he could tell, walking up and laughing. "Where's number nine?" one of them said, and Jacob knew this was Toby's jersey number. The camera did not move up to the boys but stayed instead on Trina, who stopped what she was doing and hid her face with her hair.

"Now we're fucking talking," one of guys said, and then there was a chorus of unsettling voices as the camera lost its focus, a commotion, a joining of other drunk boys to the scene, the mad crunching of gravel underfoot, and soon Trina's pleading voice somewhere in the background. Then Jacob heard something else.

A knock.

He looked up to see his father at the bedroom door.

Jacob clicked off the video. His dad was sweating inside the house and Jacob realized that he was, too. His father wore his hat, a dusty pair of jeans, and his cowboy boots.

"Hey, pardner," he said. "When did you get here?"

Jacob cleared his throat. He had no idea what to say. The scene on the video was quickly turning, he feared, into a crime, and Jacob felt as if he'd been caught.

He wanted to show it to his father, to say that he had no part of it, to confess why he was in Toby's room for the first time in months, and to tell him everything that had happened to nearly everyone he knew in what was an obviously awful world. But, before he could speak, it was like his father understood this desire and spoke the words so he didn't have to.

"Come on," his dad said. "I want to show you something."

27

Ain't It Funny How an
Old Broken Bottle Can Look
Just Like a Diamond Ring

Now, *these* were a pair of hands.

Cherilyn couldn't stop staring at them. As soon as Marian sat her down at the register and began mixing the henna dye, as soon as she felt the press of the pen against her skin, Cherilyn was transported.

She sat in her red sari, her T-shirt and shorts folded into a plastic bag beside her on the floor, and let herself be doted upon. The women at the register chatted and made sales as Alice floated around the shop fetching bits of costumes and clothing. A bowling shirt for Rex Patterson, a leotard for Amy Glick. Cherilyn pitched in, as well, using whatever free hand Marian was not drawing on. She counted change and made suggestions and assured at least five different people that, yes, she would be selling her crafts tomorrow, and that, yes, she would be at the bicentennial. And, thank you, and did they really think she looked beautiful? Thank you. Yes, birdhouses, actually. I'll have plenty.

"I told you," Alice said. "We'd make a pretty fierce combination."

"Maybe we would," Cherilyn said, and felt that this might be true. Everything, at that moment, might be true.

When Marian finished with her right hand and stood up to

stretch her back, Cherilyn held her hand up to the light. It was covered in a pattern of curved and repetitive lines, peppered by small and delicate circles that made a hypnotic but unknowable shape.

"What is it?" Cherilyn said. "I mean, I love it, but what is it?" The ink was a coppered orange color against her skin.

"It's not done yet," Marian said, and sat back down to work on her other hand. "That's what it is."

Cherilyn looked at the clock on the wall and realized she was going to be late. This idea pulled her in a couple of ways. She'd told Deuce she would meet him at three o'clock, as this would give her enough time to clean up and go to Alice's and check up on her mom before her picture. And what a picture it would be now, she realized. She delighted at the idea of showing up in this dress for Deuce. She could just imagine the look on his face.

She also knew Douglas wouldn't be home until after his lesson at four and so this gave her and Deuce two hours, which was plenty enough time for a picture and whatever else they needed to do, and Douglas wouldn't have to know a thing about it. She could explain it to him tomorrow when he saw it on the mural. They could have their talk then. And why should she feel guilty? She had to remind herself that Douglas had apparently kept something from her yesterday, too. Going out for drinks with Geoffrey? Please. If he was going to tell her a lie then, surely, she could provide a little tit for his tat. And she wasn't even lying, was she? No, she was just not saying everything. She needed to remember that.

She'd offered to meet Deuce at his house but he'd refused. He'd said the place was a mess with all his cameras and equipment and was in an overall dubious state. So, they compromised. Cherilyn told him to meet her outside her mother's house at three. She told him to park on the street and just give a couple taps on his horn when he got there.

"Ain't no way in hell I'm honking at a woman like you outside her mother's house," he said. "I don't care what year it is. I'm a gentleman."

"Just wait for me, then," she said. "Don't go inside."

"Oh, I'll wait for you," he told her. "Don't you worry."

But now there was no way she would be there at three and part of her was okay with this, too, as she'd not felt as good as she did now in a long time. The hours in the costume shop had her so busy, the delight she found in other people buying clothes for their new selves had her so stimulated, that she felt pain free. No tingling or burning or cramping, just the feeling of Marian's soft hands beneath hers. The feel of the henna drying on her wrists. It was like a vacation from herself. And every time Marian would stop to take a breath and check her phone, turn to pull a beer out of the little fridge the ladies had stashed beneath the counter, Cherilyn would thank her and it felt good to thank people. Maybe that was reason enough to go into business, she thought, to have the opportunity to say thank you again and again.

When Marian finally finished, Cherilyn stood up as the women gathered around her. They smoothed her sari at the back from where it had become wrinkled and readjusted her head scarf. Cherilyn held up her left hand and it looked very similar to her right but for her wedding ring. It disrupted the pattern, there was no doubt about it.

"I'm sorry," she said. "It's beautiful but, again, I still don't know what it is. Is it a picture of something?"

"That's the thing," Marian said, and gently touched her palms. "You have to put them together for it to make sense."

She guided Cherilyn's hands forward and placed them next to each other and there it was: a flower. On each hand, half of the bud and flowing leaves, the light orange designs climbing like tendrils up her wrists and to her forearms.

"It's a lotus flower," Marian said. "Hindu women apparently get this done on their wedding day. It's a sign of fertility and good health and all of that stuff. A fruitful life."

"Hindu?" one of the women said and made the sign of the cross. "I hope you can get that off before Sunday."

"Oh, hush," Alice said. "It's gorgeous. Marian, I had no idea you were so worldly. Perhaps we ought to get you a little henna booth in the shop. Get you doing more than stocking shelves."

"It comes off with a little lemon juice, I think," Marian said. "I just googled it. I'm not sure how worldly that makes me."

Marian held out her phone so the women could see.

Cherilyn looked to see a number of images, all of painted hands held side by side, women's hands that looked, now, very much like hers. She felt the same pleasant rush of connection with these women that she had felt with Susan of Oman and closed her eyes as Marian gently blew on her wrist to help it dry.

"I could do the palms, too, if you like," she said. "As long as I'm still getting paid for doodling."

"Fine by me," Alice said. "We all need a little more doodling in our lives, I'd say."

The woman who crossed herself said, "Well, that sounds perverse."

"That's because I was thinking of you when I said it," Alice told her.

Cherilyn smiled and looked at the clock again. It was already three-forty-five. "Actually," she said, "I have to get going." She reached down and picked up her bag and thanked Marian and Alice with a hug and, when she looked back up, realized that there was a line of people at the register. They had all been watching her, waiting patiently to check out. She adjusted her sari to hold it gently above the concrete floor and inched around the counter. The line parted for her in two distinct rows and Cherilyn smiled and said thank you as she passed between them, a few women reaching out to touch the silk fabric of her dress.

"Cherilyn," Alice said, and Cherilyn turned back to face her. "You take it easy on that good man tonight." She smiled. "He has no idea what's coming for him."

Cherilyn felt her cheeks flush. "No," she said. "I guess he doesn't, does he?" But which man was she thinking about? That was a curious question.

Cherilyn walked out of the store and into the heat outside, where the people stepped aside for her, as well. Then she stood in the grass lot looking for her car for a good two minutes, before she remembered that it wasn't her car she was driving today.

And even on the way to her mother's, she looked at her hands, placing them side by side atop Douglas's steering wheel as she sat through a surprising amount of traffic. But the traffic was okay with her. She didn't worry that she was late. In fact, a part of her was glad. If there was something she knew about Deuce Newman, it's that he would still be waiting there for her, no matter how long she took. He had waited for her his whole life, so what was an extra hour? Plus, the way she felt in that dress, the way the gold trim cast its small prisms about the car in the afternoon sun, made her feel that she was a person worth waiting for.

Much of this feeling faded, though, when she pulled on to her mom's street and saw Deuce Newman's truck parked in her driveway. It looked so ostentatious sitting there that Cherilyn experienced an immediate sense of panic. What if people had seen it? How could she explain that? Cherilyn forced down this new feeling of dread, as it was not at all what she had on her docket today. There would come a time for explanations, she knew that, but it would come later. Still, the thought of this made her stomach do a churning thing.

She parked next to his truck with its oversized tires and

silly-looking dumbbell hanging from the trailer hitch and walked into her mother's house without knocking. When she turned the corner to the kitchen, she saw her mother and Deuce sitting at the table. Her mom was dressed and looked put-together, which gave Cherilyn a great sense of relief. Her mother was having a good day, it appeared, which meant Cherilyn would not have to stay long.

When Deuce saw her walk in, he stood up from the table. "*Holy* smokes," he said, and did a little bow. "Her majesty has arrived."

Cherilyn smiled, in spite of herself, and performed a little curtsy with her dress. She was perturbed that he had come in the house when she had asked him not to, that he had not followed her instructions, and said, without too much conviction behind it, "I thought I'd asked you to wait outside."

"Cherilyn," her mother said, still not looking at her. "Who is this man in my kitchen?"

"Oh, come on, Mrs. Fuller," Deuce said. "We've been talking for half an hour."

"That's Bruce Newman, Momma," Cherilyn said, and walked over to give her mother a kiss on the forehead. "You remember him from high school, I'm sure. He's a photographer now. He's going to take some pictures of me for his art project tomorrow."

"Remember?" Deuce said. "That's why I took yours earlier. I'm doing a mural of everybody in town."

"Well," her mother said. "I don't want him in here."

Cherilyn looked at Deuce and smiled. "Oh, be nice," she said. She turned toward her mom and pulled out her sari on both sides. "Aren't you going to at least say something about my dress?"

"*You're* the work of art," Deuce said.

"Look at my hands, too," Cherilyn said, and held them out for her mother to see.

Her mother looked at her hands, then up to Cherilyn's face. "What is it," she said, "Halloween?"

Cherilyn sighed and walked to the freezer. Her plan was simple. She would heat up a frozen dinner to make sure her mother was fed and be gone.

"I was just telling your mom, she should come out to the square tomorrow and try that DNAMIX machine," Deuce said. "It might give her a little lift."

Cherilyn pulled out a Salisbury steak dinner and opened the box. "The square?" she said. "Don't you mean Johnson's?"

"Nope," he said. "Word is they're moving it out to the square tomorrow for the bicentennial. Let the tourists have a go at it. I have a feeling it's going to be a hit."

"I didn't know that," Cherilyn said. She pulled the plastic off the tray and set it in the microwave.

"I've been asking your mom what she'd want to be, you know. If she could be anything."

"And I've told him a thousand times," her mother said. "I am Mrs. Jean Fuller."

Cherilyn shut the microwave and said, "No, Momma. That's who you were when Daddy was still around. That's just your name. This thing tells you what you could be. What you *should* be."

Her mother stood up from the table and walked her glass to the sink. "I'm old, honey," she said. "I'm not ignorant."

"I just think you're missing the point," Cherilyn said, and looked at the microwave to punch in the time. It was already four-fifteen.

She was going to have to call Douglas. There were no two ways about it.

"Y'all give me a second, if you don't mind," she said, and grabbed the telephone mounted on the wall. She took it down and stretched the long cord around the door and into the laundry room. That this thing still worked was a miracle, as she remembered using it back in her high school days, whispering to Douglas on the phone late at night when her parents were asleep. And here she was calling him again.

She dialed his cell phone number and cupped her hand around the receiver. She would have to be quick, she knew, so that he couldn't hear Deuce in the background still imploring her mom to pick a better destiny.

It was noisy when Douglas answered, some music playing somewhere, and Cherilyn was surprised at his voice. He sounded happy on the other end of the line and this was something she did not expect. He called her funny pet names and she could feel him smiling out of her sight and she had to force herself not to be happy for him.

She had her reasons.

She had to remember that she was upset with him for lying to her about Geoffrey. She had to remind herself, as she looked at Deuce in the kitchen, that this was not a time for explanations. That this was a time for herself. For her true self. And she had to remind herself that this was who she was being.

So, she asked him to stop whistling for one second, to pay attention, because she had a message to deliver. She would not be at home when he expected her to be. No. Today she would not be so predictable, and he would just have to be okay with that. She then walked into the kitchen and hung up the phone. She pressed start on the microwave and looked at Deuce. "Let's go," she said.

Deuce grabbed his keys from the table and said, "Yes, ma'am." He then pretended to tip a cap that he was not wearing to her mother and said, "Mrs. Fuller, it's been a pleasure. I hope to be seeing more of you soon."

"I hope I go blind first," she said.

Cherilyn reminded her mother that her food was in the microwave and then opened the door for Deuce as he walked out to his truck.

When she turned to follow him, her mother spoke from the kitchen.

"Cherilyn," she said. "That man is not Douglas."

Cherilyn turned back to her and sighed. "I know that, Momma. You're just confused. It's okay."

Her mother walked over to her and took Cherilyn's hands into her own. They were surprisingly warm and strong and she squeezed them hard enough for Cherilyn's ring to dig into her finger. "What I mean to say," she told her, "is that man is *no* Douglas."

And was it there again between them? The buzzing? Could Cherilyn feel it coming through her mother's palms and into her own? If she could, she did not want to, and so she pulled her hands away and walked out of the door.

When she got to Deuce's truck, she looked back and saw her mom still standing there watching her. Cherilyn heard the sound of the microwave going off in the kitchen and thought to remind her again of what was there waiting for her. But, instead, she opened the truck door, lifted her dress, and climbed inside.

28

You're Up One Day and
the Next You're Down

Pete pulled out of the Johnson's Grocery parking lot with as much bravado as any priest borrowing his new friend's wife's Subaru Outback can achieve. He felt energized and near holy on his way to see Trina. He also felt a bit self-righteous, one might say, even as the pre-installed governor of Catholicism did what it could to tamp down his enthusiasm.

Why should you feel good? the voice asked him. *Trina is obviously in trouble.* Yes, he told it, but I am on my way there to make it right. Whatever it is, I'm ready to help. I was her age once. How hard can it be? I've been through some shit myself, as you may recall. I just want to be involved. I want to be of assistance. I can do this. *Careful now, Pete,* it said. *You don't know what's going on with that girl. Don't assume you can fix everything. That sounds an awful lot like pride.*

Well, whatever this is, he told it, it feels good. I've made a new friend, I believe, and I've got Anna all over my mind right now and she would want me to be doing this, too, I know. Ask her if you don't believe me. And tell her I said hello. Tell her I love her, please. She'd probably want us to take Trina in if she were here, you know that, into our own home, no matter her issues. But I feel happy right now, is all that I'm saying, with my readout and with

Douglas and with Anna and with this opportunity with Trina. I feel happy for a change. Can't I at least have that? Even if you think I'm somehow doing this for me and not for Trina. If I'm doing all of this for me. It's a bit of happiness. Can't I have it?

The voice went quiet for a moment, as if it were perhaps indeed checking with Anna, wherever she was, to make sure everything was on the up-and-up.

Very well, then, it eventually said. *A little happiness for Pete. Enjoy it while it lasts.*

And so Pete enjoyed it by driving along the shoulder of Iris Lane, bypassing the traffic in an undeniably illegal manner and turning up 61, just like any bad-ass priest on a mission might do.

He topped out at eighty miles per hour on his way to Lanny's and, just as he put on his blinker to turn into his driveway, saw a curious thing: his own pickup truck, the ancient blue Toyota that moved like a riverboat, tearing out of Lanny's driveway. It sprayed gravel all over the road, fishtailing onto the far shoulder before righting itself and heading north out of Pete's sight. It was an odd sensation to see your own car on the move without you in it, but was also, to Pete, a great relief, as he would much rather talk to Trina without Lanny there. So, he said a quick prayer for his old truck and thanked God for yet another fortunate turn in his day.

This feeling did not last long, though, as he pulled into Lanny's driveway and saw a car he did not recognize parked by the house, about ten feet away from where Lanny's blue Laplander–pit bull mix was currently chained up and losing its mind, barking itself into another dimension. The car was a small two-door coupe without any plates at all, and when Pete got out of the Outback, he realized this other car was still running. This was also a relief, as whomever Lanny had left there would not be staying long. Pete looked at the dog, who he remembered being named Ollie, and clicked his tongue at him a bit. Ollie continued to lunge against the chain, barking and growling in its obvious rage at Pete's presence, and Pete told it, "You know, Ollie. This is why y'all can't have nice things."

Pete then climbed the two steps up onto Lanny's front porch. He went to knock but saw that the door was cracked open. Always a gentleman, Pete knocked on it anyway, stepped inside, and said, "Katrina?"

As soon as his foot crossed the threshold, Pete became extremely conscious of what he was wearing. Maybe that's why Lanny's demon dog had been so rude outside. Pete was still in his work clothes, and his white collar and pressed pants looked as out of place in Lanny's foyer as would all the shiny stars and buckles of a policeman's uniform. He didn't want to appear as an authority figure to Trina, he understood, but rather as a family member or a friend, and so he went to pull off his collar.

Before he could do this, though, he was nearly knocked out by the smell of the place. It was an awful mixture, thick in the air like marijuana and burnt plastic, and Pete immediately recognized it from a time he'd smelled this exact same thing around some of the men behind the Catholic food bank. It was one of those smells, so distinct in life, that it could make you travel in time. So, Pete did the same thing now as he had done that day behind the food bank and put his hand to his nose to cover it. When he turned the corner to the living room, he saw Lanny sprawled out on the couch.

"Lanny?" he said. "That you?" But Lanny did not move.

Pete walked over to him, figuring he was passed out high but, when he got to him, saw that Lanny had been beaten. His left eye was swollen shut, his nose and mouth smeared with fresh blood. Pete checked his pulse and, when he realized he was still alive, thumbed a quick sign of the cross on Lanny's forehead and went to lift him. He then heard a noise outside, behind the house, and stood up. A crashing out in the yard, somewhere. A shed door slamming. He looked around the room. What was going on here?

Pete saw that nearly everything had been toppled over and riffled through. A lampshade on the floor, a desk drawer pulled out, a CD tower on the ground, all the cases cracked and opened. Pete, he realized, had walked into a robbery.

He left Lanny lying there and whispered Trina's name fiercely as he walked through the house. "Trina," he said. "You in here?" His adrenaline was up and he began sweating as he checked each room. He looked into the dining room to see an antique armoire, probably oak, probably Lanny's parents' at one time, maybe as old as the whole damn town, open and emptied. Broken china all over the floor, a set of opaque salt and pepper shakers sitting unmolested on the dining room table.

Pete hurried down the hall and went to the first door he supposed was Trina's, as it had a "No Trespassing: Violators Will Be Shot on Sight" sign nailed to the front of it. "Trina," he said again, and opened the door.

Pete knew this was her room immediately, not because anything in it signified that a teenage girl lived there but merely in the way the room existed in such stark contrast to the rest of the house. It was immaculate. The bed was made in almost military fashion, the school uniforms hung in perfect alignment in the closet. It looked like a picture of a room rather than an actual room any human being lived in and appeared to Pete, in a panic, like a room that nobody planned to return to. The only evidence of someone being there at all was an open laptop, set upon the desk at the far wall. Pete walked over to it, the screen still bright with a social media page that he did not know but believed to be Twitter as he recognized the little bird in the top corner of it. He stared at the screen for a moment, the feed full of #'s and @ signs, and realized he would not know how to read this document if he tried.

The fact that the screen was still bright, though, meant to him that Trina had been here recently and, also, that she might have been the one he'd seen peeling out in his truck. He hoped this was true if it meant that she was safe.

Pete then noticed the top shelf of Trina's desk, empty and clean, almost dusted-looking, except for two small piles of rocks set next to each other. The one on the left was made of at least a hundred small stones, none much bigger than a quarter, none much different than the gravel of Lanny's own driveway, all piled together neatly into the shape of a pyramid. Conversely, the pile on the right was not much of a pile at all, but instead consisted of one lone rock, a reddish one that had the flat and smooth look of a worrying stone. Taped beneath these two piles were individual index cards, which Pete lifted with his fingers to read. The one on the left, beneath the hundred stones, read only the word *Yes*. It was written so carefully by hand, Pete could tell, so thoughtfully. He looked at the card beneath the lone red stone. It read, simply, *No*.

Pete then turned to see a man so hostile behind him that he had the brief and terrifying notion that perhaps his God was not the real one at all. That perhaps the ancient pagans had it right all along and that, while Pete wasn't looking, the slobbering dog outside had simply shifted into human shape and loosed its collar and drug its pain-racked body up the stairs and into the house to finally do what it had wanted so badly to accomplish outside.

Pete did not get the chance to ask this dog anything, though, as it ran toward him, lifted the pistol in its hand, and struck Pete across the head.

Pete fell to the floor and the light that dawned upon him was not the one of heaven for which he so desperately wanted to

witness but instead merely one of the many complicated illumina-
tions of our own world. It was blinding bright and white and
served only to usher forward a pain of similar color. Pete could
still hear and feel the room around him but could not see nor move
his body and, as such, soon heard the sound of a woman's voice
that was not angelic or ethereal at all but instead panicked and
short of breath.

"Goddamn, Ricky!" she said. "What'd you do now? Kill a priest?"

"Shut up, Tessa," the man said. "I didn't know who he was."

"Well," she said. "Check his pockets for money, I guess."

Pete felt the weight of the man set upon him as he began to grab
around in his pockets, his hands hard and painful against Pete's
thighs, his fingernails sharp as claws on his skin.

"No money," the man said. "Goddamn priests don't have no
money. What the fuck is he doing here?"

"Well, what's that blue thing, then?" the woman asked him. "Is
that a credit card? Let's take it and go."

The man picked something off the ground beside him. "Just
some sort of ID," he said. "Just says 'Father' on it. Where'd that
damn girl go? And where's that shotgun you said he had? I didn't
come out here just for two lousy grams of shit."

"She's gone," the woman said. "Leave her be. She won't say anything. She can't stand Lanny, either. Does he have a phone at least?"

"I didn't come out here for no goddamn phone," the man said.

"Call nine-one-one, you dummy," she said. "I ain't going to hell
for killing a priest."

"He's not dead," the man said. "Let's go."

And with this Pete felt a tremendous weight lift off his body as
the man stood up and left the room. Pete tried to roll over but
could not yet tell if his eyes were opened or closed, so blinding was
the light, nor which way on the floor he could turn his body if he
wanted to.

He soon felt a gentler presence beside him, though, like that of a soft animal, and heard the low tones of three numbers being pushed into his phone.

"You weren't supposed to be a part of this," the woman told him. "Now look what you made us do."

Pete felt the phone drop onto his chest, heard the distant ring on the other side of it, and then only the woman's last words to him.

"I hope you're happy now."

29

Saddle in the Rain

Jacob followed the click of his father's boots down the hallway. He'd turned off Toby's phone and set it facedown on his desk like a playing card as soon as he'd seen his father standing there. What else was he to do?

He was nervous and sweating and still processing what he saw on the video and so Jacob asked his dad if he could duck into his room and change out of his uniform. He thought this might give him a private second to plan, to make some sort of decisions about the rest of his life, but it did not. Instead, his father leaned against the open doorway and crossed one boot over the other. He watched Jacob contentedly, as if all he was missing in life was a hayseed to chew on. Jacob took off his school shirt and threw on a black tee, swapped out his uniform pants for the jeans he wore yesterday, transferred everything from his pockets, and, as he did this, thought of ways to tell his father impossible things.

The sick trajectory of the video was immediately obvious to Jacob and its existence, unfortunately, not that rare. This unscrupulous form of recording was something a lot of kids at his school did, something kids everywhere did. He'd seen screenshots of his classmates undressed, grainy footage of couples making out beneath the bleachers or through car windows. He'd heard about which guys sent dick pics, which guys got revenge on their exes by saving masturbatory Skype sessions for social blackmail. It was all remarkably uncontroversial, part of the fabric of his generation, he knew, and was yet another way Jacob felt alone in the world. Rather than recording and posting images to multiple platforms, Jacob did not want to see himself at all. He hated the whole idea of it.

The desire his peers had to see themselves reflected in their screens was not only addictive, Jacob thought, but so malignant as to infect its own host. Selfies. Videos. Instagram. Snapchat. Everyone starred in a movie of their life that they mistakenly thought others wanted to see.

Each time Jacob watched a classmate lift up their phone to take a shot of their face in the school hallway, the cafeteria, the coffee shop, he did not look at their phone nor the hands that held it but only the way their face changed when they saw it reflected back in the screen. The way they altered everything about it. *Bright smile, now. Chin up. Eyes big. Life, remember, is exactly how we want it to be.* And then, after the photo, the way it dropped back into its familiar and unfortunate shape. It was a hard thing to watch. Perhaps these selfies took a bit of the person's soul, Jacob thought, the way he'd once heard Native Americans suspected cameras might do. Or, maybe, if not their soul, the photo took that person's smile for good and carried it away from them. And maybe smiles, like breaths, were of a limited number in life. If so, selfies were aptly named, he thought. They were little versions of a person's self, dolled up and wound from the back like a toy, sent out into the world to lie.

So, just telling his father about the video was not that easy. For Jacob to say something as simple as *Hey, Dad, look at this* never crossed his mind. This was partly because he knew the image of Toby and his friends, the truth of what they were perhaps doing to Trina, would crush his father as it would crush any parent, but also because he understood the great and guilty confession the video would make about his entire teenage world. His father was not ready for that. It was as if the video were too graphic for him, too mature, like he and Jacob had somehow silently switched places those last few years and now Jacob would be the one having to explain the hard truths. *Listen, Dad,* he'd have to say, *not only is this your son, but this is also not abnormal. This is what kids do. Do you understand? What you've always thought happens only elsewhere, in some other town, with some other terrible kids? That is what we call Friday night.*

So, Jacob said absolutely nothing as he laced up his shoes and pulled his Latios cap over his head.

"Ready Freddy?" his dad said.

Jacob followed him down the hall, tracing his hands along the walls as if to make sure they were actually there. So many things coming together for him, but he still couldn't see the whole picture. Trina, now, as the victim in all of this? Her anger made sense to him in a way it hadn't before. But what about the Twitter page? What about his readout? What did she want with him?

His father led him to the kitchen and took off his cowboy hat, waved it at his face like a fan to cool down. He smiled.

"You said you wanted better victuals," he said. "Your old man stepped up his game."

His father raised his eyebrows toward the sink, where Jacob saw an enormous slab of meat sitting propped in one of the basins. It stood high enough to reach the windowsill behind it and was wrapped in plastic as thick as Visqueen, dark purple veins of blood running across the front like rivers on a map. This was definitely not an option at any grocery store Jacob had ever been to.

"What the hell is that?" Jacob said.

"That, Cookie," his dad said, "is a side of grass-fed, Grade A, American Angus beef. I bought it from Otto's market today. It's something to see, ain't it?"

"What do you want me to do with it?" Jacob asked.

"That's enough chow to last us a month," his dad said. "I ordered us a book on Amazon to teach us how to take it apart, too. How to section and store it. Steaks and ribs and brisket and all. I figure I need to know how a cow works anyway, you know. I figured this was something you and I could do together. The book should be here tomorrow."

Jacob felt as if he might be hallucinating. Who was this man in his kitchen? What life had he lived, before Jacob knew him, to make him this way? What history did he hold inside? Above all, what strange urge did the universe have to pair them together? To make them partners somehow? What was its logic? In this feeling Jacob was like all children are when they finally consider their parents as individuals, when a lifetime's string of questions gets pulled up and tied into a single bow that represents the only question worth asking a parent:

Who are you?

Jacob looked at his dad.

"Is this what you wanted to show me?" he said.

"Well," he said. He looked disappointed. "Yes and no. I mean, this is just a start. Come see what else I've done."

"Let me guess," Jacob said. "You traded your truck for a mule."

His father winked and placed his hat back on top of his head. "Phil-er-up," he said, and walked toward the garage door.

As soon as he started down the steps into the garage, Jacob heard music. It was old-time saloon-style music and Jacob thought wretchedly, *Oh, God, he's found a player piano.*

Although Jacob saw no piano, he recognized immediately that their entire garage had been transformed since he was last in it. His dad had nailed wood paneling to the walls and, inside the garage door, erected a sort of cattle fence made of 2x4s. In the middle of this fence, now the only entry point to their garage, stood two swinging saloon doors. He'd spread knickknacks all around the place, as well, many of which Jacob did not recognize and could not imagine the origin of. Old-looking lamps. Metal signs advertising bygone bourbons and spirits, a "Wanted Dead or Alive" poster with Jesse James pictured on it. On one of the walls, Jacob saw a stuffed possum curled up on its back as if asleep. And at the far side of the garage, a bar probably six feet long, topped with the dark and lacquered wood he'd seen at the bottom of the trailer the day before. At its farthest end, two barstools sat side by side as if already in conversation with each other. His father, Jacob knew, had never been so productive in his life.

His dad turned to him, little sounds like bells coming off his boots, and held out his hands as if to say, *Well?* As if to say, *This is all of me.* As if to say, *Please be kind.*

"You did all of this since yesterday?" Jacob asked.

"I did," his dad said. "A feller could have used a little help, to be sure. Especially with that bar. I'm afraid I scratched up the bottom of it pretty good."

"Didn't you have some sort of important meeting today?" Jacob asked.

"I did," his dad said, and looked around the place as if he, too, were seeing it for the first time. "I was there, but I wasn't really there, if you know what I mean. My mind was sort of on the other side of town."

"I do," Jacob said, because he felt that exact same way. He knew he should say something nice to his dad. His father looked so obviously desperate for anything in his life to change that perhaps a simple pat on the head would have saved him. But all Jacob could think about was Trina. What did she have planned? As bad as Jacob thought it might be when it was Toby's life she was avenging, how brutal might it be if it were her own? Why hadn't he stopped her? Why had he let her entertain it? And soon all of the dark fantasies she'd shared with him while he thought of nothing but the possibility of the two of them together, somehow, moved to a part of his brain that made them appear not as her fantasies at all but, instead, as his own guilty memories, as if what she'd wanted to do to those boys were things he himself had already done.

Jacob said, of course, none of this.

"This is incredible, Dad," he said instead. "Totally insane, but incredible."

His dad frowned.

"How is it insane?" he said. "This made me feel, I don't know, I reckon it made me feel the opposite of insane for a change. I mean, I had a bushel of fun doing this, Son. Maybe a barrel."

"I'm sorry," Jacob said. "It's just not something a person expects to see in their garage."

His dad looked back at him as if this was the point.

"I think I'm going to call it the Sleepy Possum," he said. "The Sleepy Possum Saloon."

"Okay," Jacob said. "So, should I expect some train robbers in the house? Perhaps a gang of bandits?"

"No," his dad said. "This is just for us. This is a place for you and me, pardner. This is a place where we can talk like men."

"Like men?" Jacob said.

What did that mean?

"Come have a seat," his dad said, and walked to a stool.

When Jacob sat beside him, he saw a gun sitting on the bar.

It was the commemorative pistol from the glass case that he had moved aside the day before, when taking pictures of the blueprints of Deerfield Catholic. The one whose glass his dad must have broken the previous night. Next to it sat the single bullet that it had been mounted with.

His dad picked it up. He held it in his open palms not as if wielding it but as if offering it up for judgment. "This," he said, "is an

1884 Colt Peacemaker with a Frankford Arsenal cartridge, almost perfectly preserved. I brought it over to McGee's Gun and Pawn this morning and he oiled it up for me, said there's no reason it shouldn't still fire but, you know, I only have the one bullet. They apparently don't much make them like this anymore."

He held it out for Jacob to take.

Jacob shook his head. "I don't want to touch it," Jacob said, and this was perhaps the most honest thing he had ever said. "I don't want to touch a gun."

"Okay," his dad said, and set it back down. "I understand. I was just thinking this might serve as a sort of symbol for us, you know." He moved his chin a bit to get Jacob to look him in the eye, which Jacob did. "I've been thinking a lot about you lately, pardner," he said. "About the two of us."

Jacob felt his throat tighten in the same way it had in Toby's room, as if it were his body reminding him that he had not yet let anything out. That all of his fears and his grief were still waiting inside of him, that they weren't going anywhere until he let them.

"I've had this thing just sitting on the wall in my office for years," his dad said. "This thing that still works, that still functions. I've just had it hanging on the wall. Hung up and taken for granted. And I guess what I'm coming around to is the notion that I feel like you and me have sort of become that same way. It's just us now, you know. It's just the two of us left out in this tremendous field. This endless prairie. And there is so much work to do. So much herding and mending. And it is raining, Son. Do you understand what I'm saying? Right now, it is raining on us."

Jacob looked down at the floor. He saw his father's boot prints in the sawdust. He thought, for one brief moment, that he could hear the rain.

"But I've been acting like I'm all alone out here," his dad said. "I know I have. I've not been a good father for you lately. I've not been a good hand. Ever since your brother," he said. "I feel like I've just had you hung up on the wall. I'm sorry, Son. I want you to know that I'm sorry."

Jacob's eyes began to well as he knew without a doubt that his father was not the one who should be apologizing. And, above all the terrible things he had done lately, above and beyond what he had talked about with Trina, Jacob felt the impression he'd given his dad that *he* was somehow letting him down, not being there for him, was perhaps the worst crime of all. The idea that he had caused his father, a man who'd already suffered so much, any additional pain killed Jacob inside.

"I was thinking that we are sort of like this gun, in a way," his dad said. "That we can still work together, you know, if we stop taking each other for granted. If we start to talk about things. Like Toby, for instance. Like your mother."

"Dad," Jacob said. "There's something I need to tell you."

His dad held up his hand. "If you'll oblige me for one more second," he said. His dad picked up the bullet off the bar, rolled it around in his fingers. "I think the reason I've not talked to you as much as I should, Jacob, I want you to know, is that I've always been sort of afraid of you."

Jacob lifted his head. The comment confused him as he'd spent a lifetime, he thought, as all children do, hiding from his father the parts of himself that should scare anyone.

"Afraid?" Jacob asked.

"Heck yeah," his dad said. "Your brother was always sort of easy to understand, you know. He was sort of simple, I guess I'm saying. Not dumb, but just sort of easy. I've met a thousand people like Toby in my life. In some ways that was a comfortable thing about him. That was a thing to love. But *you*? I don't know. You've always seemed like more of a puzzle to me."

"I'm not a puzzle," Jacob said.

His dad again held up his hand. "And I think the reason for this," he said. "Is that you remind me so much of your mother."

There it was again, yet another train car of emotions ready to pull out from the station in Jacob, ready to set off from his body into the larger world. His mother, who was only photos to him, only some mysterious and untouchable DNA. He could not remember the last time they had spoken of her.

"The greatest tragedy of my life," his dad said. "And I've had my share. Is that you boys never got to meet her."

"Dad," Jacob said, but he did not know what else to say. He was torn completely between a desire to end this conversation and to extend it into a lifetime and so Jacob noticed instead only that the light had shifted in the short time he and his father had been in the garage. He looked outside and past the saloon doors to a sky both purpled and glowing with change and knew that there was a phrase for this time of day that he had learned in photography class but could not recall the name of. Yet he understood it as he looked back at his dad to see him in what seemed like a higher definition than he had ever seen him before. The way the light lit up the days-old stubble on his chin, the lines around his eyes and mouth, the veins along his hands on the bar. He looked to Jacob, in that moment, like a picture of a man.

"Did I ever tell you the story," his father asked him, "about that time your mom saved a mosquito?"

His father had told him this story, had told both he and Toby this story when they were younger, but it had been years. It was from a time before both he or Toby existed, when his parents lived in a small rental house. And, as he had done before, his dad recalled for Jacob the way he'd watched his mother follow the mosquito around from room to room, standing on chairs and tiptoes as the thing bounced dumbly from wall to wall without allowing her to touch it. He could remember what she was wearing that day, he told him, could remember so clearly what she looked like in that state of their lives together. How beautiful and strange he found her, and the point of the story was always the same.

"I thought she was trying to kill it," he said. "But the whole time she was trying to save it. The way she cupped it in her palms and walked it outside the screen door. It was like she was saving a bird. A mosquito, of all things. And I just laughed and laughed and she had this look on her face when she walked back inside. She was her own entire person, I knew, and she smiled as if to say to me, in a way, that I am going to do what I want to do, mister. And you are going to love me for it. And I've never loved anything more, I don't believe, than I loved your mother at that moment."

His dad took off his hat, held it by its top, and tapped it lightly on the bar.

"You remind me of her in that way, I suppose," he said. "It might not make sense to you, but that story reminds me. It's about the heart of you both. And I feel afraid, I reckon, because talking to you often feels like talking to her, and I don't ever want to let either one of you down."

A sense of guilt as dark as the oncoming night blanketed Jacob's chest, as it was not his father, he felt, who should be apologizing for anything.

"Dad," Jacob said. "I want to talk to you, too."

His dad perked up his eyes. He slapped Jacob lightly on the thigh. "See?" he said. "The Sleepy Possum is a magical place! Lay your saddle down, Son. I'm here."

"There's this girl," Jacob said. "A girl Toby was hanging around with. A girl named Trina."

His father nodded to say he knew of her and breathed deeply through his nose as if to acknowledge that he already recognized this would not be a happy story.

Where to begin, Jacob thought. The phone calls? The duffel bag?

The video? The Twitter account? The shotgun? The way these terrible options turned over in his mind was mirrored by the way the music in the room changed. The ragtime piano faded out and was replaced by the sound of a horse neighing again and again, until his father reached over the bar and unplugged his phone from a speaker, and Jacob realized this was his ringtone.

His dad looked at the screen and grimaced. He held the phone lightly, as if he might set it down, but then said, "Hell's bells. It's the law. I better take it."

Jacob stood up from his stool as his father opened the call and said, "Sheriff. What can I do you for?"

His dad held out his hand to ask Jacob to wait, to sit back down, but Jacob did not. Although he knew there were a thousand reasons the sheriff might call the mayor on a night like tonight, when the whole town was about to come alive in a way it hadn't before, Jacob had the awful feeling that perhaps the reason the sheriff was calling was him.

He began toward the house and saw his father look up at the old clock above the bar. "No," his father said. "I'm still at home. I know they've got the choir doing something. I know things are kicking off. I plan to be there before it's over."

Jacob walked up the steps and put his hand on the door to the kitchen. "No," his father said. "I haven't talked to Deuce since his performance at the meeting today. I know he's been calling but there's only so much a man can take on state's salary."

Jacob looked back at his dad, who furrowed his eyebrows like he was being asked something unexpected. "No," his dad said. "Jacob is here with me."

With this, Jacob opened the door and walked quickly through the house. It was all coming for him, he knew. Every part of him that he wished did not exist was finally coming to claim him and he felt torn wildly between the urge to hide everything in his possession and to show it. *This is how we got here,* he could say. *Take these from me, please. Help me understand how to put them together. Help me understand how it came to this.*

His father opened the door behind him and Jacob ran down the hall to Toby's room.

He heard his father say, "Duffel bag? I don't know, Randy. Do you know every single purse that your girls have lying around the house?"

Jacob quickly unplugged Toby's phone and stuck it in his pocket. He looked down at his backpack, which held the blue duffel bag, and picked it up, too. He saw his own phone sitting on the bed and grabbed it to see a series of messages he had missed while outside. All from Trina.

The hollow log, the first read.

7 o'clock, the second.

The last, *Somebody needs to be held responsible* . . .

Jacob saw his father's shadow approach the hall. There was no way out of the house in which Jacob could avoid him and so he went to Toby's window. He threw it open and ducked his head to crawl on the sill. If he could just get to Trina, he thought. If he could just talk to her.

"No," his father said. "You know I'm not on Twitter. What the hell do you mean, keep him here?"

Jacob gripped the ledge of the window and rocked back and forth just as he had done on his brother's bed. He then heard his father's boots in the hall, the click of his spurs, all the rain that was not even there, and into the life he now understood he had made for himself, Jacob jumped.

30

Souvenirs

There is a theory about dreams:

Some say that our dreams are so hard to describe to other people once we awake, so hard to communicate clearly, because they lack a consistent frame of reference. They are like a house of the mind with no foundation.

To put it another way, imagine yourself walking across a gigantic jigsaw puzzle. As you do this, the picture before you is clear, in all of its interlocking shapes, and so you understand where you are. Your dream, in this way, is not confusing while you are in it. Unbeknownst to you, however, these pieces are silently slid out and replaced by new images as soon as you pass them. So, when you get to the end of your dream and turn back to assess it, to recall the picture upon which you traveled, nothing is how you remembered. That's why you find yourself, that next morning, saying things like, "I had this dream where we were in our house, but it wasn't really *our* house. And *you* were there but you didn't really look like *you*. Still, I *knew* it was you. You don't understand. I could *feel* it."

Normally, this is when the other person stops listening.

Who can blame them?

Our dreams, because they are ours and ours alone, and because they are constantly shifting in a way that we pretend we are not also shifting when we are awake, are impossible to share. This is not a fault or flaw of our memory but is instead the way our minds preserve us, protect us, like our own hands automatically do, when we shade our eyes from the sun.

As for Douglas, he felt that his day was like a dream in reverse.

Everything that had transpired over the past two hours, everything he was given access to at Geoffrey's, was the stuff of his fantasies. Yet rather than this being difficult for Douglas to describe, it would have been the easiest thing in the world. He could draw this dream in every detail. The balanced weight of the trombone in his hands. The glint of light off the drummer's snare. The click of the bass player's fingers as she thumbed the upright. The sights, the sounds, the smells. They were all there for him to relay in the way that few dreams ever are.

Even what came after this, when Douglas couldn't get Pete on the phone. After he accepted a ride to his house with the band. The way he pulled down the tip of his beret and ducked his head to climb into the Bedknobs and Broomsticks' van, their name stenciled on the sides above a treble clef. The way the other residents of the Scenic Wetlands Apartments and Balconies had gathered out on the walkway, as well, to watch them load their instruments. This was the culmination of a million dream images for Douglas and he wanted, so badly, to be happy that they were so similar to what he'd always imagined. The disarray of cords and instrument cases behind the third-row seats. The bumper stickers from nightclubs with sayings like "Drummers Do It in Rhythm" used to cover up tears in the upholstery. The smell of old smoke and sweat. The way the engine cranked up as if it were several engines, rumbling to life in the parking lot, making children playfully cover their ears before they could even hear the real music which flickered to life on the radio, tuned to 90.7 WWOZ out of New Orleans. Before they could hear the opening beat of "Hey Pocky A-Way" by the Meters, circa 1974, which began on cue as if it had been waiting for them. And maybe it had, because this was a song that had a part for each person in that van to play. The drummer slapped his hands on his thighs in rhythm with the opening snare, Geoffrey fingered an imaginary piano on the seat beside Douglas, the bassist plucked at the top of the steering wheel. The way that none of them said a word but for Douglas to give directions to his house that whole time and the way that, somehow, by the end of the song, they had already arrived. All of these details were there for him to describe.

But where was Douglas in this?

Of all the outlandish turns in his afternoon, the one that Douglas would have the most difficulty describing and therefore felt the most like an unfortunate dream, was his conversation with Cherilyn. He couldn't stop thinking about it.

He'd gone back into Geoffrey's after Cherilyn hung up and listened to them play for a while but politely turned down their requests for him to jam again. The music was good and he smiled along as best he could but as soon as an hour had passed and Pete had not come back, Douglas became antsy. Something in the tone of her voice he'd not heard before. He went outside to call Pete and got no answer, but this didn't worry him. He was a priest, after all, and who knew how good they were with cell phones? After the second time he walked back into Geoffrey's apartment, still looking down at his phone, Geoffrey told the band, "That's a wrap, folks. I believe our whistler's got another gig to get to."

When they pulled into his driveway, Douglas climbed out and thanked them all, said he would see them on center stage tomorrow, and then noticed an odd thing.

His car was gone.

How had she gotten it started?

He thought to call and ask. He wanted to call and ask Cherilyn a lot of things, but he also had the distinct impression that she wanted some space. Whatever she was doing at her mother's house, he had offered to come join her and she had declined. So, he would give her that. He could give people things, couldn't he? Sure he could. As an example, he had also given his keys to Pete and so had to walk around to the backyard to get the spare, which they kept beneath a small concrete statue of a jaunty-looking frog with a fishing pole.

Douglas entered the back door of his home as he had done so many thousands of times before, hung his blazer on the back of the chair, and was overcome by the silence. He looked toward the kitchen, where it should be wine time, where he would normally see Cherilyn waiting for him. No, not waiting for him, he thought, but living her life with him. Where he would see her drawing an end to her day, like he was, so that they could share the evening. And she was not there.

Yet so much of her scattered around.

Douglas looked down at the breakfast table. Six birdhouses there, all facing one another as if arranged in a small neighborhood, and he was touched by the strange beauty of the scene. Each house basically the same structure but made unique by Cherilyn's flourishes. The roof of one was shingled entirely of plastic flower petals that Douglas recognized from the pens she had sold a couple of years ago. A large heart-shaped wreath on the front of another made entirely, it seemed, of the type of twist-ties one found on bread bags. There had to be hundreds of the little ties, Douglas realized, shaped and braided together by his wife's hands. How had he not noticed her doing this? Or, if he had, how had he not mentioned how ingenious he found her? Douglas was now struck by the image of his wife as a person who saw material everywhere: the anecdotes he told her from school, the pens that had gone unsold, the colorful ties he had so often thrown away, and then of her gathering these materials to make a better life for him, a better life for birds. This notion of her giving spirit, her generosity, filled his chest.

Then he saw something else.

Also on the table, beside the birdhouses, sat two coffee cups.

He'd not had coffee that morning. He'd been so hungover he couldn't have kept it down. He thought it was unlike her to use two cups and tilted one of them over so he could see inside of it. At the bottom, the oily dregs of black coffee. In the other, the familiar tan veneer of settled milk, how both he and Cherilyn drank it. And again how peculiar, as it had been in Tipsy's car, to think of Cherilyn's moments without him as if filled with mystery. Who had come over today? he wondered. Surely, it was not her mother, as Cherilyn would have broken her back scrubbing the place just to avoid her mother's off-handed comments about housekeeping. Maybe a girlfriend. A neighbor?

Douglas might not have entertained another question about this cup if he was the same man he was that morning. But he was not the same man. This was not because of his readout or his students or even the band, really, but because he was now a man whose wife had asked to stop whistling. And, as is the case with the vast majority of communication between spouses, it is not the words that are said that change things but the tone with which they reach you. Douglas had been bothersome to his wife on the phone, and he knew this. So, he rinsed out her cup in the sink and kept the one with black coffee sitting unwashed on the counter so that he could mention it later.

He turned and leaned against the counter. Cherilyn was right, Douglas thought; they had things to talk about. Her readout, for one, which he had again decided he would listen to. If that's what caused her to sound that way on the phone, then he wanted to do whatever he could to make sure it never happened again. He would not only hear her out but would encourage her. However she wanted to interpret the idea of being royal, whatever changes she wanted to make. He would support her. He would not say a negative thing tonight. All he wanted, he knew, was to see her happy.

As for his own readout, he would tell her that, too. No more lying. No more omissions. He would confess where he had been the night before, as well. He would come clean and tell her the terrible truth: that the person she sounded so aggravated with on the phone was the best thing he could ever become. I'm sorry, he would say, if that disappoints you.

But not in this dirty kitchen.

Douglas decided instead that, as a way of combatting the emptiness he felt in the house without her, he would fill it with expectation. He would welcome her home in the way she so often did for him. If she wanted to be royal, then he would welcome her royally. He looked at the clock and figured he still had an hour, if she was going to be a bit late. He wet a towel and quickly wiped down the counters. He organized the cooking magazines. He went to the breakfast table and carefully removed the birdhouses, then took a tan tablecloth from the pantry and laid it over the table. He placed the birdhouses back on the cloth in the same manner she had arranged them and they now looked like a little suburban oasis out in the desert somewhere.

He walked back to their bedroom and straightened his side of the room and opened the closet. He took out his nicest suit, a gray two-piece that he wore to weddings and funerals and knew Cherilyn liked. He chose a pink shirt that Cherilyn had once given him for his birthday but that he had never had the confidence to wear and hung it on the closet door.

He then reached behind his sweatshirts at the top of the closet to pull out his little lockbox. Not much in it. A ticket stub from a date he and Cherilyn went on to see *Les Misérables*, when Douglas had promised himself to dedicate more time to his art, which he had not done before last week. A few letters from his parents from before they passed and, beneath it all, two flattened coins.

The coins were two once-ordinary quarters that he and Cherilyn had run through a souvenir machine on their first date, some twenty and more years ago by now, when he had surprised her by driving her a few towns over to the carnival in Fluker, Louisiana. The coins had been hand cranked by the both of them, flattened to wafers with embossed words that read: "Where the Fun Begins!" Douglas had put the coins in his pocket and, that night, when he was at home in his parents' house and remembering her, made two small holes in the top so that they could be made into necklaces. He figured to give them to her on their next date, but it went so well that he didn't feel the need to. And this next date turned into years in which Douglas always pushed off the gift, feeling that it was growing more powerful as time passed because it wasn't what the coins said, exactly, nor even that they were from their first date that endowed them with power, but that he remembered this as the first time they had physically touched each other, when he tried cranking the wheel by himself and thought it was stuck. When she placed her hand on top of his and smiled, and said, "How about we try this together, you weakling?"

He'd recently been planning to hold off until their twenty-fifth wedding anniversary to give this to her and secretly hoped, in his greatest imaginings, that he could hold off until their fiftieth. But now, Douglas felt clearly, he wanted to give her this tonight.

He set them on top of his suit and went to the bathroom and turned on the shower. He then took off his pants and his shirt. He looked at himself in the mirror.

What he would give to trade this body for another. Or, if not another, then maybe the previous version of his own, the body Cherilyn had originally fallen for. The one he most recalled, without telling her, from a time they went tubing down a river, the name of which he couldn't remember. When she had looked at him, his face and his body, and bit her bottom lip in a way that said *I like everything about you*.

The body he looked at now, however, had an unfortunately comedic aspect. The pear shape of his hips was like soft jowls. Even his breasts, he thought, sat on his chest like two tired eyes. The hair down his stomach was laid out as if a broad nose, and his belly button, he saw clearly now, was a small and quiet mouth. His naked torso was like a separate face entirely, looking back at him, and when did it become this way? He cupped his hands around his love handles and gave them a shake. How many meals in the school cafeteria? How many skillet-burger Wednesdays? He looked down and pressed at the sides of his belly button as if to make it speak. He gave it a belly-button voice.

"Well, now," it said. "Fancy meeting you here."

Holy shit, Douglas thought. *I have become ridiculous. What woman could a body like this seduce?* He looked back up at himself in the mirror and cracked up laughing. He couldn't help it.

He had forgotten to take off his beret.

"Let's try this for a start," Douglas said, and took off the beret, hung it on the doorknob, and hopped in the shower. He scrubbed himself clean and even did some light calisthenics as he bathed. No better time to start than the present, he figured. He curled the bar of soap in his hand like a dumbbell. He held on to the wall and did some calf raises while rinsing out his sparse hair. He flexed his stomach muscles that he realized were still embarrassingly sore from his and Cherilyn's dalliance the other night and, reminded of this, Douglas felt the burn.

He hopped out and toweled off and dressed in his suit, put on his cologne. He then went into the den and dimmed the lights. He flipped through his CD selection and chose Ella Fitzgerald's *Ella for Lovers* as the perfect mood music but when he went to put it in the CD player, saw that there was already an Elton John disc in there, the little EP with "Candle in the Wind 1997" on it. Okay, then, he thought, if this is what she wants, let's do it, and hit play.

He walked to the kitchen and whistled along to the song, which he had not heard in years. He took down two nice wineglasses and set them beside the bottle he'd bought yesterday. He placed the corkscrew next to this. Douglas then opened the bag he'd seen before when he was cleaning, a number of candles in it, and arranged them throughout the house but did not light them. He looked at the clock. It had grown dark outside but he didn't want to light them too early. So, he fished out a box of matches from the drawer and took one out. He wanted to time it all perfectly and so he stood with a match in one hand and the box in the other and looked through the kitchen window, waiting to see her pull up.

He stayed this way until the phone rang and, on the small display of his caller ID, he saw Bruce Newman's name.

31

You've Got Gold

Had she ever sat so high off the ground?

The sheer altitude alone made Cherilyn woozy, not to mention the speed they were going. She believed she could likely reach out and tap the top of each car they passed, so high was Deuce's truck. She could definitely look down into the windows and see the other drivers' laps, which had an almost perverse feel to it, and believed that Deuce could likely just cruise over the medians if he chose to, such were the size of his tires, which had, she must admit, a rather powerful effect.

Overall, Cherilyn was now inside an impressive machine. It had a big broad dashboard with silver buttons and blue lights, black leather seats which were comfortable and new, and a whole row of seats behind them, as well. This was a pickup truck with a lot of bells and whistles and space to do whatever a person wanted. It made her Outback feel bland and outdated and yet, Cherilyn knew, that car was the nicest thing she and Douglas owned. It cost so much that Douglas had put off getting a new car of his own those last five years but that was a train of thought for another time and place and not, Cherilyn reminded herself, for today. Today was not about Douglas. It was about her.

Deuce hadn't said a thing since leaving her mother's place, which was uncharacteristic for him. And as they wove through traffic Cherilyn appreciated, at least, that she was too high up for anyone to see her in a car that was acting so rudely or, perhaps, for anyone to see her in the car with Deuce. The silence had become uncomfortable, though, and Cherilyn got the impression that Deuce was nervous. He kept rubbing the breast pocket of his shirt, fluffing his hair back over his ears, adjusting the way he was sitting. So, she wanted to say something. She had to fight her natural impulses to compliment him on the truck, but she was not going to behave like some teenager on a first date, she told herself, because that's not what this was.

Instead, she said, "Where's the fire, Deuce? Seems like you've got a heavy foot."

"We're chasing the daylight," he told her. "It's what all the best photographers do. No better time than sunrise and sunset to capture the real beauty of the world."

"Is that what you're trying to capture?" she said, and smoothed the dress on her legs. "You have a place in mind?"

"You know me," he said. "I'm always thinking ahead. Not much longer now. You want some music or something? I've got two hundred and fifty-six digital radio stations."

The mention of music made her think quickly of Douglas, which she was not pleased about. The strange music she heard in the background when she spoke to him on the phone earlier, the way he let her choose whatever station she wanted when they were in the car together although she knew he preferred that jazz station from New Orleans, which she didn't much care for. The way she would come home to find him sitting among a circle of records, playing vinyl on the LP player they kept in the bottom cabinet of their bookshelf. And, mainly, the way he was constantly making his own music around the house, whistling bits and pieces of things as he stepped out of the shower, sat at the table, or tied his shoes. How much music was inside of him? she wondered. Music that she didn't even know, had never even heard, and yet nobody knew Douglas better than her. She didn't want to think about it.

So, "No," she said, "silence is good," and looked around his truck a bit more.

It was obvious he'd done a lazy man's job of cleaning. The back seat was full of junk, as if he'd just shoved everything back there to make room. She saw boxes for all sorts of equipment she wasn't sure she understood: modems and printers and cartons of paper and toner. Tripods and webcams. A projector and a garden hose. A little teller bag of money and receipts. It looked like a thousand things that might make up a photographer's day-to-day life but what caught Cherilyn's eye, what seemed most out of place, was a small gift about the size of a shoebox. It was wrapped in gold paper with a silver bow. Cherilyn typically would have asked about this, so out of place it looked sitting there, but did not for her fear that the gift might be for her. Or, she wondered, was she afraid that it wasn't? With which outcome would she feel more disappointed? So, instead, she turned back toward the front seat and said, "Looks like a junkyard in here. Don't you have a place to store all that stuff?"

"Believe it or not," Deuce told her. "There's not one piece of junk back there. It just looks like that because it's in separate pieces. It's like your birdhouses, for example. Some people just see twigs in the yard and glue in the drawer, but you see this whole possible world. I'm the same way." He turned the truck on a side street and said, "Not long now."

Cherilyn knew where they were going. The only thing on this side of town was Parker Field. This was the place people came to try and sight the deer who sometimes grazed on the grasses that grew there, descendants of the same family of deer the town was named after, legend had it, which Cherilyn knew to be untrue.

Deer have to wander. It's what they do. So, if these were still the same family of deer that some settlers spotted nearly two hundred years ago, then it wasn't because the deer lived there, Cherilyn knew, or that they considered Deerfield home, but merely because it was a place they liked to visit from time to time on their way to another place they liked to visit from time to time.

Cherilyn knew Parker Field mainly as the place the town held the annual Fish Festival and the Labor Day BBQ and where sometimes men would come out to fly their remote-control airplanes. It was left unmown but for the major holidays and Cherilyn liked it this way best, when the butterflies were all over the place feeding on flowers while also, she realized, making their way to someplace else. This made Cherilyn wonder why everything else in the world seemed only to visit Deerfield and yet there she was living in it. Why wasn't she on her way to someplace else? Maybe she could be.

As Deuce slowed the truck Cherilyn pulled down the visor to look at herself, and the hands that did this for her were like that of a stranger. The henna had grown darker on her skin in the last hour and Cherilyn placed them together again to see the pretty picture they made. She then opened the mirror and adjusted her head scarf and said, "Oh my goodness," as she could see behind her now and into the bed of the pickup.

"Bruce Newman," she said. "Is that a mattress in the back of your truck? Because I will get out of this vehicle right now if that's what you're thinking. I mean it."

Deuce smiled. "Well, look who's got the dirty mind," he said.

"I most certainly do not," she said.

"Relax," he said. "I'm just moving it back to storage. Had a friend staying with me the past few days but his wife's coming in for tomorrow and so they got a hotel outside of town." He held up two fingers. "Scout's honor," he said.

"I've known you nearly your whole life," she told him. "And you haven't ever been a Boy Scout."

"Well," Deuce said, and smiled again. "You've got me there."

Deuce then pulled off the road and onto the tall grass of Parker Field. He drove out to the middle as quietly and easily as the truck was made for him to do and parked. He looked at the clock on the dashboard. "Twenty minutes to sunset," he said. "Perfect timing. This is what photographers call the Golden Hour."

"How is it an hour if it's only twenty minutes?" she said.

"I guess that's what makes it special," Deuce said. "Let's go."

Cherilyn opened the door. She noticed a small step slide out for her from beneath the cab and so she lifted her dress and stepped down into the high grass. She looked toward the west, where the sun was setting behind the dense woods that edged the field, and understood why this would be called the Golden Hour. The setting sun had lit the sky behind the trees a pink so vibrant as to look otherworldly. She walked around the front of the truck and saw Deuce digging around in the truck bed.

"I swear to God," she said. "If you pull out that mattress, I'm going to yell for the sheriff."

Deuce looked back at her and slowly lifted a tripod with one hand and a milk crate with the other. He held them above his head like one might do their wallet and hat through a metal detector. "Head out to the middle there," he said. "I want to get some wide-angle shots before we do the close-ups."

Cherilyn walked to the middle of the field. The wind moving across that empty space lifted the dress in her hands to make it brush across her thighs and calves in a way that felt soft and wonderful against her skin.

Deuce waddled up behind her with a camera around his neck and set the milk crate on the ground. "Stand on this," he said. "You won't be able to see it beneath the grass. It'll make you look like you're floating."

"That sounds nice," she said.

"I know what I'm doing," he told her. "Don't you worry."

So, Cherilyn stood on top of the milk crate and steadied herself. She looked out toward the forest that she realized could have ended anywhere. What was on the other side of it? she wondered. If she were just to walk out into those woods, to do something totally unlike herself, where would she end up? In what town? In what city? In what state?

"Okay," Deuce said. "Turn around for me."

Cherilyn held her dress and turned carefully on the milk crate to where Deuce had set up his tripod a good twenty yards away. He was adjusting the angle on it, tightening all sorts of things with his hands and looking through the camera. "That's good," he said, and already she heard the soft sounds of the camera clicking.

"Do you want me to smile or something?" she asked him. "I'm not sure what I should do."

"Just do whatever feels natural," he told her. "Just be yourself."

And although she tried it briefly, Cherilyn soon realized that smiling did not feel natural at all to her at that moment. No, what she wanted was to be taken seriously for a change, if not from anyone else but herself. She wanted to look on the outside the way she sometimes felt in her heart, like she was important to the world, that she was a major part of it. So, instead of forcing the smile that she had happily done for a thousand other pictures in her lifetime, Cherilyn closed her eyes and let go of her dress and lifted her arms out to the sides. She wanted to feel the warm wind in the same way she felt it in her dream of fine sand and, as if she had summoned this herself, she did feel it. The breeze took hold of her dress and blew it gently to the side. It flitted the head scarf around her face and Cherilyn breathed through her nose what she felt to be pure oxygen. She stood that way for a long time.

"Oh my God," she heard Deuce whisper. "Don't move an inch."

So Cherilyn, as if a model of herself, did not move at all on the outside. But, on the inside of her, there was almost unbearable movement. She heard the caravan approaching now, all of the hopes and dreams of the past weeks coming to her, her hands outstretched and painted with two distinct parts of a picture that only she could place together and make whole. She heard the quick clicking of the camera like the sounds of small sticks breaking underfoot and she said, quietly, "This feels so, damn, good."

"Shh," Deuce whispered. "Don't say anything. Just turn around. Slowly. Just look behind you."

Cherilyn opened her eyes to see Deuce pointing behind her. She turned around carefully and, beneath purpling sky, saw what was to her the most beautiful scene she'd ever come across. In front of the tree line, as if glowing, three deer stood grazing in the field. The light tan of their fur rendered by the Golden Hour to look like fine fabric and, when they noticed her turn, each animal looked up from their meal to appraise her. Their long and careful faces, the gorgeous geography of their bodies as they considered her. They were not afraid, it seemed, and neither was she, so Cherilyn stretched her arms out to them as if they might abandon all reality and allow themselves to be pet by her alone, to be fed from her soft hand.

She then heard the door to Deuce's truck quietly open and shut behind her, to which the deer flicked their ears, set their haunches, and bounded back into a wilderness to which Cherilyn knew no end. As they disappeared Cherilyn was overcome by the enormous potential of what was already around her, what was always around but that she could not always see. The myriad possibilities of what could step out of the woods and present itself to you on any given day, if only you had the patience to wait for it.

She turned back around, smiling, to see Deuce standing before her with the gift box in his hand.

"I want to give this to you," he said. He knelt heavily down on one knee and bowed his head as he presented it. "I have a feeling you're going to like it."

And, surprising to herself even, Cherilyn did not say anything to him. She was so far away from that place now, her body filling with emotions that she did not understand yet was so powerless to stop, that she did not know if she would ever speak again. She reached out and took the box automatically and was puzzled by how light it was in her palms, by how it felt like nothing at all and, as she untied the bow, she realized that it felt this way because her hands had gone numb.

She said nothing about this as she lifted the lid of the box and looked inside to where sat a small crown of gold.

And all of those unfortunate feelings, as if the backside of everything good she had felt just seconds ago, returned to her.

"It's for you," Deuce said.

She touched the small crown, which did not appear to be costume jewelry at all but rather real gold with tiny shards of bright blue and green glass along the edges. Beneath her fingers, it too felt like nothing at all and Cherilyn's legs began to grow heavy. She experienced a tingling up her spine and into her neck as undeniable as if beset by invisible hands.

"I don't understand," she said, and she didn't. Not what was happening inside of her body nor how Deuce could have known the exact thoughts running through her mind those past weeks. Not what she was doing out in that field nor what was coming for her. She began to feel nauseated and held the box to her stomach.

"It's all for you, Cherilyn," he told her. "Everything I've ever done. That's what I'm trying to tell you. It can all be different now."

She looked down to see Deuce reach up and place one of his hands on her calf, beneath her dress, and reach the other hand to his breast pocket. "I have something I want to show you," he said, but Cherilyn had the sudden sensation that her heart was no longer beating, that she was no longer breathing, that something was going terribly wrong, and she wondered wildly if the source of this feeling was shame.

She bent over and placed her hand on Deuce's shoulder. She dropped the box on the ground. "I don't feel right," she said, and toppled over the milk crate.

Deuce caught her and said, "I know. I'm here for you. We can do this together."

Cherilyn fell to her knees and looked up at Deuce. Her eyes were wide and frightened, appearing almost angry at him for bringing her there, as if he had caused this whole thing. She could feel her consciousness leaving her, her body going away from this field and this man, and it took an enormous effort for her to say the only thing she could think of to say.

"No, you idiot," she said, and put her hand on the ground. "Call Douglas. Call Douglas right now."

Cherilyn then fell into the grass, where the last thing she recalled hearing were the gentle footsteps of every living thing she could not see.

You and Me, Sitting in the Back of My Memory

Douglas was in no mood for small talk. He'd told Tipsy only the basic facts: Cherilyn was in the hospital and he needed a ride.

"I'm flipping a U right now," Tipsy said. "I'll have you in ten."

In that ten minutes, Douglas did what all jealous men do.

He devolved.

The majority of his confusion had turned to anger as he replayed Deuce's voice in his head, and anger was not a good look for Douglas. He kept rubbing his own face, pacing around the kitchen in his suit like some drug-addled attorney. He'd had virtually no practice at being jealous, he realized. Maybe he should have been feeling this way a long time before? This odd form of paranoia rewired his circuits so completely that nearly every good thing he'd thought about his life reversed course to store itself in some dark battery within his heart he was not previously aware of.

He'd stood like a moron throughout the entire conversation, holding the phone in one hand and the unlit matchstick in the other.

"The hospital?" he said. "Is she okay?"

"Yeah," Deuce told him. "She had a sort of spell, I guess. The doctors are in with her now. Did you know she was having something going on? I sure as hell didn't."

Douglas looked at his own reflection in the kitchen window, as if he was talking to himself on the phone.

"I don't understand," he said. "Why are you the one telling me this, Bruce? Are you at the hospital, too?"

"Well," Deuce said, and took a while before finishing.

"Well, what?" Douglas said.

"Well," he said. "I'm the one that drove her here."

"But she's at her mom's," Douglas said. "I talked to her just a couple of hours ago."

"Yeah," Deuce said. "That's sort of true. We were over there first, for a bit. But then we went out to Parker Field and, I don't know. You should have seen her. It was scary, to be honest."

Douglas leaned closer to the window, so close for his nose to touch the glass, for him to see only his own eyes.

"You were with Cherilyn?" he said. "Cherilyn was with you?"

"Look," Deuce said. "I figure we both have some explaining to do."

"We?" Douglas said. "I don't believe I have any explaining to do."

"No," Deuce said. "I mean, me and Cherilyn. But just come down here, for now. She's asking for you."

Deuce hung up the phone and Douglas didn't move. He was too curious about his own reflection. Who was that fool staring back at him in the glass? Who was that total and complete asshole? A number of scenes from his recent memory returned to him as poisoned in almost an instant. The way Deuce had mentioned Wick Bart's wife going so crazy after an affair, how he'd warned them to look out for sudden changes in a person. This story became ominous when paired with Cherilyn's unexpected request for an encore the other night. Was Douglas, he thought sickly, receiving only the collateral benefits of Cherilyn's outside love? Impossible. But even the way she had been so short with him on the phone, the way she had asked him to stop whistling for the first time in her life. It was all there. Maybe this wasn't about her readout at all. Maybe it was all much bigger, much worse than Douglas ever allowed himself to consider. How was it possible, he wondered, that every fear in one's life, every nightmare, stood always at the ready?

He tried calling Pete to get his car but got no answer. He then called Cherilyn's mother, hoping Cherilyn might be there, hoping that it might all be some awful joke. When her mother picked up the phone, Douglas didn't even say hello.

"Is Cherilyn there?" he asked, and something in the tone of his voice must have given his position away. He heard her mother let out a long sigh.

"Oh, Lord," she said. "I told her this wasn't a good idea."

"Is she there?" he said again.

"No, Douglas," she said. "They've gone off about an hour ago. If it makes you feel better, I thought she looked like an imbecile."

"She's in the hospital," he told her. "Did you know that?"

"Hospital?" her mom said and let out a little huff. "She didn't look sick to me."

Douglas hung up the phone and, after getting a hold of Tipsy, spent the next ten minutes wondering what he should break. He looked down at the coffee cup, now fully assured of all its horrible possibilities, and thought, with total clarity: What would happen if I threw this out the window? He did not, though, and instead walked over to the kitchen table. He looked at the nice little village of birdhouses he had set out for Cherilyn to come home to and picked one up. He held it between his palms and thought to squeeze it, to crush it in his own hands, to just leave it there scattered to bits for when she returned. He thought of making glorious and broken metaphors of all her crafts but saw instead the way the glue was so carefully lined between the sticks, the way it looked as if some miniature mason had run its trowel along every joint and junction of that house, and he set it back down.

He stormed to their office to look for what? He did not know, exactly. Some emails, perhaps, some awful pictures. He leaned over the desk and moved the mouse but the machine made such an obvious objection to what he was doing that he had no patience for it.

He went into their bedroom and looked around. When was the last time it had been so clean? He had straightened up his side, he knew, trying so foolishly to impress her, trying to be the best version of himself. But why was her side so clean? Was she also doing that for him or was she, perhaps, doing it to hide things from him? Had she scrubbed the area like a crime scene? Is that what it had become? He walked into the bathroom and dug through the drawers and saw his beret hanging on the doorknob where he had taken it off before. He picked it up and studied it. How pitiful was he? Who was he to think that he was meant for something special, that he had some untapped potential? What arrogance. What selfishness. There was no great destiny for him, he thought. He was exactly what the readout said he was, and nothing more. He saw it clearly now.

He was a jester who had fallen for a queen.

So, he folded the beret in his hand and dropped it into the bathroom trash can.

He looked back into their room at her dresser and Douglas knew what she kept in there. A little lockbox of her personal things. A little cache of evidence. He walked over and opened the drawer and dug around in her clothes until he found it.

He set it down on the dresser and put his finger on the latch.

As if to save him, however, Douglas felt his teacher mode coming on. What lesson had he ever taught about history, after all, more than its maniacal commitment to repeating itself? And since Douglas had never opened this box before in all their lives together he understood that doing so would create for him a new

history, one that he would be allowing, or assuring, really, to repeat itself.

Yet the only history Douglas wanted to repeat was the one he'd
always thought he'd known, where his allowance of Cherilyn's privacy was like her allowance of his own and, he believed, one of the
cornerstones of their marriage. This unspoken agreement oper-
ated as silently and powerfully as many other unspoken agree-
ments they shared, ones he believed distinguished them from
many other couples he knew. The way they never mentioned the
word *divorce*, even teasingly, to each other or around friends. The
way they never made the other one the butt of a joke to other people. The way they never talked about other people they found attractive, the way they did not complain about the other's family or
friends. The way they never said anything intentionally that they
knew might hurt the other, even in some small way. This did not
mean that they were dishonest with each other. It meant, Douglas
felt, they were instead honoring the other, depending on the other.
It did not mean that they were perfect, either. It meant only that,
when one of them felt petty and small, as humans are apt to do,
they relied on a simple but underutilized trick to bring them out of
it. Instead of trying to shrink the other person down to their size,
they asked, instead, for their love to make them big again.

Yet Douglas felt undeniably small with his hand on the latch. If
there was anything in that box that Cherilyn did not want him to
see, he knew, then there had to be a reason, just as he had his reasons for keeping his box with its two flattened coins from her. And
since so much of this history was filled with overwhelming evidence that his wife was the kindest person he knew, he had to
trust that the odds of her having something hidden in that box
that would diminish his love were not nearly as great as the odds
it would make it grow.

So, he put the box back in the drawer and walked out his front door, where he saw Tipsy driving up the street, flashing the head-lights like his own little siren.

Tipsy cut through the back of the neighborhood to get out to the highway as Douglas sat in the passenger seat, kneading his knuckles against his suit pants.

"I'm not even going to bother with town," Tipsy said. "It's a zoo. We can make up time with a little speed, I think."

"Whatever it takes," Douglas told him. "Just drive."

"I was just over there, actually," he said. "Not even an hour ago. I didn't see Ms. Cherilyn but had heard about Father Pete on my police scanner so I just went to say hey."

"Police scanner?" Douglas said.

"Shoot, yeah," Tipsy told him, and nodded at a little box beneath the dash. "I'm a volunteer firefighter. Two years now. Not a single fire. Plus, when things are slow, this helps me keep up on my gos-sip. People depend on me for that type of information, you know. You wouldn't believe some of the things people do in this town."

"Tipsy," Douglas said. "Focus, please. What about Pete?"

"You haven't heard?" Tipsy said. "He got robbed out at Lanny's, sounds like. Has a big old lump on his head. Lanny's there, too, out of his mind on something. Couple of druggies did it, is the word. I didn't get a chance to talk to him. Just sort of waved at him through the window like this. Anyway, they got cops all over town looking for them."

"Jesus," Douglas said. "What in the living hell is wrong with this day?"

Tipsy hit the gas a bit more and said, "I'll get you there. I know you're worried. I hope she's okay. There's nobody in this town peo-ple like more than Cherilyn, I don't believe. She hasn't hurt a fly. The both of you, really. People look up to you. You just have a sort of love that people see."

Douglas looked over at him. He agreed with at least part of what he'd said. He did hope she was okay. But what would okay even mean now?

"Let's just drive, if you don't mind," he said. "Let's just get there."

"Roger that," Tipsy said.

Tipsy got to the hospital in no time and dropped Douglas off in the parking lot. On his way to the door, he passed Deuce's truck parked in a handicapped spot and looked inside of it. On the seat he saw a small golden crown, and this turned his insides. It was too dark to see much of what was in the back seat, but then Douglas noticed a mattress in the truck bed. He put his head on the side of the truck and squeezed his eyes shut. Be logical, he told himself. Be open.

He then turned and walked through the door to reception, where a woman named Pamela Walker was working the desk. Once a student of his, she was now nearly thirty years old.

Pamela looked up at him and smiled. "Hey, Mr. Hubbard," she said. "She's in room twelve down the hall to the right. Gave us a little scare, didn't she?"

Douglas was so warped with worry that he did not know how to respond. He should have said thank you, of course, but for some reason said only, "I remember that paper you wrote about Jean Lafitte."

Pamela smiled as if she were suddenly much older than Douglas and said, "She's going to be fine, Mr. Hubbard. Dr. Granger is back with her now. Room twelve. Right that way."

Douglas took the right and walked down the hall to see Deuce Newman sitting on a chair and thumbing at his phone. Deuce stood up when he approached, and Douglas held up his hand.

"Not one word," Douglas said. "Not one word out of your big enormous face."

Deuce showed his palms as if in surrender and, without knocking, Douglas opened the door to room twelve and walked in.

33

Your Boy Is Here

Jacob was no athlete. Yet, in this moment, he pretended.

He ran down the quiet streets of his neighborhood as if timed. He stopped only once to catch his breath and duck behind a neighbor's tool shed. He wanted to see if his father was coming down the road in his truck, but he was not, so Jacob pulled the phone from his pocket and swiped it open. Six-thirty. He still had time if he hustled.

He wanted to make it to the log before seven o'clock, before the choir started up, before everyone was in their seats and, most important, while there might still be people milling around on the trail. Random people, witnesses, not involved in any of this. Not *every single one of them* nor the dickheads but just ordinary people who jangled keys in their pockets and placed them in doors, who sat on sofas next to people they loved and did not say much at all, who had jobs and pets and were sane. Enough of these normal people around, maybe, that Jacob could talk her out of it, could tell her that he *knew* now, that he understood.

He texted her back.

On my way.

He ran again before getting an answer and in this effort could think only of the times that must have surrounded the video. He imagined Trina in Toby's car on the way to that party and realized, sickly, the reason she was not in it when he crashed. All this time, he'd thought maybe Trina had abandoned Toby, had let him drive, but now there was the possibility that Toby had left her. That he had been a witness to something horrible, that he may have even caused or allowed it, and yet left her there to suffer. It was too much to imagine, what great distance there was between what she thought her night would be and what it turned into. This idea of distance led him to think about the stretch of time after the video, as well. And as Jacob felt his own feet pound against the pavement he could only imagine the sounds of Trina's feet against the gravel as she began her own trek home. Such a long walk for her by herself, he imagined, likely full of the realization that she was now a different person than the one she had been just hours before. Her past was different. Her future was different. And in that stretch of time, alone in the dark, Jacob knew she had the opportunity to hatch a million plans, all of them justified, Jacob felt, by each solitary step she was forced to take. This idea broke Jacob's heart for the world and for Trina, and for everyone made to walk alone in life, and he decided that he would no longer be a part of that. Loneliness. He would do away with it. It did not matter that he was no longer a twin, that he was an only child; whatever Jacob could do to travel in pairs, from there on out, he would do. He and his father. They could be something together, Jacob knew, if he would begin to allow it.

When he finally reached the square, he thought he might have turned in the wrong direction. He stopped to catch his breath. Nothing was how he remembered it.

All the lights.

Where had they come from?

The square before him was strung with glowing bulbs, sagging from lengths of cable hung between tents and craft booths and food stands. He watched people move about below these lights, carrying boxes and pulling carts as if the earliest settlers of a place they'd just invented. And the way Jacob had felt at Toby's door that afternoon, about perhaps living in a world where every possibility was open, that every step you took could perhaps be a step toward a different life than the one you thought you knew, appeared very real to him.

On his right, two women crossed the street wearing corseted Victorian dresses. They twirled umbrellas in their hands and waved at a teenaged boy painting a sign that read "TAX ADVICE AND SHRIMP." Jacob watched a man across the street from him sit heavily upon an old ice chest, taking a break from the work, it seemed, with a squirrel on his shoulder. He had no idea if he knew these people or not. Regardless, he took a deep breath, pulled his cap low over his head and made his hasty way through the crowd.

He would stop her, he thought. He would listen to her. He would help her in whatever way that he could and, with these thoughts, Jacob felt physically strong as he navigated the square. He reached the other side and jogged across the street, where he finally saw the hand-painted sign that arrowed him toward the Crane Lane.

He neared the mouth of the trail and all the strangeness of the glowing square was doubled over by the darkness now before him. He bent to catch his breath and heard an engine turn. On the far shoulder of the road, about thirty yards from him near the woods, he saw a truck flick on its lights. Jacob thought in a panic that his father had beaten him there but then realized this was another truck he had seen before. It was Father Pete's truck.

This possibility thrilled him as he had the sudden notion that Father Pete may be the only other person in the world he could talk to about what was happening. The only other person who could make it stop. Trina's uncle. A witness. A priest.

Jacob lifted one hand to block the glare of the lights and tried to wave him down with the other. As soon as he started toward it, though, the driver threw the truck into gear and drove up the gravel shoulder. Jacob yelled, "Hey!" and waved his arms, but the truck did not stop. He watched it head out into the parish and could not see who was in it, only the small square light of a phone that the driver held by the wheel.

"Come back!" Jacob said, but not loud enough for anyone to hear him. He bent again, with his palms on his knees. He looked into the trail like one might do a deep well. He heard no one in it. He then stood and took off at a jog, trying to both listen and run at the same time, and felt himself nearly trip on every oak root and divot available to him. He pulled out his phone and turned on the flashlight, the world seemingly darker beneath this tunnel of trees than any other place he'd known. He pointed the small cone of light to the ground and counted all the roots and colored rocks that he passed.

Before long, he could hear it. In the distance, his school. The bicentennial kickoff. The choir. The football team. He heard car doors opening and closing in the parking lot, the low hum of activity as parents filed into the gym to watch their kids sing and get trophies or perhaps, if Trina had her way, Jacob feared, to watch them die. The immense gravity of the sick situation took hold of him and everything he heard was transformed. Their innocent conversations and small talk rearranged their sound in Jacob's head to become like screams and, with only a few more steps, he had reached the hollowed log.

He stopped to look for her. "Trina," he whispered, and scanned the woods with his light. "I'm here," he said. "I'm here."

There was no answer. So, Jacob bent to the ground, took off his backpack, and angled his light to the log.

Inside of it sat a blue duffel bag as fat and ancient-looking as a snake. Jacob unzipped his backpack and gave the woods another worried glance before pulling out his own bag, an exact replica of the one inside the log. What did it mean? Two identical bags, two totally different possibilities.

Jacob reached in and grabbed the bag inside the log that had, from the first touch, a terrible weight. He unzipped it and saw what he knew he would see: the barrel of a shotgun. And with this sight Jacob felt that every train in the station had now pulled up inside of him. He stuffed his duffel bag inside the other, his eyes beginning to blur, and was careful not to touch the gun. As he went to slide it back in the log, he felt his phone go off in his hand.

He looked to the screen to see a message from Trina. The last one, he remembered, said *Someone needs to be held responsible.*

This one read, simply... *Who better than you?*

Jacob closed his eyes to try and think. Who better than him to be held responsible for what? he wondered. Toby's death, or Toby's life? He did not want to feel responsible for either but yet could not ignore the idea that maybe all men should be held responsible for their inaction. That perhaps he should be held responsible for his. The way he'd watched girls go in and out of Toby's life knowing that he did not care for them yet said nothing, the way he listened to Trina talk about payback and guns but was too hung up on a kiss to see it, the way he'd heard guys talk in awful ways about girls that he never condemned in any manner stronger than silence. But if only he could *think* instead of feel, he thought, that would be helpful. If he could solve this simple equation, connect all these dots, think his way out of this particular moment right now before he took on the rest of his life, he might come upon a solution. But Jacob could not. Instead, what he *felt* was that he had been acting like the only boy in the world, as if he was a stranger everywhere he went, and that no one would ever understand him. And through this machinery of feeling instead of thinking, Jacob was overcome with the urge to call his father. He wanted to tell him everything, to confess all that he had thought and done, even if the connections between these things made little sense. He wanted to take the blame for it all.

In the distance, though, he heard something coming.

It was a soft crunching of leaves and shifting of sticks, an almost impossibly slow sound, more light and careful than any human could be. Jacob looked behind him but saw nothing. He then stood up and turned his light to the path before him and in it, where it had not been before, stood a giant bird.

It was an egret, tall and feathered white, taking its gentle evening stroll across the path before him with no knowledge of anything at all. Its head rocked back and forth atop its long neck and the bird eyed Jacob in a way that seemed, to him, without judgment. The careful footsteps and gentle grace of its body were so out of place that Jacob felt run over by all of life's potential. The fact that this animal could lift and take flight whenever it chose to, that it could be, in many ways, whatever it chose to be. The physics of it nearly paralyzed him.

Jacob watched it cross the path until his vision blurred almost completely. He was crying, he knew, and yet was determined not to blink. He wanted to witness this small thing, this leisurely stroll across a path of terrible possibility, before the rest of his life began. As he did this, the sharp outline of the bird's body went from defined to hazy and white, the cone of his flashlight growing to glow around the crane until it was no longer a bird at all but only a bright notion.

And then a series of lights around him, he realized, from white to red, as the bird was evolving from one form into another. He heard the graceful hitch of its wings, felt the air displaced by its decision to fly, and watched the red crane squat and take off toward whatever future awaited it.

In its wake, other incoming sounds.

The sounds of men in the lights that Jacob heard now.

The white, the red, the blue lights.

34

That's What Happens, When Two Worlds Collide

Douglas entered the room to see Cherilyn sitting upright on a hospital bed, wearing a thin gown with blue flowers on it. Dr. Granger stood before her with his fingers pressed gently beneath her neck as if checking her glands.

Cherilyn looked over at Douglas without moving her head.

"Oh, Douglas," she said, and reached out her hand as if expecting an embrace.

Douglas stood at the far end of the room and did not say a thing. All he could do was look at his wife's hands. He had no idea what was all over them: dark brown lines and circles of what he first thought to be an infection. Cherilyn must have noticed his look of disgust as she put her hand to her lap and wrapped it in her thin gown.

"I'm glad you're here," she said.

Douglas could hardly bear to look at her in that moment. It physically hurt him to do so, and so he very intentionally looked at Dr. Granger.

He was a handsome man in his sixties, still fit, with salt-and-pepper hair and a pair of fashionable tortoiseshell glasses. He was not the type of doctor you saw around town but one that appeared so intelligent that he could exist in only two places: at a hospital or at brunch.

"What's going on?" Douglas asked him.

Dr. Granger asked Cherilyn to stand up and raise her arms.

"What's going on," he said, "is that I have a patient who's been keeping secrets from me."

"Is that a fact?" Douglas said.

"Douglas," Cherilyn said.

"Hold your arms out," Dr. Granger said. "Try to keep them up. Don't let me push them down."

Dr. Granger placed his hands on top of Cherilyn's and began pushing down on her arms. He did one until he had forced her arm down to her side and then did the other.

"Close your eyes," he said, and took his stethoscope from around his neck. "I want you to tell me when you feel pressure on your arms, okay?"

Cherilyn closed her eyes and said, "Okay."

Dr. Granger took his stethoscope and ran it lightly down her right arm from her shoulder to her elbow.

"I feel that," she said. "It's cold."

"I'm sorry," Dr. Granger said, and blew on it with an open mouth, rubbed it a few times with his sleeve. He then moved it down to her right leg.

"Oh," she said. "My leg. I feel that."

"Good," Dr. Granger said, and moved it over to her left leg. Cherilyn stood with her eyes closed. He then moved it up to her arm, tracing from her elbow down to her forearm, and put the stethoscope back around his neck.

Cherilyn opened her eyes. "Are you going to do the other side?" she asked.

She looked at Dr. Granger and then over at Douglas and the expression Douglas saw in her face was one he'd never seen before.

The look was one of open and unabashed fear and rendered her so vulnerable that Douglas had the sensation it was his own life being threatened. He felt his chest tighten around this image, as if saving it in his new dark battery for any time he might run low on worry.

"I didn't feel anything," Cherilyn said, as if talking only to Douglas. Her eyes began to well. "What is happening to me?"

Douglas had to fight the urge to approach her. He wanted to, but also thought that what he needed to do at that moment was to *think* instead of feel.

"How did you get here?" Douglas asked her.

"I'd also like to know how long this has been going on," Dr. Granger said.

"No," Douglas said. "I mean, who drove you here?"

Cherilyn lowered her chin to her chest and began weeping in a way that told Douglas all that he thought he needed to know.

Douglas suddenly saw his own past as one he might never recover and so, rather than going to console Cherilyn, walked out of the door to see Deuce still sitting across the hall.

Without saying a word, Douglas attacked him to the best of his ability.

He grabbed Deuce by the shirt and pulled him to the floor. He knelt on top of him and went to punch another human being for the first time in his life. Deuce moved his head to the side and Douglas cracked his knuckles on the floor, but this did not stop him. He went to hit him again. "What did you do to her?" he yelled.

"Come on, now!" Deuce said, and blocked Douglas's weak punches with his arms. He then grabbed Douglas by the coat and rolled over on top of him, kneeling on his chest and trying to grab his arms as Douglas flailed against him, his thin hair out of order and all over his face.

"Don't make me put you down, now," Deuce said. "This wouldn't ever be a fair fight."

35

How Lucky Can One Man Get?

Hank was lucky to still have his toe.

This was the consensus, at least, of all the smiling nurses and doctors who'd come through the ER to help bandage his foot. A man can live, of course, without a pinkie toe, but it was not the preferred way of going about things. And so wasn't this big strong cowboy, they said, this rugged Marlboro Man on their hospital bed, this Lone Ranger, lucky to still have his toe?

Jacob did not see the humor.

His jeans were still wet from the panic he'd had in the woods where he stood shaking and unable to speak, unable to drop his phone, even, as the police commanded him to. He could still smell the rank odor of adrenaline on his shirt and in his armpits from where he'd sweat like a mute before those lights. He was no hero in that moment and he knew this. What he also knew was that Trina hadn't ever planned to walk in that building with a gun or do anything to those boys. There were no shells in the bag, the police had said, no ammunition at all, yet they had been tipped off by an anonymous call to check the Crane Lane for a shooter. She'd then tweeted out the video of him at his locker, as well. And so what Trina had hoped was for Jacob to be there at the same time the cops were, to be holding the gun and perhaps die right there in those woods, to take the blame, he realized, for a crime his brother never got the chance to. That her readout for him was not one of hope but perhaps some strange form of confession she would not be around to deliver herself. And, Jacob knew, Trina had almost gotten the exact thing she wanted. The only calculation she had not made, it seemed, was for Jacob's father.

Jacob remembered little other than the sound of his dad's voice among the lights, coming from behind him, though, as if he had followed him up the trail. So much yelling, Jacob remembered, and in such a rough way that he had never heard adults yelling before. Drop things. Turn around. Hands up. So many conflicting commands that Jacob could not have obeyed if he tried. And, finally, the one line he remembered, because the nurses kept repeating it now.

"Ain't nobody draws a gun on my boy!"

The shot that followed this sent Jacob to the ground, sure he was to be jettisoned from this life and into another. It also sent the four policeman to the ground, each of them down to a knee with their guns drawn.

The only person who didn't fall was his father, whose hand was still on his holster.

"That," his dad said, "was an accident."

"It was those good boots that saved the toe," one of the nurses said. "You know, Nikes aren't really built for that type of thing."

Jacob now sat beside his father in the ER with the full knowledge that there were a million possible ways in which he could have died that night. If his father had not shown up, if he had been wearing different clothes, perhaps, said a different thing, looked a different person, if just one officer had sneezed. The horrible possibilities terrified him. Yet the way the nurses acted toward him was as if it was high time Jacob realized everyone on this planet is just one stranger's decision away from eternity. They barely paid him any attention at all and doted, instead, on his father. Jacob rubbed the growing bruises on his wrists from where he had been immediately cuffed and dragged to a squad car that sat idling on the gravel entrance to the trail. Where, through the car window, hopping like he was crossing a bed of coals, he saw his father coming, too.

The officer set them both in the back of the squad car, where his father politely bled all the way to the hospital, and Jacob did not let him get a word out. He instead leaned his head against the cage in front of him and confessed to his dad everything he could think to confess. He let it all come out. From the beginning, with Trina. What she'd said the dickheads had done to Toby that night and the anger he'd had not just about Toby and the kids at school but about his mom and how he felt that there was nobody at all in the world and even the way she had kissed him and talked about terrible things without him ever trying to stop her and how he had ultimately, like an idiot, let it all get out of hand.

His dad did nothing other than rub Jacob's shoulder as he blubbered. He kneaded it back and forth as if he were expressing some deep sore, squeezing all of the guilt out of him. It was a motion so strange and unrehearsed as Jacob spoke like a child, cried like a child, that Jacob didn't know what to make of it. But something in his father's rough touch he enjoyed. The way it felt like his father was perhaps not trying to get something out but rather trying to join him there, in Jacob's body, to be one with him when the trains rolled out. He wanted to feel it again.

The attending officer drove without hurry and said only, "It's funny you should mention Trina Todd," he said. "There's an APB out on her right now for Grand Auto. Not sure what good it'll do with all of us over at the school but, I mean, it's like a full moon tonight."

So, Jacob thought, more men were going after Trina.

God help them.

Jacob looked up at his dad, who was now lying in the hospital with his left boot still on and his right foot wrapped like a package. He had his hat resting on his chest and looked unmistakably pleased with himself. He took small sips of apple juice through a straw from a carton and seemed to know everyone in the place. Oddly, the amount of people who came by to wish his father well gave Jacob a sense of pride. His father was admired, Jacob knew, and why shouldn't he be?

Jacob should tell him that he admired him, too, at some point, and he would tell him, he decided, but knew he had plenty of time. Whether they shipped him off to some detention center for troubled youth or threw him in jail or just let him sit in that hospital room forever, Jacob knew that what his father told him earlier was true. It was just the two of them now, out in the field, out in the rain, and they would have plenty of time to talk.

The person Jacob most wanted to talk to now, though, he'd heard, was also in a room in the hospital. Jacob stood up from his chair and stretched out his back. His father looked over to him and smiled. He made a little pistol with his finger and blew off the smoke. "What did I say, pardner?" he told him. "That thing still works."

Jacob did not smile but walked down the hall. When he turned the corner, he saw Sheriff Bates standing against the far wall and thumbing his phone.

"Where do you think you're going?" he said.

"I heard Father Pete was here," Jacob said. "He works at my school. He's Trina's uncle. I was going to go tell him something."

Sheriff Bates nodded to a door at the far end of the hall and then let out a big puff of breath. "Boy," he said. "If you weren't your daddy's son. No telling what would have happened to you tonight."

Jacob turned to him. He'd never heard anything so true.

"I understand," Jacob said. "I'm sorry. I got pretty lucky, I guess."

"I'd say it's the opposite of luck," he said. "Everything y'all have been through. Your brother. Your mom, who was a woman I knew and still miss, by the way. It's not that your dad is the mayor that helped you out. It's that everybody knows he can't take any more. That he doesn't deserve any more. I believe it's given you a sort of currency, if you catch my drift. Don't waste it."

"I understand," Jacob said, and he did. His mission now would be the same as the sheriff's in many ways. He would do what he could to protect his father from here out.

Sheriff Bates looked back at his phone. "Let me ask you one thing I *don't* understand," he said. "All of these tweets. You're saying you didn't send these? And this bag you're holding here. It's not the same one? You're saying this is all just her, pretending to be you? Setting you up?"

Jacob nodded.

"People do it all the time," he said. "Fake accounts. Alters. Catfishing. Nobody really knows who anyone is. We just sort of go around pretending. I probably should have paid more attention."

"I'm telling you," the sheriff said, and looked as if he was scrolling through hundreds of posts at a time, "this makes me feel like I am in over my head. It's like we've got a criminal mastermind on our hands."

"You don't," Jacob said. "What she did makes perfect sense. It wasn't complicated."

"Well," the sheriff said. "It makes me feel like I'm in a movie, and that's not a feeling I enjoy. It's a sad feeling."

Jacob turned to walk down the hall. It was a sad feeling, he thought, to believe yourself in a movie like this one. He passed a closed door to his left where it sounded like someone was singing. It was a man's voice, high and light, from a song he did not recognize. When he passed the next door on his right, Jacob heard his own name.

He turned to look in the room and saw his History teacher, Mr. Hubbard, sitting on an examining table. A nurse was wrapping his wrist with a bag of ice and Mr. Hubbard was wearing a suit, for some reason. He still had that black eye from before. And whether or not it was the pure surprise of seeing him there that did this to him, Jacob did not know, but all he understood at that moment was that he cared for Mr. Hubbard. He had affection for him. Perhaps it was still the run of adrenaline opening all of his veins and neural pathways, but Jacob did not mind. What he knew instead was that he cared what Mr. Hubbard thought of him and the reality of what Jacob had done, without ever even touching a gun, crashed upon him again. Strings of emotional connection seemed to unfurl from inside him and roll out to attach themselves to every person in the world that Jacob could have hurt by his inaction. What a glorious and invisible map. How had it been so difficult for him to see this before? All of us connected in so many silent ways. Our friends. Our families. The people we are soon to meet. The people we need to call again.

And sweet Mr. Hubbard, here, with his missing mustache.

Jacob felt so ashamed he could barely look at him.

"I heard about what happened," Mr. Hubbard said.

"I'm so sorry," Jacob told him.

"No," Mr. Hubbard said. "*I'm* sorry. You tried to tell me today after class, didn't you, that something was going on, and I didn't listen. I've been thinking about that moment ever since I heard. How clearly upset you looked to me, and I didn't stop what I was doing to ask you."

"It's okay," Jacob said.

"No, it's not," he said. "You have to understand, Jacob, that it's not okay for me. That's the exact opposite of the type of teacher I'd like to be. Do you understand that? Everything I did in class today, actually," he said. "I want to tell you that *I'm* sorry."

"It's okay," Jacob said. "A lot of those readouts obviously don't make any sense. I don't think anybody knows what they are doing. Everyone is just trying to be something else, don't you think?"

"Are you asking me that," Mr. Hubbard said, "or telling me? Are you asking me if anyone knows what they are doing? Or is your thesis, here, that nobody knows what they are doing?"

Jacob looked at him. He said nothing.

"Either way," Mr. Hubbard said. "You get an A. Just don't ever scare us like that again."

"I never thought it would go that far," Jacob said.

"Nobody ever does," Mr. Hubbard said. "But, look, let me know if I can vouch for you with the police or whoever. You're a good kid. Not just a good student. I can see it a mile away. It's like a wise carpenter once told me, Jacob. Some people are no great mystery."

Jacob cocked his head. "That's a Jesus quote, I'm guessing?"

"No," Douglas said. "Principal Pat, oddly enough."

"Weird," Jacob said.

"Agreed," Mr. Hubbard said.

Jacob thanked him and walked down the hall, his eyes burning again as if to let Jacob know they stood ready to cry at any moment henceforth. It would not be a bother to them, not be a burden. They could just go at their discretion. Was this, Jacob suspected, adulthood?

He looked into the next room and, as if to confirm his suspicions, saw a woman through the small glass window of the door, sitting on a table and weeping openly into her hands. Something all over her arms, Jacob thought, like flowered tattoos.

When he reached the far room, Jacob saw Father Pete in bed with a gown on. He had a large bandage wrapped around his head and his eyes were closed. He was not sleeping, though. Instead his face was pulled together tightly at the corners, as if he had a headache. He looked to be repeating something under his breath, rocking gently back and forth, and Jacob had to watch him awhile until he understood that he was praying. Jacob felt for a moment that he had never seen a person do this. Surely not his classmates, even those who pretended to care about all the memorized chants and incantations they went through in Mass each week. Not even his own dad. No, Father Pete was actually praying. He was in conversation with something. It looked to Jacob, very much, like a skill.

Jacob knocked gently on the door until Pete opened his eyes, turned his head toward the door.

"I'm Jacob Richieu," he said.

"I know who you are," Father Pete said. "I see you at school every day. I said the Mass for your brother's funeral."

"That's right," Jacob said. "I don't know why I introduced myself."

"Do you know where she is, Jacob?" Father Pete asked him. "Do you know where Trina went?"

Jacob shook his head. "I don't," he said. "I think the police are looking for her."

"I know they are," Father Pete said. "I'm the one who called in the missing plates. I'm just hoping they find her safe and sound somewhere. I'm trying not to listen to too much of what I hear in the halls, you know, until I hear it from her. I'm trying not to assume anything."

"It's not going to be good," Jacob said. "No matter where they find her. Trina is not going to be okay."

Jacob pulled his brother's phone from his pocket. It felt to him as cold and distant as any stranger's belonging and he did what he had come there to do. He walked over to the bed and punched in the code and handed it over to Pete. "I think you should see this," he said, and set the screen to the video.

Jacob did not bother to sit as he watched Father Pete take in what he had already seen for himself. He could hear only the awful voices of the boys in the woods on that night. *Now we're talking, number nine!* His brother's number. A brother he loved but who had made different choices than he had, and his choices on the video were soon washed up into the chorus of terrible choices that generations of boys had made and continued to make as Jacob heard the phone in the video drop to the ground as the almost congratulatory sound of those boys turned to confusion. Toby's voice, which he could barely make out, now just one in a sea of voices drowning out what were obvious and urgent pleas from Trina. Her voice, too, soon lost in the sound of gravel underfoot until finally someone yelled out that the cops were there. And Jacob watched Pete strain his eyes at the phone as if to see anything of value as it was picked back up and put in his brother's pocket. They heard the hoof of Toby's footsteps out to the car with no words at all, no apologies whatsoever to the person he had left behind. And then the slamming of the car door and the revving of the engine and who could know what made the video stop? Had it run out of memory? Had Toby shut it all down without even knowing? Or did the phone somehow know that, by showing what it had already shown, it would play on forever?

Father Pete set the phone on the table beside him.

"I'm guessing this is your brother's phone?" he said. "Not yours."

"Yes, sir," Jacob said.

Pete laced his fingers across his chest and breathed so deeply into his lungs that it suggested he was discovering an entirely new way of breathing.

Behind Jacob, a nurse walked into the room and began to busy herself as if they weren't even there. She opened a drawer, checked the notes on a legal pad on the desk.

"Did she ever say anything to you," Pete asked Jacob, "about her mom?"

"No," Jacob said. "She never really talked to me about anything. In some ways, I think I was the last person she ever wanted to talk to."

"I think," Pete said, "that I might also be pretty low on that list."

"You think that's where she is?" Jacob said. "With her mom?"

"If that's the case," Pete said, "I might be heading to Natchez to look for a dwarf."

The nurse walked over to Father Pete and put a small clamp on his finger.

"I know that place," she said. "Me and my husband went there last year for the Christmas lights."

"Went where?" Pete said.

"To Natchez," she said. "There's a bar there. I think it's called the Bar Under the Hill. There's a dwarf who owns it, or a little person, I believe is the right nomenclature, Father. But, anyway, every night at closing time, by way of letting people know, he climbs up on the speakers and sings 'House of the Rising Sun.' It's something to see. I cried like a baby."

Pete looked over at Jacob as if to confirm that he was not dreaming.

"I don't understand," Pete asked the nurse. "Is this a real story you're telling me?"

"You're at ninety-nine percent," the nurse said, and pulled off the pulse ox. "Healthy as a horse with a bump on its head. And, yeah, it's a real place. I wouldn't just make something like that up. Some things are too great to make up."

The nurse wrapped the pulse ox in a tight bundle and put it back in a drawer. "I bet they'll let you go home tonight," she said. "Now I have to go tell your friend that they've got some news about his wife."

The nurse walked past Jacob and down the hall and Jacob looked back at Father Pete.

"If you find her," Jacob said, and walked toward him. He pulled out the misfiled Pikachu card from his pocket and handed it to him. "If you find her, give her this. Tell her I'm not my brother. I'm not ever going to be my brother. I never would have been my brother."

"I will," Father Pete said. "But I think I'll hold off on telling her anything except that I am glad to see her. As for the rest, I'm just going to listen. Does that sound all right with you? Sometimes we just need to listen."

Jacob walked back to the door. He turned and stood without saying anything.

"Jacob?" Father Pete said.

"Yes, sir," Jacob said. "I'm listening."

36

If You Need a Fool Who Loves You . . .

What hurt her most was that Douglas was there. He had to be.

He wouldn't leave her like that, would he? In a hospital room? With so much to discuss? The idea was too awful to consider.

Surely he was right around the corner, about to walk in any moment.

So why hadn't he?

The last Cherilyn had seen him was when he rushed out the door to accost Deuce. And wasn't that a silly sight. Cherilyn poked her head around the corner and saw Douglas sitting on top of Deuce as if he were a Jet Ski, flailing his arms at his head like Deuce's ears were on fire. She then hurried back to her bed to sit down before she even knew how it ended. She was terrified, for some reason, that Douglas would see her watching this fight. But why?

Weren't scenes like this akin to her recent fantasies, after all? Hadn't she bandied about images of young boys vying for her attention, running past her as if to draw her eye? And not only young men in these fantasies but grown men, as well, she knew, grown men in their hundreds and thousands to protect her royal honor. Nations, armies. All fighting for her. And not only grown men, she realized, but the women, too, at the costume shop, whose attention and praise she had craved and received. So many people to surround her. Hadn't she wanted all of that? Yes, she knew, she had.

So why didn't she want it now?

Perhaps it was because, instead of being royal, instead of being a person who launched a thousand ships, Cherilyn realized she had simply set into motion the most lopsided battle in history. That Douglas would trounce Deuce Newman in every way that mattered was not the source of her shame, however. This, instead, came from the fact that she had made Douglas feel that his greatness was something he needed to prove in the first place. How had she let him forget? And, with this, she understood that it was perhaps her own silent motivations that had made him feel that way. So, she decided, she would no longer feel any need to dress up for Deuce Newman nor allow him to continue thinking that there might be any chance on this earth that she would ever love anyone but her husband. She would throw away his key. Keeping it was something she had done in her past, and everyone has a past. All she would concern herself with from here on, she determined, would be her present.

So, she shied away from the fight in the hallway not so that she wouldn't see Douglas, but so that Douglas wouldn't see that former version of her. She listened to their argument through the open doorway, to the doctors and nurses trying to pull them apart and felt nothing but crystallized guilt. She knew she could explain it enough, the trip out to Parker Field with Deuce, the strange clothes. She knew she hadn't gone too far in any of her mental journeys to make a permanent dent on Douglas's heart, but she expected him to be hurt. He had a right to be hurt.

What she did not expect, however, was how long he would stay gone.

The fight was over. Had been for probably thirty minutes. A

nurse told her that Douglas was getting some ice for his wrist, but even that shouldn't have taken so long. She walked to the door and looked down the hall and the nurse said she was sure it would just be another minute or two, but people like her, Cherilyn thought, just didn't get it.

When a person needs the person they love, time doesn't work the same.

And so the minutes Cherilyn waited alone in that room took physical form to stretch like tentacles throughout her memory and reconnected her to every other time she had been without him. They reached through her past to cup and open little pictures for her to review: an odd stretch of minutes when Douglas was late from work one day and she worried, a time he had gone off to find ice cream when they were on vacation in Florida and left her there for what seemed like too long and she worried. Hundreds of these little memory photos of Cherilyn watching herself without Douglas, seeing herself like she did in the bikini picture he took just a few years ago. It was her there, yes, but it was not the version of her she most liked. And these tentacles in her memory connected her to all of the times in her life without him, traveling from high school all the way up to these moments in the waiting room as if only to say, *These, Cherilyn. You see, these are the miserable times*. And she did see it.

So, Cherilyn sat on the bed, put her hands to her face, and let it all out.

When Douglas finally came back to the room, he entered it as if a stranger. He stood at the door almost hesitantly, like he wasn't sure if he was in the right place. How long had he been pacing around out there? she wondered. How long has he been preparing what he wanted to say to her? When he finally got his body all the way through the frame, he had something of the traveling salesman to him, Cherilyn thought, his suit coat laid over his arm.

Why on earth, she wondered, was he wearing a suit?

And where was his little hat?

She recognized the pink shirt she had bought him and had the strange notion that Douglas had wrapped himself up like a gift she did not deserve. She smiled at him, but he did not smile back.

"Douglas," she said. "I can explain everything."

He closed the door behind him and stood at the handle. His hair was neatly swept. His eye still had its bruise. He had a big bag of ice wrapped around his hand.

Cherilyn turned toward him on the table and was surprised that he didn't approach her. He instead was looking at the far wall, above her head, and Cherilyn realized he was holding his body in an odd way. He stood up on his heels as if making his back as straight as it could be, and Cherilyn recognized this from the times she had seen Douglas speak in public. From toasts he'd given at weddings to little impromptu speeches at school fundraisers. The way he looked at himself in the mirror that very morning. His face was so serious.

Douglas, she realized, was in teacher mode.

"First, Cherilyn," he said. "Please know that I am sorry you are not feeling well and that I acted the way I did, but before we can get into any of that you need to know that I have a few questions."

Cherilyn put her hands on her thighs. "Okay," she said.

Douglas was as grave as she had ever seen him. His hand, beneath his blazer, looked like it was shaking.

"What I need to know, Cherilyn, I suppose," he said, still looking at the wall, "is if all of my nightmares are coming true. I need to know, I guess, if I should be preparing myself for every awful thing I've ever imagined."

"Oh, Douglas," she said. "No. Not at all. Your nightmares are not coming true. Are mine?"

Douglas shuffled his feet as if he was not the one who was

supposed to be answering questions. He paced to the side to try it again from a new spot in the room.

"Let me rephrase the question," he said. "What I need to know, Cherilyn Hubbard, is if you have been running around with my mortal enemy."

Cherilyn smiled at the phrasing.

"I'm not laughing, Mrs. Hubbard," Douglas said, and she could see that she had indeed hurt him. Here was her own personal king, she thought, afraid an enemy had infiltrated his castle.

"No, sir," Cherilyn said, though she had no idea why she said *sir*. She wanted to speak clearly, she supposed, to make sure there was no confusion. "I am not running around with anyone. I am as in love with my husband as I have ever been."

Douglas paced back and forth as if taking the information in, sorting through the many ways that he could yet again clarify what it was he needed to assure himself of.

"All right, then," he said. "That is good. Very good indeed. Then, what I need to know now, I suppose," he said, "is what the hell is going on with your hands."

"Oh, Douglas," she said, and held out her arms. "Come here."

Before she could pull him in, though, and before she could even tell if he would let her, the door opened, and Dr. Granger walked inside looking down at his phone. Douglas shuffled to the back of the room as if hiding. She heard him rearrange the coat in his arms and take in a few deep Douglas breaths.

Dr. Granger lifted up his nice tortoiseshell glasses to take a closer look at his phone and squinted his eyes at the screen.

"I'm telling you," he said. "That man is lucky to still have his toe."

He then sat down in his little rolling chair and scooted up to Cherilyn. He put the phone in his breast pocket and looked up at Douglas.

"Douglas," he said. "You may want to have a seat."

"I'll stand," Douglas said.

"Well," Dr. Granger said. "Come stand by your wife, then."

Cherilyn did not like, at all, the gravity of the doctor's voice and looked back at Douglas, who did indeed come stand beside her. He stepped forward and placed his hand on her shoulder and, with this, it was as if the whole of her life clicked back in place.

Cherilyn felt that she could read through her skin everything that Douglas wanted to tell her, even more so than if she had tried to read his face. The pressure from his palm as it had been through so many years that he had comforted her about both enormous and minor difficulties. The way he moved his thumb back and forth on her back as if imprinting a code to let her know that although he was still thinking about all of this, although there was still a lot to clear up, everything would be okay. The pressure and beat of his thumb to let her know that no matter what they were about to hear from the doctor, it was nothing compared to the conversation they had not yet finished, nothing compared to what they both still needed to know, to sanctify, which was that they, the two of them, their hearts together, were still all right. That their lives did not have to change from something they cherished to something they never wanted. All of this communication as clear to her through his thumb as if he had spoken the words but yet invisible, Cherilyn knew, to everyone else on the earth.

And with this hand on her shoulder, with this constant communication, Cherilyn looked at the doctor and thought, *Let's do this. Tell me everything. Douglas is with me now. I can handle it.*

In love, Cherilyn knew, there is no fooling the skin.

37

...I Know One

What Douglas needed her to know was this:

All that mattered to him was her. No matter what the doctor said, no matter what she still needed to tell him, all that mattered was their future together.

He wanted so desperately to tell her this but, before he could, had to step aside for the doctor. When it seemed as if the news he was delivering would be bad, Douglas came forward and put his hand on Cherilyn's back. If only he could tell her, he thought, and moved his thumb back and forth across her skin.

Dr. Granger shined a little light into Cherilyn's eyes.

"Your body," he told Cherilyn, "has been *busy*."

Douglas did not like the sound of this at all. He rubbed her back a bit faster and began to prepare himself to argue against nearly anything this doctor would say that might suggest there was something not perfect about his wife. "What does that mean?" he heard Cherilyn ask.

"Well," he said. "Do you want the definite good news or the possible bad news?"

Douglas recognized that he was still in teacher mode as this question struck him as the most asinine thing he had ever heard.

Who in their right mind, he thought, *would ever favor possible bad news over definite good news?* The question was not, for him, even a question at all.

"We want them both," Cherilyn said. "I can take it."

"Okay," Dr. Granger said. "The passing out is not good, nor is the loss of sensation in your hands and arms. Especially with a pregnancy."

Even the supposition, Douglas thought, that the chance of bad news, no matter how minor it might be, could ever compare to the comfort, could come close to the definite good news one already had in their pocket, was outrageous.

"What are you saying?" he heard Cherilyn ask. "Are you saying we're pregnant?"

"What I am saying," Dr. Granger told her, "is that you, Cherilyn Hubbard, contain multitudes. And, according to your urine, one of these multitudes is a baby."

Douglas took his hand off Cherilyn's back as if he had decided something. He crossed his arms and took a quick breath through his nose.

"I want the definite good news," he said. "That is what I always want."

Both Cherilyn and Dr. Granger looked at Douglas in a way that let him know he had said something confusing, and when Cherilyn reached out and took his arm into her own, it was like the living world clarified. Time then did its funny thing to a man in love and rewound the last few minutes for him to review again.

"A child?" Douglas said. "Did you say a child?"

He felt Cherilyn squeeze him. He had not yet looked at her and was, for some reason, afraid to.

"How does that happen?" Cherilyn said. "I mean, we sort of thought that ship had sailed."

"Bodies are weird," Dr. Granger said. He held out his hand and made a little bulb like a flower. "Sometimes they just sort of . . ." He made his fingers pop open. "Wake up."

Douglas scrambled in many different mental directions, only a few of which pointed to the future. He instead went back to the past, to his own personal history, to try and figure out how they had arrived here. In his calculations he was first brought back to the scene only two nights before, when he had been asked for an encore. Yet in this memory he did not feel the shame he had felt on that night but instead the press of his wife's ankles against his back, the way she drew shapes along his shoulders when they had finished. These shapes led him to the shape of their living room couch, of all places, where they'd made love just months before. If this was the one that did it, after all those years of trying, if that was the one that stuck, their impromptu session that seemed to have no plan behind it all, then what did it mean? Hooray for the living room couch?

Is that enough for something to mean?

What Douglas's mind did not do, however, did not even consider doing, was wonder if the child were not his own. Douglas was lucky in this way. If his mind were like the minds of many men and had gone in that direction, if he would have thought instead of felt and asked the question, even suggested it, then his would be a life he could never get back. And so, as if to protect him, his heart took his mind by the hand and led it down the proper hall.

As it did, Douglas recalled other times on their living room couch. The way Cherilyn had sat next to him and read that book about kings and queens, perhaps wishing she could be somewhere else entirely. The way he had seen her sitting at the table so often, lately, with her head in her hands, rubbing her thumb against the pad of her palm. The way she had unscrewed aspirin bottles that seemed to be lying all over the house. The way she had stopped working around town, had seemed so exhausted. His mind turned up an array of these scenes, and where had Douglas been in them? he wondered. How was she alone in each of these memories that he could only have access to if he was there with her? Why didn't he see himself beside her?

All of this reminded him that there was no such thing as only positive news and so Douglas asked the question he felt he needed to ask.

"What's the possible bad news?" he said. "What else is going on?"

"Is the baby okay?" Cherilyn said.

"I'm sure it is," Dr. Granger said. "All I have is the test. It's probably no bigger than a red bean right now. Just a little ball of DNA. We'll have plenty of time to see what it's up to, and you'll be seeing plenty of me, so don't worry about that right now."

"I'm confused," Douglas said. "What are we supposed to be worried about?"

"Well," Dr. Granger said. "The neurological stuff is worrisome. I don't like the dizziness, although that could be on account of the baby stuff, and I don't like the passing out or headaches, although that could possibly be from the baby stuff, too."

Douglas put his hand on Cherilyn's back. He got his thumb going again.

Dr. Granger stood up and placed his hands in his pockets. "What worries me," he said, "is the loss of feeling."

He then turned toward the desk behind them and took out a stack of brochures.

"I'm going to order some tests," he said. "I'd love to tell you that they're all precautionary but, you know, any doctor who tells a patient he knows what's coming is, how to say it . . ."

"Full of shit?" Douglas said.

Dr. Granger smiled and set down a little stack of papers that Douglas saw had headlines such as "What Is MS?" and "What Is Neuropathy?" and, last, "When a Tingle Is More Than a Tingle."

"Let me put it this way, Mr. Hubbard," he said. "No matter what, I think you and your wife are off on a brand-new adventure."

He then patted Cherilyn on the knee and left the room and Douglas watched him go.

Douglas set his jacket down on the bed beside Cherilyn. He walked around her to the stool Dr. Granger had just sat upon and did not say a word. He smoothed his hair on his head, set his elbows on his knees, and did what he had not done in far too long. He looked at her.

The two of them sat looking into each other's eyes for so long that, to anyone out in the hallway, they may have appeared frozen. But what Douglas was doing, and what he knew Cherilyn was doing, was the opposite of freezing. They were instead melting into each other. They were checking in. They were studying each other's face, reminding themselves of the other's physical presence. They did not smile or frown but simply stared until each felt it okay to move their vision beyond their physical presence and into the invisible places of this person that they knew better than anyone else.

And whenever Douglas had seen all that he needed to see inside of her, whenever he affirmed all that he wanted to affirm, he bent forward in the chair and put his head on Cherilyn's lap. She placed her warm hands on his head and stroked his thin hair and they sat together not knowing what they would say when the time came but knowing only that it would come, and they stayed that way until they heard a knock on the door.

"Hey, Hubbard," a man said.

Douglas picked his head off Cherilyn's lap and looked to the doorway. Pete was standing there in his work clothes, a huge bandage across his forehead. He had his arm around Hank, who had on his hat, one good boot, and a cast the size of a special delivery.

"We were just curious," Hank said. "Have you heard the one about us?"

Douglas had pictures of himself taking care of Cherilyn if the bad news was true, and Cherilyn of taking care of Douglas if her bad news was true. Of both of them, of all three of them, taking care of her mother. Of everyone taking care of one another. What did the reason for caring, the *specifics* of caring, matter, if they were together? And as the firetruck turned around the courthouse they saw only one last artisan in attendance. A man they all knew as Bill, who worked at the bank, standing over an upturned bucket and practicing one final routine, it appeared, with a marionette.

He looked up to wave at the small parade coming through the lit square, invisible strings hanging from his fingers, and they all waved back.

And although, in their homes, many did sleep, there were others like Deuce Newman who also saw the night as the day as he sat hunched in front of his computer, clicking from image to image and loading them into a database as he had been doing those past weeks. Faces standing in front of a curtain in the DNAMIX booth, waiting to learn whatever future he gave them, faces grumpy and put out in front of a broken window, faces old and disappointed sitting by an ancient kitchen table. He now entered them all into a collage that made up what he thought was the greatest picture, the silhouette of a woman whose arms were stretched out to her sides in a field. An image, he thought, of a person finally getting what they deserved from the world, which was all of it in its entirety. And so, once he was done, he shut down the computer and webcam he had spent so many hours documenting as people stepped in the booth and he typed out whatever struck his fancy, having his fun with them, before finally just putting the thing on random. And, with this project complete, he knew that this night meant his next day was finally here, and that it might launch him into a thousand new directions. That it might finally take him out of Deerfield and into the larger world, which was a fate he felt was long overdue. He had so many ideas for the future that he could not sleep, so many possibilities of what he could do with his little invention. There were so many ways to change his life that it felt to him now that only one thing was impossible: Cherilyn. But he had tried for that thing. There was a comfort in that. He had tried for her and he had failed, so he would move on. He would set out on new missions. All he needed, he figured, was water and light.

And if anyone thought that what he had done was outlandish, that it was such an overly complicated way to try and win the heart of a girl, then, Deuce knew, that person had never been in love.

And on one of the quietest streets in Deerfield, as Douglas helped Cherilyn down from the firetruck, the Hubbards also knew that this night was not an end to their day.

They walked together through the front door, something they rarely did, and took two unexpectedly different routes to the kitchen, where they found themselves together again.

Cherilyn took off Douglas's coat, folded it neatly beside the sink. She then took up a coffee cup, turned on the water, and, without saying a word, washed it out with a stiff sponge. She set it on the rack, dried her hands, and looked at Douglas. "Now," she said. "How about some music?"

Douglas watched her walk to the pantry door and open it, as it was well past midnight and neither of them had eaten. *How* about *some music*, he thought, and before he started to whistle or even think of his trombone, walked over to Cherilyn and held her from behind. It had been far too long, he thought, even though it hadn't been very long at all, since he had held her. Cherilyn leaned her head back against his shoulder and they stood that way in the pantry door for minutes, not speaking at all, only moving back and forth to a song that no one else could hear.

about their home. It ran through the vent and into the air-conditioning and spread itself throughout the house. It slid beneath doorways and climbed up walls. It wrapped itself around curtains and settled into bedsheets. It scented all they would touch from there out, and everything that would remain out of reach.

Answer:

How can you know that your whole life will change on a day the sun rises at the agreed-upon time by science or God or what-have-you and the morning birds go about their usual bouncing for worms?

How can you know?

You cannot. No one can.

So, then. What do you do?

The answer is simple.

You close the book.

You look up.

You see me standing here. You see all of us standing here, loving you.

You *recognize* us.

And together, into the unknowable day, we venture out.

ACKNOWLEDGMENTS

The first person I would like to thank is you, whoever you may be, for taking the time to read this. Our lives are made of hours and you lent me some. I won't forget it. Thank you for every book you've ever read and will read from anyone at any time on anything. It's important; what passes between humans on pages. Never stop.

Otherworldly thanks go to Renee Zuckerbot and Sally Kim, both for your trust in me and for your kindness. Also, of course, for your belief in this novel, which would just be another file on my computer without you. You both mean more to me than you know. Thanks to Ivan Held and G. P. Putnam's Sons, as well, and to Katie McKee, Alexis Welby, and Gabriella Mongelli for your continued faith and energy.

Thanks also to librarians and booksellers; the safeguards of joy.

Aside from my kitchen counter, this book was written in two specific places I am extremely grateful for. The first is the Sundress Fine Arts Academy in Tennessee. Thanks to Erin Smith for letting me feed the animals. Enormous thanks, as well, to Mary Ann O'Gorman and the Twisted Run Retreat in Mississippi, where huge chunks of this novel were written. The quiet there saved me. Again and again. I had so much fun in my head.

I am also thankful to John Prine, whom I never met, yet who seemed to know me better than I do. Mr. Prine, if you can hear me up there, your songs are the soundtrack to my best memories. Your lyrics are like friends. Not a day goes by without one of your phrases spinning through my head and brightening my world in some way. On behalf of all the whistlers, strummers, and hummers who feel the same: I thank you.

I am also thankful to my students and colleagues at the Creative Workshop at UNO and The Yokshop in Oxford, MS. To every wonderful weirdo at The Parkview Tavern. Y'all keep me going. To Sean Ennis, as well, the first person I let read this whole thing, who kindly laughed at all the right parts before asking all the right questions. To every writer who believes in Art as the empathy machine. Come on, now. We've got this.

Most importantly, I thank my parents and stepparents, sisters and grandparents. The whole smiling and supportive lot, both here and away. What did I do to deserve you?

And, as always and forever, to Sarah and Magnolia and Sherwood:

My growing hearts.

My best blue tickets.

THE BIG DOOR PRIZE

M. O. WALSH

DISCUSSION GUIDE

THE BIG DOOR PRIZE **COMPLETE PLAYLIST**

BOOK ENDS

PUTNAM
— EST. 1838 —

to be a sort of benchmark for being a good person. You have to be level on the level. Prine frequently guides me in this way. And, of course, Prine fans know why Grandpa voted for Eisenhower.

3. **"Oh My Stars"**   CHAPTER 8

This snippet is from "Linda Goes to Mars" (*German Afternoons*, 1986) which Bill Murray referenced as being the first thing to make him laugh when he was stuck in a long depression. In my novel, it references masturbation. Sorry.

4. **"I Hate it When That Happens to Me"**   CHAPTER 11

One of my favorite Prine lyrics of all time comes from this song (*Fair and Square*, 2005) and displays what I see as his remarkable ability to match an odd visual detail with a human emotion, as it starts: "Well, I once knew a man who was going insane. He let love chase him right up a tree." Whenever I think of that man in a tree, and all the crazy ways love has made me act, I feel some kindred spirit at work.

5. **"I'm Taking A Walk"**   CHAPTER 12

Well, in this chapter, a character is just taking a walk so it might be a bit on the nose. Still, it's a great song, also off *Fair and Square*, 2005. On April 7, 2020, when I found out John Prine had passed away from Covid, this was the first tune I put on my headphones as I went to wander the neighborhood with my dog.

6. **"They Ought to Name a Drink After You"**   CHAPTER 13

This chapter is simply a scene with men at a bar. I mean, what else could I call it? (*Diamonds in the Rough*, 1972)

7. "Up in the Morning, Work Like a Dog" CHAPTER 15
The opening lines to "It's A Big Old Goofy World" (*The Missing Years*, 1991) which Prine said came about as an attempt to get as many similes in a song as he could. Out of curiosity, I counted, and it uses the words "like" or "as" 19 times (19!) yet still ends up tender enough to be a motto for life itself.

8. "My Picture in a Picture Show" CHAPTER 16
This song is most notable for me as an example of Prine's ability to turn seemingly nonsensical lyrics into incantations in my head. How else to explain the way that every time I see a menu with the words "Hamburgers" and "Cheeseburgers" on it, I feel compelled to say aloud "Wilbur and Orville Wright?" I imagine this habit has confused my children for years.

9. "There's Flies in the Kitchen, I Can Hear Them A-Buzzin'" CHAPTER 17
If a listener doesn't feel what the woman in "Angel from Montgomery" feels when she wonders about her husband: "How the hell can a person go to work in the morning, come home in the evening, and have nothing to say?" then that listener might be dead. In the novel, our main female character has a visitor in her kitchen, as well.

10. "The Caravan of Fools" CHAPTER 18
This chapter has Douglas, our main male character, confronting his class of high school students and nearly losing his mind at their naivety. The chapter, I hope, is funny. The song (*The Tree of Forgiveness*, 2018) is not at all funny.

undeniable masterpiece. I probably would have just retired if I ever wrote something that good. So glad he didn't.

19. **"Ain't It Funny How an Old Broken Bottle, Can Look Just Like a Diamond Ring"**   CHAPTER 27
"Far From Me" (*John Prine*, 1971), is also clinic in storytelling. Just three verses and a universal truth, "I guess a question ain't really a question when you know the answer, too." It's a perfect song.

20. **"You're Up One Day and The Next You're Down"**   CHAPTER 28
"That's the Way that World Goes Round" (*Bruised Orange*, 1978) is such a mixture of comedy and pathos that you can't help but laugh at how pathetic we are. It doesn't get any better than the scene of a man in sitting in the bathtub in this tune, counting his toes while "naked as the eyes of a clown."

21. **"Saddle in The Rain"**   CHAPTER 29
I love this song, not only because it's the only time I've ever heard the word "afterneath" but just because of how scorching the lyrics are. "Peace of mind? Try spending the night some time, all alone in a frozen room, afterneath you've lain, your saddle in the rain."

22. **"Souvenirs"**   CHAPTER 30
This chapter has our main character on the precipice of perhaps losing his wife to another man, going through all of the things they've collected and saved in their home over time. Hard to find a better chorus than Prine and Goodman singing, "It took me years, to get those souvenirs, and I don't know how they slipped away from me."

23. You've Got Gold   CHAPTER 31

A love song that makes no attempt to hide in irony or in sarcasm (*The Missing Years*, 1991). The narrator loves this woman. He believes she has gold inside of her. He believes he has it inside of him, too. It is as simple as it is powerful.

24. "You and Me, Sitting in the Back of My Memory"
CHAPTER 32

This ("Long Monday") is one of the few songs that get multiple mentions in the novel. See above for the way it makes me think of my wife. I can't be blamed for hitting repeat.

25. "Your Boy Is Here"   CHAPTER 33

This line is from "Mexican Home" (*Sweet Revenge, 1973*). The heat lightning burning the sky like alcohol, the car lights passing over the kitchen wall, all the vivid details of the song combine with its strange chorus of "Mama dear, your boy is here, far across the sea, waiting for that sacred core to burn inside of me" to create some sort of inexplicable emotion in my heart. I love the song.

26. "That's What Happens When Two Worlds Collide"
CHAPTER 34

Some of my favorite Prine recordings are covers he sang as duets on albums like *In Spite of Ourselves* (1999) and *For Better, or Worse* (2016). So, although he didn't originally write this, it felt fitting to nod to the many times he also honored his favorite artists by covering their songs, most often with women who had much better voices than he did.

27. How Lucky Can One Man Get?   CHAPTER 35

This is from his song "How Lucky" (Pink Cadillac, 1979), in